...ly

Susanna ...., New ... . author

"Part mystery, part gothic suspense…. An atmospheric and provocative tale of love, lies, and the secrets a family keeps. *The Lucky Ones* is masterfully crafted. I highly recommend."

—Kerry Lonsdale, *Wall Street Journal* bestselling author

"Tiffany Reisz reinvents gothic suspense for the present with this unforgettable story about a family with secrets more dangerous than dragons."

—Gwenda Bond, author of *Girl in the Shadows*, on *The Lucky Ones*

"You will find yourself falling in love with every character… [Y]ou'll wait with bated breath just to see in which direction the author will turn; and at the end you'll find yourself not being able to go a minute without thinking of the journey and glorious storytelling of Tiffany Reisz."

—*RT Book Reviews* on *The Night Mark*, Top Pick!

"This time-travel romance is swoon-worthy and lovely. Reisz is a powerful writer who hits all the high romance you can ask for, while creating a fascinating yet believable plot that makes us believe that love can conquer all, even time and death."

—*Kirkus Reviews* on *The Night Mark*

"A dark, twisty tale of love, lust, betrayal, and murder…this novel is not one to be missed."

—*Bustle* on *The Night Mark*

"[Reisz's] prose is quite beautiful, and she can weave a wonderful tight story."

—*New York Times* and *USA TODAY* bestselling author Jennifer Probst

"Reisz fills the narrative with rich historic details; memorable, if vile, characters; and enough surprises to keep the plot moving and readers hooked until the final drop of bourbon is spilled."

—*Booklist* on *The Bourbon Thief*

"Beautifully written and delightfully insane…. Reisz vividly captures the American South with a brutal honestly that only enhances the dark material."

—*RT Book Reviews* on *The Bourbon Thief*, Top Pick!

Also by Tiffany Reisz

THE LUCKY ONES
THE NIGHT MARK
THE BOURBON THIEF

The Original Sinners series

The White Years

*

THE QUEEN
THE VIRGIN
THE KING
THE SAINT

The Red Years

*

THE MISTRESS
THE PRINCE
THE ANGEL
THE SIREN

THE

ROSE

TIFFANY REISZ

mira

Recycling programs
for this product may
not exist in your area.

ISBN-13: 978-0-7783-0792-1

The Rose

Copyright © 2019 by Tiffany Reisz

For questions and comments about the quality of this book, please contact us at
CustomerService@Harlequin.com.

BookClubbish.com

Printed in U.S.A.

*For Mary Renault, who put me on a ship with Theseus
and showed me how to sail into unknown waters.*

THE

ROSE

Come, Erato, come lovely Muse,
stand by me and take up the tale...

—Apollonius of Rhodes

PART ONE

Aphrodite & the Rose

CHAPTER ONE

Lady Ophelia Anne Fitzroy Godwick—Lia to her friends—called the emergency meeting of the Young Ladies' Gardening & Tennis Club of Wingthorn Hall to order.

"If I could have your attention, please," Lia said to the three young ladies in her bedroom. "We might have a problem here."

"No alcohol at this meeting," Georgy muttered as she scrolled through her phone. "That's a massive problem."

"I'm not joking," Lia said.

She met their eyes, one by one, so they could see she was serious.

Georgy—blonde, buxom and wearing strapless yellow tulle—sat prettily in Lia's armchair. Rani, brown-skinned, dark-eyed, tall and slender, lay in her red satin best across

Lia's bed. Jane, the bookish brunette with secret talents hidden behind cat-eye glasses, leaned against Lia's bedpost in off-the-shoulder ivory.

Lia, in a vintage party dress of palest rose pink, stood with her back to the fireplace facing all three of them—a general addressing her troops, a knitting needle in her hand in lieu of a swagger stick.

"What's the problem, boss?" Rani asked.

"Fourteen," Lia said. "The three of you and fourteen of them."

Rani's eyes widened.

"Fourteen of our clients are coming?" she repeated.

That got the ladies' attention. For the Young Ladies' Gardening & Tennis Club of Wingthorn Hall was not a gardening club, and they didn't play much tennis, either. The YLG&T Club was, in fact, an escort agency.

"Which ones?" Jane asked.

Lia quickly rattled off their names, ranks and identifying proclivities.

Georgy tucked her iPhone into the bodice of her gown, muttering, "If Sir Trevor tries to lick my feet during dinner, I'm not going to be happy."

"Nobody is licking anybody's feet at dinner," Lia said. "Except maybe Gogo."

Her dog, an enormous gray deerhound who looked perpetually confused, raised his head at the sound of his name.

"Go back to sleep, boy." Obedient to his mistress, he laid his long face down onto his paws and closed his eyes. "As I was saying, we have clients coming here tonight so we need to be on our best behavior. When you go downstairs, just remember, this is my graduation party, not an orgy. And this is Wingthorn Hall, not a brothel."

"Could have fooled me," Georgy said. Lia ignored her.

"Not only are fourteen clients coming here…so are their wives. Thus, you've never met these men before, right? When you do 'meet' them, be polite and then disengage quickly. Feel free to fake food poisoning and run for it. Stick together. Don't post any pictures online. And whatever you do—" and here Lia paused to look directly into Georgy's eyes "—do not flirt with anyone."

"What?" Georgy sat up straighter. "No flirting? You mean, at all?"

"At. All." Lia punctuated those two syllables by slapping her palm with the knitting needle.

"But, boss, what if he's *really* handsome?" Georgy asked.

Lia shook her head.

"What if he's literally the most handsome man in the world?" Rani asked. "*And* rich."

"Flirting is banned until further notice."

"What if," Jane said, "he's handsome, rich *and* DTFMEL?"

"DTFMEL?" Lia knew the DTF. She wasn't sure about the MEL.

"Down to Fund My Extravagant Lifestyle," Rani translated.

Lia considered that. After all, while she handled the appointments and the money in the YLG&T Club, she didn't own the ladies. And this was the job. She could hardly begrudge them for making a living.

"We'll take it on a case-by-case basis," she said. "All I want is to get through tonight without ending up in the back of a police car or on the front page of the *Sun*."

Earl's Daughter in the Streets, Madam in the Sheets: The Scandal of the Century…

She could see the headlines now. And the think pieces on women and sex work. And the tweets.

Oh God, not the tweets.

"All right, boss," Jane said with a jaunty salute. "We'll behave. Promise."

"Another thing—let's drop the 'boss.' I'm Lia. I'm your friend. I am not, I repeat, *not* your boss. Right?" She grinned and nodded. "Yes? Agree with me, please."

"Right, boss," Georgy said. *Smart-arse.*

"I hear prison isn't all that bad these days," Lia said. "I'll catch up on my knitting."

Unless they didn't allow knitting needles behind bars.

"Why didn't you tell your parents 'no party'?" Rani asked. A fair question.

"Trust me, I did. They are, unfortunately, *proud of me* and couldn't be stopped. I asked them not to invite anyone except family. Also didn't work. I asked them for no gifts. I'm guessing there's a table covered in gifts down there." Which would all be going to a charity shop tomorrow, if Lia had her way.

"Loads of them," Georgy said. "How awful."

Rani met Lia's eyes. "I'm sure it'll be fine." Lia wanted to believe Rani. "Nothing's going to happen tonight. They're more scared of us than we are of them."

Lia nodded. However…she couldn't quite shake the feeling that something bad, very bad, was going to happen tonight. She didn't tell her "young ladies" that. Once they'd been her friends but now they worked for her, and she couldn't have them seeing her rattled for no good reason.

Or was there a good reason?

"I'm sure you're right," Lia said, faking a smile. "Now… Escorts dismissed."

"Come on, birdies," said Georgy as she rose from the armchair. "Time to face the music."

The three of them filed out of Lia's bedroom. Gogo attempted to follow them.

"Not you, boy. Unless there's something you need to tell me," Lia said.

Gogo trotted back to his dog bed.

Once she was again alone in her room, Lia's shoulders sagged. She put her hands to her face and breathed through her fingers. If she had a time machine or even a friendly neighborhood wormhole, she'd hop into it in an instant and go back about three years ago to the night when she'd had the bright idea of starting an escort agency with her friends. She'd find herself, grab herself by the arms and tell herself, "Lia, pet, you're going to regret that…"

Would she have taken her own advice? Probably not.

Lia knew she needed to go downstairs. Guests were arriving already, and she couldn't play the fashionably late game forever. Still, she didn't leave her bedroom. She paced her floor, trying to calm her nerves.

As she passed her fireplace mantel, she laid eyes on a statue, a marble Aphrodite Anadyomene that had once belonged to her great-grandfather Malcolm, the thirteenth Earl of Godwick. According to family legend, her notorious rake of a great-grandfather had worshipped Aphrodite, goddess of romantic love and passion—"the one deity I have any respect for," he'd said. Fitting, then, that Lia had this particular goddess on her mantel. Aphrodite was probably the only deity around who'd answer the prayers of a frazzled madam.

Although she hadn't said a prayer to Aphrodite in years, Lia decided to give it a go. She doubted it would help but it certainly couldn't hurt, could it? She found her sewing scissors on her dressing table and took a candle from the candle box by the grate.

Lia lit the candle and, with the little scissors, she cut one gingerbread-colored curl from her hair. As her hair caught in the flame and burned, she whispered, "Aphrodite, goddess

of love, lust and badly behaved women, please protect your
daughters tonight—Georgy, Jane and Rani. And me, too, I
suppose, if you don't mind."

Then Lia added, "If you run into my great-grandfather Malcolm in the afterworld, please tell him he's a bad influence."

She blew out the candle and found that she felt a little better. At least she could say she did all she could. Outside she
heard the beginnings of a fierce rainstorm. Odd. Rain hadn't
been in the forecast. Lia glanced at the lovely and placid countenance of Aphrodite on her mantel.

"Your doing?" she asked with a smile. Of course Aphrodite did not answer. Lia left her bedroom. If luck or Aphrodite were on her side tonight and that rain kept up, the house
might flood and then the party would be canceled.

A madam could hope.

CHAPTER TWO

As soon as Lia left her suite, she heard voices, laughter, the clinking of champagne flutes and the clicking of high heels on marble floors. She descended the curving main staircase to the entryway of Wingthorn Hall, the ancestral home of the earls of Godwick. Her mother, Mona, the Countess of Godwick, stood by the door, resplendent in a strapless evening gown as scarlet as her reputation.

She grinned broadly as Lia came to stand at her side for door duty.

"You look beautiful, darling." Her smile turned quickly to a scowl. "When did you get so old?"

"I'm twenty-one, Mother."

"Impossible," the countess said. "I'm thirty."

"You're for—"

Her mother raised her hand to silence her. "We do not say the *F* word in this house."

The *F* word was *forty*. Lia's mother was the *F* word plus seven. "Sorry."

Thunder rumbled outside. The ancient windows shivered. Temporary "footmen" waited at the door, armed with black umbrellas to shield the arriving guests.

"Maybe we should cancel the party," Lia said. "For safety reasons."

The safety of her sanity.

"Too late for that," her mother said. "Here we go again."

The grand oak front doors of Wingthorn yawned open. A man entered. Lia couldn't see who he was at first, as his face was hidden behind an umbrella held by a footman. The footman lowered the umbrella, and Lia had one thought at the first sight of the man.

Oh no.

The man, whoever he was, wore a dark blue three-piece suit that perfectly complemented his olive-brown skin. The umbrella had gotten to him a second too late. His hair was rain-damp, dark and curling. His age? Lia guessed thirty, thirty-three tops. Too young to be friends with her parents, too old to be friends with her.

Whoever he was, Lia knew she'd never seen him before. Yet when he looked at her, it seemed he knew her. He gave her the slightest little winking smile as her father shook his hand.

That wink. That smile. Pure mischief. It made Lia's toes clench in her shoes. She ordered her toes to unclench, which they did, but under protest.

"Blink, child," her mother whispered, "before your eyes dry out."

"Who is he?" Lia asked, blinking.

"Has to be Augustine Bowman."

"What's the gossip?" Lia had to know all about him at once and even immediately. Stat.

"Supposedly his mother's a famous Greek beauty. His father is military or something. Divides his time between London and Athens. He's been buying up ancient artifacts and taking them home to Greece."

Lia watched her father, Spencer, the fifteenth Earl of Godwick, chatting with Augustine Bowman, no doubt talking of important manly things like football, old Scotch and how very grand it was to go through life with a penis. Mr. Bowman was nearly as tall as her very tall father, but broader in the chest and shoulders. She bet he had good legs, too, like a football player. She needed to find something about him to loathe and quickly, or she'd be staring at him all night.

"Do you think he beats his servants?" Lia asked.

"If they ask him nicely enough."

"Mother."

"You should show him the tapestry you're working on, dear," her mother, eternal matchmaker, said. "I hear he loves Greek mythology as much as you do."

"I am not going to show him my tapestry," Lia said. "Or anything else."

"Sex really is very fun, darling."

"My kingdom for a normal mother."

"Tsst." Her mother snapped her fingers. "Here he comes. Smile on. Tits out."

They straightened their backs and put on their best smiles as the man approached.

"Mr. Bowman, isn't it?" her mother said. "How do you do?"

"A pleasure, Lady Godwick," he said. Then he turned to Lia. "And you must be Lady Ophelia."

"No one on earth calls me Ophelia," she said at once. Ha. She'd show him.

"Shall we go to Venus, then, if I wish to speak to you?" Mr. Bowman asked.

A joke. Unexpected. She didn't like it. And an accent, too. Greek obviously. And nice. It perfumed his words like a subtle incense. She could give credit where credit was due.

"Call me Lia," she said, when what she wanted to say was, *Please leave before Georgy sees you, because if any man here is rich, handsome and DTFMEL, it's you.*

"And you must call me August, please," he said. "I have a gift for you." He offered her a box wrapped in plain brown paper and twine.

Lia saw her mother flashing her the old side-eye. Lia ignored it.

"You didn't have to bring me anything," she said. "I have everything I want or need."

"But you don't have this," he said, and there it was again—that winking smile, that smiling wink. She'd heard a phrase before—*That one looks like trouble*—and Lia never knew what it meant until this moment.

Now she knew exactly what trouble looked like. It looked like him.

"Thank you," she said. "I'll put it with the others."

She'd meant to go alone to the gift table in the morning room, but Mr. August Bowman had other ideas, apparently. He followed her, which was the exact opposite of what she wanted him to do.

Double trouble, this one. She was determined to ignore him and his obnoxious good looks. They would not get to know each other. She would not, on pain of death, chat him up.

"So…you're a friend of my father's, Mr. Bowman?" she asked, unable to stop herself.

Damn her. Damn her to Hades.

"August, please."

"August." She did like the feel of his name in her mouth. August, the hottest month of the year. She'd told the other ladies not to flirt and here she was, flirting her head off.

"I'd call your father and I more friendly adversaries than friends," he said. "At auctions, I mean. Usually I win the duels. He bested me last time. But I haven't surrendered."

"Good luck. With my father, you'll need it."

"I don't believe in luck," he said. "Perhaps divine intervention."

"Do you know any divinities?"

"I'm looking at one."

Lia met his eyes. His mouth quirked as if trying not to laugh at her.

"You're flirting." She pointed at him.

"Oh, you noticed."

Lia was about to tell Mr. Bowman a few other things she'd noticed when their housekeeper, Mrs. Banks, bustled down the long hallway, looking as angry as any woman in a pink cardigan and tweed skirt has ever looked. A young woman accompanied Mrs. Banks, a young woman who looked as if she'd been crying.

"Miss Lia," Mrs. Banks said. "I need a word. Sir." She nodded an apology to Mr. Bowman.

"What is it?" Lia asked.

"You know this girl?" Mrs. Banks pointed at the pretty young woman who wore the black-and-white uniform of the catering staff. Her name tag read Rita.

"Yes, that's Rita," Lia said. She had never seen the girl before in her life.

"Did you give her this?" Mrs. Banks held up a bottle of Hermès perfume still in the packaging. Lia understood the situation at once—a member of the catering staff had nicked one of her graduation gifts. "Found her stuffing it down in her bag. She said it was hers."

"It's hers," Lia said.

"Really?" Mrs. Banks asked. "Can you explain why it was in a wrapped box with a tag on it that said, 'To Lia, with love and adoration, from XL'?"

Lia blushed crimson. Mr. Bowman said not a word, but the slight arch of his left eyebrow spoke volumes.

"I don't like that perfume," Lia said. "It makes me sneeze. Makes Mum sneeze, too."

"Really, I thought this was your mother's scent?" Mrs. Banks asked.

"I'm sure you must be mistaken." Lia stood up as straight as she could. She didn't like being haughty but she could do it when she had to. "I don't like the perfume. I gave it to Rita. End of discussion."

"All right. I see," Mrs. Banks said. "Just a misunderstanding, then. Apologies for the interruption. Back to work, girl."

Rita mouthed a "Thank you" to Lia before turning and running down the hallway, Mrs. Banks following behind her.

Lia glanced at August, who was eyeing her with intense interest.

"We should go in to dinner," she said. August offered her his arm and, against her better judgment, she took it.

They walked side by side down the long main hall, toward the large salon where dinner would be held.

"XL," August said. "Xavier Lloyd? That's your father's attorney, isn't it? Or perhaps XL is someone's very flattering nickname?"

"No idea. Just one of Daddy's friends, I'm sure."

Xavier Lloyd *was* her father's attorney. He was also Rani's best client. Big tipper. Always sent flowers and very expensive gifts.

"That was kind of you not to get that girl sacked for stealing," August said.

"I gave her the perfume. You heard me."

"Poor girl." August sighed as they walked to the salon. "Waiting tables in high heels. Easier ways for a pretty girl to make money."

Lia stiffened. "What's that supposed to mean?"

"Answering phones. Web design. Driving Formula 1 race cars," he said. "What did you think I meant?"

Lia didn't answer. She just walked on. The vague looming something she'd been dreading tonight? Good chance it was the man walking right next to her. He definitely had an ulterior motive for attending the party—that she knew. But what?

"Would you allow me to sit with you at dinner?" August asked as they entered the salon.

Lia was impressed by his audacity. She'd met the man all of five minutes ago.

"I have to sit with Mum and Daddy."

"Ah, of course. I'll just sit over there with those lovely young ladies," he said, which was once again the exact opposite of what she wanted him to do. "Enjoy your dinner."

He left her with a wave and sat at the very same table as Jane, Rani and Georgy—Rani and Jane on his left, Georgy on his right.

August leaned over and whispered something in Georgy's ear. She laughed and whispered something back. Rani moved her chair closer. Jane took off her glasses. The flirting had begun.

He glanced once Lia's way and gave her that winking smile again.

Augustine Bowman.

Trouble with a capital *T*.

CHAPTER THREE

Dinner went as well as could be expected considering Lia was trussed up so tightly in her grandmother's vintage corset she had to pray before every bite that there'd be room for it when it landed. People were much thinner in the past. Probably because of war rationing.

As Lia picked at her food, she kept one eye on the other tables. She wanted this party to be over yesterday, but even she had to admit to herself that everyone had mostly behaved themselves. The sense of dread slowly released its stranglehold on her heart. Even her father had been good so far—proof miracles did occasionally happen.

"Daddy," Lia said as her father poured her a glass of chardonnay. "Why did you invite Mr. Bowman to the party? Are you two friends?"

"We run into each other at the auctions. I scooped up... *something* he wanted. Told him I was 'sorry not sorry'—"

"Daddy, don't *ever* use internetspeak in my presence again."

"Sorry, darling. Anyway, I felt bad for beating him to the prize, so I asked him to the party as a peace offering."

"And to show off how rich you are?" she teased.

"How lucky I am." He kissed her cheek, and Lia managed a smile. "He's a nice enough lad, but keep an eye on him. He might very well try to steal your graduation gift. You know, since I stole it out from under him first."

Lia glanced over at August Bowman and found he was already looking at her. How could she keep an eye on him when he was already keeping an eye on her?

Her father stood up and clinked his wineglass with his fork. The room fell silent.

Oh God. The toast. Not the toast. Lia picked up her glass and drank deeply. Not enough chardonnay in the world.

"Thank you all so much for coming to Lia's graduation party tonight," he began. Nothing good ever came of her father giving toasts. She scanned the room for the closest emergency exit. "Lia hates me right now for throwing her such a large party when she would have been happy with an extra chocolate biscuit at tea and a gentle pat on the back."

"Yes, why couldn't we do that?" she asked. That scored a laugh from the room.

"Because I'm a monster," her father said. "Just ask your brothers."

Another laugh.

"I'm not joking," her father said to the assembled guests. "They caught Lia's mum and I shagging in the kitchen and for some reason took offense to that."

"Toast over!" Lia called out.

"I'll make it quick, I promise. And no stories about shagging your mum. Other than that one," he said, shuffling through his notecards. "No, wait, there's one more."

Lia gently banged her head on the table. Mum patted her back to comfort her. It didn't work.

The toast continued.

"Lia," her father said, "was conceived on our wedding night."

And it was all downhill from there.

She survived her father's musings on her conception, her birth, her childhood, her first car—a 1980 red Austin Mini Metro, which, he said, "Can go from zero to ninety-seven if you roll it down a very steep hill and get a good tailwind behind you. And to think, I was going to buy her a Jag."

"I like my Mini better," Lia said. Hardly a Jag, but she'd paid for it herself.

"Ungrateful children," her father said. "Scourge of the modern era."

"Embarrassing story time over, please," she called out to more laughter.

"In conclusion," he said, and Lia sagged with relief, "I have the best daughter in the world. No surprise as I also have the best wife and the best house."

"Daddy."

"The best art collection."

"Daddy!"

"The best wine cellar."

"Daddy, stop or I'll shoot." She had a spoon full of caviar in hand, and she wasn't afraid to use it.

"Sorry, sorry." He raised a hand in surrender. "I'll draw this to a close before Lia puts a hit out on me. Lia has always had a passion for Greek mythology. For years now she's even been weaving mythological tapestries. One of these days I'm going to walk into her room and catch her ritually sacrific-ing one of her brothers to Zeus. Or both of them, I hope."

All the parents of teenagers in the crowd laughed. Lia was glad her brothers were still away at school.

"So, as a small token of my love for my daughter, I give her this..."

He put a red wrapped box in front of her. Of course her father was going to make her open it in front of everyone.

She stood up, tore off the paper and lifted the lid. The box wasn't cardboard but solid wood. That meant the gift was fragile, very fragile. And expensive.

Very expensive.

She pushed through the packing material until she found the object. She lifted it out and looked at it.

Lia gazed in wonder at the cup in her hands. She'd never seen a more beautiful Greek relic. The stem was short and the bowl wide and shallow. The colors were black and golden amber. Inside the bowl was painted a beautiful girl who lay seemingly dead on the ground. From her side, a rose grew. Roses were painted on the stem, too. And a continuous three-petal rose motif adorned the lip while the twin handles were painted with vines.

"This," her father said, "is a kylix. A wine cup, dated to 500 BC. Supposedly used in temple ceremonies to the god-dess Aphrodite. A little piece of real Greek mythology just for you, my love."

Lia was stunned speechless. Her hands shook so badly she could barely hang on to the exquisite 2,500-year-old artifact. Carefully she put the cup down and wrapped her arms around her father, tears hot in her eyes.

The guests said, "Aww..." all at once.

Her father pulled back from the hug but kept his arm around her back so she couldn't escape.

"Lia got her first drink of wine from a two-thousand-year-old kylix when we took her to Athens a few years ago," her father said. "She's been asking for a good drinking cup ever since. Hope this one is good enough for you."

"It'll do," Lia said, laughing and crying.

"A toast to Lia." He raised his wineglass. "If she's half as happy in life as she's made her parents, she'll be the happiest young woman alive."

Lia lifted her kylix. The guests called out, "To Lia!" and "Cheers!"

Lia looked around the room and saw everyone had their glasses raised in her honor.

Everyone but August Bowman.

CHAPTER FOUR

After dinner, the guests dispersed to various rooms in the house—the music room, the front parlor, the Wingthorn Hall portrait gallery. The rain had picked up, and it beat hard against the roof and windows. People were going to be trapped at the house until the storm was over.

"Aphrodite," Lia muttered on her way to the music room, "you are useless."

"Watch out. She probably heard that."

Lia spun around and found August walking behind her.

He grinned and caught up to her.

"Stop eavesdropping when I talk to myself," she said. "It's rude."

"You were talking to Aphrodite."

Lia glared at him. "Don't be right when I want you to be wrong, please."

He laughed, low and throaty.

"Where are you going?" he asked.

"The music room."

"May I join you?"

"I'd prefer if you didn't."

"I've offended you." He didn't look hurt by this realization. Lia was annoyed to find he looked rather pleased with himself. He leaned back against the wall, hands in his trouser pockets, looking the very picture of casual elegance.

"No, I just don't like parties very much."

"Why not?"

"The usual reasons. Strangers. Awkward chitchat." She was the madam of an illegal escort agency, and her parents had unwittingly invited three of Lia's escorts and half their client list.

"Let's go and have some unawkward chitchat." He nodded toward the morning room.

"I need to mingle," she said. "Sorry."

She turned away from him and started down the hall again, toward the music room. August, of course, walked right at her side.

"We need to talk." His tone was no longer flippant and flirtatious. In fact, he sounded almost scared. "Please believe me when I say it's important."

"Leave your card with the butler," she said. "My visiting day is the fifth Tuesday of every month."

"We could be friends, Lia," he said. "We have a lot in common, after all."

"I highly doubt that."

"You have wealthy, powerful parents. I have wealthy, powerful parents. You love Greek mythology. I eat, sleep and breathe Greek mythology. I'm handsome. You're beautiful. We're practically twins."

"We are not amused."

"Will you at least open your gift?" This man was determined. She gave him credit for that.

Lia looked at him. "Now?" This was her graduation party, not a child's birthday party.

He nodded. "It's nothing indecent, I promise. You'll like it."

"And you'll stop flirting with me if I open it?"

"If you want me to," he said. "Do you want me to?"

Lia didn't answer.

"Well?" he asked.

"Let me get back to you on that."

"Open your gift. Then you can tell me if I can keep flirting with you or not."

Too intrigued to say no, Lia crossed the hall to the morning room. She found his gift in its plain brown wrapper. She tore off the paper, lifted the lid and pushed the gold foil tissue aside.

"Oh," she said, unable to mask the delight in her voice.

He'd given her a copy of *The Wind in the Willows* by Kenneth Grahame, her favorite novel of all time. The cover was a deep forest green with the Greek god Pan engraved on the front in gilt. This wasn't simply a copy of her favorite book of all time—this was a rare first edition of her favorite book of all time.

"How did you know?" she asked him.

"It's my favorite book, too," he said.

"It is?" She didn't know anyone who read it anymore, except children.

"I love the part where Ratty and Mole set out by boat at night on a search-and-rescue mission for the missing baby otter, and they accidentally end up—"

"Yes, on Pan's Island," Lia said, running her fingertips gently over the golden lines of Pan on the cover. "I love when they find Pan himself sitting there with the otter asleep at his feet."

"And Ratty and Mole are overwhelmed by wonder and love," August said.

"Yes, right." She smiled like a child. "That's my favorite part, too. I could recite the whole passage, I've read it so many times."

"Surely not," he said, a smile lurking at the corner of his mouth. He was teasing her, she knew it, but she didn't care anymore. He'd knocked her guards down with one little gift. Without her meaning to do it, the words of her most precious story tumbled out.

"'He looked in the very eyes of the Friend and Helper,'" Lia recited, "'saw the backward sweep of the curved horns, gleaming in the growing daylight; saw the stern, hooked nose between the kindly eyes that were looking down on them humorously, while the bearded mouth broke into a half-smile at the corners…'"

Lia paused and flipped open the book to the exact page, handed it to him so he could read along and see that she didn't miss a single word.

"'All this he saw,'" she continued, "'for one moment breathless and intense, vivid on the morning sky; and still, as he looked, he lived; and still, as he lived, he wondered.'

"'"Rat!" he found breath to whisper, shaking. "Are you afraid?"'

"'"Afraid?" murmured the Rat, his eyes shining with unutterable love. "Afraid! Of him? O, never, never! And yet—and yet—"'"

"'"O, Mole, I am afraid!"'" August finished as he closed the book with a gentle thud and passed it back to Lia. She took it carefully from him and held it to her chest. Then he raised a hand to her face and, with a flick of his thumb, wiped a tear off the arch of her cheek.

"I stand corrected. You know your *Willows*."

"Oh, sorry," she said. She put the book back into the tissue paper and hid it away in the box like she did with so many of the things that brought tears to her eyes. "Daddy used to read that book to me every night. Every summer day when I was little, we'd walk in the woods, looking for Pan's Island."

"Did you find it?" he asked.

"No," she said. "But finding it wasn't so much the point as looking for it with Daddy." She laughed to stop herself from shedding another tear. "Anyway, if I'd found it I wouldn't be here. I'd still be there."

"You'll find it someday."

She wasn't sure why, but when he said that, she almost believed him. Must have been his Greek accent.

"Thank you very much," Lia said. She was determined to take control of this conversation again. "This was very kind of you, Mr. Bowman." He arched his eyebrow. "Sorry, August."

He looked to the left, looked to the right. He crooked two fingers at her, beckoning her to step forward to hear a secret. She leaned in so close she could have kissed him. He bent his head and put his lips to her ear.

"*Timeo Danaos et dona ferentes,*" he said. She wasn't sure what it meant but it made her knees weak to hear it, and her thighs weren't holding up all that well, either.

"Um…my Latin's a little rusty," she said, meeting his eyes, the wild color of storm clouds.

He put his hand to his mouth as if to tell her a secret.

"Beware Greeks bearing gifts," he said. His breath tickled the sensitive skin of her shoulder.

Lia raised a finger and wagged it at his face.

"You're trouble."

"You don't know the half of it," he said.

"I'm going now. Thank you for the gift. Flirting over."

Lia couldn't believe she'd cried in front of the man. It had been years since she'd shed a single tear over anyone or anything. She'd forgotten how much she hated being vulnerable in front of someone. Thanks to August Bowman, she remembered.

Wanting to put distance between them quickly, Lia strode across the hallway, stepped into the music room and stopped dead in her tracks.

Across the room, at the fireplace, stood her mother with a man Lia had not seen in four years and had hoped to never, ever see again. The second he saw her, he smiled and raised his glass of red wine to her in a mocking toast.

David.

Here it was. This. The thing she'd been dreading. The knot in her stomach. The hand wrapped around her heart. She'd been right. Something monumentally bad had happened tonight, was happening right that second.

David Bell was here, in her home.

Her mother spotted Lia at the same instant and waved her over.

"Lia? Are you all right?" August suddenly stood at her side.

She was too scared to lie. "No." Her breathing was so fast she thought she might faint. "Help me. Please?"

As if answering her "please," the house reverberated with a clap of thunder. The windows turned white as lightning split apart the sky.

The power went out and they were all plunged into darkness.

"I wish I could take the credit," August said. "But that wasn't me."

CHAPTER FIVE

L ia felt a strong arm around her waist. She let August pull her from the room and down the hall. He took out his phone, turned on its torchlight and led her away.

"Your room's upstairs?" he asked.

Lia nodded. They took the stairs quickly, despite the dark and the chaos in the house as the hundred guests laughed nervously and fumbled around for phones and candles and torches.

"Left," Lia said as they reached the top of the staircase. He half pulled, half carried her down the long hallway. "Here."

They'd reached her suite. Lia was still shaking when August opened the door and led her inside. He put her on the love seat in her sitting room.

"We need wine and candles," he said. "What would you like first?"

"Candles in the box on the mantel," she said, hoping that was true. Her suite included a sitting room with a large stone fireplace, only decorative these days, and her bedroom with a smaller working fireplace. She'd prefer to keep August out of her bedroom. August went to the sitting room fireplace and, by the light of his phone, found the candles, candlesticks and matches.

"Are you going to tell me who that man was downstairs?" Quickly he lit four candles and set them around the room—two on the stone mantel, one on her side table by the love seat, one on her sewing table by her weaving loom.

"Just an ex," she said.

"Ex what? Ex-con?" he asked. "You're terrified of him, I can tell."

Lia stood up and took a candle from her mantel. By the light of it, she pulled two wineglasses from her cabinet and a bottle of Syrah from the wine rack.

"Not terrified. I just... I didn't want to talk to him. He's not a nice person."

Understatement of the century.

Flustered, Lia broke the cork off when twisting in the screw. The corkscrew landed with a metallic clatter onto the table.

"Damn." Lia put her hands over her face and breathed. She faked a smile, dropped her hands, muttered a "Sorry."

"Let me help you." August walked to her and picked up the wine bottle, examining the broken cork as Lia rubbed her forehead. He slapped the base of it once, twice, three times with the palm of his hand. The broken cork wriggled its way to the top of the bottle and, with his fingertips, August pulled it out.

"Voilà," he said.

Lia stared at him, wide-eyed. "How did you do that?"

He raised his right hand. "It's my spanking hand."

Lia shook her head as she poured the wine. If mischief were a kingdom, this man would be the prince of it.

"Who is he?" August asked. "Really?"

"His name is David," Lia said softly. "A few years ago we spent the night together. I was serious about him. He wasn't about me, apparently. Next day—literally the next day, he slept with someone else. He's a bit older than I am. My parents have no idea we were involved. They don't know some of the things I know about him. Seeing him out of the blue tonight with my mother was…a bad surprise."

A very bad surprise. The worst of all surprises. But she couldn't and wouldn't go into that. David was a wound far too tender to touch.

"Do you want me to toss him out of the house?" August asked.

Lia was so shocked by that question that she laughed.

"What? Why would *you* toss him out of my house? You don't know him."

"Because he hurt you," he said. "And that's all the reason I need."

"You don't know me, either," she said.

"But I'd like to." He raised his wineglass to his lips. In the flickering candlelight, his fingertips looked dipped in gold.

Lia wanted to say something to him, something like *I'd like to know you, too*. But that would be stupid, and Lia didn't say stupid things to men anymore.

Instead she said, "I need more wine."

She turned away from him to top off her glass. When she turned back, she found he'd taken the cover off her loom and was examining her tapestry.

"I keep that covered for a reason," she said as she came to stand by him. The reason was Gogo's wiry hairs. And embarrassment.

"Lia," August breathed her name, "your work is magnificent."

She blushed in the dark. "Thank you. Still learning."

She'd woven the ocean, the dark red evening ocean, from one corner of the fabric to the top edge. A shadow lurked near the right center. The candlelight fluttered across the surface of her tapestry and tricked her eye into seeing the wine-dark ocean moving in flickering waves.

"This is Andromeda and Perseus," August said. "Yes?"

"How did you know that? I haven't put in Perseus yet. Or his Pegasus."

"I know my mythology," he said. "This is Cetus, yes? The shadow? The monster about to emerge." He pointed at the shape lurking in the red water. "But where's Andromeda, the teenage maiden being sacrificed to Zeus's sea monster?"

"That would be me," Lia said. "Or you. The viewer."

"This is what Andromeda sees?" August waved his hand over the tapestry, the red evening sea, the shadow in the water about to rise and devour her.

"I wanted to weave the scene through her eyes, what she saw as she was waiting to be killed. Hope I got it right."

"Let's find out," he said. "May I?" He raised his hands and Lia put hers into them without thinking. Or...without thinking anything except that she wanted to put her hands in his.

August pulled her closer, moving her to stand directly in front of him. From behind her, he clasped her wrists.

"You are now Andromeda, daughter of Cepheus, the king of Aethiopia, who dotes upon his daughter and Queen Cassiopeia, who like so many mothers in mythology was jealous of her daughter's beauty."

August lifted her arms up and over her head. He held both her wrists in his one large, strong hand. They rested lightly in his grip, and she knew she could pull them away in an instant.

She didn't.

"You are Andromeda," he said again. "And your hands are chained over your head with another chain wrapped around your stomach." He wrapped his arm around her hips and pulled her back against him. "Tightly. You can't move at all."

"At all?"

"No," he said into her ear. "This was done at your request, Andromeda. Remember? Long or loose chains meant you could possibly cower when the Cetus came for you. And you will not cower in death but stand up straight and meet it face-to-face. You ordered your mother to lock the final chain to the rock."

"Why did I do that?" Lia asked, her voice low and breathless, her wrists still held in his hand, above her head. His voice was deep and low and rumbled like a gentle earthquake. He became a different person to her as he told the story, like an ancient bard, singing his tales at the feasts of long-dead kings.

"The priests at the temple said you must be chained naked to the rock to await the ravaging of Cetus. It was to be your wedding night, and you would be married to Death. Your death alone would appease the wrath of Poseidon."

"Yes, in all art, she's naked," Lia said. "Thought that was because the artists were perverts."

"You poor girl, Andromeda. You wanted your mother's arms, your mother's protection and love. But you also wanted to punish your mother, as well. It was your mother's fault you had to be sacrificed."

"Was it her fault?" Lia asked, already knowing the answer.

"Queen Cassiopeia had bragged about you, saying her daughter was more beautiful than the Nereids, the water nymphs who served in Poseidon's temple. I say bragged, but in truth she lamented. Once she'd been the most beautiful woman in the kingdom, and then you usurped her. While chained to that rock, did you think perhaps your mother hadn't secretly hoped this would happen? After all, once you were dead and gone, perhaps she would be the most beautiful woman in the kingdom again. 'Look well, Mother,' you said to her. 'Look well at your child. Am I beautiful now, in these chains? Is this the marriage you arranged for me? Your daughter wed to Death? Will you brag that you're the most beautiful woman in Father's kingdom when I'm gone? Was that your plan all along?'"

Lia could hear the girl's voice ringing in her ears. She could hear the hiss and rasp of her fury and her fear.

"How do you know all this?" Lia asked. "I read everything I could on Andromeda before I started the tapestry. I never read she made her mother chain her, or what she said to her."

"I'm Greek. You weave these stories into your tapestries with wood and thread. We are born with them carved onto our very bones, like scrimshaw. I know them as I know my own name. And yours, Lia."

Lia had never been more aware of her body and her breathing than she was then, wrists in his hands, back to his chest, lips panting, knees trembling, stomach quivering, her breasts pressed hard against the fabric of her dress. She knew if she could touch herself inside, she would be wet.

"But where is handsome Perseus in your tapestry?" August whispered the words into her ear. "Where is his winged horse and our hero come to save you, Andromeda?"

"He's coming," Lia said. "But not yet. I'll weave him in last. I wanted Andromeda to wait, to be afraid, to believe no one is coming for her, that no one is going to save me. I mean, save her."

"Cruel," he said. "You have a pagan soul, my lady."

"That's not—"

August laughed. She felt his chest move against her back.

"Mercy is one of the Christian virtues, and I am no Christian, either." The arm around her stomach tightened as he molded her body to his. Lia shuddered, shocked at the pleasure of being held against him.

"Am I hurting you?" he asked.

"A little," she said. "But don't stop. I want to know what it was like to be her."

"Is that why you weave from her perspective?"

"That's how I do all my tapestries."

"You leave room in the myth for yourself," he said. "You want to be in the story."

"I know that sounds stupid." She blushed.

"Not at all. There is no shame in wanting to live inside your favorite stories."

"I'm getting too old for fairy tales."

"Fairy tales aren't real. These myths, they did happen," August insisted. "Andromeda was real. She should be remembered. Always."

"You won't see the Duchess of Cambridge tied to London Bridge to stop the ice caps from melting and flooding London," Lia said, joking to hide her arousal. "I wish I really could live in Andromeda's shoes. Well, sandals."

"I could put you into her sandals," August said.

He released her hands and she turned and faced him.

"What do you mean?" she asked.

"We need to talk about the kylix your father gave you tonight. It's not what you think it is."

"What is it, then?"

"Something very, very dangerous."

CHAPTER SIX

L ia stared at August with narrowed eyes.
  "Dangerous?"

"Maybe," he said. "I need to see it to be certain."

"I don't know about that. Daddy said you tried to buy it, but he beat you to it. If this is all a ploy to steal it—"

"I will not steal it. I have no desire to steal it. But I need to know if it's what I think it is. That's all. For your sake. I promise."

She exhaled heavily. "Fine."

Lia took her candle and led him to her bedroom, where she'd put the kylix for safekeeping after dinner. August went to her bedroom fireplace and lit several more candles.

"Is that Aphrodite?" he asked, staring at the statue on her bedroom fireplace mantel.

"Oh, yes, it is." Lia walked over to him. "She was my great-grandfather's, the thirteenth Earl of Godwick—Old Number Thirteen, we call him. Notorious rake. Loved fine art and even finer sex."

"I like the man already," August said.

He took the statue by the base and turned it so Aphrodite faced the wall.

"No offense," he said, and Lia wasn't sure if he was speaking to her or Aphrodite. He pointed at a black-and-white photograph that was also on her mantel. "Who's this?"

"That's him—Old Number Thirteen. That photo was taken in 1933 at the Pearl, a brothel in London," she said. "Lord Malcolm's favorite haunt."

"These women with him are all prostitutes?" he asked. Three glamorous young women in exquisite evening dress sat arrayed around her smiling handsome grandfather.

"I told you he was notorious," she said.

He moved down the mantel to a second photograph.

"I know these ladies," August said. "My dinner companions."

"Friends of mine. I've known Georgy for donkey's years. She's from the village of Thornhill, just down the way. I met Rani and Jane at King's. And that's me, of course."

In the photograph, Lia sat on a green velvet divan with her friends clustered around her.

"Thick as thieves," August said. "Same setting? The Pearl?"

"We were out shopping, stopped by the hotel, had the clerk take our photo there. You know, since my great-grandfather used to practically run the place. We were just being silly."
Silly, silly, silly…

She could tell August was about to ask another question, but he was interrupted by Gogo sliding his enormous length out from under her bed and immediately scampering to him. Gogo whimpered to be petted.

"Lia…there's a horse in your room," August said as he gazed down.

"Gogo," Lia chided. "Get back in your bed. You'll get hair on Mr. Bowman's suit."

"Gogo?" August repeated. "Is he a club dancer?"

"Gogo, short for Argos," Lia said.

August laughed softly and squatted on his haunches to meet Gogo face-to-face.

"Poor lad, named for the most loyal hound in Greek mythology and your mistress calls you Gogo."

"When I was little, Mum had a cat named for the painter Toulouse-Lautrec. She called him Tou-Tou. Women, right? No respect for the dignity of men and other beasts."

August only smiled and kept petting Gogo. She liked that, that he was nice to her dog. But she didn't like liking it.

"Gogo, go-go to your bed now," Lia said. Gogo hesitated before obeying. She was also impressed that Gogo had warmed to August so quickly. He tended to hide from strangers, especially men, and August was certainly one strange man.

"You wanted to see the kylix, right?" she asked.

"Please," August said.

Lia returned to her bed and passed him the wooden box.

She watched as he opened it, watched as his lips parted when he looked down at the kylix nestled in the packing straw. His eyes widened as he stared at it without touching. Gray eyes, gray like a mercurial sky that couldn't decide if it wanted to break into sunlight or let loose a storm. She really needed to stop staring at his eyes.

"Gods…" he said with a long breath. "May I?" He nodded at the kylix.

"Go ahead."

He pulled a handkerchief from his pocket and, with it, carefully eased the kylix from the box, lifting it as if it were a newborn baby sparrow.

"This, Lia, is not an ordinary kylix."

"It's 2,500 years old. Is there such a thing as an ordinary kylix?"

"Yes," he said. "I have dozens of them in my flat. You can buy them at auctions for a few hundred. But this is different. This…is something special."

"Why so?" she asked, studying the kylix as he turned it in his large hands.

"It's the Rose Kylix." August pointed at the three-petal rose motif painted on the lip of the kylix.

"It has a name?"

"A name, a legend and a secret. Your father has his story wrong. The cup wasn't used in Aphrodite's temple. It was used in worship by the Cult of Eros."

"Is it as old as Daddy thought?"

"A great deal older, in fact. Do you know this myth?" He pointed at the woman painted inside the kylix bowl and the rose that grew from her chest.

"Girl. Rose. Aphrodite?"

"Not quite," August said. "Although she is part of the story. It begins with Chloris, goddess of flowers. She was walking through the verdant spring woods she called home when she happened to stumble across the body of a nymph lying dead on the forest floor. She wept for the beautiful creature and determined to raise her again to life. As she was the goddess of flowers, she transformed the fallen nymph into a flower. She called upon the other gods to bless her new creation. Apollo shone down on the flower with the healing rays of the sun. Dionysus granted it an intoxicating scent. The three Graces blessed it with beauty and splendor and charm. Aphrodite named it Rose in honor of her son—Eros. Rose. E-*ros*."

"I didn't know the Greek gods played word games," Lia said, enchanted by the story and even more enchanted by her handsome storyteller.

"The gods play any and all games they wish to—word games, beauty contests, bets and dares," August said. "Immortality gets boring otherwise." He pointed at the image in the center of the bowl. "You see this painting...the young nymph lying dead on the ground. And from her body blooms a rose. From death, new life. It's fitting that the new flower was named after Eros, the son of Aphrodite and Ares. The goddess of love and the god of war. Beautiful petals. Vicious thorns. That was Eros. Beautiful and lovely. And very, very dangerous. Like this cup."

"Dangerous?" Lia stepped back from him, from the cup. "What do you mean? Is it poisoned or something?" She knew old paints and old glazes could make people quite ill.

"In a way, yes," August said. "Though it's not what you think. The cup was glazed with the same 'poison' that tipped the arrows of Eros. If you drink from this cup you will have extraordinarily heightened sexual experiences."

"So there's traces of aphrodisiac or something in it?" she asked.

"No, Lia, you don't understand." He shook his head. "I mean, the Rose Kylix is literally the cup of Eros. If you drink from it, you will *experience* your erotic fantasies. You will enter them, live them."

"That's insane," she said. "The gods weren't real."

"You break my heart to say that. Of course they were real. And this cup was a gift from Aphrodite to her son Eros. Until she took it back."

"Why?"

"His worshippers were having more fun than hers because of it," he said. "She's got a jealous streak wide as the Mediterranean Sea."

"How do you know all this?" she demanded.

He yanked his shirt out of his trousers.

"Stop undressing right now," Lia said, shocked and yet not displeased.

"Look." He lifted his shirt and pulled the waist of his trousers down two inches. On his lower stomach, right above the left hip, he had a tattoo. A tattoo of a rose identical to the three-petal rose tattoo motif on the kylix, done in thick red lines.

"What is that?" Lia asked, staring at the artwork. She felt an overpowering urge to touch it.

With her tongue.

He playfully bowed to her.

"Augustine Bowman, prostitute in the Temple of Eros, at your service, my lady."

"You're telling me," Lia said, "that you're a prostitute."

He smiled at her. "I told you we had a lot in common."

CHAPTER SEVEN

"I have no idea what you're talking about," Lia said, standing up straighter.

August took his phone out of his trouser pocket, and from its leather case he pulled a small pink business card with the words *The Young Ladies' Gardening & Tennis Club of Wingthorn Hall* printed on the front. On the back was a phone number in black, next to a rose and tennis racquet logo.

"Just a moment," he said. "Have to make a call. Trying to schedule a tennis match."

He sent the call.

On the fireplace mantel, Lia's phone buzzed like an angry bee.

"Your friend Georgy likes me," August said. "She asked if I played tennis and then she winked at me. I said I was game for a game. She gave me this card. Odd that it rings to your phone. Then again, maybe you really love tennis and gardening."

"What's wrong with tennis? Or gardening?" Lia asked.

August rang off. "No one home," he said. Her phone immediately ceased buzzing. "Guess you're out playing tennis. Let's try again."

He dialed. Lia's phone buzzed. And buzzed. And buzzed. If Lia had a gun, she'd use it to shoot her phone.

August rang off once more.

Her phone stopped buzzing.

"One more time," August said. "She must be out gardening…" He dialed again. Lia's phone buzzed again.

"Fine. Fine. You can stop now," Lia said. August slipped his phone back into his pocket.

"Forget it," he said. "I've never played tennis in my life."

"The Young Ladies' Gardening & Tennis Club of Wingthorn Hall isn't a gardening or tennis club."

"You don't say."

"I happen to manage the 'appointments' and the money of some friends of mine who are in the business of pleasure," Lia explained. "That's all. That's why her number rings to me. If you want to see her, you come through me first."

"You know it's illegal," he said. "Not being an escort. That's legal. I would know. But you…*running* an escort service is considered pandering and that is a crime in this country, you wicked tart."

"I know the law," Lia said. "Two of our best customers are barristers."

"Tell me something. Why does a wealthy peer's daughter need to have her own escort service? Your parents are filthy rich."

"My parents have an open marriage. My grandfather had the largest vintage porn collection in Europe. My grandmother collected the lingerie of famous courtesans. My great-grandfather slept with hundreds of prostitutes in his life. He even died in the bed of his teenage mistress—exactly how he wanted to leave the world. The Godwicks have been playful deviants for centuries. You could call sex the family business if you want." There was more to the story—much more—but she wasn't about to give August more of her secrets than she had to. "Why do you do it?" she asked him.

"I love making love," he said. "Friends, Romans, country-men. All of them. Line them up and lay them out. That's me."

"Got a tart card?" she asked.

"Do you wish to hire me? My week is fairly open," he said.

"You make a lot of money at it?"

He tilted his head to the side, raised his hands slightly, gave her a look that said, *Really?*

"Right. Stupid question," she said. Lia walked over to the mantel. She turned Aphrodite back around. "So let me guess, you're blackmailing me?"

"I would never blackmail you. It would be an utter betrayal of who I am and what *we* do," he said.

She didn't miss the pointed "we" in his statement.

"I'm attempting to get your attention, Lia. I need you to take me very seriously."

If she hadn't been taking him seriously before, she certainly was now.

"All right, you have my attention."

"Good. I promise, I don't like being the bad guy, Lia. And I hate being serious. I'd much rather we take our clothes off and jump into bed than have a serious talk. Sometimes it can't be avoided, however. This is one of those unfortunate times."

Lia ignored the comment about bed and jumping and her. At least, she tried to ignore it.

"Now..." August continued, "whether you like it or not,

you need to either sell me the Rose Kylix or put it into my safekeeping."

"Daddy was right about you. I should have listened."

"Your father knows nothing about me, I promise," August said. "If he knew what I knew, he never would have given that kylix to you. It is an *extremely* dangerous artifact. It can't simply be left sitting around your rooms, waiting for someone to get pissed and drink a toast out of it for laughs and end up in an asylum because Zeus showed up in their bedroom five minutes later in the form of a giant swan with a raging stiffie."

"That's a vivid image." Lia could not believe for one second that he was telling her the truth. A god's magical wine cup? That was plain nonsense.

"Whatever you want to believe," he said, "the fact is, that cup rightly belongs to Eros and those who serve in the Temple of Eros." He pointed at himself.

"There is no Temple of Eros. It's 2019, not…19."

"How can you say that? You have a shrine to Aphrodite." He gestured at her mantel while staring at her.

She sighed. "Fair point. But my shrine is just for fun."

"So is mine," he said. "Sacred fun."

Lia turned away from him. This was madness. Absolute insanity.

"Lia, I need you to believe me," he said. "The Rose Kylix can be very dangerous if you don't know what you're doing. And you don't."

"You want me to give you the cup."

"Sell it to me. Name your price."

"No." She shook her head. "No, absolutely not. My father gave that to me for my graduation. He'd be heartbroken if I sold it."

"I'll trade you one of mine for it. I have kylikes galore."

"Then you don't need mine. Now…are you going to go tell on me or not?" she demanded.

"Never. On my honor."

"Do you have any honor?"

"Somewhere…" He patted his pockets. "Left it at home. Probably next to my stack of tart cards."

"I don't like you," she said.

"Yes, you do."

"Fine, but I've never had good judgment when it comes to men."

He held out his hand to her and she looked at it. Then she put her hand in his. He turned it palm up and stroked the lines of her life. It tickled deliciously, his rougher male fingertips against her soft tender skin.

"Tell me a sexual fantasy you have," he said.

"What?" She laughed, too shocked to slap him.

"I want to prove to you that I'm telling the truth about the cup."

"Did you not just say it was extremely dangerous?"

"Not if I'm with you," he said. "I know how to use it. I know all its secrets."

"Oh, of course. Makes perfect sense."

If he'd detected her sarcasm, he didn't let on.

"I want to prove myself to you. Let me, please."

"That's a little personal."

"Would you like to know one of mine?" he asked, then went on before she could tell him no. "It's 1780, and I'm a much-used and abused cabin boy on a passenger ship heading to France, and the exquisite teenage daughter of an indebted courtesan is being sent off to marry an ogre three times her age. When she sees poor me, she takes pity on me and buys me from my wicked captain and makes me her own personal—"

"No. Stop. Do not continue."

"I was just getting to the good part. Don't you want to hear the good part?" August looked positively crushed he wouldn't get to tell her the good part.

"No," she said, though a small part of her did want to hear the good part.

"Tell me yours, Lia." He smiled. "Just a little hint."

He caressed the lines on her palm again. She didn't realize how sensual that could feel, how intimate, like he was caressing her whole life with one fingertip...

"You're serious about this?" she asked.

"As serious as I will ever be about anything in my life. If you're willing to drink from the cup with me, you will have an experience that you will never forget. All you must do is tell me what you want, and I can give it to you. I can give you your ultimate fantasy without even leaving this room."

"This is mad," she said. "Insane. Absolutely barmy."

"One sip," he said. "That's all. And if I'm wrong or I'm lying, the worst that will have happened is that you will have drunk dusty wine from an ancient kylix. And if I'm telling the truth, we can negotiate for the return of the cup. Surely that's a reasonable offer?"

"One sip?" she asked.

"One sip," he said.

Lia raised her hands. "All right. You've made me curious. And I'm up for anything that'll keep me away from the party."

"Thank you," he said. "But I want you to enjoy it. So... fantasy?"

She didn't have to think for a long time before she had an answer.

"My first time was not wonderful." Classic English understatement.

August's eyes widened. She shook her head.

"Not that," she said. "I wasn't raped, wasn't drunk, wasn't

violated. I was in love with him. It was just…bad. Sometimes I imagine a much better first time. With anyone but him. Not really a fantasy. More like a wish."

"Your friend David downstairs?" he asked.

She said nothing, did nothing. He nodded. Message received.

"You know who had a wonderful time losing her virginity?" August asked.

"Who?"

August pointed at her tapestry. "Andromeda."

"Did she?"

"Perseus was quite a lover. No surprise, as he was Zeus's son by a mortal mother."

"Lucky Andromeda."

"Would you like to be her? Just for a night?"

"You can do that?" Lia asked.

"The Rose Kylix can do that."

Something about the way he looked at her… Lia almost believed he was telling the truth. And what if he was? What then?

"We won't be…you know…" she asked.

"Having sex? No. Not in our bodies, anyway."

"Oh, well, as long as we're not in our bodies." She rolled her eyes.

"Wine?" August suggested.

"I'll get it," Lia said. She didn't want him drugging it. If she was going to drink, she would be in charge of the pour.

On her way from the bedroom she paused and turned around.

"Do you think I should wash it first? The kylix?"

"What are you going to do?" August asked. "Put it through the dishwasher? It's one sip."

She sighed and fetched a new bottle of wine and opened it. He held out the kylix.

"How much?" she asked.

"Just a splash."

She poured enough for two swallows into the kylix. She set the bottle aside and waited. She expected August to make a joke, say "bottoms up" or something, but he didn't.

He cradled the kylix in his two large hands and closed his eyes. He murmured something in Greek, something strange and lovely, as strange and lovely as he was.

"What did you pray?"

"I prayed for you. That you would enjoy worshipping with me."

"Who are we worshipping?" she asked. "Eros?"

"Each other, of course," he said. Then he sipped from the cup and passed it to her.

She stared at it, suddenly frightened.

"I'll protect you," August assured her. "Whatever happens, you'll be safe."

Lia took a deep long breath. She drank from the cup.

The wine tasted a little dusty but still sweet and warm and potent. She set the cup carefully on the bedside table.

"Now what do we do?" she asked.

"Kiss me," August said.

"What?"

"Kiss me. I dare you."

"What'll happen when I kiss you?"

"Good things will happen."

"Like what?" she demanded.

"I'll put my tongue in your mouth, for starters."

"And after that?"

"You'll see," he said. "If you dare."

She wanted his tongue in her mouth. And she wanted to see.

Lia dared.

The kiss was wine-flavored and heady. August didn't wait to keep his promise. He pressed his tongue into her mouth to open and deepen the kiss. Lia wound her arms around his neck. He kissed a path from her mouth to her throat, then put his lips to her ear.

"Don't be afraid," he said.

"Of what?"

"The sea monster," he said. "I'll be right there."

"Where?"

Before he could answer, the bottom fell out of her world.

PART TWO

Andromeda & Perseus

CHAPTER EIGHT

L ia stood in a room made all of stone, though how she got there she didn't know. Stone floors. Stone walls. Stone firepit. Tapestries hung on the walls, but they were nothing like hers. The colors were bold and bright, but they were simple color blocks. No patterns. No people or creatures embroidered on them. Why was she dreaming about tapestries?

She knew the answer. She wasn't dreaming about tapestries. She wasn't dreaming at all.

The stone blocks of the floor were warm under her bare feet and she felt the grit of sand between her toes. In the distance, not far at all, she heard the rush and roar of the sea.

Closer, far too close, she heard voices and footsteps approaching, sandals on stone. Had she ever heard that sound before? Wooden soles on rock floors? No. Yet, she recognized it immediately.

Lia walked to a window, which was nothing but a square cut out in the stone wall. There was no glass windowpane. Why was there no glass in the window?

Oh. She knew why.

Glass hadn't been invented yet.

This should have terrified her, but it didn't. What did terrify her had nothing to do with the glass.

She was going to die today.

And the footsteps approaching belonged to those who would carry her to her death.

But she would not be carried. Nor would she be dragged. She was the virgin daughter of King Cepheus and Queen Cassiopeia.

"I am Andromeda..." Lia said, and knew it was true. She was, somehow, that ancient princess. She wasn't dreaming it. Nor was she hallucinating. A black ant peeked in her window, twitched his antennae left and right before marching onward up the side of the palace.

Was this real?

The sun was near to setting. It hung so low in the sky, if it had been an apple she could have picked it without having to stand on her toes. Or asking her father to pluck it for her as he had done a thousand times. And he would have bowed when he presented it to her, as if it were one of the golden apples of King Atlas. How did she know this? The man in her memory was dark of skin with a beaming smile that he wore only for his daughter. He still called her away from her sewing in the evenings to play draughts with him on the terrace by the sea. Men came to seek her hand in marriage and he welcomed them warmly, saying, "If I beat her at this game, you may have her as a bride. If she wins, however, I'm afraid she'll have to stay a maid."

Then he would lose on purpose.

No daughter in the world was more loved than she, Andromeda, by her father, Cepheus.

And perhaps that was what had made her mother say what she said…

They had entertained a desert prince one week ago, a handsome dark-skinned, amber-eyed suitor who'd made the mistake of saying to her mother, Queen Cassiopeia, "Princess Andromeda is the most beautiful lady in all the kingdom."

Her mother had once worn that title and worn it proudly, too proudly. And surely it had stung to see that crown transferred to her daughter. The wine had flowed too freely that night. The words even more freely.

"Oh, she is," her mother said. "So beautiful my own husband the king would rather gaze at his daughter across the checkerboard than his own wife in his bedchamber. Her beauty surpasses even Poseidon's lovely little Nereids. Perhaps Poseidon would like to come and take our Andromeda to his realm for a game of checkers. Then perhaps the king will remember he has a wife."

The danger when speaking of a god by name is this—the god hears.

Poseidon heard.

The door, solid wood with hinges of iron, opened behind Lia-Andromeda.

The empty room was at once filled with ten of her father's guards, the king and the queen. The king's eyes were so red it looked as if, had he blinked, he would bleed from them. Tears had formed furrows on the cheeks of his dark and lovely face. The queen's eyes were clear, though she shook like a flower in a storm.

"What news?" Lia asked, though it was not her voice that came from her lips or even her language. Ancient words. An ancient tongue. How was she speaking words she didn't know? How was she understanding them? Was she really here, in ancient Aethiopia? She felt like a marionette on a string and there was even a string on her tongue, making her speak. Who was pulling the strings?

"The offering was made," her father said. "Ten bulls slaughtered, twenty calves. No matter. Fourteen more houses fell today. Thirty-seven dead, if not more."

Lia nodded. She had already accepted her fate, but she had held out hope that her courage would appease Poseidon's wrath. It seemed that, no, her death alone would do. Since the night of her mother's "boast," the city had been pummeled with storms, with waves, even earthquakes. The great city of temples and trade and markets and gardens was quickly being reduced to rubble. Nearly three hundred had died already.

And so Andromeda had to die, too.

"We mustn't wait another day, then," Lia said. Lia? Andromeda? They had become one and the same, as if Lia had slipped inside Andromeda's skin or Andromeda's spirit had inhabited Lia's body. What strange magic was this? "We should go now, before the sun sets."

"Darling," her mother said, and took a step toward her. Lia held up her hand.

"No one touches me," Lia said. Her father, a great and mighty king, turned away so his soldiers would not see him weeping.

"But, my love..." her mother said.

"I will die a maid," she said. "And the next hand to touch me will be that of Hades. I hear he seeks a bride. Wish me well, Mother. This is my wedding night."

Lia swept past her father, past her mother, past the guards

who had come to ensure that she would not run or hide from her fate.

That morning she had bathed in spring water and had anointed herself with rich oils. Her maids had prepared her hair as if for a wedding, plaiting anemones into the black waves. Her gown was white and belted with blue. Around her neck she wore a cord and on the cord hung a silver coin to pay Charon, the ferryman who would take her across the River Styx. Hades would receive a fine bride tonight. She prayed she would please him and he her.

As Lia walked down the palace steps to the front doors held wide open by guards, she prayed.

Artemis, grant this virgin your courage. Grant this maiden your protection. Grant your servant a quick death. Grant my people long life. Grant that Hades is a tender lover to his unwilling bride.

A retinue formed behind her as she walked down the palace steps toward the sea. She had seen a hundred bridal parties like this, except always it was the guests who celebrated and danced and the bride who wept. This evening, the eyes of Andromeda were dry and all who followed her to her fate wailed a funeral dirge.

Lia saw a girl, only nine or ten, break free from her mother's hands and rush toward her.

"Princess!" the little girl called. She was weeping now, and it was clear from the furrows of dirt on her tender cheeks that she had been crying all day. "Don't do this, my lady. Throw your mother into the sea. You should be our queen, not her. I'll die if you die."

Lia smiled down at the dark and comely little girl who knelt at her feet, weeping as if her own life were forfeit tonight.

"Beautiful child," Lia said. "You must not weep for me. I do not die tonight. I'm getting married."

"You are?" the girl asked. "But…"

"It was a lie you were told. Your princess will not die. Go home with your mother." Lia nodded toward the woman running toward them. "Weave a wreath of flowers and offer it to Artemis in honor of my marriage tomorrow. Will you do that for me? Right now? A fine wreath of ivy and anemones and…and…?"

"Roses?"

"Yes, yes, roses, if you can find them."

"I know where they grow, Princess. Who do you marry?"

"A great hero," Lia said. "Handsome as the night is dark with a smile like the first bright rays of dawn."

"Does he love you very much?" the little girl asked.

"Oh, yes," Lia said. "He loves me…very much."

The little girl smiled, delighted. Lia blinked the tears from her eyes.

The girl's mother looked at her with gratitude and sorrow.

"You are a great lady," she whispered as she bowed her head. "Surely your name will be written in the stars."

The woman took her daughter by the hand, and it was a sword in Lia's heart to hear the girl calling out to all who would listen. "It's a lie! It's a lie! She's getting married. The princess won't die tonight! Do you hear? She's not going to die! She's marrying a hero who's as handsome as the night is dark! And he loves her, too!"

Old men muttered "Madness" and "Poor fool" and "Silly girl" as the child skipped down the lane back to her home.

Forgive your maiden one last lie, Artemis, Lia prayed as she walked on. *I could not bear to see the child cry.*

As she neared the edge of the sea, the water grew wilder. The sand shifted under her feet, and somewhere she heard what sounded like boulders falling off the cliffs and into the ocean. They were not boulders, however, but houses.

This wrath must end.

The sun was near its setting, so low its belly brushed the top of the water. The sea was red as blood, the blood dark as wine. Lia turned and saw one of the king's guards holding a length of iron chain.

"Is it heavy, sir?" Lia asked him.

"It is a far lighter burden than you bear, my princess."

"If it is so light," Lia said, "then my mother could carry it."

Her mother stepped forward. Her head was low, her eyes downcast.

"Andromeda…" The queen's voice clutched at her like a hand. "Please…"

"Take the chain, Mother. You shall bind me," Lia said.

"But—"

"Do as your daughter tells you," her father ordered. "And be grateful she will speak to you at all."

The fury in his voice roused the queen's dignity. She stepped forward quickly, took the chain from the guard and approached her daughter. They walked to the spot chosen for the sacrifice. Hooks had already been driven deep into the rock face closest to the sea. Lia brought her fingertips to her lips and then knelt to touch the water.

"A kiss, Poseidon," she said to the sea. "If you want more, I am here waiting for you."

She rose.

Lia looked back over her shoulder at the faces of the hundreds gathered.

"Please," she said to the guard who had declared her burden so heavy. "Turn away."

The guard bowed once to her and obeyed.

"Away!" he cried. "Look away!"

She watched until every last man had turned his back to her.

Lia, as Andromeda, unbelted her dress. She unhooked the

pins from her shoulders. The gown whispered to the ground. Naked, she faced her mother.

"I was born naked," she said. "How fitting I will die naked, as well. By your labor I came into this world. By your labor I will leave it."

Her mother's hands did not shake as she bound her daughter to the black rock. And no matter how tightly her mother bound her, Lia demanded she be bound tighter.

"I want to die quickly," she said. "Not cowering. Tighter."

Her mother bound her tighter.

"Look well, Mother. Look well at your child. Am I beautiful now, in these chains? Is this the marriage you arranged for me? Your daughter wed to Death? Will you brag that you're the most beautiful woman in Father's kingdom when I'm gone? Was that your plan all along?"

Her mother wept and did not speak.

"Why do you weep?" Lia asked.

"You can't imagine what it is like to be unloved," the queen said. "To be unwanted by your husband. He would rather play games with you than make love to me."

"Now you can have Father all to yourself. Be careful, Mother. He cheats at draughts. He plays to lose so he has an excuse to say, 'Let's play again. Surely I'll win this time.'"

"Forgive me," she said. "I have been a fool…"

"You have. All my life I have known this one thing…that my mother, in my eyes, was the most beautiful woman in all the world."

A sob caught in her mother's throat. Her knees buckled, and she went down to the sand.

"Leave me," Lia said. "It is time to meet my husband, and a bride and her groom should be left alone."

Her mother stretched her long and lovely arm to touch the

toes of Lia's feet. But a soldier came forward then and gently pulled the queen away.

"Andromeda…" she called out.

"I forgive you, Mother. Now leave me to my fate."

Alone and chained to the rock, Lia waited.

And before her, the dark water began to boil.

Lia wanted free from this madness, but she was as bound to it as Andromeda to the rock. The iron chafed her wrists. Tears streaked down her face, and she would have given anything for her father to come and wipe them away. But he was far behind her. The last she'd seen of him, four guards held him back from flinging himself into the sea in his grief.

A dark form appeared under the water's surface.

Long and dark, serpentine but not a snake, for surely no snake was as wide as her father's throne room, nor as long as the path from the sea to the palace. She had thought Poseidon would send a wave to drown her or a stone to crush her.

But no, he sent Cetus…to devour her.

Artemis, let it be merciful, she prayed. *Warn Hades his bride comes soon. Tell him to prepare our bedchamber. I pray his dark kingdom is kinder to me than this one has been.*

A thing with gray skin surfaced, breached and sunk down again.

Almost time.

Lia looked up at the sky in the hopes of seeing a star before she died, for there were no stars in Hades's underworld. And she did see a star, the evening star, glowing like a white dove. The star most certainly had feathers.

But, no, it wasn't a star falling from the sky. What was this? A horse with wings? A winged horse and a man astride it?

In the blink of an eye, the horse dropped its hooves hard into the sand and raised its proud head.

"I have gone mad," Lia, who was Andromeda, said to herself. "Terror has driven me to see things that cannot be."

A man in a white tunic stood next to the horse, holding it by the bridle. He gazed at her in wide wonder.

"What is your name, maiden?" he asked. "And why are you thus chained? A lady of your great beauty should be bound in sweeter chains, those of lovers, not of criminals."

"I am no criminal, my lord." Her voice shook, and she could not look at the man for her humiliation. Why didn't he turn his head like the other men?

"Who are you? Tell me? I may have service to render to you. Or are you here out of some secret shame?" he asked.

"There is shame, but it is not mine," she said.

"Who are you? Tell me all. Tell me now."

"I am Andromeda and my mother is the queen Cassiopeia, who foolishly boasted and brought the wrath of Poseidon upon us. The priests of the temple say I must die to appease him. So you must leave me now to my fate or my kingdom will suffer evermore. Three hundred have died already and all because of idle words. Go now, my lord. It is too late for me, but not for you. Cetus comes and there is none who can stop him."

"Andromeda…" the man said. "Look at me."

Lia couldn't do it.

"You have courage enough to face Cetus but not to look at me?" he asked.

How could he tease her at a time like this? But his words had pricked her pride. She turned her head and, for the first time, saw him truly.

August… She knew it was him the moment she met his eyes. Yet it wasn't him. He was too young. He looked no more than twenty-five, if that. Thinner; his hair longer and lighter in color, almost bronze. But those were August's eyes, shining like silver. The hand that touched her face was August's hand. The voice that spoke to her was August's voice.

Even if he didn't know himself, she knew him.

"I am Perseus," he said. "And there is no time for tears now, my lady. I am a son of Zeus by a mortal mother. I have slain the Gorgon and I will slay your Cetus. Surely that will make me an acceptable suitor."

"Death alone is my suitor. This is my last night on earth. Leave me to the evening stars. I will never see a morning star again."

He smiled, and on any other man she would have called it too proud. But he wore it well.

"Dry your tears, my lady. You may live to see the morning star, after all. And I hope from my bed."

She would have laughed at him but for the earnest tone of his voice.

"Save me," she said, "and I will marry you tonight. My father would far prefer to pay a bride's dowry than hold a funeral banquet."

"Stay brave, Andromeda," he said. "I will come to you again."

She meant to speak and wish him well, to thank him for trying even if he failed. But that was when the monster rose from the deep.

Lia screamed.

The beast was enormous, rising and writhing from the water. It had flesh like a week-old corpse, bloated and gray, a thousand teeth in a head large as a house, and huge eyes, big as a soldier's shield. When it screamed, birds fell from the sky, felled by its foul and poisoned breath.

She would have fallen to her knees if the chains had not held her. But Perseus did not pause once, even to take in the enormity of his task. He mounted his strange horse and, with a cry and a kick and a beating of wings, they rose into the air.

The beast, Cetus, snapped at the horse as it flew around its head. And despite her terror, Lia couldn't look away.

Artemis, guardian of virgins, protect this man who dares to guard me from certain death. If he has his way, I will live and, by dawn, no longer be under your protection. But as I am a maid still, I am your maid, and I beg of you, protect this man.

Did Artemis hear her prayer or did Perseus defeat the beast all on his own? Or was it Zeus who intervened to save his half-mortal son? She could not say. All she recalled ever after was that one moment Cetus's head and body danced side to side, snapping at the horse and its rider like a scorpion. And then it simply…stopped.

It went still as a statue. And nothing had scared her more than that moment when everything, even the endless rushing sea, went completely and utterly silent.

Then the beast began to crumble.

A fin fell from its back. A tooth broke out of its head. Piece by piece it came apart, like a stone watchtower in an earthquake. Perseus, she saw, held something in his hand. A horrible thing, so hideous that to look on it would turn anyone to stone.

Lia closed her eyes, closed them tight, and waited.

She did not open them when she heard the beast's shattering cry. She did not open them when she heard a thousand voices rising in a cheer. She did not open them when she heard hoofbeats on the sand.

She heard the voice of Perseus whispering into her ear.

"Andromeda, the gods have spared you. Open your eyes."

She obeyed. How could she not?

"I am saved?" she wondered. Perseus stood before her, hands on either side of her body. Sweat and seawater drenched his hair, and there was blood on his tunic. His skin was flushed and his eyes wild with victory. She had never seen a more beautiful man.

"Yes, my lady. You are saved. I saved you for myself. Am I yours?"

She smiled. "As I am yours, my lord."

He brought his sword, gleaming and gold, and with it he broke her chains.

Next, he pulled off his tunic and helped her into it. She stepped forward off the rocks and nearly stumbled in her relief and her shock. She clung to his bare chest, his arms, and felt the flesh of him under her cheek. The mad pounding of his heart betrayed that he, too, had fought in mortal fear.

"You are safe now, my lady. Now let us go rejoicing into the city. You will be my bride by morning."

"I can't... I can't stand." Though she believed him when he said she was safe, her body would not obey her commands to move, to walk, to accept she was free.

"Then you shall ride."

He lifted her like she weighed nothing and set her on the back of his winged horse. She took hold of the bridle and Perseus led her and his beast from the edge of the water up the path to where the guards waited and stared, and the citizens of the city waited and stared, and her father waited and stared, and her mother stared and wept.

"Andromeda..." her father breathed as he came forward and touched her bare foot with his hand.

"I live, Father. I live. And you have this man, Perseus, to thank."

He looked at Perseus, shining like copper in the light of the guards' torches.

"How can I repay you for my daughter's life?" her father

asked, eyes wide and beseeching. She had never seen the mighty man so humbled.

"With her heart," Perseus said. "I will wed her tonight."

"She was…before all this… She was to be wed to her uncle, my brother Phineas."

"Where is he, then?" Perseus demanded. "Was he the man who slayed the serpent of Poseidon and saved your daughter? Or was it another man, perhaps?"

Her father nodded. His word was law.

"You shall have her," the king said.

"Yes, he shall," Lia confirmed. "But not at your word. At mine."

"I wish you luck with her," her mother said. "With a tongue as sharp as hers, you will need your shield as much as your sword."

"The most beautiful maiden in this kingdom and the next wishes to have me as her husband," Perseus retorted. "What man can ask for more luck than that?"

Chastened, her mother dropped her gaze to the ground.

At the top of the path, where sand met stone and the palace loomed, Perseus took a torch and stood upon a high step. To the waiting assembly, he called out in a voice deep as thunder, strong as lightning.

"I am Perseus, son of Zeus by a mortal mother, and tonight I have slain the serpent to save your princess and your kingdom. Tonight, I wed Andromeda. Tomorrow…ah, tomorrow you will not see us. And perhaps not the day after, either. The gods saw her beauty and her courage and chose to reward it. Your kingdom is saved and, far more than that, your princess is saved! Rejoice!"

A cheer rose up, so loud it shook the rafters of the firmament. The stars shivered. Lia shivered. Perseus took his winged horse by the lead rope once more and guided her into the palace grounds. Behind them people streamed in the gates, singing and dancing and wailing in joy. Every torch was lit. Every voice cried out to bring food and wine, to light offerings at the temple, to rouse all the children from their beds.

Perseus led her and his steed all the way up the high stone steps and through the open palace doors.

"You!" he called out to one of Andromeda's maids who had hidden herself in the palace to mourn her lady in private. She came forward, joy in her face.

"My lady," she said, and it was all she could say.

"Yes, your lady is saved," Perseus said. "And I saved her. And she is my bride. Go prepare a chamber for us. And then make yourself scarce. I will see no face but hers until morning."

Into the great glittering throne room, the people poured cheering, amazed by the sight of a horse with wings, at the man who dared name himself a son of Zeus, at the sight of their princess, still living and breathing, and at the madness that, though they had planned a funeral, they were attending a wedding instead.

Her father uttered a few simple words that acted as a magic incantation. One moment, she was a daughter. The next moment, she'd become a wife.

It all happened so quickly that Lia didn't realize it was over until she was being led upstairs to the chamber Perseus had ordered prepared for them. Up the wide stone stairway, servants with torches ahead and behind her. Outside the palace, in the streets and the hills, fires bloomed like anemones in spring as word spread that the princess had been saved, the kingdom had been saved.

But if she had been saved, why did her heart beat so hard? Hard as it had when she'd been chained to that rock? Was this fear she felt? Fear of her new husband? Or something

else that felt like fear and made her heart beat wild as fear…
but far sweeter?

The chamber the servants brought her to, she had seen before but never slept in. A chamber for honored guests with
a bed large enough for three, swathed in white netting and
heaped high with red pillows fringed with gold. The lamps
had been lit and the room glowed warm and bright. She
looked at the window, the wall, the tapestries, the bed and
floor, even her own hands and feet, and thought, *I should not
be here.*

Her maid brought her water, washed and perfumed her face
and hands and feet and helped her into a simple gown of white.

The maid had just finished taking down her hair when the
door opened and a male voice said simply, "Out."

She glanced once into Lia's eyes before bobbing a quick
bow and departing without a word.

Alone with Perseus, Lia caught herself blushing. Surely any
moment now this…what? Dream? Memory? Hallucination?
Surely it would end.

Perseus stood before her, resplendent in his red wedding
cloak, gazing at her with August's eyes.

"How are you, my lady?"

"Alive," she said, then smiled.

Then she cried.

She hadn't meant to weep. Surely, she'd spent all her tears on
that rock. And this was her wedding night. She'd been saved
by a son of Zeus. He would be furious at her tears, expecting
gratitude at the very least, worship more likely.

"Poor lady," he said, and took her face in his hands. "Why
do you weep?"

"I'm still afraid."

"Of me?" he asked.

"Yes," she whispered. "Forgive me."

He smiled at her, and she knew she'd never seen a more handsome man.

"Nothing to fear. And nothing to forgive."

"You are gracious," she said, swallowing tears.

"Here." Perseus lifted a corner of his cloak to her face and used it to dry her cheeks. Her father had done the same a thousand times as a child. Then Perseus wrapped the cloak over her nose and said, "Now blow."

Lia burst into startled laughter.

"Ah, that's better!" He smiled like the sun she'd thought she'd never see again.

"My husband is…strange."

"Forgive a little foolishness," he said. "I would face Cetus again to make you laugh."

"No need," she said, and laughed. "See? All you must do is ask."

"Is that so?" He crossed his arms over his broad chest, not so broad as August's but in ten years it would be. He furrowed his brow and gazed down at her, his face so serious she could hardly stop herself from laughing again.

"It is, my lord."

"I say laugh and you laugh?"

She laughed.

"I say smile and you smile?"

She smiled.

"I say swoon and you—"

She fell into his arms in a faint. He wasn't expecting it and almost didn't catch her in time. But he did and he held her, laughing so loudly they must have heard him in the streets.

"What will they think of us? These are not the sorts of sounds that should be echoing from a bridal chamber. They'll think we've both gone mad."

"We have," she said. "Haven't we? I think I have."

She put her hand to her forehead and sobbed through a smile.

Perseus held her close and caressed her hair.

"Cry if you have need of it. I will wait."

"You deserve reward for your heroics," she said. "Not a bride who can't stop weeping."

"I am a stranger to you."

"What husband isn't to his wife on their wedding night?"

"Oh, I can name a few," he said. "But not us. Though I would not like to stay a stranger to you. Perhaps we could be…friends?"

"You saved my life. And the kingdom. I will withhold nothing from you. Certainly not my friendship."

He lifted her hair off the back of her neck, stroked her cheek with careful fingers, careful not to hurt her, careful not to startle his skittish bride.

"Shall we be close friends?" he asked. "The best of friends? Intimate friends?"

"No foe has ever risked his life to save me as you did."

"Then we'll be friends," he said. "As only soldiers who fought side by side in the same battle can be friends. Friends who would die for each other. Friends who would ask anything of each other."

"Ask anything of me," she said.

"Would you lie with me? Now?"

She nodded, no hesitation, though the fear was in her heart again.

The bed was high on its marble pedestals and he had to lift her to put her on it. She sat on the edge and watched as Perseus, her husband and her friend, took off his clothes. It was done quickly and simply. She turned away, blushing.

"No." He took her chin in hand. "We are friends, remember? We have battled together and defeated the Cetus. We cannot be shy with each other."

"Ah," she said. "But it was only my first battle."

"Not mine," he said. "So I will teach you how to fight. As friends do?"

She looked at his face. That she could do without blushing.

"Give me your hand," he said.

She held out her hand and he caught it and kissed it.

"Is this how soldiers behave in battle?" she asked.

"Oh, but you would be surprised."

"I have heard stories," she said. "You hear things from servants when they think you aren't listening."

She stared steadily at his shoulder. Her fingers were in his hands, his thumbs rubbing her palms.

"Do you know what happens between us tonight?" he asked. "Have you seen it happen?"

"I..." She laughed, nervous. "Horses in Father's stable. The groom couldn't cover my eyes in time."

He dropped his head back and roared a laugh. *Gods, what those listening out in the hall must think...*

"If horses are what you've seen, then you'll either be relieved tonight or very disappointed." He glanced down, and she did, too.

She shook her head.

"Well? What is it? Relieved or disappointed?"

"Relieved you aren't a horse from the waist down? Yes," she said. "I'd rather we not have centaurs for children."

"Not disappointed, then," he said. "Good. Very good." He kissed her hand again, met her gaze. "Perhaps...pleased?"

As she looked into his eyes and he into hers, he lowered their joined hands and wrapped her fingers around him. She tensed in surprise, blushed deeper. He was hard in her hand, hard and soft at the same time. The flesh was soft, smooth, like a woman's skin, but stiff, a core like iron.

"There," he said. "Like that." With his hand around her wrist he guided her fingers where he would have them go. Around the center of the shaft, holding firmly. Then he let go of her wrist, but she did not release him.

"What do I—"

"Just touch," he said softly. "That's all."

With both hands she lightly, ever so lightly, stroked his organ. It was upturned, which she'd heard tell of—one of the girls had joked that the statues in the courtyard were never happy to see her. Upturned and moving, shifting in her hand like it had a will of its own. She pushed against it and it pushed back. Perseus made a sound in his throat, a pained sound, and she looked at him, questioning, but he replied, "Don't stop."

He seemed to like it when she gripped it, so she did again, and he inhaled once and sharply before laughing at himself. As she stroked him he touched her hair, her cheek, with his fingertips. His gaze was intent and almost tender.

"I will put it inside you," he said. "You understand that?"

"I...think so?"

"From where you bleed," he said. "Do you bleed?"

She nodded. How strange it was to talk of these things with a man. For her whole life it had been forbidden and now, with the speaking of a few words, it was no longer forbidden but, it seemed, required.

"For some time now. Father's turned away all the suitors. His brother made the best claim on me."

"Until I made a better claim."

She smiled, kept stroking. The flesh was darkening. He had thick hair around the bottom and a line of it to his strong navel. She touched it, the hair, with the back of her hand and found it soft and warm.

"It may hurt," he said. "When I go inside you."

"Will it?"

"You've heard it will. Surely."

"I have heard. But those are women who…"

"Who what?" he asked. He tugged her earlobe to make her smile.

"Who didn't want their husbands," she said.

"And you do?"

She dropped her gaze to the floor, embarrassed.

"Speak true," he said. "Do you?"

"I think I do."

"The place between your legs, does it ever ache?" he asked.

"Ache?"

"To be touched? Do you touch it yourself?"

"My lord?"

He grinned. "Do you ache now?"

"I…"

"I want you to ache," he said. "And the gods do say women feel more pleasure in the act than men. When there is pleasure, that is, women have the better time of it."

"Do we?"

"You will see. I will make certain you see."

She squeezed him tighter in her fingers and pulled a little. A small tug, but it did something to him. A few drops of wetness emerged from the slit at the end. Her lips parted in a silent gasp.

"Seed," he said. He wrapped his hand around the back of her neck, his other hand on her shoulder. His hips moved forward, and his face changed. Eyes fluttered and closed, eyes fluttered and opened again. Lips parted. Quick breaths followed by another smile, a smile to make her drip onto the bed.

"Seed…" she said, and touched the wetness.

"Taste it."

Her gaze flashed upward.

"It's all right. Taste it. It is done, I promise. Wives taste their husbands. Husbands taste their brides. You should know me, the feel and taste of me, as I will know you."

She raised her fingertips to her lips.

"Salt," she said when it touched her tongue.

"Ah, it pleases me to the ends of the earth to see you taste me."

"What else would please you, my lord?"

"To kiss you," he said. "To enter you. To fill you."

"I am yours," she said. "I cannot refuse anything you ask of me."

He lowered his head to kiss her lips. She gasped and laughed when he nipped her bottom lip with his teeth. Her fingers flew to her mouth in shock.

"You bit me," she said. Luckily her lip wasn't bleeding, but the surprise had certainly made her squeal.

"I'm trying to confuse everyone listening outside," he said. "I'm so tempted to make bird noises."

Lia laughed so hard she fell back in bed. Perseus laughed, too, even as he jumped onto the bed and pulled her into his arms.

"Shall we?" he asked.

"What? Make bird noises?"

"I'm a son of Zeus," he said. "They'll probably think I've turned myself into a bird and am ravishing you midair. Or I've turned you into a bird. Or we're both birds. Ah…the stories they'll tell about us for ages and ages hence. We'll be legends. Could you hoot like an owl, please?"

"I am not making bird noises," she said, still laughing. Why did no one ever tell her she would laugh with her husband on her wedding night? All she'd ever heard, all her life, was warnings about how awful and frightening and painful it was. She would get married every night if she could.

"You know you want to," he said. "Serves them right for listening to a couple on their wedding night."

"Are you sure they are?" she asked.

"Why wouldn't they? Here. Let me prove it."

"Prove it?"

"Moan," he said. "Moan like you do when the servants rub oil into your feet."

She stared at him, wide-eyed.

"Go on," he urged. "Trust me."

"I have married an unusual man," she said. But she did as she was told. She lay back on the bed and began to murmur and moan softly as if she were receiving the most decadent delicious foot massage ever given.

Perseus slid off the bed and tiptoed over to the door. He waved his hand at her, indicating she ought to keep moaning. She did. She moaned as she watched him walk silently to the door. He raised a fist and then…

Bam! Bam! Bam! He hit the door so hard she thought it would splinter.

Lia heard screams. Men and women both screaming in shock and right outside the door.

"That's what you get for eavesdropping," Perseus called out. "Go away!"

Lia had tears running down her face she was laughing so hard. And then Perseus made it even worse by running to the bed, naked, and leaping on it like she used to do as a girl.

"That was very good," she said. "You almost flew over the bed."

"The running bed mount should be an event in the next Olympic games," he said.

"You are sure to win the laurel crown."

"Ah, who needs a crown on his head with a prize like this in his bed?"

He touched her face, turned her to kiss him, and she did kiss him then. A kiss of teeth and tongue and deepest gratitude for saving her and the kingdom. And desire, too. She did want him, though she scarcely understood what that meant.

"Are they gone?" she asked.

"I'm sure they are. And if they aren't, fine, we'll simply be very quiet." He lowered his voice to a whisper. "Won't we?"

"Yes, my lord," she mouthed.

He grinned, pleased with her. And it pleased her to please him.

"I want to do something to you," he said. He still whispered, and she knew they would whisper all night like this. She felt like a little girl again, hiding with her girl cousins under the covers and telling secrets and ghost tales all night.

"Do anything to me," she said.

"Put your hands over your head."

She obeyed.

"Now I'm going to tie your wrists to the bed."

"But why?" she asked, in full voice. He put a finger over her lips.

"Don't you see? It's to spite Poseidon, who ordered you chained to that rock to be ravished by his Cetus."

"Is it safe to spite him?"

"I'm a son of Zeus," he said. "He'd never dare try anything against me. My father wouldn't allow it. Poseidon must know he has no power over you anymore. No one else does but I."

From no other man would she believe such boasting. But she had seen herself today the miracle of his winged horse, the wonder of his defeat of the Cetus.

"As you say," she said softly.

He untied the cord from around her hips and it was the

work of mere seconds before he had her wrists bound to the bar of the bed.

"I'll tell you a secret," he said, "if you promise to tell no one."

"I'll tell no one."

"No one has power over you but I," he repeated. "And no one has power over me but my father." He kissed her. "And you."

"I? Power over you? How so?"

"You wish to find out?"

"More than anything. Tell me my powers."

"You have the power to render me speechless," he said.

"Do I?"

Perseus smiled tenderly down at her. Then he pulled her gown down to her waist and looked longingly at her naked breasts.

He said nothing.

"Ah," she said. "I do have power over you."

He still said nothing. He met her eyes and kept her gaze as he lowered his head to kiss the tip of her breast. She inhaled as his tongue touched the nipple, froze in something like fear when he drew it into his mouth. He sucked her gently at first and then harder. He made a sound, a quiet moan, and she felt the power over him again. She tried to hold him and remembered her tied wrists and his power over her. He was tongue-tied. She was hand-tied. They were equal, then. What a wonder.

He moved on top of her and drew her gown all the way off her body. She lay naked under him. This was a thing that she knew happened to brides, that their husbands would undress them. And she'd feared it all her life. But Perseus had already seen her naked on the rock today. She feared nothing anymore. And certainly not him.

Never him.

Perseus touched her between her legs and his fingers quickly found the place, the little hole where she bled from. He rubbed it with his fingertips, and she was surprised to find she wanted that. His mouth moved over her breasts again and again while his fingers plied the hole until it had opened up for him. He pressed his knees wide, forcing her thighs to part and the hole opened up even more for him. He took himself in hand and pressed his manhood into the furrow of her flesh.

He didn't enter her, though she'd braced herself for it. Instead he rubbed her with his organ, rubbed along that seam. It seemed he was working himself into some sort of frenzy. His hips moved quickly against her and though he still didn't enter her, she felt as if this was the moment she'd been waiting for and warned about. With his hands on either side of her and his head resting between her breasts, he pushed against her. She hadn't known it would feel like this—good. More than good. She didn't want it to end, though it seemed to be reaching a sort of finale. As his organ slid through the folds of her body, she grew wet and then wetter and the little knot of tissue that ached sometimes when she lay alone in bed…it swelled and throbbed. She caught herself moving under him and with him, seeking more than he was giving her. When she released a hoarse moan, Perseus placed his hand over her mouth. Yes, of course. Silence. They might have people still listening in the hall. And she didn't want them to hear what they did. This was for their ears alone. And her ears heard sweet sounds—Perseus and his quiet rough breathing, her own breaths hitching in her throat, the slight movement of the bed under them and her heart in her ears, her wild beating heart.

Perseus pushed himself off her, and she didn't know what was happening until he grasped his organ in his hand and pressed the head of it into her. Only the head and then only barely. Enough to pinch a little or tear but not enough to really hurt.

She watched him, fascinated, as he shuddered without moving. Something was happening. She felt even more wetness than before on her. He sighed long, long, long, until it seemed like he'd sighed the very breath from his bones.

Then it was over. He lay at her side, his head on her breast. His organ rested on her hip, soft now and dripping. She shifted her legs slightly and felt liquid between them.

Ah, he had entered her but a little and released his seed inside her, filled her up with it. And she was now very, very wet.

"I have an ocean between my legs," she said. "Or a river."

"Ocean, definitely," Perseus said. "Salt water."

"Why did you do that?"

"So I could do this." He moved over her, and she saw he was stiff again.

"Already?" She'd been warned by an old handmaiden of her mother that once a man spent, he was done for the night.

"I'm a son of Zeus," he said. "I can't turn you into a bird, but I'm not entirely without powers."

He nestled between her open thighs and placed the tip of his manhood again inside her. And then he pushed. She was so slick and wet inside that his organ went in without causing her much pain at all. No pain, really. Nothing more than a sensation of stretching, of being pleasantly filled.

"There," he said into her ear as he settled his body on top of hers. "You like it?"

"Yes," she whispered. "It's, ah…it's nice."

He laughed, burying his mouth into the pillow to muffle the sound. Then he lifted his head and looked down at her, grinning. He touched her cheek, stroked her hair.

"We'll have to do better than nice."

Slowly he withdrew from her before entering her again

fully. The seed inside her made the movement easy for him and her. He withdrew again and entered her again, faster this time, and still she felt no pain.

"Move with me," he instructed. "When I push in, you lift up." He pushed in. She lifted her hips.

"Ah…" she said, her chest fluttering.

"More than nice?"

She nodded. "Much more."

He settled himself into her and began to take her in earnest. She closed her eyes when she found it helped her concentrate on the sensation of being filled over and over again. And such a delicious wanton sensation it was…all that seed inside her, so much wetness and his organ thrusting into her.

Perseus sucked her nipples again, fondled and pinched them. They grew hard in his fingers, and her breasts ached. The shaft of his manhood rubbed against the swollen knot where he entered her. She twisted under him, seeking more contact.

Perseus seemed to understand how to give her what she needed. With both hands on either side of her shoulders, he lifted himself up, looming over her with no parts of their bodies touching each other except where they were so intimately joined. He thrust harder now, giving his organ to her and not holding anything back from her. She lay beneath him, speared, her breasts rising and falling with his thrusts.

Now they made no attempt to silence or mute their cries of pleasure. They echoed through the room—his desperate breaths, her moans and whimpers. She couldn't bear to wait anymore, though what she was waiting for, she didn't know. Perseus must have known because he kept at her, pounding himself into her, rattling the bed, rattling the walls, shaking the world down to its foundations.

"Take it," he said. "I can give it to you as long as you can take it."

She squirmed under him, seeking the release she craved. The organ spearing her was bliss, but it wasn't enough, not nearly enough. She lifted her head and, red-faced, tears streaming from her eyes, begged a quiet "Please…" He reached between their bodies and found her knot, her swollen aching throbbing knot, and touched it.

Her head fell back on the pillow and she arched under him. He rubbed her knot, rubbed it quickly, roughly, endlessly, as she lifted her hips under him once, twice, and then on three she was overtaken by a release that felt ages in the making. She shuddered, frozen stiff as a statue while her body went mad around the pulsing organ inside her. There was lightning in her belly, thunder in her hips, a storm all through her body. A thousand miles away Perseus was still on top of her, rutting into her. He found his own release and pushed it in hers, and for a tight, tense, aching moment they were joined so completely she thought there would be no parting their bodies ever again.

But the storm passed as all storms must, and a few seconds or years later, Perseus lay with his eyes closed, his head on her heart, weak as a newborn babe. She twisted her hands and freed herself from the cord he'd wrapped around her wrists. When she put her arms around Perseus, he smiled in his half sleep.

"My wife…" he said.

"Why," she whispered, "does it feel like you have always been my husband?"

"Because I will always be your husband," he said, "and eternity is a river that runs all ways."

CHAPTER NINE

L ia sat up.

All the lights were on in the room again. Lights. Electric lights. She nearly cried with relief at the sight of them.

Her heart pounded so hard in her chest she thought it was trying to escape. Where was she? Her bedroom? Yes, this was her pink-and-white rose-print bedspread. That was her fireplace mantel, painted white. Aphrodite sat upon it and smiled benevolently down at her. And there was the door to the bathroom…that Lia ran through so she could promptly throw up her dinner.

That helped.

She rinsed her mouth out and brushed her teeth. When she looked at herself in the mirror, she saw a pink-cheeked woman of twenty-one with pale brown hair partly braided into a crown, partly down and curling. Midnight blue eyes, just like her father. Annoyingly large breasts, just like her mother. A tiny gap between her top two front teeth.

It was her. Not anyone but Lady Ophelia Godwick, Lia to her friends.

What the hell had just happened?

The kylix. August. The world turning inside out.

The rock. The monster. Perseus.

She'd married Perseus and they'd made love. Twice. She could still feel his hands on her breasts, hear his laughing voice, his cock inside her, his come…

His come.

Panicking, Lia slipped her hand under her dress and pushed her fingers into her knickers. She was wet. Extremely wet, like she always was after having an orgasm. She pulled her hand out of her pants and looked at the wet shimmer on her fingertips. Only her wetness. No semen.

And she felt…normal? Not like she'd had sex with someone. She knew what that felt like, even though it had been a long time.

All right. So whatever had happened, she was pretty sure she hadn't actually had sex with August Bowman. But something had happened between them.

Where was August?

Lia stumbled into the sitting room. "August?"

No answer. She saw the Rose Kylix sitting on the fireplace mantel, next to her statue of Aphrodite that August had yet again turned to the wall.

Under the kylix was a note.

Lia—

The disorientation will pass quickly and you'll be feeling on top of the world very soon. I've left you the Rose Kylix as it

*is legally yours, but please, I beg of you, do not drink from it
again. It's very unsafe to drink from it alone. I'll explain more
if you'll see me again. Apologies for leaving you. There's a side
effect to drinking from the cup that I thought we ought to avoid.
I have to say, I loved playing Perseus to your Andromeda. We
should have made the bird noises.*

Love,

August

Bird noises.

August knew about the bird noises.

That meant she hadn't dreamed it. Two people couldn't
have the same dream.

It had happened. It was real.

But it couldn't be. It just…couldn't.

Yet, what if it was?

Lia read the rest of the note.

*PS: The Moirai, otherwise known as the Three Fates, who
weave our destinies just as you weave stories on your loom, have
a bad habit of getting their threads tangled sometimes. The thread
of your life and the thread of mine are knotted together for reasons unknown to me. Don't fight fate, Lia. You will not win.*

Lia jumped when she heard a sudden knock on her door.
She put the cup back into the box and went to answer it.

"Yes?" she called out. Her mother poked her head into
Lia's sitting room.

"Darling? You all right? You've been gone almost an hour."

An hour? Lia thought half the night had passed.

"I threw up, Mum," she said, *a* truth if not the *whole* truth.

"Threw up?" Her mother came in and put her hands on

Lia's face, her skin was cool against Lia's flushed cheeks. "Too much to drink?"

"Empty stomach plus wine," she said. "Sorry."

"It's all right. You can go to bed. Party's almost over, anyway. Most people left as soon as the lights came back on."

"What about David? Is he still here?" she asked. "I should say hello to him."

An hour ago, she would have hidden behind the wallpaper to avoid David Bell. Now she wasn't just ready to face him, she was eager.

"He had to run," her mother said. "You really look flushed, sweetheart. Why don't you go to bed?"

"No, no, no, no, no," she said. "I'll come down."

"Are you sure?" Her mother laughed a little. Lia might have been acting a little odd, not that she cared.

"I want to," Lia said. August had been right—she did feel suddenly…heavenly. She blinked and smiled. "I'm fine. Very fine. Just had to get that out of my system."

"All right. We'll serve the coffee, though. That should get everyone else packing," her mother said.

They left her suite together and walked down the stairs.

"You didn't see where August went, did you?"

"August?"

"Um… Mr. Bowman?"

"He told us goodbye. Said he had to work tomorrow. Thanked us for a nice evening. Why do you ask?" Her mother wore a devilish little smirk on her lips. She probably thought Lia and August had sneaked out of the party and had sex.

Well, they had.

Sort of.

"No reason." There was a reason, and the reason was that she wanted to jump on top of him and stay on top of him until dawn. Dawn of next year. Ohh…that must have been the other side effect August had warned her about in the note.

"Are you sure?" her mother asked. "He was paying you quite a bit of attention tonight. Couldn't take his eyes off you."

"We were just talking, that's all. About the kylix Daddy gave me."

"Did he have any insight on it?"

"A little. He said it's from the Cult of Eros, not Aphrodite."

"Eros was the son of Aphrodite, right?" her mother asked. Lia nodded. "Can you imagine having the goddess of love and passion for a mother? That would have to be awkward, wouldn't it?"

"I wouldn't know," she said. She would know.

Lia laughed. For no reason. None. At all. A laugh just bur-bled up out of her stomach like a cork from a champagne bot-tle. Pop and it was out.

"Lia?"

"Nothing," she said. Then she giggled.

"Good to hear you laugh. Even if it is alcohol-induced."

Well, she'd had that one sip from the Rose Kylix. She could blame the wine.

"Mum…" Lia said.

"What?"

She giggled again. "I love you."

"I love you, too, darling," her mother said, shaking her head. "But let's go and get this party over with."

They turned a corner to the main staircase, and she saw her father passing by at the bottom of the steps.

"Daddy!" Lia skipped down the stairs and launched herself into his arms. He caught her, just barely.

"Lia? You all right?" he asked, holding her tightly to him.

"I'm…wonderful," she said, grinning. She kissed his hand-some cheek, ruffled his salt-and-pepper hair and rested her head on his strong shoulder. He really was the most handsome papa in the kingdom.

"Did you enjoy your party? Too much, maybe?" he asked, laughing as he patted her back.

"I have to tell you something, Daddy." She pulled back and took his face in her hands. "Something very, very important."

She patted his cheeks, his dear cheeks, his dear old darling cheeks.

"And that is, love?" She could tell he was trying very hard not to laugh in her face. Apparently, he and her mother thought she was drunk. Well, fine. She was. Drunk on happiness and magic and Perseus and bird noises and August and… and…and…

"Daddy, I'm being serious," she said. "You have to be serious with me." She put her thumbs on the edges of his lips and forced his smile into a frown.

"Better," she said.

"Mrph," he replied, unable to open his lips now.

"It's about my graduation present," Lia said. She released his face and now held him by both shoulders. She raised two fingers to his eyes and then to her eyes to make sure she had his entire attention.

"The kylix? What about it?" he asked.

"The thing with my graduation present…"

"And that is?"

"Daddy… I *love* it."

PART THREE

Briseis & Achilles

CHAPTER TEN

That night, Lia slept better than she had in years. She woke up the next morning still buzzing with a low-level sort of euphoria. By 8:00 a.m.—the day after her graduation party when she should have been sleeping off a hangover until noon—she was out on the lawns of Wingthorn playing with Gogo. They tramped through the woods. They launched a little boat onto the little river that bordered the property. Lia even sang a sea shanty to Gogo, who looked at her with his head cocked as if to say, "My human has lost her marbles."

She spent the rest of the morning and afternoon in various happy pursuits. Part of her wanted to chalk it up to being out of university after three long hard years at the academic grindstone, but she knew it was August, all August, she had to thank for her newfound bliss. Unfortunately, all good moods came to an end eventually, and Lia's did when she returned to the house by midafternoon. She'd stopped in the kitchen for lunch, but on her way out she ran into her father.

"Hello, sweet papa," she said, and kissed his cheek.

"Hello, bizarre child," he replied. "How are we feeling this morning? Mostly recovered?"

"Completely recovered. Gogo and I went out in the dinghy on the river."

"Did he row?"

"He called coxswain again," she said. "Lazy arse."

"Did he enjoy the party last night?" her father asked.

"He spent most of it under my bed hiding."

"Did you enjoy it?"

She sighed, shrugged. "It was fine. Alcohol helped."

"I shouldn't have thrown the big party." He winced. "I know you hate them."

"I didn't hate it," she said. A true statement.

"You spent half the party in your room."

That was true. She couldn't argue with that. "Sorry," she said. "I don't mean to disappoint you."

Her father took her face in his hands.

"Are you alive?" he asked.

She grinned, rolled her eyes.

"Yes, obviously."

"If you want to disappoint me, you'll die before I do. Nothing else will work," he said. "And then I'd never forgive you, and you'd be written right out of the will. I'll leave everything to the Virgins just to spite you for dying on me."

"Daddy, you have to stop calling Art and Charlie 'the Virgins.' They despise you enough as it is."

"Ungrateful children, I swear. I'll call those two anything I want. You know what they call me, don't you?" he demanded.

"The Sexual Predator."

"The Sexual Predator," he said, carrying on as if he hadn't heard her. "They don't say, 'Where's Dad gone?' or 'What's our father—who pays all our bills and puts a roof over our heads—want us to do now to show him our gratitude?' It's 'Where's the Sexual Predator? What's ye olde Predator up to now?' And all because once, just once, they caught me and your mother...in our own damn house."

"They caught you in *the kitchen*. That we all use."

"They were supposed to be out," her father said.

"There are sixty rooms in the house and you picked the kitchen to..." She fluttered her hand. "There are things boys do not need to see their father doing to their mother. Can you blame them for thinking you're a pervert?"

"God only knows what they call your mother," he said.

"Stockholm Syndrome."

Her father chuckled. "Well, it is clever."

"You're barmy," she said.

"And you're my favorite," he said. "Don't tell the boys. I want to be the one to tell them."

He kissed her forehead and walked to the door. On the threshold, he paused and looked back at her.

"Oh, forgot to tell you. David Bell stopped by last night. He's back in the country."

"I heard," Lia said, keeping her expression neutral.

"He left you a gift," her father said. "It's in your sitting room. And we're all going to his opening Friday. Please don't make other plans."

Lia was too shocked to speak.

"That won't be a problem, will it?" he asked.

"No," she said, forcing herself to answer. "I don't have plans Friday."

"You'll make the showing?"

"Sure," she said. "Right." She faked a smile. "Sounds lovely."

She and Gogo went upstairs to her suite. As soon as she entered her sitting room, she saw David's "gift." A small box, the perfect size for a bracelet or necklace.

She knew that, whatever was in there, it wasn't anything she would want.

With shaking hands, she tore off the red wrapping paper and lifted the lid of the box.

She found a small envelope inside. When she opened it, a lock of gingerbread-colored hair fell out into her hand.

Her hair.

On the notecard, in his sloping looping handwriting she remembered so well, he'd written her a little note. The stationery was elegant, embossed with his name and a stylized *DB* on it. It seemed someone was moving up in the world.

Dear Ophelia,
I'm back. Call me tomorrow. We should talk.
David
P.S. If you don't call me, I will call you. So call me.

Lia stared at the note.

Call him tomorrow…that was today. What the hell would he want with her now? And what was he doing back, hanging around Wingthorn and her parents like nothing had happened?

Lia knew she had to call. She'd go mad wondering what he wanted from her if she didn't. Her hands shook so hard she could barely tap the numbers on her phone. But she managed to do it. She heard the rings and held her breath.

"Hello, Ophelia," David said when he answered. God, she hated caller ID.

"What do you want?" she asked.

"That's not very friendly."

"I'm not very friendly. What do you want?"

"You still haven't told your parents," David said. "Why is that?"

"They don't need to know." And Lia would die before she told them.

"So… I hear you've started a gardening and tennis club," he said.

Lia froze. She had to force herself to speak.

"You want to join?" she asked. "The dues are out of your price range, I promise."

"Doesn't seem much point in joining when you don't do any gardening. And when's the last time you picked up a tennis racquet?"

Lia didn't answer.

"I know what your little club is," David continued. "And I'm going to tell your parents. I'm going to tell the police. And I'm going to tell the papers. Earl's daughter starts her own escort agency? What a story."

Lia said nothing. She tried and nothing came out.

"Here's the deal," he said. "My show opens Friday. You give me a million pounds before the show, and I'll forget what I know about this little erotic cottage industry you and your friends are running. If you don't have it Friday, I'm calling the police and the papers, and you get to be as famous as Heidi Fleiss. That scandal was over twenty years ago, and people still know her name. You want the world to know your name?"

"A million pounds?" Lia repeated.

"That's how much money I lost in work when you had your tantrum, little girl. You owe me."

Lia put her hand over her mouth.

"You understand everything I've said?" he prompted.

"Yes," Lia said, nodding though they were on the phone.

"What were you thinking?" he asked, then tut-tutted at her

like a maiden aunt. "This is the new Victorian era, sweetheart. Nobody gets to have any fun anymore, didn't you know that?"

She knew now.

"See you Friday," he said. "Goodbye, Ophelia. Don't go swimming in any rivers."

He rang off.

Lia dropped the phone.

She sat on her love seat and held Gogo until her racing heart calmed. Pure hatred coursed through her veins. She imagined David on the floor in front of her and how she would put on steel-tipped boots and kick and kick and kick his face until no one could tell a face had been there. Then she'd start in on his testicles.

Lia let herself hate him for thirty whole seconds, let herself entertain the most gruesome violent scenarios that all ended the same way: with David in a coma.

After thirty seconds, she pushed the thoughts away. She wasn't violent. She would never hurt anyone. And she needed to figure out what to do.

And fast.

All her life she'd prided herself on being intelligent and resourceful, no shrinking violet but an English rose, hardy and hale with thorns aplenty. Usually no matter the mess she got into, she could get herself out of it.

This time, though, she had no idea what to do.

Lia stood up to pace her sitting room. So David was back and out for blood.

She had some cash from her work but not a million, not even close. She took 10 percent from the ladies, and she was always lending her cut to them when they were skint. At most, she could scrape together fifty thousand if she had to. Her father had the money—last week he'd dropped a million on a Brueghel—but there was no chance she'd be asking him for the cash. He'd give it to her in a heartbeat, but not unless she told him why she needed it.

And that was never going to happen.

Maybe she had something she could sell? Her suite was full of antiques, but even if she sold every stick of furniture in the place, every knickknack, every painting, she wouldn't get to one million and certainly not by Friday.

And then she'd have to explain to her parents why she'd suddenly sold everything she owned.

Also never going to happen.

Lia kicked her shoes across the floor as she cursed her arrogance and her stupidity. Why hadn't she quit while she was ahead?

She ordered herself not to panic, though it was true her heart was racing so hard she thought it would run right out of her body.

"A million pounds," she said aloud. "A million bloody pounds…"

On the love seat, Gogo raised his head off his paws and looked at her, ears cocked.

"And we were having such a good morning, weren't we, boy?" she said with a sigh.

A good morning because of a miraculous last night.

August.

Name your price.

That's what he'd said when trying to buy the Rose Kylix from her.

Name her price?

Lia found her phone still lying on the floor. Thank God August had called her three times. She sent him a message sure to get his attention.

I need to talk to you, please. I'm interested in selling you the kylix. —Lia

August Bowman replied immediately.

My house at nine Monday night? Bring the kylix, please.

He sent her his address.

Can't we do it now? she wrote back, ready to have this over with. If he turned her down, she'd need to find a plan B immediately.

Can't, he replied. My mother's here. Help.

Is your mother as bizarre as my mother? she asked.

You have no idea, August wrote. See you tomorrow.

Lia started to set her phone aside when August sent her one more message.

An emoji of a singing bird.

CHAPTER ELEVEN

Lia was a wreck from Sunday afternoon until Monday evening. She stayed away from her parents as much as she could without raising their suspicions. She went on long walks with Gogo, invented excuses to run errands, holed up in her bedroom trying and failing to read even so much as a page or two of a novel.

Finally, Monday evening rolled around. Lia took a quick shower and put on her favorite summer frock and brown boots. Carefully she packed up the kylix, and by eight she was on her way to London in her little red Mini Metro, which purred like an asthmatic kitten.

August lived in Camden and Lia found the address easily, though parking took a little longer. A pretty three-story Georgian house, the last in the row on the corner of the street. A nice house but not at all ostentatious. She went to the front entrance and buzzed. August opened the door a crack.

"August?" Lia could see his eyes peeking around the edge of the door. "Hello?"

"Has it passed?"

"You mean the urge to shag you until bits break off?" she asked.

"That one."

"Yes," she said. "Was that a side effect of drinking from the cup?"

"No," he said. "Just a side effect of meeting me."

She glared at him, a glare to melt brick like candle wax.

"Yes, it's definitely passed," he said. He held open the door for her.

He let her into the front hallway, and the desire to do erotic violence to the man came back in almost full force. At the party, he'd worn a three-piece suit. Tonight, he wore artfully faded jeans, black T-shirt, black jacket. No shoes. Bare feet. Sexy arches.

Sexy arches?

She'd never found feet sexy before. What was this man doing to her?

"Did you bring the Rose Kylix?" he asked.

"I did."

"And you are interested in selling it to me?"

"For the right price," she said.

"Why the sudden change of heart?"

"Does it matter?"

"Guess not," he said, though his searching eyes said otherwise. "Let's go up to my office."

He led her down the front hallway and past a reception room. Crisp white-painted walls and pale gray tile floors. He led her to the front room, and she found the furniture all the same shade of elegant blue gray. Clean lines. Square tables. Many right angles.

"I hope you approve," he said on the stairs going up.

"Very nice," she said. "I didn't expect you to go so modern, though. Antiques collectors usually have museums for houses."

"You know what they called the Pantheon when it was first built?" August asked.

"What?"

"Modern architecture."

Lia harrumphed. "We are amused."

They walked down a short hallway. August paused outside an open door and ushered her inside. She started to enter but stopped on the threshold.

Lia looked at him. "You said your office."

"This bedroom is my office."

They stood inches apart from each other. He wore a too-innocent look on his too-handsome face.

She pointed her finger at that face. "We are *not* amused."

Lia entered his bedroom, keeping one eye on him the entire time.

Luckily, she wouldn't have to sit on the bed. Not that it wasn't a nice bed. It was a very nice bed. Not a king-size like she'd expected. A double only. An elegant low platform bed with a deep mattress and a thick gray suede comforter. A black metal frame surrounded it, like a canopy bed without the canopy. Very modern, almost space-age. And at each side sat two perfect black cubes for nightstands, bearing identical silver lamps. In front of the bed sat two tufted leather club chairs in front of a long gas fireplace. The whole setup put her in mind of a hotel room, a high-priced five-star modernist hotel room, tailor-made for deviant yet impersonal sex.

"You like it?" August asked.

"It's quite…symmetrical."

"Thank you," he said. "This is where I have a lot of serious private conversations. The walls are soundproof."

"Because of all the private conversations?"

"And the screaming orgasms."

He said it so matter-of-factly that Lia knew he hadn't made a joke. Well, she admired a man who was good at his work.

Lia sat down in one of the two club chairs. He sat, too, but on the opposite chair arm, not in the seat. Trying to take the high ground in negotiations? She appreciated the tactic.

"Is that a real fireplace?" She eyed the long black rectangle that seemed built into the wall. "Or a fish tank...full of fire?"

"It's an electric landscape fireplace. Marvelous invention. It's blue fire. I love blue fire." He sounded positively delighted.

"Is that what you spend your sacred prostitution money on? Blue fires?"

"If I push a button I can turn it purple or orange, if you prefer," August said.

"Blue will do."

"Blue it is, then," he said. "My business is your pleasure."

"You're making this less easy," she said.

"Harder?"

"I wasn't going to say that word around you."

"Wise woman," he said. "I suppose you'd like to talk about what happened between us Saturday night?"

"I would like to do that, yes," she said. "Could you explain to me exactly what happened in terms I will understand and will not cause me to go mad?"

August didn't answer at first. "I'll try," he finally said. "But I can't promise either of those things."

"Do your best."

"First," he said, "I have to ask if you can accept the possibility that you are living in a world where the Olympic gods—Zeus, Hera, Apollo, Aphrodite, Artemis, the whole crew—were real gods who existed in a very real way and wielded very real power. If you can, that's the answer. If you can't, this conversation won't go very well."

Lia took a deep breath. "I rode the Pegasus bareback. I've never ridden a horse bareback, always with a saddle. But now I know how it feels, and I think if I had to do it again I'd know how to hold my knees…" she said. "Let's just say I'm willing to suspend disbelief for the time being."

"All I ask," he said.

"What about the sex?"

"What about it?"

"Did we have it?" she asked, wincing slightly.

"Not in the traditional sense of the word."

"You didn't put any bits of yours into any bits of mine?"

"Apart from when I kissed you and put my tongue in your mouth."

"I didn't think we did," she said. "I didn't feel like it after. It just felt like I'd…" She waved her hand.

"Had an orgasm?" August asked.

"That. You?" He held up two fingers. "Twice?" He nodded. "Nice."

"I'll send you my dry-cleaning bill," he said.

"We didn't have sex, but we both came," she said.

"Mind over matter." August shrugged. "Ask any teenage boy about that phenomenon."

Lia had teenage brothers. She didn't have to ask.

"The power of the Rose Kylix," he said simply and with another shrug. "The Greeks have always believed in other realms of existence. Plato's world of the 'forms' where the ideal form of all things exist. The physical Mount Olympus and the Olympus where the gods lived and reigned. And a realm of fantasy—Arcadia, as the Renaissance painters have called that world."

"We were in Arcadia?" she asked. Next, he'd tell her they'd taken a detour through Narnia.

"In a way, yes. In mind," he said. "Not in body. It's like a dreamworld except a million billion times more real, more vivid. Literally we experienced a metanoia—going beyond one's mind."

"And we had sex there…?"

"Andromeda and Perseus did," he said. "And in that world, you were Andromeda, and I was Perseus."

"I was her, August," she breathed. "I really was. Everything I said was in Andromeda's voice, her words, her thoughts. Everything I did was her. It wasn't me. But it was me." She looked up at the ceiling and shook her head, still lost in the wonder of it all. "It was incredible."

"I enjoyed it, too," August said. "More than I can say."

"So this is all…magic?" she asked. "That's your theory?"

"The gods aren't magicians," he corrected. "They're gods. But even gods have toys. Word of advice: don't play with a god's toy without permission."

"But you played with it."

"I have permission," he said. "Do you believe me?"

"No. But I believe you believe it, so I won't accuse you of lying."

"How do you explain it, then?"

"Greek fire," she said. "There are accounts of it being used, historical accounts, but the formula for Greek fire is lost to history. Discoveries and inventions get made and sometimes lost over time, yes?"

"This is true," August said.

"I would assume," Lia continued, trying to sound as scientific and rational as she could, "that the ancient followers of Eros discovered a flower or an herb or a combination of them, maybe now extinct, that had hallucinogenic and aphrodisiac powers and there's residue of it in the cup. Or perhaps it's a drug that puts you into a highly suggestible state. I know you're good at telling stories. I was drugged and suggestible and you whispered in my ear what you wanted me to see and feel and think…like you did when you were looking at my tapestry."

"So, your theory on what happened Saturday night was simply…"

"I was tripping balls," Lia said.

August politely applauded. "You feel better now that you've completely explained away the most incredible experience of your life?"

"Yes," she said. "Much."

"You're wrong, by the way, but if you need to tell yourself that rational nonsense to avoid a break with reality, it's fine."

"Thank you. I will."

"Should I assume that you were terrified by the experience and that's why you want to get rid of the kylix?"

She held up her hands. "We're not negotiating yet."

"We aren't?"

"First, I need to ask you some questions, and I'd like you to not ask me why I'm asking them. Can you do that?"

"I'll try," he said.

"Do you like what you do?" she asked.

"You mean…buy antiques, go to parties, travel, read, keep up with my archery and see what's new on Netflix?"

"Your 'work,'" she said. "Do you like it?"

"Selling my body?"

"Yes, that was the work to which I was referring." The man did violence to her syntax.

"Enough that it rarely feels like work," he said. "I wish I hadn't agreed to not ask why you want to know, because I really do want to know."

"I'm not telling you. Yet. What about your clients? Who are they?"

"We're a religion, not a business," August said. "They're not 'clients' to me. They're patrons."

"Who are your patrons, then?"

"There are a few people left in this world who still worship the Olympians. Like you, for example, with your statue of Aphrodite on your mantel. And others who still believe. We find each other."

"Just women?"

"Men and women. Both. Neither."

"Like androgynous and nonbinary people?"

He shrugged. "Them, too. But also fawns, satyrs, nymphs, one particularly amorous cloud."

"I am going to proceed," she said, "on the assumption that you are a sane person who occasionally says insane things like 'the Greek gods exist' and 'I've had sex with a cloud.'"

"A safe assumption," he said.

She wasn't entirely sure about that.

"So…you have sex with worshippers of Eros?"

"Correct."

"And your patrons pay you in tribute to Eros, and you use that money to buy, among other things, cubist furniture and fish tank fireplaces."

"And lost, missing and stolen Greek artifacts," he said. "Especially anything related to the Cult of Eros. The bulk of them were destroyed when the temples were torn down, but sometimes they turn up at the auction houses or in museums."

"Noble," she said. "I can certainly respect wanting your treasures returned to your country."

"Whatever happened to a good old-fashioned conquering, Lia? Finders keepers, stealers reapers, and all that?" he said, his tone mocking but not cruel.

"When I was a little girl, I thought the Elgin Marbles were toy marbles that a security guard at the British Museum had confiscated from a Greek boy named Elgin. I could never figure out why there was an international incident over a little boy's marbles. I felt like an idiot when I got older and learned the Elgin Marbles were stolen Greek statues."

"That's the most adorable thing I've ever heard," August said. "Is it strange that's given me an erection?"

Sane man. Insane statements. Lia pressed on.

"Are you careful with your patrons?"

"Do you mean do I break them, lose them in airports or spill wine on their white trousers?" he asked.

She stared at him, lips in a straight line.

"I have no venereal diseases," he assured. "Wait. That's not what they're called anymore, is it? I assume that was your question."

"That was my question."

"Any other questions about my genitals?" he asked. "I'm happy to discuss them with you. Display them. Show you pictures. Work up a PowerPoint presentation."

"No more questions there, thank you. As for money, you have it, I assume?"

"I'm comfortable."

She raised her eyebrow.

"It's safe to say I won't need to be visiting the employment office anytime soon."

"Thank you for answering my questions. I would now like to begin negotiations."

"Yes, let's. Please."

He sounded hopeful, eager. She liked eager. She needed eager.

"I have settled on a price. The price is not negotiable, though other aspects of this transaction are."

"Go ahead," he said.

"One million pounds."

August's eyes widened but he didn't laugh, gasp or kick her right out on her tailbone.

"One million," he said. "That's a lot of money, Lia."

"I know, and I am sorry," she said. She did know and she was sorry.

"Hmm…" He raised a dark eyebrow, pointed a finger at her, wagged it. "Sudden change of heart about selling. Non-negotiable money. Deer in the headlights look in your eyes. You're being blackmailed, aren't you?"

"Doesn't matter."

"Does to me," he said. "I'm a sacred prostitute. You're a madam. It's all the same game. When someone comes at one of us, they come at all of us."

"I appreciate that," she said, and was surprised to find she did truly appreciate his allegiance. "Let's say you're right, and I am being blackmailed. What of it? You want the Rose Kylix. I need the money."

"You should reconsider paying off your blackmailer. They can keep coming at you even after you've kept up your end of the bargain."

"I have no other choice." Not if she wanted to protect Rani, Georgy and Jane.

"Can't you talk to your parents?"

"Absolutely not and for reasons I won't discuss with you."

He held up his hands in surrender. "Forget I mentioned it."

"What about the deal?" she asked. "I don't have a lot of time. If you don't want to buy the kylix, I'll find someone who will."

He sighed. "Considering I spent nearly that much on antiques at Christie's two weeks ago, I can hardly complain that you're pricing yourself out of the market. I suppose we have a deal," he said, and held out his hand to shake.

She did not shake his hand. "That's not all I want."

"There's more?" Now she'd gotten to him. Finally, he sat down in the chair opposite her and leaned forward as if he hadn't quite heard her right. "Your father paid fifty grand for the cup. Now you want twenty times that, and you're saying there's more?"

"Yes." Lia carried on, ignoring his protest. She sat up straighter in her chair and casually, too casually, twirled the little silver ring she wore around her index finger. "In addition to the one million, I would like to employ your services."

"My services?" August repeated. He blinked. Twice.

"Yes," she said. "Specifically, I would like us to repeat Saturday night's…event. I want us to drink from the kylix again. And again. And again. Really, as often as we safely can in the next week before we make our trade. Do you agree to that?"

"Of course," he said. "It would be my pleasure."

"And also…" Lia cleared her throat. "I would like us to, you know."

"I know?"

"You know…"

August sat back, rested his elbow on the chair arm and stroked his chin.

He had lovely fingers. Made for stroking.

She was going to pretend she hadn't noticed that.

"Lia, Lia, Lia," he said. "You do surprise me."

He had the audacity to grin at her, smugly. As if he'd been expecting her request.

"You're a male escort," she reminded him. "I don't believe for one second you're surprised that someone wants to employ you for that purpose."

"Employ me for that purpose? You really are the prissiest madam I've ever met. And I've met my fair share of madams."

"We're negotiating," Lia said. "I take my negotiations seriously."

"You do. I respect that. And you are certainly your father's daughter at the negotiating table. Quite ruthless. I'm shivering in my shoes."

"You're barefoot."

He held out his naked foot and wiggled his toes. "You noticed."

She was very tired of his dancing around the subject.

"Do we have a deal or not?" she asked.

"On Friday, you give me the Rose Kylix for good, and I give you one million pounds. Until then, you wish to drink from the kylix and explore your fantasies—with me. And you want us to make love all week, in *this* world, as well. I have all that correct?"

"That's correct," she said. "Before you say yes or no, let me remind you that all I have to do is take the Rose Kylix to any one of Daddy's wealthy art collector friends and show them what it can do. I'll have offers of five, six, seven million or more by end of business on Tuesday. Once they feel its effects like I did."

"Then why don't you?"

"They'd try to understand why it does what it does, and they might destroy it while analyzing it."

"Very likely," August said.

"And it's a Greek artifact and you're Greek. It belonged to the religion you profess to be a member of. It should go to you and your...church? If at all possible, I mean. Good form and all that."

"Very good form. And you definitely want me to make love to you?"

"If you don't mind," she said. "I was thinking it might be… therapeutic."

"I can't say I'd mind that at all. I'd say we have a deal."

He held out his hand again, and Lia shook it. When she tried to pull hers back, he held on to it.

"Now…" he said, "get your kit off. Meet you in bed in nine seconds."

August stood up. He took his jacket off and threw it over the back of his chair.

"What? Right now?" she asked, suddenly panicking.

"Why not? Can you think of a better way to seal the deal?"

"You want to have sex with me right this second?"

"You on my cock will take the sting out of the million pounds I'm paying you," he said.

"I need to prepare myself."

August shook his head. "I don't care if you're waxed or not."

If Lia had the Rose Kylix in her hands at that moment, she might have thrown it at him.

"That is *not* what I was talking about." Lia took a deep breath, tried to calm her rising panic. "I meant I needed to *emotionally* prepare myself. Mind-body connection, you know."

"I'm not going to put my cock in your brain," he said. "Although in certain positions it can feel like that, I hear. Your ankles on my shoulders, for example. Can get very deep. Want to try it?"

Lia tried not to picture that. She failed. August unbuckled his belt. So much for calming her wild breathing.

"Please stop that," she said.

He took his hands off his belt and held them up like a suspect surrendering to the police.

"It was your idea—and a very good idea at that. Why are you so scared?"

"Haven't done it in a long time. I barely know you. You're older than I am. You've had sex with a cloud. Shall I go on?"

"Yes, go on," he said.

"I thought we could wait until after we drank from the kylix. Saturday night when I came to it was like…if you'd been in my room, I might have done something illegal to your body. Possibly even lethal."

"Oh my." His eyes went wide. He looked positively scandalized. "You realize if we'd made love after, we would have been doing it under the influence. I'd rather we make love the first time in our right minds."

This was a good point. Lia wished he would stop making good points.

She paused, took a breath. "Despite my profession—and yes, I know how prissy that sounds—I don't have a lot of confidence in this arena. I've been with a couple men but I never could, you know, get there."

"No orgasms?"

"Not with someone. I mean, to do that you really have to trust someone, right? Let down your guard? I'm not good at that."

"And that's why you're hiring me, yes? To help you learn how to let your guard down?"

"I can't remember the last time I cried about anything," Lia said. "You know, until Saturday night when you gave me my book. I'd started to think I couldn't cry anymore. Maybe you can help with that other problem, too."

August gave her a long searching look. His strange stormy eyes were full of what appeared to be compassion. "He didn't just cheat on you, did he? What did he do?"

"Nothing I can talk about," she said. "It was very bad. All you need to know."

He didn't press, and she appreciated that.

"You've been hurt," he surmised. "The sooner you sleep with me, the sooner you'll start to feel much, much better, I promise. I'm not being glib. I do this job for a reason, and that reason is I'm very good at making my patrons feel very good."

August touched her chin, gently, and tilted her face up to meet his gaze.

"I changed my mind," she said. "I'll just sell the Rose Kylix to the highest bidder. Rule, Britannia."

She slapped the arms of her chair and stood up.

"Or you can sit there and watch me take my clothes off," he said.

"Also a viable option." She sat down again. She could always leave *after* he took his clothes off. And she would. But she ought to see what she was paying for first. Right?

August pulled off his shirt, and she stared, as if hypnotized, as he tossed it onto his jacket. The jeans next. There were no underclothes to bother with.

He stepped in front of her completely naked.

He was magnificent. There existed no other word for him in any language. He had an athlete's form and a boy's beauty and a man's cock. He held out both arms to his sides and slowly turned in a circle—displaying himself to her like goods on the auction block. And where was her bidding paddle when she needed it?

Muscled arms etched with veins. Broad, long, smooth back. Narrow waist. A perfect arse. Endless legs with thighs corded with muscle. There was no comparing his skin to velvet or silk or stone or steel. He was smooth hard male flesh, all of him. His pulse beat at the base of his throat. She tried to meet his eyes, but her gaze wandered down to the tattoo of the three-petal rose on his lower stomach. The urge to press her tongue to it was almost overwhelming. Her stomach contracted, her breaths grew short and shallow, and her fingernails dug into the leather chair arm when she allowed herself the pleasure of looking at his cock.

Beautiful cock, hard and erect, large enough to frighten her but not to frighten her away. She had thought she'd felt lust before, but that had been like a child dipping her toes into a wading pool. Now Lia threw herself, naked, into the deepest end of the ocean. August was not simply a beautiful man. August was a god.

He met her eyes. "Shall we?" he asked.

"All right," Lia said, swallowing. "You talked me into it."

CHAPTER TWELVE

August said nothing as he stepped forward and stood in front of her, naked and lovely and waiting.

She still sat on her leather club chair. Shaking and nervous, she lifted her eyes to his and found he was looking down at her with love. *Love?* Yes, she couldn't call it anything else. The tenderness in his eyes, the kindness, the desire…it looked like she'd always imagined love would look in a man's eyes.

No wonder he made a fortune doing this.

He reached out and stroked her burning face with his fingertips.

"Touch me," he said.

"God," she said, heaving a breath. "Where?"

"Anywhere. Touch me anywhere and any way you like."

He was fully aroused. His cock was thick and red and inches

from her face. Lia did want to touch him. She absolutely did. She wanted to touch every inch of him and she knew exactly which inch she wanted to start with...

"Please, Lia," August said softly.

She heard true need in his voice. Well, if he wanted her to...

Lia shook a little in her chair. She was so close to him she could feel the heat emanating from his body. His fingers were still stroking her cheek. She glanced up at him again and saw him watching her, waiting, eager for her to make the first move, to break the tension, to open Pandora's box and see what flew out...

Lia leaned forward and pressed her fingertips against the three-petal rose tattoo. They were thick lines, deep, like scars, not like ink. Like burns. Like a...

With a gasp, she pulled her head back and met his eyes.

"It's a brand," she said.

He nodded.

"Did it hurt?"

"You ever been branded? Of course it hurt."

"I'm sorry."

"I'm not. I was branded after I was with my first patron," August said. "First time in my life I felt truly alive, truly... human."

She touched the brand again, as gently as she could, tracing the lines of it, the beautiful wound...

"Lia, Lia," he whispered, "you are going to make my life very interesting this week."

She sat back and put some space between them.

"Will I have to share you with other patrons?"

He shook his head. "For you I'm clearing my whole calendar."

She smiled, though she tried not to let him see it.

"You're so beautiful," she said.

"That's kind of you to say."

"Credit where credit's due," she said, and cleared her throat.

He slid his hand under her chin, lifted it.

"I'm not going to force you to do anything you don't want to do this week," he said. "I don't force. I seduce. But I will seduce you, and by the end of the week you will have done things with me you never dreamed you wanted to do. You understand?"

She slowly nodded.

"Let's get into bed," he said. "I want you on my cock."

She took another heaving breath. She might have squeaked.

"You're a grown woman, Lia. You're allowed to have sex and enjoy it."

"It was so easy to be with you before."

"Because I was someone else?"

"Because *I* was someone else," she said. "I don't know if I can…"

"You can. You will. But we can go slowly. Bring the cup. I'll fetch the wine."

Lia relaxed slightly when August stepped away from her. She busied herself opening her bag and taking out the kylix, which she'd wrapped up carefully in clean linen. She carried it over to the bed.

August came up behind and pressed himself against her back. He took the cup from her hand and set it on the black square nightstand, next to an open bottle of red wine. He wrapped his arms around her stomach and kissed the side of her neck.

The warmth of his body seeped through the fabric of her dress and into her skin. She stood still, too nervous to move, as he nibbled the pulse point in her neck and ran his hands slowly up and down her back. She liked it but didn't know how to respond. And she wanted to respond. She wanted him to know she wanted him.

"Relax," he said into her ear, as if he'd read her thoughts. "Let me do my job. And let me show you why I love my work."

She smiled, nodded, still nervous but relieved she wouldn't be expected to perform.

"But first, let us bid adieu to your clothes."

"No," she said, turning to face him. "No. No, no, no."

He narrowed his eyes at her. "You do know how sex works, yes?"

She held up her hand and pushed the air, demanding some room between them. He obliged and took one step back.

Lia unzipped her dress, pulled it off and laid it over the back of a chair. Under it, she wore a simple ivory slip, one that had belonged to her grandmother in the '60s.

"Better." He stepped forward and ran his hands over her back again and Lia shivered pleasantly as his skin warmed her through the silk. "This is very pretty. It will look even prettier on my floor…"

"Give me time," she said.

"All the time you need," he said, and kissed her neck again. "But we're getting rid of the knickers right this second."

She made a sound halfway between a whimper and a squeak. They had a deal, she reminded herself.

"All right."

August pulled her knickers down her legs and with a dainty lift of her feet she was out of them.

"Not so bad, was it?" he asked after tossing her underwear all the way across the room.

"I survived."

"Now would you be so kind as to bend over the bed?"

"Why?"

"It will make lubricating your vagina easier."

Another small sound came out of Lia's throat, like air escaping a balloon.

"Or you could lie on your back," he suggested.

He was trying to be helpful.

"I'll just...um...do the first one," she said.

With as much grace and dignity as she could muster under the circumstances—weird bed, weird bedroom, weird yet incredibly attractive naked male prostitute standing behind her with an erection—Lia bent over the bed.

"I'm not going to spank your arse," he said as he lifted the back of her slip.

"Thank you."

"Unless you want me to."

"Let's table that for now."

He didn't say anything. That troubled her. Deeply.

"You're looking at my vagina, aren't you?" she asked.

"Yes."

She sighed.

"It's very pretty." He touched the seam of her vulva and lightly stroked it with his fingertip. It parted at his touch and Lia's fingers curled into the bedspread. "Beautiful cunt."

Lia grimaced. "Do you really have to call it that?"

"Yes. You should, too. It's sexy."

"It's rude."

"Sexy."

"Crude."

"Prissiest madam ever, I swear to the gods."

Lia heard him opening a drawer and felt the first touch of warm liquid on her body.

"I thought it would be cold," she said.

"I have a lube-warmer."

"Of course you do."

She tensed as he spread her labia open wider. He made a sound like "Hmm..."—the sound of an art critic judging a painting.

"What?" she demanded.

"Your cunt looks like a rose," he said.

"Does not."

"Pink-red petals, dark little center, bit dewy."

Lia buried her burning face against the cool suede of his bedspread.

August touched a tender spot inside her.

Lia gasped as her vagina clenched around his fingers.

August laughed. Wonderful laugh.

"I'm falling in love with you already," he said.

"Well. Stop," she said. "Please and thank you."

"Prude."

"Are you finished now?"

"I am," he said. "And you really didn't need the lube. You were soaking wet before I got there."

He pulled his fingers out of her—bad—and Lia stood up—good.

She turned to face August, who was using a little white towel to wipe his fingers clean.

"Now what?" she asked. She was feeling quite...slippery.

"I need to know what sexual fantasy you'd like to experience tonight."

"Don't rush me," she said. "This is my session, isn't it?"

He put his hands together in a prayer position. "I am all yours."

"Thank you. I thought so."

"What would you like to do, Lia?" he asked, the picture of submission.

Damn him...he'd called her bluff.

"Well… I'm open to suggestions," she said. August managed not to laugh at her too loudly.

"Probably a good idea to get started," he said. "Before you lose your nerve."

Lia nodded. "Agreed."

He slipped into bed and propped himself against the tufted leather headboard. How was he so comfortable being naked while she was shaking in her slip?

"Could you pass the condoms, please?" he asked.

He'd put an entire box of them on the nightstand. Felt rude, like bragging. Surely they wouldn't need more than one. She passed him one.

One.

"Lia? You're there." He pointed at the floor. "I require your presence here." He patted his stomach. Lia slowly crawled onto the bed, wishing the entire time August had a much bigger bed.

"Why is your bed so small?" she asked.

"More intimate. You can hide from someone in a king-size. Not in this bed. No hiding places at all…"

He reached for her and, with his hands on her waist, pulled her on top of him. She sat on his stomach and found herself *very* aware of her wet bare vulva pressing against his warm flesh. She was trying to ignore his cock, though it certainly wasn't ignoring her.

Lia was of two minds. One mind wanted to get her things and rush straight home and pretend she'd never had this terrible idea. The other mind wanted to press her entire body to August's entire body and stay there a few millennia. August took her face in his hands, stroked her cheeks, her neck. Then he smiled at her.

Might as well stay, she decided.

"It won't hurt," he said.

"I'm not a virgin."

"That's not what I meant, and you know it." He brushed her hair over her shoulder and leaned in to kiss her. His lips met hers and Lia shivered. She clung awkwardly to his shoulders as she returned the kiss, tentatively at first but with growing confidence. August ran his fingertips up her arms and over her shoulders, across her back and down to her waist. The man kissed like he'd invented kissing, patented it and made a fortune off the patent. He nipped her bottom lip, dipped his tongue into her mouth and retreated, pushed and retreated, teasing her until there was nothing for her to do but put her own tongue in his mouth. That would show him.

When her tongue met his, August moaned softly. He pulled her closer and Lia could almost swear he wanted her as much as she wanted him. Of course he didn't. This was the job, and she knew how it worked. And that was fine. She wasn't here to fall in love. She knew better than that, and even if she didn't, she knew she couldn't.

But…she could enjoy herself while it lasted, right?

"You're a good kisser," August whispered.

"I was thinking the same about you."

He smiled again, and looked in her eyes again, making her blush again.

"What?" she asked.

"You're insanely beautiful."

"Shut up. I have a gap in my two front teeth."

"Like Isabella Rossellini."

"Like David Letterman," she retorted.

"It's a sign of a strong libido. Ask the Wife of Bath. And very, very sexy."

He kissed her again, before she could tell him all the ways he was wrong about that. And as he kissed her, he slowly and with the utmost care moved her so that she was on top of his cock.

"Take your time," he said.

Lia pushed a lock of hair out of her face and tucked it behind her ear.

"So…" she began. "Help?"

He really had the most wonderful smile when he was trying not to laugh at her. Lia could get used to that smile—when she got over the urge to wipe it off his face.

"Allow me," he said. He took her by the waist and gently pulled her down until she was sitting on his erection.

He reached under her slip and took himself in hand. With one hand on her and the other on his cock, and with a judicious lift of his hips, the tip found the entrance of her body and pressed against the tender hole. With her hands on his shoulders, she moved up and then forward.

Accidentally—she was trying to look anywhere but at August—she met his eyes while steadying herself against the headboard. And once he had her attention, he didn't let her look away.

He wasn't smiling now, but the expression on his face was somehow better than a smile. His eyes were soft as he gazed at her face, and his hands gentle as he lifted her hips and guided her onto him. Lia felt pressure as she lowered herself onto his cock. Pressure and penetration as he entered her slowly, inch by inch, until she'd taken as much of him as she could. She rocked back and forth simply to make herself more comfortable.

August must have liked it because his eyelids fluttered, and his back arched against the pillows. Beautiful man.

"There," he said, panting slightly. He put his hand on the side of her face and stroked her cheek with this thumb. "That's not so bad, is it?"

Lia swallowed. "It's all right. Not bad."

The lacy hem of her slip lay over her thighs as she knelt on him. August slid his hands under it again.

"Do you want to make love?" he asked. "Or talk about your fantasies?"

"You're a man. Don't you need to come?"

"I'm not a normal man. I can stay hard for a very long time. Especially if a beautiful young woman is sitting on my cock and blushing pink as a rose. If I start to get soft, I'll just peek."

"Peek?"

He lifted her hem, and she slapped it back down again.

"Do not peek."

"Lia, I'm literally penetrating you right this moment. We are having sexual intercourse. We are fornicating."

"Fine," she said. "You can peek." He really did feel very good inside her. The cock in her throbbed and her flesh surrounding it throbbed in time. She placed her hands flat on his chest and rocked her hips into his. She was rewarded with a deep spasm inside her stomach, a spasm that traveled up her spine and down into her thighs. She braced herself, her hands flat on August's broad chest, and did it again.

"Take your slip off," he said, his voice hoarse. He was already inside her. There was no reason for her to feel modest, but her fingers were shaking as she tried for the zipper in back. He grew impatient with her fumbling fingers and pulled it down for her. When he'd bared her breasts, he looked at them so long and so longingly Lia blushed.

"You're staring," she said.

"Phryne of Athens," he said. "The courtesan. When she was charged with impiety and taken before the courts, she bared her breasts to the judges. At the sight of them, they acquitted her. At the sight of your breasts, they would have crowned you empress."

He squeezed them, molded them into his palms, fondled the nipples until they were so hard she hurt. He wrapped his arms around her waist. Her head fell back and she arched for him, gasping as he licked her left nipple, placed his lips to it and sucked it into his mouth. The slow draw, the tug, the moist heat on her breast, was bliss.

For the first time, Lia felt the line, the red cord of nerves that ran from her breasts to her sex. As he sucked the nipple, drew it deep into his mouth, her vagina grew wetter, riper, swollen.

She pressed her hips against him and felt the pleasure run down her back and into her hips. August pulled her against him again and pushed his hand between her thighs. Lia's vagina ached around the thick organ inside her, and she moaned against his shoulder.

Never had she felt this good before, not in her own body. He took her breasts in his hands again—his large, strong male hands—and held them firmly. She covered his hands with hers, wanting to feel him touching her. Lowering her head, she pressed a quick kiss onto his knuckles. That one kiss, no matter how devout, wasn't nearly enough for August. He grinned that wild dangerous grin of his again. He kissed her again with that wild dangerous kiss of his.

August wrapped an arm around her and scored her back with his rough fingertips. She'd never felt something so sensuous. Every time she moved, even the slightest bit, her clitoris brushed the shaft of his cock.

"August," she said.

"Yes?"

"What?" she asked.

"You said my name."

"I did?"

He slowly nodded. She forced her eyes to focus.

"Stop gloating." She'd been clinging to the headboard, but August took her hands by the wrists and brought them down to his stomach.

"I can't help it," he said. "You're beautiful and I'm arrogant. This is so much fun I can't believe I get paid for it."

"Are you really enjoying this?"

In lieu of answering, he rolled her onto her back on the bed.

"August—"

He took her legs and wrapped them around his lower back. Then he pried her hands off his upper arms and pressed them into the bed. To make matters worse, he put his hands over her hands, and locked their fingers together.

"You're trying to make me feel something for you," Lia said. "I know all the tricks."

"I feel something for you already," August said. "And this isn't a trick."

Slowly, and very deliberately, he began to thrust into her.

Slowly, and very deliberately, he let his full weight rest on her until she could think of nothing and no one but him.

"Remember what I said about the Fates?" he asked. A kiss on her lips. A kiss on her cheek. A kiss on her neck. "About the threads of our destinies being tangled together?"

"You really believe that?" Her voice was breathless. His thrusts were so incredibly deep and slow she couldn't help but move with him.

"We're tangled together right now. Can't you feel it?"

She nodded, too turned on to speak. He released her right hand and brushed her hair off her cheek and then cradled the back of her head. August pushed his knees in until they were at her hips. He'd tangled them together in a tight, tense knot of arms and legs and a hundred deep kisses.

"How's this for a Gordian knot?" he said into her ear as he thrust into her again. Lia arched under him.

He kissed her mouth, deeper even than before. Their tongues touched and mingled as August moved in her with long slow strokes of his cock.

"We can stop if you want to," he said. "Do you?"

She shook her head. "No."

August smiled down at her, caressed her cheek with the back of his knuckles.

"I don't know what he did to you," he said, "but I'm going to enjoy undoing it."

"You can't change the past."

"No, but I can give you a very good present." He thrust into her again.

She laughed, a real laugh, deep and throaty and sensual. She sounded like a woman who was enjoying herself. He laughed with her, dropping dozens of tender kisses on her neck and along her collarbone. All right…so maybe he did want her. She relaxed underneath him and spread her thighs a little wider.

"Shall we play?" he asked. "I think the wine's breathed enough."

"What do I do?"

"Tell me your sexual fantasy you want to explore tonight."

Lia tensed again. Two steps forward, one step back.

"You first," she said.

"I'm a wicked king," he said immediately.

"Oh my God." How many of these insane sexual fantasies did he have?

"And a very powerful king at that," he continued. "And there's another lesser king who has to send tribute to me. But this poor king has no gold or silver or diamonds to send me. All he has that I might desire is…"

"His daughter?"

"His *only* daughter," August said. "She's sent to me to be my concubine."

"It's never a secretary, is it? Or a juggler? The tribute always has to be a concubine."

"And when she arrives at my palace, because I am so very wicked, I make her strip naked and show herself to me in front of the entire court."

"You're an absolute bastard. Worst king since Nero."

"Nero was an emperor, not a king," he said. "But don't worry, she gets her revenge. When I make love to her the first night...she tries to stab me with a dagger she's hidden under the pillow."

"Good girl. I like her spirit."

"But I'm not deterred."

"Quitters never win," she said.

"I decide that I can't simply overwhelm her with power and might. I must make her love me. So begins my attempt to win her heart and obedience through a strict regimen of hand-feeding, spankings followed by forced orgasms, and tender poetry."

"Poetry?"

"Yes, I tie her to the royal bed and recite poems to her until her heart—and thighs—melt."

"This is an actual sexual fantasy you get off to?" Lia asked.

"Often." August nodded. "Though there are variations. Sometimes it's the king's son instead of his daughter. And instead of poetry, it's near-constant oral sex."

"I'm speechless."

"Your turn," he said, his voice tender and coaxing. "I'm dying to hear what you dream about in that deep dark little corner of your mind, the one with all the locks on the door and Cerberus guarding it with all three of his vicious heads..."

He massaged her breasts as he spoke, and she did find herself strangely melting into his hands.

"Close your eyes, Lia," he said as he then pushed his hands

gently into her hair and tugged her head back to bare her throat to another hundred soft kisses.

She closed her eyes and sighed at the bliss of the moment— his beautiful cock embedded in her body, his fingers wound into her hair, his warm lips licking and sucking her neck and his hot breath on her skin… And his words, his perfect words.

"Tell me your secrets, Lia…tell me everything you want. I won't laugh. I won't judge. Whatever you desire, I can give it to you, but you have to tell me what it is…"

"You won't laugh?"

"I really won't laugh."

"Well, to be honest… I wouldn't mind playing in your fantasy."

"You'd make a wonderful wicked king."

She opened her eyes and looked at him. "The bloody concubine, August."

He pulled back, his eyes wide. "You disgust me."

Lia pushed him off her. That act of rebellion was quickly quashed. August grabbed her around the waist, wrenched her slip off her and threw it across the room. Then he dragged her on top of him, and it took no convincing at all to get her to straddle him.

"So she wants to be a concubine," August said. He took her by the hips and eased her down onto him again.

"No, I don't want to be a bloody concubine," she said. "It's a fancy word for being a victim of kidnapping and rape."

"But you fantasize about being kidnapped and raped."

"In a nice way." She let her head fall back and smiled dreamily up at the ceiling. "A sexy way. A not-at-all-real-in-any-way way. That's what I meant."

He ran his hands up her arms and drew her down to his chest.

"Who do you imagine being your keeper? Your captor?"

"Achilles," she said.

"Ah, does that make you Briseis?" he asked.

"I think I'd make a very good captive queen."

Achilles and his best friend and shield-bearer Patroclus were her two favorite characters in *The Iliad*. She loved how much they loved each other, protected each other. And from her first reading, she'd secretly envied Briseis, the enemy queen who Achilles took as his personal concubine.

"Let's find out."

Still underneath her, August reached for the kylix and wine bottle on the bedside table. He splashed in a little wine and offered the cup to her. Lia's heart beat madly as she took it from him and cradled it in her hands.

"Ready?" he asked. She took a shuddering breath.

"Ready as I'll ever be."

Her toes were already curling in anticipation and excitement. But fear, too. Real fear. What on earth was about to happen to her?

Lia lifted the kylix to her lips and drank deeply. Her hands shook so badly August took the cup back from her. He drank from it and set it on the table again. Then he rolled them over so that he lay on top of her again.

"Nervous?" he asked.

"Very."

"You'll be safe," he said. "I won't let anything happen to you except the preauthorized capture and very pleasant rape."

"Good, thank you."

"Until then…" He kissed her deeply on the mouth, and his tongue tasted of wine. She wrapped her arms around his back and held on to him tightly. Before she knew what she was doing, Lia opened her thighs for him again.

August entered her with a thrust.

"My lovely concubine," he said.

"You're more my concubine than I'm yours. I bought you."

"Rented," he said. "Do you really want to play my concubine, or did you just want to see me in a leather kilt?"

"It's called a pteruges," Lia said.

August laughed softly into her ear. "I know what it's called, and you didn't answer my question."

Lia started to answer it, but before she could speak another word, the world went dark.

CHAPTER THIRTEEN

L ia ran.

She didn't need a torch to light her path. She knew the fastest way from the palace to the temple. Those had been her servant's last words to her as the old woman lay dying on the floor by the great stone hearth.

"Hide in the temple. They may fear the gods. They fear nothing else, it seems," Hagnes had said, coughing on the last word, blood on her lips. She died before she could take her next breath.

The temple, just ahead, gleamed like polished silver in the moonlight. Behind her, the battle sounds raged on. She heard the screams of men and wondered if any of the sounds belonged to her brothers. She did not wonder about her father or her husband. They had been among the first to fall under the sword of Achilles.

She reached the temple and found it eerily silent, eerily dark. No fires burned in the braziers. The priests were all hidden. Or dead, too.

Lia ran up the marble stairs and searched for shelter. Under the great altar, perhaps. There was a room that led deep into the bowels of the temple, where the sacrifices were offered. She saw the altar ahead. The eternal flame on the wide table still burned. But for how long?

She ran toward it, naked feet slapping the mosaic floor. As she neared, a shadow moved, coming out of the dark, and seized her by the arms.

A man. A soldier. An enemy, likely Athenian.

He asked her no questions. He simply looked at her face as she writhed in his iron grasp, trying to free herself. A beast of a man, grizzled doglike face, breath like rotten meat. Lia braced herself for death, expecting he would run her through with the short sword on his hip. Instead he threw her over his shoulder. As he started off with her, she reached for the handle of the iron brazier burning on the altar. She yanked it with all her strength and brought it down to the temple floor where the smoldering coals inside struck the soldier's feet and legs. He screamed and dropped her. She hit the ground running. Hagnes had been wrong. There was no safety here. There was no sanctuary to be found anywhere but in death.

Lia raced through the temple, hoping to make her way to the mountains, the trees, somewhere she could hide until the army returned to their ships. Male voices shouting, barking orders, and still more screams followed her into the dark night.

Another man appeared, another soldier in armor with a sword. Lia threw herself behind the marble column next to her and clung to it for life. She crouched, column in front of her, trying to hide, to will herself invisible.

Wide-eyed, panting and panicking, she glanced around, searching her surroundings for a better hiding place.

She heard footsteps, the flat of sandals ringing against the marble steps. Men approached.

She counted five Greek hoplites, two carrying torches, the other three carrying their swords. They stood at the top of the steps, at the entrance to the temple, speaking in low tones. She tried to creep around the column but either her white gown was too bright in the moonlight or they heard her breathing…but one of the soldiers sprang forward and captured her, quick as a hare. She struggled in his grasp, but there was no use. She went limp to avoid getting run through with his blade.

"What's that?" one of the other soldiers called to the one who held her.

"Pretty girl," the soldier said, laughing.

"I'll be the judge of that," said a man with a booming voice.

She was dragged by the hoplite to the men holding the torches. Their faces were grotesque to her. Under other circumstances they might have been handsome, or at least not repellent. But even the oldest man, old enough to be her father, stared at her with a rapacious hateful gaze. She'd seen that same look in her husband's eyes right before he put a spear through a stag's heart or a crueler spear in whatever poor slave girl he ordered to his chambers every night.

"Who wants to be first?" asked the soldier who held her with arms pinned behind her back—so that if she were to try to run, he'd wrench her arms out of her shoulders. "I went first last time."

The oldest soldier, who wore a gray beard and was heaviest around the chest, stared at her face in the torchlight.

"I know that face," he said. "Gods…it's the little queen. Aren't you?"

The soldier who held her kneed her lightly in the back.

"The general asked you a question, wench. Answer him."

Lia swallowed. "Briseis," she whispered.

The old general boomed a laugh like thunder.

"Briseis…" he hissed like a snake. "Caught us a queen."

"Can I keep her?" the soldier holding her asked.

"What would a shit like you do with a queen?" the general demanded. "Even a slave, she still outranks you."

That got the other three soldiers to laughing.

"What we going to do with her, then?" another soldier asked.

The general seemed to puzzle that over, eyes narrowed, fingers stroking his ratty gray beard.

"I know," he said at last. He turned and stood at the edge of the temple stairs. He put two fingers into his mouth and blew a piercing whistle, loud as the cry of a hunting horn.

Lia went still as a statue in the grip of her captor. But though her body was frozen with terror, her mind ran wild. She was no fool. She knew her fate had been decided. As queen, she could be valuable. If her soldiers had taken any high-ranking Athenian or Ithacan prisoners, she might be ransomed for them. She might be given to Agamemnon, their king. She might be executed, publicly, in front of the remaining citizens in order to quell any rebellion.

Hera, Lia prayed. *I, too, am the wife of an unfaithful husband. Protect your child. Deliver me from harm. Whomever takes me into captivity, let him be better than this disgusting rabble. And let him be a better man than my dead husband. You know I am asking for little in that.*

The general had called someone up to the temple, and he now approached. She sensed the change in the soldiers surrounding her. Their backs straightened. Their chins rose. Their faces hardened to stone. They weren't standing at attention out of respect.

They were afraid.

A man stepped into the temple.

The general walked to his side. The man was tall, taller than any of the other soldiers, including the general. Broader in the chest, too, with powerful arms and a king's bearing. He wore magnificent armor—a bronze breastplate with an owl engraved on the gleaming metal and a bronze helmet with violet plumes.

As they approached, Lia composed herself. She sensed that this man, far more than the general, held her fate in his hands.

"Here she is," the general said as they came to her.

Lia raised her face to the new soldier. He took off his helmet and stepped forward.

She met August's gray eyes. She searched his face and saw August's strong jaw, his nose, his olive skin—but his hair was short, a soldier's haircut. In this world he was Achilles, not August, and though she knew him, he did not seem to know her.

Lia felt true fear.

"Achilles," the general said. "Thought you'd like to meet one of the widows you made today. Briseis, meet Achilles, the man who killed your lord and husband."

The five soldiers laughed. Achilles did not laugh. And when they saw he did not laugh, they stopped laughing.

"Your husband died honorably," Achilles said. It was August's voice, though with a new roughness to it.

"Are you sure it was my husband, then?" Lia, who had become Briseis, asked.

The five soldiers stared stupidly at her, not understanding the meaning of her question. But Achilles understood and, this time, he laughed.

She knew well of Achilles. They said he was the greatest warrior who ever lived. They said he was a favorite of the gods. They said he was immortal. They said he was merciless. They said he was loyal to no one but his own honor and his shield-bearer, Patroclus.

They said many things about the great Achilles.

They'd never said he was handsome.

Achilles looked at the general.

"She's mine," he said. Then, without another word, he grabbed her around the thighs and hoisted her over his shoulder. Lia went limp against his back, too terrified to scream or speak or fight. His steps were light and easy on the marble stairs leading down. Her weight on his shoulder didn't slow him down one bit.

Achilles carried her for what felt like a mile before he put her on her feet by a stone hut at the edge of the city. He barked an order and an old woman in the worn wool garb of a laundress was brought forward.

"Sir?" the old woman asked.

"I want her washed and brought to my tent," Achilles said.

"Yes, sir."

Achilles walked off, and Lia faced the laundress.

The woman, though aged and stooped, was no fool. She tied a cord around Lia's wrists and wound it around her waist and then around her ankles. Lia had to take short hobbling steps or she'd trip. With this humiliating mincing gait, she was escorted to a square wooden hut.

The woman opened a door with an iron latch and pushed Lia gently inside. She saw three women in the room, all busy at work—tending the fire in a large stone hearth or folding and rolling freshly washed and dried fabric. Words were quietly exchanged, instructions given and received.

The oldest woman, with white hair under a gray veil, came

to Lia and looked her up and down. She was left standing, stupidly staring, while the trio untied the rope. Things happened so quickly after that, Lia had no chance to fight or run. She was led from the hut to a courtyard around the back, surrounded by high walls. The gray-haired washerwoman pushed her to stand in a sort of large wooden bucket or tub. Another woman pulled her bloodstained gown off her. Lia started to scream but the third woman immediately doused her with water, pouring it from a large clay pot over her head and shoulders. Before she could recover from the first dousing, she was doused a second time.

After, she was dried with a rough towel held in rough hands. A loose robe was thrown over Lia's shoulders and she was taken back into the hut. The three women made her stand by the fire as they anointed her body with some sort of floral-scented oil, sparing no part of her. They were practiced in their work and it was done in seconds, it seemed. Then Lia's wet hair was combed back, braided and laid over her right shoulder.

A gauzy linen dress, so sheer Lia could see her own nipples through the fabric, was pinned over her naked body—leaving her just as exposed as before. The three women looked her up and down and seemed to admire their quick handiwork. Lia wanted to vomit.

The eldest of the women tied Lia's wrists together again, looped the rope around each ankle again to hobble her.

Another soldier waited for them outside the hut. Lia hadn't seen him among the five soldiers who'd captured her. He looked to be in his late thirties, about ten years older than Achilles. He bowed his head to her when he approached. Bowed his head?

"You are Briseis?" His tone was respectful, measured.

"I am Queen Briseis, yes."

His eyes gleamed as she claimed her title but he did not laugh at her, nor smile.

"I am Patroclus. I've come to escort you to the tent of Achilles. Are you ready?"

She took a step forward and nearly stumbled, forgetting she'd been hobbled with rope.

"May I?" Patroclus asked.

Thinking he meant to untie her she quickly answered, "Yes."

But he didn't untie her. He simply swept her up and into his arms to carry her through the soldiers' camp.

They called out jokes and suggestions for what Patroclus should do to the girl in his arms until he shouted back, "She's meant for Achilles."

All were silent.

"Fools and heathens," Patroclus said to her as they passed through an endless sea of round wooden huts and smaller leather tents. "If you serve Achilles well, he will do right by you and marry you when the war ends. He is noble to the sinew and bone."

"It speaks much that his shield-bearer speaks so highly of him," Lia said, amazed that, just like last time, the words she needed to say came to her so easily, like she had memorized a script.

"We are like brothers," he said. "More so in some ways."

As they passed one of the smaller stone huts, Lia was able to see inside through a gap in a curtain. A buxom young dark-haired woman lay on her back, naked, breasts bouncing, as an older man rutted on top of her, grunting. She panted under him, writhing.

Lia wanted to look away but couldn't. The woman laughed with the man, and Lia prayed she was a camp prostitute and not a prisoner like herself. She found herself clinging harder to the neck of Patroclus.

"Forgive me," he said. "Some sights are not fit for a young lady's eyes."

"I am no maid," she told him. "And have you forgotten where you are taking me? And why?"

"I suppose I have," he said, and laughed softly. He held her closer, like a father with a child. He, too, seemed noble, noble to the sinew, noble to the bone.

She caught herself staring at his profile, an elegant profile. Gray hair at the temples, a neatly trimmed brown-and-gray beard, and eyes just the same, brown with flecks of gray.

"We are nearly there," he said.

"How do I please him?" she asked. "I have enemies enough in this camp. I wouldn't like to make another."

"You will please him," he assured.

"How are you so certain, sir?"

"You please me," he said. "And he and I share the same soul between us."

"Do you share his tent?"

He paused, looked at her, smiled slightly. "I almost wish I did."

They reached their destination, the tent nearest the battle-front. The position of greatest vulnerability in an army camp—it spoke of Achilles's confidence that he'd chosen it. A man stood guard outside the largest of the soldiers' tents. More a hut than a tent. The quarters of a wealthy soldier, indeed.

Patroclus opened the leather flap of the door, and carried her into the hut and set her gently onto her feet. Lia immediately collapsed onto the nearest pillow. She saw bronze shields and swords piled in a corner of the hut, a bow and quiver of arrows, boxes filled to overflowing with silver and gold coins, richly painted amphorae, and yards and yards of silk and other fine cloth. A fortune in war spoils.

Patroclus knelt in front of her and untied the rope from her wrists. He worked slowly when untying the rope from her ankles, and as he pulled them from her body, his fingertips brushed across the tops of her small bare feet. The touch was deliberate. She knew it. He knew it. She met his eyes; he met hers. Immediately he stood, putting distance between them.

"Do you require anything before I leave you? Food? Water? Wine?"

"No, thank you," she said. "You have excellent manners for a soldier."

"Soldier, yes," he said. "Not savage."

"My servant, a stooped and sickly woman of sixty years or more who tended me from my birth, had a sword put through her belly today. I buried her with a sprinkling of ashes from the fire grate."

"I am sorry for her death, but it is good and right that wars are so vile," he said. "Otherwise there would be more of them."

"Strange words from a soldier."

"I wish nothing more for the world than the time comes when it has no need for my services. I promise you, I can find better things to do with my days and nights than waging war." He looked down at her. "Be well, my lady. I shall be just outside, standing guard."

"Will you listen when he takes me?" she asked him.

"I will not listen," he said. "But I might hear."

"Then I hope he gives me pleasure," she said, "so that you will enjoy what you hear."

He stared at her, and she could not fathom the look in his eyes. It was a long look, long and longing. Then he turned and left her alone. Lia gathered the fabric of her gown around her as best she could and once more tried to make herself small and invisible.

She heard male voices outside the hut, softly talking. She strained her ears but couldn't make out the words.

The door of the hut opened.

Achilles entered.

He'd removed his cuirass and now wore only the stripped leather pteruges of the hoplite and a loose tunic. His hair looked damp and he carried with him the scent of salt water. He'd bathed in the sea.

He glanced at her, sitting still and small on the red silk pillow. She'd had a pillow like this in the women's quarters of the palace. Was this her pillow? The palace had been sacked. How much of the loot in the corner of his tent had been her husband's? Her father's? Hers?

"Were you touched by anyone?" he asked.

"The women who bathed me," she said. "And Patroclus, who carried me here."

"Did he take you?"

"No. He honors you. He…he touched my foot. That's all."

Achilles nodded, pleased.

"I fight all day," he said. "I have no interest in fighting in my own tent."

"I will not fight you, sir."

"No," he said. "You will not."

Lia gazed at him as he pulled off his tunic and dropped it to the floor. He brought his fingers to a small leather tie at his hip, unknotted it and dropped his battle skirt to the floor, as well. He stepped toward her, naked but for the sheen of oil on his dark olive skin.

"Lie back," he ordered, and she did as instructed. Lia's heart pounded in her throat. She tried to tell herself this was a fantasy—that this man was August Bowman and she was Lia

Godwick—but no matter what her mind said, her body knew this was very, very real. This was real, and she was Briseis, a slave of war, and it was Achilles who now owned her body.

On her back, she panted, nearly hyperventilating.

Achilles loomed over her. "Show me your cunt," he said.

She knew disobedience would win her nothing but a quick death but that wasn't the reason she obeyed. She lifted her sheer gown up to her stomach and spread her thighs wide. She gazed at the high white moon that shone through the small square in the roof of the hut where the smoke from the fire was meant to escape. She obeyed Achilles because this was nothing new for her. For three years, she'd been little more than a concubine to her husband, the king. She was well versed in the art of submitting to survive. What wife in this cruel era was not?

And at least Achilles had a face and form handsome enough not to repulse her.

He took his organ in his hand and stroked it as she slipped her hands between her open thighs and opened the folds of her body to him. With the moon so high and white, the room was bright enough she knew he could see all he wished to see. A slight smile spread across his lips. Not a cruel smile, however.

"Beautiful," he said.

She said nothing. With her husband, she had learned silence was her salvation. He wanted her breasts and her holes—no part of her was spared—but a woman's mouth was for taking cocks and not conversation, in his opinion. It was easy enough with her husband to will her mind far away. When he took her body, her mind ran free in verdant forests, playing hide-and-seek with nymphs and gentle-eyed does unafraid of the hands of wounded women. But though she tried again and again to cast her mind away to the sacred woods where she hid from men, it kept coming back to this moment of Achilles standing over her, staring down at her spread-open sex.

He knelt between her thighs, still stroking himself. She couldn't help but glance at his organ, though she regretted it immediately. He was larger than her husband by far, the organ so thick his fingers could barely encompass it and his hand so much larger than hers. What did that mean for her body, she didn't want to wonder.

"You don't weep," he said. "I wonder why that is."

She still did not speak. Some men loved the sound of their own voices and found their words sweeter music than anything wrung from the harp or lyre. Best not to interrupt.

He took her by the hips and pulled her closer to him. He found the entrance to her body with two fingers and pushed into it all the way, to the knuckles of his hand. Lia flinched and whimpered but held her tongue.

"You're very young," he said. "And small. I am neither."

He removed his fingers from inside her and put them in his mouth, wetting them before pushing them back into her. He pushed his thumb into her to join the first two fingers, and Lia had to spread her legs wider to take it. Achilles parted his fingers, prying her open from the inside. Lia gasped in pleasure and pain as he widened her opening, then pried her apart even more. A low grunt escaped her throat.

"Better like this," he said, "than tear you apart with my cock."

He pulled his hand out and wet his fingers again in his mouth. This time her body yielded more readily to the intrusion. His fingers moved inside her, probed and pushed until she was open enough for him.

The tips of two fingers found a knot inside her, a tender tensed muscle and kneaded it. Lia's eyes rolled back in her head.

"Good," Achilles said.

She tried to breathe as he went about preparing her for his cock. He rubbed along the front wall, rubbed along the back. When she made a certain sound, a tiny gasp or quick inhalation, he stopped, as if he could simply take no more.

"Enough," she heard Achilles say to himself. Abruptly he pulled his fingers from her and replaced them with the tip of his organ. With his large hands, he gripped her by her waist, lifted her, and then with a stroke he impaled her.

On her bed of silk, so incongruous in this rough wood and leather hut, she lay still as Achilles rutted into her with long rough thrusts. She willed herself to not move, to let him take all while she gave nothing.

At first her strategy worked. The huge phallus splitting her demanded nothing of her but that she yield to it. And Achilles was careful to not let his full weight rest on her and crush her. He crouched over her, hands and elbows on either side of her head, knees holding her legs apart as he pumped into her. He exhaled in rough, ragged breaths that tickled her shoulder and neck.

Only when he pressed his lips to the tendon of her throat did her body respond. It shocked her when he kissed her, shocked her enough that she gasped. And when he kissed her again, a longer kiss that lingered at her throat and ear, she felt her sex unexpectedly begin to swell.

She'd borne his thrusts until then and now…suddenly and strangely…she almost welcomed them. She grew slick. Her fingers gripped the silk beneath her harder, and her toes curled against Achilles's iron thighs.

"Look at me," he demanded, and she obeyed without thinking. As soon as she'd turned her head, he caught her lips in a kiss. His tongue plundered her helpless mouth as the cock inside her throbbed. She whimpered, but he gave no quarter, neither with his kisses nor his bruising thrusts.

At once he sat up on his knees and tore the sheer linen gown from her body as if it were made of parchment. He took her breasts in his hands, and though they were full breasts they seemed small in his palms. He held them hard and squeezed them, pinched the nipples and tugged them until they felt sore and heavy. He rubbed the pads of his thumbs over the nipples until they grew painfully, yet deliciously tender.

"Good," he breathed as she began, for the first time since he'd entered her, to move under him. She hadn't meant to, hadn't wanted to, but her body took over from her will. As he rolled her nipples, her breasts swelled, and her sex grew even wetter. Her thighs seemed to spread farther apart of their own accord. The cock shifted in her, going deeper until the tip kissed her womb and she shuddered in pleasure and shame.

"You take my cock well," he said. She heard pleasure in his tone, but mockery, too.

"I am no maiden. You give me nothing I have not taken before."

This desire, unwanted and unexpected, had loosened her tongue. She half expected him to slap her for her words. Instead he laughed, a low and heady sound.

"The silk under you is soaked and I've yet to spill in you. Don't pretend you hate this. Your body tells me otherwise," he said as he squeezed her breasts to the point of pain. They were like twin hearts on her chest, throbbing from his brutal attentions.

She opened her mouth to protest but he covered her lips with one massive hand. His right hand. She could smell the salt water on his skin from the sea and the subtler scent of her own body on the fingers that had penetrated her.

"This is my sword hand," he said as he pressed his first finger into her mouth. "I killed your husband and king today with this hand."

If he'd thought to hurt her with that taunt or goad her into biting him, he did not know her husband. She would have thanked him if she could speak. Since she couldn't, she closed her eyes and sucked the finger deeper in her mouth. Achilles moaned his pleasure, and at the sound, her raw inner muscles clenched around his cock.

Achilles pulled his finger from her mouth and grabbed her hips with both hands. He worked her up and down on his shaft. It would end soon. She knew it would end. And she willed herself to endure it until that end. But she failed there, made a fatal mistake. She looked at him again, looked at his head thrown back in pleasure and the long line of his bare throat, the pulse throbbing at the base. His chest, harder and stronger than any bronze breastplate that could shield it. The stomach, so hard and flat that she could count the ridges of his muscles under the smooth brown flesh. And his manhood, thick and slick with her juices, pumping in and out of her body, nearly lifting her hips off the pillow with its urgent thrusts.

"Please." She sobbed the word as her head fell back on the pillow. It seemed Achilles had been waiting for her to surrender to him and he took that as her white flag waving. Through eyes hooded and heavy with desire, she watched him lick his fingertips and press them against the sore and swollen knot of flesh at the entrance of her body. He bore down on her with quick pumps of his hips as he stroked that knot. How did he know to do it? She alone had ever touched herself there, in the quiet of the night when all who were about her slept. He stroked it and she swelled even more and pulsed against his fingers. Sharp pleasure radiated through her sex, through her belly and back. Fluid trickled out of her, dampening her thighs as she worked herself up and down the cock that pierced her. As big as Achilles was, she could have taken a cock twice its size at that moment. She could not get enough of him. She cried out as her climax took her by force and left her shuddering in her innermost parts.

Arching, eyes wide open, she saw the shadow of a two-headed, two-backed beast moving on the walls of the tent. Lia went limp beneath him, his cock still embedded in her deep as a knife.

Though she lay limp, half dead, half asleep, he had not finished with her. He placed his hands on either side of her head and he rose and rose, his back arched and his pelvis flush with hers—and the sigh that came out of him was a sound of purest, most erotic male pleasure. She ran her hands from his stomach all the way to his neck and down again. Lia felt sealed to him, soft to hard, wet to wet. Her sex continued to give little spasms as he moved slowly in her, not thrusting but rolling his hips into her hips. Her thighs were damp, as was the pillow underneath her, though he hadn't come inside her yet. It was her pleasure that perfumed the room, her arousal combined with the sweat of Achilles's body and the oil—a primal scent.

He lowered his head and licked the sweat from her body from her belly to her breasts to her throat. Then he rose up again, pressing his hips into hers, sealing them together again.

He thrust three times, hard, harder, hardest, then cried out as he released inside her, spurting his seed into her, against the mouth of her womb.

When it was done, he exhaled, a deep groan from the back of his throat. He rested on his elbows over her, his cock still inside her. Slowly he withdrew from her, almost reluctantly. She closed her legs as he rolled onto his side, propped his head on his fist and looked at her.

"Water?" Achilles asked. "Wine?"

"Wine, please," she said. He stroked her cheek once before standing. He found a clay jug and poured wine into a rough clay cup and passed it to her. She sipped the sweet wine, then passed the cup back to him. He took it from her and remained standing.

"Thank you, sir," she said.

"Palace born and bred," he said as he filled the cup again. "I killed your husband today, made you my concubine and you thank me for a sip of wine."

"You did me a favor," she said.

"You did not love your husband?"

"No." He loomed over her, but she didn't look up at him when she replied.

"Was he cruel to you?"

"He is dead. I will not speak ill of him anymore."

"He *was* cruel to you. You should know I killed your brothers, as well. All three of them. And your father. Will you still say 'please' and 'thank you' to me now?"

"My father forced me to marry. My brothers served as my husband's lapdogs. If you wish me to shed tears for them, I'll require a sharp knife and a fresh onion."

He laughed.

"I seem to amuse you, sir," she said.

"You delight me," he said. "Briseis."

She shivered as he spoke her name. His Greek tongue made the syllables into music—Briss-eee-uss…

"Achilles," she replied.

He nodded. "Do you know who I am?"

"The world knows who you are."

He smiled, pleased. He squatted in front of her, his powerful thighs holding him still as a statue as he looked long at her face.

"You are very beautiful," he said as he took the cord from her braid. "But young."

"This is my twentieth summer," she said.

He ran his fingers through the plaits of her braid and loosed it into soft waves.

"Too young to be a widow," he said.

"But the proper age to be a concubine?"

"I think you might be. Though I won't force you to stay with me against your will."

"You would set me free?" she asked, heart racing with hope.

"No, but if you despise my attentions, I can send you to the laundresses. Though I think you will prefer my tent to scrubbing Spartan seed off woolen bedrolls."

"Is Spartan seed worse somehow than Athenian seed?" she asked.

"It puts up much more of a fight."

A jest. The great warrior Achilles had made a jest. She smiled, almost laughed.

"You choose my tent, then?" he asked.

"Yes, sir," she said.

"You did seem to enjoy coupling with me." He lay back on the bedroll and drank deep from the wine cup. "Whether you wanted to or not."

She thought of lying, thought better of it. He twirled her hair in his fingers, tugged it lightly to make her speak.

"That is true," she confessed.

"Am I simply too handsome for you to resist?"

"I pretended you were Patroclus."

A jest to mock Achilles for his arrogance. He laughed like a man so certain of his prowess there was nothing to do but laugh at such a statement. Laugh and call for Patroclus.

"Patroclus!"

No. Surely, he wouldn't…

Lia looked around in terror, saw the scarlet cloak of Achilles and hastily wrapped it around her naked body.

Patroclus entered the tent and did his noble best to not look at her, though she did see his eyes dart her way once before looking away again. Achilles made no move to cover himself nor did Patroclus seem shocked by his friend's nakedness.

"You have need of me?"

"I need your good company," Achilles said.

"You have company already."

"Which I have enjoyed to the hilt."

"I know," Patroclus said. "Half the camp knows."

Achilles looked at her. "You were too loud, my lady," he said.

"I meant you, young fool," Patroclus said to Achilles.

He raised his wine cup in salute. "You know this man is the other half of me when I let him speak to me that way," he said to her as he pointed at Patroclus.

"The better half." Patroclus's eyes glinted with amusement.

"No greater truth has ever been uttered," Achilles said. "Not by the prophets or the priests. And Briseis agrees. Don't you?"

Lia said nothing. He rolled to his feet and poured new wine for Patroclus.

"Don't play shy, little queen," Achilles urged. "Tell Patroclus what you told me."

"What did she tell you?" Patroclus asked.

"This one," Achilles said, pointing at her, wine cup still in hand, "said she pretended I was you while I took her."

Patroclus roared with laughter. "She only said that to take you down a peg, you arrogant child."

"It didn't work," Achilles said. Lia blushed to have her words repeated to Patroclus. "But even I am able to yield when bested. She thinks you're the better-looking man, apparently. It must be the beard." Achilles yanked on Patroclus's chin hair.

"I told you to grow one," he said, slapping Achilles's hand away.

"I tried," Achilles replied.

"Try harder," Patroclus said. "I'm tired of old men thinking you're my son."

"Brother." Both men looked at Lia. "You look like his older brother. His wiser, kinder, older brother."

"See?" Achilles said. "I told you she likes you better. But no matter. We share a heart and a soul between us. Might as well share a prize."

"She is your prize," Patroclus said. "Not mine. She was given to you."

"And as she is mine, she is mine to share. So now I—" Achilles pointed at his chest "—share her with you. Come, little queen. There is war enough for all by day. Let us make peace by night."

Achilles waved at her, beckoning her to rise. She stood slowly, and as she did Achilles pulled his cloak off her body, revealing her to Patroclus.

How is this happening? she thought as Patroclus raised his hand to her face and stroked it.

"You've scared her now, boy," he said.

"It'll pass," Achilles assured. "Help him with his armor, little queen. Earn your keep."

Achilles had propped himself up on his elbows, crossed his long and muscled legs at the ankle. He seemed quite happy to be watching the entertainment unfold before him. She knew little of men's armor, so Patroclus had to whisper instructions to her.

"There's a tie behind the shoulders," he said very softly as she stepped in front of him. He looked past her as she raised her hands to unknot the leather straps of his breastplate. She heard him breathe in sharply as she lifted her arms to the shoulder strap.

When her head was next to his, he lowered his mouth to

her ear and whispered, "Forgive me." He raised his hands to her back and stroked her there. "I should not take you, but he wants this... I spoil him like a firstborn son."

"Do you want this?" she whispered back.

"Can you doubt it?" he asked.

She didn't doubt it. Patroclus desired her. She'd known that from the moment he'd touched her foot when he'd removed the rope that bound her.

But how had August known?

Lia hadn't told him this was part of her fantasy about Achilles. She'd told him about her desire to be a concubine to Achilles, but not the other half of the fantasy—where Achilles shared her with Patroclus, his soul mate and shield-bearer. And if she hadn't told August that...how did he know to make it happen?

"Go on, my lady," Achilles said. "You wanted him. Now you have him."

Lia ignored the taunting and concentrated on her task. At last she succeeded in unknotting the straps of the breastplate. She removed it and set it next to Achilles's armor, propped against the hut wall.

Patroclus pulled off his tunic and stood bare chested before her. Broad, dark patch of hair in the center—some brown, some gray—and muscle to spare. Hard flat broad stomach.

"Touch him, little queen," Achilles ordered.

She raised her hands and pressed her palms lightly to the hard flat plane of his stomach. Patroclus looked down at her small hands on his body and took a labored breath. She wondered how long it had been since he'd felt a woman's hand. A pity as he was a pleasure to touch. She stroked his sides, feeling the hard rib cage underneath his skin. She touched his chest, the bones of his throat and collar...and then the shoulders that had carried her weight so easily through the camp.

Patroclus lowered his head and kissed her mouth. He ran his hands down her back to grip her by the hips and pull her to him. She sensed he was on the verge of losing control of his desire. It seemed Achilles sensed it, too.

"Briseis." Achilles gestured to his hip, wagging his finger there as if trying to tell her something. She narrowed her eyes at him.

"What, sir?" she asked.

Achilles sighed dramatically.

"He's trying to tell you to do this." Patroclus stepped back to untie the leather thongs on the pteruges. She moved to obey, but Patroclus finished before she could help. His clothes landed on the floor and he kicked them away.

She gazed at his entire body. Achilles was the greater warrior, it was said. He was lithe and quick as a striking cobra, but Patroclus was the larger of the two men, the heavier. He had massive thighs, a huge chest, broad back and powerful hips. But it was his arousal she could not look away from, the red, thick, straining organ.

"To serve him is to serve me," Achilles said.

"How would you have me serve?" Lia asked, though she already knew the answer. She knew because she'd been here before, in her mind. She knew what Achilles would say...

"As a slave should serve. On your knees, of course."

And she knew what Patroclus would say...

"Achilles." Patroclus's tone was chiding. "She's a queen, not one of your whores."

And she knew what she would say...

"I'm not a queen anymore."

And with that, Lia went down onto her knees as Achilles laughed in his delight. She looked up once at Patroclus before she took his cock in hand and brought it to her mouth. As she surrounded it, drawing it in, Patroclus shuddered. He

gently cupped the back of her head. Lia felt his hands stroke
her hair, and she turned her gaze upward to see his head fall
back in pleasure as she sucked him. As if he sensed her gaze,
he looked down at her and lightly lifted her hair, held it fisted
in his hand as she took him deeper into her mouth.

Lia wrapped her arms around his waist and sucked him
hard, hungrily, moving her mouth on him in rhythm with
his quick rasping breaths. She dug her fingers into the flesh
of his lower back and sucked until the swollen tip of his cock
pressed against the very back of her throat.

She turned her head just slightly and saw Achilles—August—
stretched out on his side, stroking himself as he watched them,
his body bathed in the flicking light of the fire. He was hard
again already.

"Lovely," Patroclus said with a low groan. He lowered his
hands to her hair and cupped the back of her head. On his
wrists he still wore his leather vambraces, and she wrapped
her small hands around them.

Lia had imagined them in her fantasies about him, but this
was the first time she ever truly felt the stiff leather under her
fingers and the zigzag pattern of the thongs that tied them
and held them in place. Suddenly she became aware of Achilles standing next to her. She'd been so lost in the pleasure of
touching and sucking Patroclus that she hadn't known he was
there until she felt a third hand on her head.

"Lovely queen…" Achilles softly whispered. Patroclus gently
withdrew his cock and Achilles took his place in her mouth.

She sucked him deep, still clinging to Patroclus's wrist to
steady herself as Achilles fucked her mouth. Lia knew she
should feel ashamed of herself—and she did—and she knew
she should be terrified to be used by these two lethal men—
and she was. But the shame and the fear were two little drops
of rain falling onto the ocean of her desire.

Patroclus knelt behind her as she licked Achilles's organ from the base to the tip. His strong arms came around her and his lips kissed her neck as he held her breasts in his hands, squeezing and lifting and holding them hard. She felt his cock seeking the entrance of her body. It pressed and pushed into her wet folds. A primal instinct she didn't know she possessed set her arching her back and spreading her thighs. The head of his cock found her hole and she sank down onto him as he pushed up and into her.

Speared as she was—a cock in mouth, a cock against her womb—she could hardly move. The men held her pinned in place. Achilles held her head as he pushed himself into her throat. Patroclus held her kneeling back against his chest. Nothing in her fantasies had prepared her for the sensations of being taken by two men at once. The scent of their bodies— salt and sweat—and the incredible heat of their skin, the taste of male flesh in her mouth and the sound of low hard breathing in her ears. And Patroclus's hands all over her, groping at her breasts, pulling her nipples as his mouth licked and lapped and bit at her neck and shoulders.

The grip on her hair tightened. Achilles thrust into her mouth faster. He grunted softly, rapidly, in time with his thrusts as he worked himself toward his climax. Patroclus wrapped one hand gently around her throat and tilted her head back against his shoulder, holding her in place for Achilles to use. Her jaw ached, and her sex clenched around the cock inside her. Patroclus whispered, "You'll have my seed next."

Achilles grunted loudly, whimpered that way grown men did when undone. His seed, hot and thick, filled her mouth. Her throat moved against Patroclus's strong palm as she swallowed every drop as it came.

When Achilles had emptied himself into her mouth, he pulled out and dramatically dropped to his knees.

"She sucked the life out of me," he said with a sigh as he collapsed onto his side on the pillows.

Patroclus laughed softly as he pulled Lia back against him again, holding her tightly to his chest. She looked at her own body and saw his impossibly thick strong arms imprisoning her, the vambraces on his wrists, the veins popping in the hands that squeezed her breasts and the cock inside her, spearing her from behind.

"They say he's immortal," Patroclus rasped into her ear, loud enough for Achilles to hear. "But you and I know his mortal weakness. Suck his cock and he's done for."

"Don't let that get out," Achilles said, propping himself up on his elbow again. "Bad enough I have every Trojan soldier aiming for my heart. I don't need them trying to get under my pteruges, as well."

"I'd pay a month's wages to see one try," Patroclus said. "I might bribe a Trojan tomorrow, if I can find one that won't run from me at first sight."

"Are you going to mock me or fuck her?" Achilles asked.

"I can't do both?"

Achilles patted the pillow next to him. "Come here."

"Me or her?" Patroclus asked.

"Both, old man."

Patroclus lightly pushed her forward onto her hands. He pulled out of her, and as soon as he was out, her body clenched on the sudden emptiness inside her.

Lia crawled to the pillow and Achilles took her by the chin and kissed her. Patroclus laid on his side behind her, stroking her back while Achilles pinched her nipples.

"You like Patroclus?" Achilles asked as he looked at the breast he held in his hand.

"Yes, sir," she said.

"Good. I love the man," he said. "It pleases me to please

him. And you're doing a very good job pleasing him. But I think we could do better."

"A worthy goal." Patroclus kissed her shoulder and caressed it. Lia shivered. God, it was exactly like her fantasies. Exactly like them—down to every single touch, every word they said.

Achilles pushed her gently onto her back and took her nipple into his mouth. Patroclus needed no urging to take her other nipple into his. She lay beneath them as they suckled her tender breasts, overwhelmed by their male hunger. It seemed they'd devour her if they could.

"Patroclus, lie on your back," Achilles said.

"Do I have to? I'm enjoying this." He said that as he stroked her wet folds and slipped two, three, four fingers inside her...

"You'll like this more," Achilles assured. "On your back."

With a much put-upon sigh, Patroclus rolled onto his back. He picked up a dainty blue pillow and propped it under his head.

"On top of him," Achilles ordered Lia.

She turned and straddled Patroclus. He pulled her to him and kissed her roughly as he gripped her by the hips and settled her onto his cock. She sank down onto it, taking every inch. With his strong hands on her narrow waist, he made her ride him. He lifted her and brought her down on his cock, lifted her and brought her down again. Achilles watched at first, but he wasn't content to merely watch for long.

He touched Lia where Patroclus entered her, touched her tender, spread-wide labia, touched her throbbing knot.

But Achilles wasn't content to simply touch. He lowered his head and licked her clitoris. She gasped at the shock of pleasure as he brought his mouth down onto her.

And Achilles wasn't content to simply lick her. He lowered his head farther and licked Patroclus, as well.

"Gods," Patroclus said. His hands gripped her breasts so

hard she knew she'd have bruises on them. Achilles licked them both as they coupled, licked the cock that slid in and out of her body, licked her open flesh. She writhed in pleasure and Patroclus took her by the waist once more, to hold her still as he fucked her. Meanwhile, Achilles lapped at her, at both of them. Patroclus panted underneath her, his chest rising and falling fast as Achilles rubbed them both with lips and tongue. Lia's inner muscles twisted up into knots and tightened around the shaft inside her. Patroclus pumped into her and Achilles worked her clitoris with his tongue. For the span of a stroke of lightning she met the dark eyes of Achilles…and they weren't dark anymore, but the wild gray of storm clouds. Patroclus grunted as his hips came off the floor and he filled her and filled her with his semen.

Achilles lifted her off Patroclus and pushed her onto her back again. He mounted her, entered her and pounded her into oblivion. She was too spent to even move. She lay limp as a rag doll under him as he used her for his own pleasure. She felt nothing except Patroclus stroking her thigh one more time before he rose, dressed and left her alone with Achilles again. Achilles spent himself inside her with a low cry that branded her memory. After, he remained on top of her—his cock still inside her, this a temporary respite before he would use her again.

And again.

And again.

Ah, love truly was a far better game than war.

CHAPTER FOURTEEN

Lia came to with a gasp, as if she'd been submerged in water and had finally broken the surface.

She looked over and found August next to her, eyes closed. She called his name and received no answer.

He was sound asleep.

"Typical," she said, shaking her head.

She hoped he'd stay asleep for a good long while. She had no desire to face him quite yet. As soon as he woke up he'd want to have sex with her, or worse, talk. The need to get out and get home was overwhelming. Lia dressed quickly in the dark and fled his house.

Once in her car she checked her phone. Half-ten. She'd been with August an hour and a half, though in her mind it felt like she'd spent half the night with him. How bizarre…

When she checked her rearview mirror before starting out into the street, she saw a mark on her neck. She rose up and touched the mark. It was red and tender, like a bite mark. A love bite. At the sight of it, memories flooded her mind… memories of kneeling in front of Achilles, his cock in her mouth as Patroclus knelt behind her, his hands holding her breasts and his mouth on her neck—kissing and suckling the very spot where she now wore an inch-wide red bite mark.

"Patroclus…" she breathed. She could still feel him inside her. She could still taste Achilles in her mouth.

Lia shivered as a fresh wave of desire washed over her. She had to distract herself. She put the car into Drive and cracked the window to let in the cool air. It soothed her burning flesh. A light rain started to fall, a gentle late-spring drizzle that set the sidewalks to shimmering in the hazy lamplight.

At a stoplight, she giggled.

Lia was giggling so hard she forgot to drive on when the light changed. A car honked behind her and she waved an apology and sped off into the night. The kylix had worked its strange powers on her again, and she felt high as a kite. Higher. She'd smoked pot once with some friends and it had done little more than make her sleepy and paranoid. This, however, was heaven. This was bliss. This was a thousand elves dancing jigs around a thousand trees and all of them—elves and trees and jigs—all lived inside her dancing head.

Nothing could hurt her. Nothing could touch her.

Throw her off the top of London Bridge and watch her fly…

The rational part of Lia's brain warned her this was nothing but the side effect of the Rose Kylix. She wasn't really bullet-proof. She couldn't really fly.

But maybe…maybe she was untouchable. She certainly felt strong enough to take on the world. Her toes tingled and her heart leaped and she danced in her seat, though she hadn't turned on her Mini's ancient radio.

She wanted to test her joy, to find out if it was as ironclad as it felt.

At the next stoplight she dug her phone out of her bag and Googled an address. A short detour and worth it if it worked for her.

She made it to the Attic Gallery without incident and parked her car in a nearby alley. She couldn't simply drive by and take a peek. She had to get up close and personal. Usually Lia avoided walking in unfamiliar London neighborhoods at night, even posh ones. But that night she walked with her head high, her spine solid steel as she strode down the sidewalk, her boot heels banging the pavement with every confident step. Let a mugger try anything with her. She'd just been fucked by Achilles—and Patroclus, too—and lived to tell the tale. Who else could say that?

Lia braced herself as she came to the front windows of the gallery. Just as she'd suspected, they were already advertising David's new show called *Rare Bones: Exploring the Interior— The Work of David Bell*. Rare bones? Instead of bare bones? Lia rolled her eyes. A pun? David couldn't do better than a pun for his art show?

Disgraceful.

The Attic was going all out for David's show. Posters, four feet high, filled each window. Three of the four posters were just images of his art cropped in artful ways: a mural of surrealistic skeleton horses running through the streets of New York—pure wank; a reverse Hamlet with a skeleton holding a human head—must be a theme; and a massive pink rose, blooming erotically out of the pelvic bone of a woman—August had been right about the rose/vagina connection.

In the fourth and final poster, David's face—so solemn and serious and handsome—stared right at her through the glass.

The gallery knew what it was doing by advertising David along with his art. He wasn't just handsome, he was striking, a work of art himself, the poster seemed to imply. Lia met the eyes of the photographic David. She stared at him and he stared at her. Her lover. Her enemy. The man who held her fate in his paint-spattered hands.

She flashed him the V-sign and walked away. Friday night after she paid David off, she'd do exactly that.

Still flying with the hardest case of afterglow she'd ever been hit with, Lia drove home to Wingthorn and arrived by midnight. She parked and went in through the kitchen entrance. The light was on, and she found her mother in her dressing gown and her father wearing half of a suit—trousers and shirt but no jacket, tie or shoes—fighting over a bottle of wine.

"You broke the cork," her mother said. "How have you managed to father three children when you can't even work a corkscrew?"

"I don't follow your logic, spouse, unless you rate all forms of penetration on the same scale. Just push the broken cork into the bottle."

"Then we'll have cork bits in our wine," Lia's mother said. "Unacceptable."

Lia shook her head, sighed and stepped out of the shadows and into the kitchen.

"Lia," her father said. "Where have you been all evening?"

"I was kidnapped and forced to have a threesome with Greek soldiers."

"Hope you had a nice time," her mother said.

Lia picked up the wine bottle and slapped the base of it twice and hard. The cork popped out.

"How did you do that?" Her father's eyes went wide.

Lia walked out of the kitchen. "That was my spanking hand."

The last thing she heard as she stepped into the hall was her mother saying, "Has she been acting strange lately? Or is it just me?"

Lia did not wait around to hear her father's answer.

She skipped up the stairs, desperately in need of a long bath. Tomorrow when her mind was back to normal and not doing cartwheels off the ceiling, Lia would call August and ask him about what had happened tonight. For the moment, however, she was going to do nothing but enjoy the high-flying feeling as long as she could. She wasn't going to work or weave or talk to anyone. Instead she would simply lie in bed and remember the seawater scent of Achilles's skin and the feel of Patroclus inside her, and the intensity of the orgasms that had probably done permanent damage to some vitally important area of her cerebellum.

Lia opened the door to her suite—and found August sitting by the fireplace, playing tug-of-war with Gogo.

"August?" Lia said, shocked silly.

He looked up at her and smiled.

"Did you miss me?"

PART FOUR

Eros & Psyche

CHAPTER FIFTEEN

"What the hell are you doing here?" Lia demanded. "How did you get in?"

"I knocked on the front door. Mrs. Banks let me in."

"She let you in? She just opened the door and let you in? I'm having a word with her tomorrow."

"Women love me. And deerhounds, too, apparently."

He said that at precisely the moment Gogo began licking his cheek.

"This is disgusting." August winced. "But weirdly pleasant."

"Don't get an erection," Lia said. "Gogo, bed."

Gogo whined but he behaved and slipped through the door to her bedroom.

"Are you going to tell me why you're here?" she asked August. "I didn't invite you."

"I'm not a vampire," he said. "I can go anywhere I like, no invitation required. Plus, I told your housekeeper you were expecting me."

"Just because they let you loose in the house doesn't mean you can come into my room whenever you like."

"You're right. I'm wrong. I'll send roses tomorrow. Wait. You live in a house with a rose garden. Never mind. Your rooms are very Victorian, by the way. I feel like I'm sitting in at teapot. " He eyed her pink-and-white chintz furniture with suspicion and possible vertigo.

"My grandmother and great-grandmother both lived in this suite. And you've been in here before," Lia reminded him. She refused to admit August had a point. Her suite was a bit fussy. On purpose. No one expected a madam to live in a suite this twee.

"In the dark," he said. Then, quieter, "I think I liked it better in the dark."

Lia kicked off her shoes and walked to her rose chintz love seat, keeping it between her and August like a security barrier. He remained sitting on the floor where he'd been playing with Gogo.

"Let's forget about my suite for a moment, and you breaking into it. What I want to know is…how did you get into my head like that?"

"Get into your head?" August asked. "Oh, you mean the threesome, you saucy trollop, you tricky minx, you delicious tart?"

Lia glared at him. "Yes," she said. "That."

"There's no reason to be embarrassed. Do you really think you're the first person ever to fantasize about a threesome?"

"I didn't *tell* you any of that," she said as she walked over and dropped down onto the love seat. "So, what I want to know is how it happened."

"Do I need to draw you a chart?" Lia's glare became more glaring. "It was your fantasy."

"Yes, but you guide the fantasies."

"You *think* I do," he corrected. "You want to believe it's all guided hypnosis or whatever other rational nonsense you've come up with. But I already told you, the cup belongs to Eros, and when you drink out of it, it lets you experience *your* fantasies. You wanted a threesome with Achilles and Patroclus, the Rose Kylix gave you a threesome with Achilles and Patroclus."

"You still believe in Father Christmas, too?" she asked him.

"Are you trying to tell me it's the tooth fairy who puts all those gifts under my tree? Balderdash." August sat back against the armchair, facing her.

"You could sit *in* the chair." She pointed. "As opposed to sitting *against* the chair."

"I don't like chairs," he said. "I only sit in them when I have to. We need to bring back Greek couches. Better for digestion. And making love. Missed opportunity for IKEA."

"I'll trade my love seat for your chair," she said.

"Done."

They swapped positions. She sat in the armchair and he took the love seat across from it. And, of course, he didn't sit in it. He lounged on his side, and reposed himself like Caravaggio's *Sleeping Cupid*.

"Much better." He grinned. "Oh, by the way, I did something else you're going to be very angry about."

"What now?" she asked.

"I found your note." He pulled the envelope from his jeans pocket and opened it.

"You read the note from David?" she asked.

"I did." He wrinkled his nose. Why was that so bloody

adorable? She ought to be clawing his eyes out, not thinking of ripping his clothes off.

"Wonderful," she said.

"But you shouldn't be angry at me for reading your note. It was out in plain sight under a book on your side table. And when I see a note, I have to read it. It's a religious precept," he insisted. "Catholics eat fish on Friday during Lent. Muslims must give alms to the poor. Erotic cultists have to open secret notes they find."

"I'm filing that information away in the same mental folder as the one that holds your 'sex with a cloud' comment."

August rolled onto his back and propped his bare feet on the arm of her love seat.

"Come to think of it," he said, pointing at the ceiling, then her. "It was really more of a thick fog than a cloud." He turned his head and looked at her. "So it's David Bell who's blackmailing you."

August held out the note to her as if she didn't already know what it said. Lia stood and snatched the card from him.

"You know him?" she asked.

"The mural painter? The next Rex Whistler?" Lia nodded. "Don't know him personally. What the hell could you have done to a muralist to make him come after you for a million pounds? Break his paintbrush?"

Lia sat back in the chair and started to raise her legs, planning to sit lotus-style. She quickly put her legs back on the floor and clamped her thighs together.

"I left my knickers on the floor of your office, didn't I?"

"I brought them back," August said.

"Where are they?"

"Gogo grabbed them from me. They're, ah…on the floor."

Lia peeked behind her chair and found her knickers, now damp with dog drool and full of teeth marks, on the rug.

"Lovely," she said. "Just lovely. You break into my house. You read my letters. You let my dog eat my knickers. It's really a good thing you're attractive or I'd sack you."

"You won't tell me about David Bell?" August asked. "Before you sack me?"

Lia tugged her skirt a bit to cover herself. "I told you everything you need to know about him."

"I don't think so," he said. "You said he was older than you, yes? How much older?"

"Twenty years older." She waited for August to blink or raise an eyebrow. Nothing. The man was hard to shock.

"And when did you sleep with him?"

"Four years ago."

"You were seventeen and he was thirty-seven?" August asked.

"You have run the numbers correctly," she said. "Well done."

"I'm not just a pretty face," he said. "Though I am that, too."

Lia smiled, hoped he'd drop it. He didn't.

"Go on, Lia. Tell me all."

Lia wanted to tell him. It shocked her how much she wanted to tell him, though she'd told no one in her life about her and David. Not a soul.

August came and sat at her feet, then kissed her bare thigh.

"What was that for?"

"For you." He smiled up at her. "I need to know the truth and you need to speak it. This is what therapy is, Lia—telling our story to someone who will listen and understand. Tell me your story. Let me help you."

Hard to say no to a beautiful man sitting at her feet. Hard to say no when she thought maybe she had finally found someone who she could maybe, possibly, trust.

"David couldn't make it in New York apparently. Art scene's murder there, I hear. Mum met him at a showing and took pity on a fellow New Yorker exiled to England. She and Daddy invited him to dinner one night," she said, pressing on before she lost her courage. "Mum absolutely loved his work, so…to surprise her, Daddy hired David to paint a mural in Mum's bedroom. He worked for weeks on it the summer I was seventeen. A mural takes forever, especially a big one. They moved him into the house. They set up showings for his work, paid his travel expenses, set him up with potential clients. They were perfect patrons, the sort any artist dreams of having. Daddy even got him a commission from Prince Charles for a mural at one of his charities."

"What about you?" August asked.

"He taught me some sketching techniques," she said. "Every evening. He said I was good."

"Ah, the art teacher. That old story." August nodded sagely.

"He was so…" She stopped to catch her breath. "Oh God, he was handsome. He called me Ophelia. Made it sound so pretty the way he said it. I wanted to marry him," she said. "How insane is that?"

David Bell was a perfect-looking man. Her ideal. At least, he had been when she was seventeen and good biceps in a tight T-shirt, unruly ginger hair and intense brown eyes could turn her head. His clothes were always paint-spattered. Always. Jeans and white tees covered in a rainbow of paint. She'd found that sexy once. After a few years, however, Lia realized the paint splotches on his clothes had been an affectation as ridiculous as a man wearing a tuxedo all the time—*Look at me, Mr. Very Serious Artist, too busy painting to stop by Tesco and pick up a clean shirt.*

"One day during our art lesson," she continued, "I admitted to him that I was in love with him. I just said it, not expecting anything. I tried to make it a joke, told him, 'David, you might have noticed I'm madly in love with you, but I hope that won't make things awkward. When I try to seduce you, feel free to ignore me and carry on with your life.'"

"Very smooth. That would have worked on me."

"It worked on him, too," Lia said. "He came to my room that night about midnight."

"How was the sex?" August asked. She appreciated his matter-of-fact manner about the whole ordeal, asking questions, not judging her.

"Painful," she admitted. "And I didn't come. He was nice about it, though. He promised it got better with practice. He held me after. That was lovely." She gave August a wan smile. "He didn't stay long, though. Said he needed to get back to his room before we got caught together. Mum and Daddy are pretty open-minded about sex, but their seventeen-year-old daughter with a thirty-seven-year-old man? Daddy would have killed him. Then Mum would have resurrected him just to kill him again."

"Twenty-year age difference," August said. "Hard for modern parents to swallow."

"It happened in Ancient Greece all the time. Right?"

"So did exposing unwanted baby girls to the elements."

A fair point.

"Did you get caught?" August asked.

"I wish. I wish that's all it was. I'd be fine today if that's what had happened." She blinked back tears.

August took her hand in his. He turned it palm up and caressed the lines on her hand, traveling them as roads with his fingertips.

"Once wasn't enough, of course," she said. "I was in love with him. The morning after, I even gave him a lock of my hair."

"Traditional virgin offering in the Cult of Artemis."

"Was it?" Lia asked.

He nodded. "Girls were supposed to apologize to Artemis when they lost their virginities. Artemis has always been such a cockblock."

"I should have listened to her," she said.

"What happened with you and David?"

Lia took a long shuddering breath. "I left my room the next night, around midnight. I was going to his bedroom. I wanted to be with him again. If anybody caught me, I was just going to say I wanted a midnight snack. I thought I'd find David in his room, but he wasn't there. I heard his voice outside the house. And Mum's and Daddy's. They were on the patio by the rose garden, talking. I went through the music room. All the lights were off in there and the door was cracked open. If the lights are off in the music room, you can't see into it from the garden. They didn't see me, but I saw them. And I heard them."

August stroked her wrist now, the beating veins, and she tingled everywhere he touched her. Was this a side effect of drinking from the Rose Kylix? If so, she was already regretting selling him that bloody cup.

"I don't know what held me back," Lia said. "Why I didn't just walk out and say hello… Something about the way they were laughing made me nervous. So I hid at the door and spied on them."

She could still hear their laughs ringing in her ears.

Her mother's laugh, like she'd just been pinched in a tender spot.

Her father's laugh, like he'd won a hand of poker and was raking in the chips.

David's laugh, like he'd gotten away with murder.

"Mum was wearing this red-and-black dressing gown

Daddy had got her for Christmas. She looked beautiful, as always. Daddy was there, too, sitting in a chair, Mum on his lap. David walked over to her with a rose he'd cut from the garden and presented it to Mum like a knight to his lady. And Mum took it from him and said thank you. And then David leaned in and kissed her on the mouth. A deep kiss. And Daddy said…"

Something twisted in Lia's side, a pain like a rose thorn lodged between her ribs and into a lung.

"Daddy said, 'Behave, boy. You had more than enough of her already tonight.'"

"God, Lia…" August breathed. He sounded like he'd been punched in the stomach. She knew how he felt. Lia dug her fingers into the smooth leather of the armchair. The pain in her side was growing sharper, like she'd had to sprint for her life and had a vicious stitch. She couldn't get comfortable, couldn't take a full breath, couldn't move.

"I already knew Mum and Daddy played around with other people—when I was old enough, they'd warned me in case I heard the gossip. I didn't like it, but it's their marriage, not mine. If they wanted to have threesomes or foursomes or ten-somes, that was between them and whoever. But…ah, this was about me. It was…um…" She took a quick pained breath. "I thought I was going to die, August. I really thought I might die."

"Lia, Lia…" August said, kissing the back of her hand.

Two hot tears rolled down her cheeks.

Discovering David—who she would have gone off with to Gretna Green if he'd so much as crooked his littlest finger at her—had slept with her own mother the night after she'd given him her virginity had fundamentally altered Lia down to the very marrow of her bones. She had liked people before, trusted them, thought the world was a playground and she had no job other than to swing on the swings and slide down the slides, eat biscuits, pet puppies, drink tea—that was her life until then. But it turned out the playground was built over toxic waste, and seeing that kiss had sliced her open so that the poison in the soil seeped into her bloodstream.

Lia didn't trust men anymore. Her father alone was the exception to the rule, but even with him, as much as she loved and adored him… She never let her girlfriends alone with him. Not because she thought he'd flirt with them, but because… what if he did, though? She'd been accidentally betrayed by one parent. She didn't think her heart could take it if it happened again.

"What did you do?" August asked. His voice was soft, cautious.

"Ran back to my room and threw up a couple times. Not the best way to handle it. I should have burst out and yelled, 'What the hell do you think you're doing?' But I couldn't do it. I was a coward." Lia felt a fist in her throat. She didn't bother to try swallowing it away. It wasn't going anywhere.

"No, not a coward. Not you."

"I was, though," she said. "I couldn't face him. I slipped a note under his door that said if he didn't leave and cut off contact with my parents forever, I would tell them about us. Mum and Daddy know literally everyone who matters in the art world. They own all or part of at least twenty galleries in London, Glasgow, Dublin, New York and Los Angeles. They could have blackballed him if they'd wanted. Daddy's got friends in the Home Office. He could have had David's visa revoked. He could have ruined David's life, easily. It was a real threat."

"Did he leave like you told him to?"

"That day," Lia said, "my parents had taken my brothers to London for a football match or something. David came to my suite and pounded on my bedroom door, screaming at me to face him."

"And you couldn't?" August asked.

She slowly shook her head. "Picture me. Seventeen years old, curled up on the floor, wrapped tight as a ball, crying. I was terrified he was going to break the door down and kill me."

"Kill you?"

"You should have heard him," she said. "He shouted at me and shouted and shouted… I will never forget the names he called me, the things he said to me. 'I'm leaving, you jealous stupid bitch, you ugly boring nothing. Of course I fucked your mother. Who wouldn't? She's a goddess and you're nothing compared to her and you'll always be nothing, you little whore.' And I just sat there on the floor with my hands over my ears, rocking back and forth and wishing I were anywhere but there. Then he left. That was it until last Saturday night when I saw him in the music room with Mum. Smiling at me."

August opened his mouth, no doubt planning on saying something comforting. She raised her hand to silence him.

"It's all right. I know I'm not as beautiful as my mother. It's fine."

"Your mother is a lovely woman, but she is not a goddess."

"You know how my parents met?" Lia asked. "Daddy went to her little art gallery in New York to buy a painting from her—somehow she'd gotten hold of a painting of my great-grandfather, Malcolm. When she wouldn't sell it to Daddy, he picked her up, threw her over his shoulder and carried her out to his car. They eloped just like that." Lia snapped her fingers. "One day she was a New Yorker running a gallery. The next day she was an English countess. But that's how beautiful Mum is—men take one look at her and want to carry her off. Nobody's ever going to carry me off."

"Achilles and Briseis," August said. "Now I see the appeal." He kissed her knuckles. "Lia, I would choose you over your mother every time, every night for a thousand years. And my taste is impeccable."

"Thank you," she said in a small voice. She shouldn't have been happy to hear that, but she was.

"David said what he said to hurt you, not because he believed it."

"He called me boring," Lia said with a bitter half smile. "Maybe at seventeen I was. But I'm not boring anymore." She couldn't quite hide the pride in her voice.

"Never met a boring madam," August agreed. "Is that why you became one? To prove David Bell wrong?"

She laughed softly. "Maybe? Possibly? Let's just say when I was given the chance to have that very interesting career, I took it."

"So how does a wealthy earl's daughter get around to starting her own, ah…gardening and tennis club?"

"Georgy, of course." Lia grinned. "We've been getting into scrapes together since we were toddlers. She heard about a party for some Hollywood bigwig who was in town to film a movie. They were trying to get as many pretty legal-aged girls at the party as possible. And it was at the Pearl Hotel. Had to go, right?"

The Pearl was her great-grandfather Malcolm's favorite brothel back in the '30s, after all. She couldn't resist a chance to get tarted up and see Old Number Thirteen's former playground.

"Nice party?" August smiled as if he already knew the answer.

"Nice party," she said. "I met someone. But that's the point, isn't it? Load the party with pretty girls and horny men and odds are somebody's going to get off with somebody else."

"How was the sex?" August asked.

"Better than with David, though that's not saying much. When we were about to leave the hotel room, he gave me his card and said he wanted to see me again the next night. I said I was busy. He said he had five hundred pounds to get me unbusy. I said I'd think about it. I didn't need the money, but it was flattering. You know, my great-grandfather loved prostitutes. 'Whore' was a compliment when he said it. He only respected women who knew their own worth—no sane woman would let a man so much as shake her hand for less than a hundred pounds, and all that."

"Who was he?" August asked. "Your gentleman friend?"

"An actor," Lia said. "Great hair. Fantastic cheekbones. One of those congenial perverts. Too busy to date. Too horny to go without. You know the sort."

"I know exactly who you're talking about. I did body shots with him in Malta last summer. Unless you're talking about a different set of fantastic cheekbones..."

Lia would never tell. She smiled a little to herself at the memory.

"Georgy was *so* jealous. When I told her about his offer, that I didn't want to do it again, she said she'd do it in a heart-beat, especially for five hundred."

"You offered her in your place?"

"I let him know I was too busy but said a friend of mine might be interested. Texted him a pic. He texted back a thumbs-up. I told him I was the daughter of a very rich earl with connections everywhere, and if he didn't want to get his face on the front pages of the papers for all the wrong reasons, he'd take good care of her. He swore he would. And he did. It was only after I'd set the 'date' up that I realized I'd sort of rather inadvertently..."

"Pimped out your best friend to a near-stranger?"

"Yes, that." Lia winced. "Didn't stop me from doing it again. Week after, he called me and asked if I had any *other* amiable friends for some of his amiable friends who were in town—five hundred an hour if they were pretty and could keep a secret. After that, it sort of grew and grew…until there were five women working for me and fifty or more men who were regular clients."

"Not bad. Not bad at all."

Lia nervously twirled her ring. "I would always tell myself I was doing it to protect the ladies. If I were handling the money and the appointments and vetting the men—thanks to my parents I know almost every toff in the country—they'd be a lot safer than meeting total strangers. And they *were* safer, and they did make more money, and nobody ever got hurt. But, if I'm honest, I do it because it's fun, it makes me feel important…and it's definitely not boring." Lia smiled at that. She'd had a good run, that's for certain.

"And now David Bell knows?" August asked.

"He knows," Lia said. "My guess is he heard a rumor from a friend, hired a detective or something to verify it. I wouldn't put it past him. He's probably been looking for something to hold over me for four years. And I handed it to him on a silver platter."

"He'd go that far? Really?"

"When I sent him packing, he had to cancel a lot of commissions. A million pounds' worth. I called him, after he left that note, and he said I'd have to pay him the money by Friday or he'd call the police and the papers on me. So yes, he'd go that far."

"I wouldn't worry about the police. At most they'll get you on evading tax."

"I'm no shirker. I would never evade tax," she said with pride.

"Really? What do you put down as your source of income?"

Lia pointed at her loom. "Selling tapestries."

"Ah…shrewd as Penelope." He applauded.

"If I were shrewd as Penelope, I wouldn't have gotten caught by David," she said. "Daddy's titled and rich as Croesus. He's even related to the queen—distantly but still… There's no way it won't be the scandal heard round the world. Jane's family might kill her. Georgy's family might kill me. Rani wants to be a barrister. This could ruin their lives, too. Not just mine. My parents are rich. I can fly away and start over somewhere. They can't. God, August, it'll be a nightmare. I'm so stupid."

"You aren't stupid." August spoke firmly, sounding almost angry at the very idea. "And I won't let that arseface ruin any-one's life. If I have to put an arrow through his liver, I will. Two arrows."

"One for me and one for Mum."

"One for you. And another one for you."

He feigned shooting an arrow. Lia felt a sudden knot in her throat. How did August always know exactly the right thing to say to her?

"Now I get it," he said, meeting her eyes again.

"What?"

"Andromeda…accidentally betrayed by her mother."

"It's not my mother's fault," Lia said, though there was a time—a humiliating time—when she had blamed her mother. But now she knew better. "Women always—*always*, August—they always pay the price when men act like bastards. David used her just as much as he used me, and I'd rather die than let her find out."

"You're a very noble soul, Lia. I still think you should tell your parents, but I admire you for wanting to protect her."

"Even if I told Mum and Daddy, what can they do? Other than shoot David, hide his corpse in the cellar, what is there to do? He had sex with me when I was seventeen. So what?

It's not illegal here. And then I blackmailed him—and that *is* illegal. 'Leave the country or my father will destroy your art career'? That's bad."

"You were a heartbroken teenager, too hurt to know any better."

"I was a coward," Lia said. "I wasn't kicking him out of the country because I thought it was a just and fair punishment for his crime. I was kicking him out because I couldn't bear the thought of ever seeing him again. And if I didn't kick him out, he would go on his merry way, living under our roof, eating our food—"

"Shagging your mother."

"Yes, thank you for putting it so delicately."

August took her hand in his and kissed it.

"Come on," he said. "Let's go to bed."

"Bed? My bed?"

"Your bed. Us. In it. Now."

"No."

"Why not?"

"Many good reasons," she said. "Starting with...no."

She'd given him way too much of herself tonight. If he stayed another minute, she'd be weeping in his arms. Not a chance.

"Good reason." August stood up off the floor and bowed at the waist to her. "I'll see you tomorrow at nine?"

"You will," she said. "If I don't come to my senses first."

He walked to her door.

"August?"

He turned on his heel, eager as a puppy.

"Why did you come here tonight?" she asked. "You could have called."

"I had to return your knickers."

"I could have got them tomorrow night."

"We needed to talk about what happened."

"Again, something that could have been done over the phone."

He stuffed his hands in his jeans pockets, shrugged.

"Something odd happened tonight," he said.

"You think?"

"No, I mean…when I woke up, you were already gone."

"I'm allowed to leave, right? No rule against it?"

"No rule against it. It's just…I wanted you there. I came to, and you were gone. I didn't want you here," he said, pointing at the floor. "I wanted you there." He pointed in the general direction of London. "And you weren't, so now I am here."

"You barely know me." She smiled.

"True, but as soon as I saw you were gone, I drove over here to see you again."

Lia got out of her chair and walked over to him.

"I'm going. I'm going," he assured.

"You don't steal the covers, do you?" she asked. "You seem like blanket thief."

He grinned hugely. "I've never stolen so much as a pillow-case. Only a sheet once and that was for a toga party. Or as they were called in Ancient Greece—a party."

"Fine, then." She waved her hand toward her bedroom door.

"I can stay the night?" he asked.

"If you don't mind sharing a bedroom with a snoring deer-hound."

"After the cloud I slept with, a deerhound is nothing."

"You said it was a fog." She took him by the hand and led him to her bedroom.

"Upon further reflection," he said, "it might have been a stiff breeze."

CHAPTER SIXTEEN

Lia led August into her bedroom. She had a feeling she would regret letting him sleep over, but the truth was—not that she'd tell him this—she wanted him to spend the night with her.

"Where did you go?" he asked. "After you left me. I know it wasn't straight home. I was here half an hour before you made it back."

"Testing myself," she said. "Went by the Attic Gallery. Don't know why. Guess I just needed a practice run for Friday when I have to face David again."

"How did it go?"

"Huge poster of him in the window." Lia turned on her bedside lamp. "I flipped him the V and walked off. Didn't cry. We'll call that progress."

Gogo lay diagonally across her covers. He lifted his head and barked a happy greeting.

"Get in *your* bed, silly boy, not mine," Lia said as she reached out and gently tugged her dog's ear. Gogo reluctantly returned to his own bed as August stripped out of his T-shirt. He had such a long, lean, lovely body, and yet with muscles in his arms that made her wonder what he did when he wasn't busy shagging half the kingdom.

He caught her looking at him and reached for her. Once she felt the heat of his body through the fabric of her dress, she knew she wanted more of it. She leaned against his chest and wrapped her arms around his back. August drew her close and held her tightly. Her head fit so perfectly against his bare shoulder she felt like she'd been made to rest against it.

Out of nowhere, Lia began to cry.

At first she tried to cry in silence, but a whimper betrayed her. August must have heard her, because he kissed the top of her head and held her even tighter against him.

"Tell me," he whispered.

"My heart died when he did that to me. It just…it died. I loved him. God, I loved him so stupid much. I can't believe how stupid I was."

"You're not stupid. He was handsome, older, and he made you feel good about yourself. You'd have to have a heart of stone not to fall in love under those circumstances."

"He'd pinch my nose when he saw me. Isn't that the stupidest thing you ever heard? Daughter of a rich earl, and he's this nobody American painter with seventeen dollars to his name, and he pinches my nose and I fall for it like he put a spell on me. What's wrong with me?"

"Falling in love is brave and dangerous," August said. "Like climbing a mountain or going to war. Foolish, too, just like climbing a mountain and going to war. You shouldn't hate yourself for doing something brave and dangerous."

"He told me I was ugly and stupid, shite in bed, and he wanted my mother more than me."

August stroked her hair. "When a girl doesn't worship a man the way he feels entitled to be worshipped, it unleashes the beast inside him. Beasts are at their most dangerous when wounded and cornered. You'd wounded him, and you had him cornered. That's why he lashed out so viciously. He didn't mean what he said. You aren't ugly—obviously. You're stunningly beautiful. You aren't stupid. You graduated with honors from King's. You're talented, artistic. Your cunt is tight as a rosebud, and I'd happily spend the rest of my life balls-deep in you."

"Thank you? I think?"

"You're welcome," he said.

"There is absolutely no reason for you to like me," she said, though she still clung to him tightly with her arms even as she tried to push him away with her words.

"Why not?"

"I'm surly."

"You're charmingly surly."

"I'm bitter."

"Not bitter. Just tart."

"I have a heart of ice."

"A heart of ice cream," he said. "You're like a kitten with a switchblade."

"A kitten with a switchblade?"

"Give a switchblade to a kitten and the kitten somehow gets cuter, and also, even the switchblade becomes cute. That's you."

She didn't have a switchblade so she stabbed at his rib cage with her finger. August's chest moved under her head when he laughed. She loved feeling his laugh as she heard it. She turned her head to him and kissed the center of his chest. He heaved a little breath. He lowered his head and kissed her mouth.

She would have let him kiss her all night, but her face was soaked with tears and itched. She pulled away and started to dry her face, but he stopped her, picked up his T-shirt and used it to wipe her tears.

Then he held it to her nose and said, "Blow."

Lia grabbed the T-shirt, swatted his arse with it and tossed it to Gogo, who immediately sank his teeth into it and trotted off with it to his dog bed.

"I deserved that," August said as he unbuttoned his jeans.

"Are you planning on sleeping naked?" she asked.

"What other option is there?"

Lia sighed. He dropped his jeans and kicked them off.

"I have seen so much of your penis today," she said. "So much."

"I should take a shower. I'm covered in dog kisses."

"Bathroom's over there."

"Aren't you going to order me washed and brought to your tent?"

She glared at him.

"I'll be in the shower if you need me," he said.

When she heard the water turn on, Lia went to work. First things first—she stripped the covers off the bed and replaced them with fresh pink sheets, a clean white quilt. No dog hair. She dug through her chest of drawers, looking for a nightdress that was both cute but covered all her bits, and found a pink cotton nightie that would do.

By the time August returned from his shower, she was tucked up in bed, propped up on her pillows and hard at work on a drawing in her sketchbook. August, now naked and damp, stood in the doorway of her bedroom, toweling his brown hair, which had turned black from the water.

"What are you drawing?" he asked.

Lia smiled and turned the picture around to him—a tiny cat clutching a knife in one paw.

"Kitten with a switchblade," he said, grinning. "You're good."

"At least I got something out of my art lessons with David. Other than a broken heart." She quickly sketched a heart with an arrow through it. She added a few drops of blood. Then more blood. Then more. Total bloodbath.

August crawled into bed next to her.

"May I see?" he asked, holding out his hand for her sketchbook.

"There's nothing interesting in there," she said, handing over the book. "Just outlines for tapestries."

August took the book from her and turned through every single page slowly, examining each sketch with an appraiser's eye. He said little except to name the myths she'd been toying with as possible new subjects.

In one drawing, a girl lay on a bed, naked, as thick drops of rain fell from the ceiling.

"Zeus and Danaë," August said. "The original golden shower."

In the next drawing, a woman knelt in a nighttime temple as a man too massive to be human loomed over her from behind.

"Poseidon," he said. "And that's… Aethra?"

"Right," she said. "Mother of Theseus." In that myth, Aethra was summoned to the temple on her wedding night where she was impregnated by Poseidon.

"Penelope and Odysseus," he said, turning a page to a drawing of a woman's hand clinging to a bedpost—except the bedpost was not a bedpost but the slim trunk of a tree. "When Athena held back the dawn so they could have more time together in bed getting reacquainted."

August laughed softly.

"What?" Lia demanded. "You don't like them?"

"I love them. All your subjects are erotic."

Lia blushed pink.

"Not all of them," she said. "There's this one."

She turned a page to another sketch.

In it a girl slept on her side in a woodland glade. A shadow fell over her, the shadow of a man. Or was it a man?

"Ariadne," Lia explained. "After Theseus rejected her and left her abandoned on the island of Naxos."

"Ah," August said. "The most famous unexplained breakup in all of Greek mythology."

"Theseus just dumped her," Lia said. "Discarded her completely. And that was after she gave him the thread and helped him through the labyrinth, saved his life when he killed the Minotaur... Why take her away from her home and family and then leave her alone on some random island? And he didn't even have the decency to break up with her properly. He sailed off while she slept."

"She's you."

"She is not," Lia said.

"They're all you. Briseis, so beautiful she's taken captive. Andromeda, betrayed by her mother. Ariadne, betrayed by her lover. You weave your heartache and longing onto your loom."

"My mother didn't betray me," she insisted. "She had no idea about me and him."

"But it felt like betrayal, didn't it?"

"I'm over it." Lia closed the sketchbook and put it back in the drawer of her nightstand.

She switched off the lamp and settled down into the sheets.

August pulled her to him, her back to his chest. Lia sighed as August lifted her hair and pressed a hundred kisses onto her neck and shoulders.

"Are you trying to shag me?" Lia asked.

"I'm kissing. Just kissing."

"You have an erection, and I can feel it. It's poking me."

"Just because someone knocks on your door, doesn't mean you have to answer."

August kissed her gently on the lips.

"Go to sleep, you wicked kitten, before I force myself on you like Achilles. And then Patroclus. And then Achilles again. And then Patroclus again. And then Achilles after that…"

"Yes, I remember it, August. Thank you for reminding me what a massive whore I am."

"Wasn't it so much fun?" he asked, grinning in the dark so that it seemed that the darkness itself smiled at her.

Lia flipped onto her side and returned the grin.

"It really was," she said. "The most fun. Ever."

"Ah…" August ran a fingertip over her lips. "There it is."

"What?"

"That smile—that's why I do this job. This…" He tapped her cheek. "This is a happy girl."

Lia touched his smile in return. "You are very good at your job."

"But you don't want me to make love to you?" he asked.

"Why do you always call it that?"

"What? As opposed to fucking, shagging, screwing, banging?"

"Right. It's very…old-fashioned. You don't seem old-fashioned."

"Greek has multiple words for 'love.' *Philia* is love between friends, as you should know, O-*phelia*. *Agape* is unconditional love, like the love of a parent to a child or a god to a worshipper. And *eros* is sexual love."

"Lust?"

"Not the same. Lust is a destructive force. Like cheating, obsession, unhealthy infatuation. There's no English equivalent to 'eros.' English-speakers like to separate love from sex. I don't. That's why I call it making love instead of something violent like 'banging.' Not there's anything wrong with a good headboard banging."

"But you can't possibly be in love with everyone you sleep with," Lia said.

"Not *in* love. Not romantically in love. But I do love them," August said. "Giving someone an orgasm or a beautiful night or a lovely memory is an act of love. It's not an act of hate, is it? Or indifference?"

"It's selfish, though. Love is supposed to be selfless and having sex isn't selfless. Both people experience pleasure. Well, ideally, I guess."

"Would you call it 'selfless' if I gave you an orgasm by mouth but didn't have one myself?" August asked.

"A little."

"Wrong," he said, and poked the tip of her nose. "Making love to you with my mouth would be a completely selfish act on my part. My face buried in your lovely cunt? Ah, the most selfish thing I could do all week…"

He rolled onto his back as if in ecstasy.

"You're saying I'd be doing you a favor if I let you go down on me?"

"The kindest act you could do for me," he said. "Kind, loving, caring, merciful… It would be an act of true heroism on your part. You would be a martyr to the cause of Eros. You would be sainted." August took her chin in his hand, caressed her bottom lip with this thumb. "Would you please allow me to give you an orgasm?" he asked. "Please?"

She poked his chest. "You have, remember?"

"Perseus made Andromeda orgasm. Achilles and Patroclus made Briseis. But not you and me."

"What if I can't?" she asked.

"I'm very good."

"David told me I was crap in bed," she reminded.

"You were a virgin," August said. "And he was twenty years older. If a man with that much experience can't give an orgasm to a girl out of her mind with hormones, madly in love and dying to sleep with him, then he's the one who's worthless in bed." He shook his head in disgust and disdain.

"I wish I believed that."

"Lia, I could make you come so hard that your body floats three feet off the sheets and lightning will explode from your belly. You will see smells and hear colors. The heavens will break open and you will touch the face of God when I make you come. And I could do it with my hands tied behind my back."

Lia stared at him.

"Hear colors?" she repeated.

"You will hear colors *and* smell sounds," he said.

"Your hands tied behind your back?"

"Where do you keep your rope?"

She admired his confidence. There was nothing she could do with her hands tied behind her back. Nothing she'd brag about, anyway.

"I don't have any rope," she said. "How about a bathrobe tie?"

CHAPTER SEVENTEEN

August was out of bed in an instant. He switched on the little bedside lamp. Then he picked up her armchair and moved it next to the bed.

He started to sit. "Don't you dare!" Lia said.

"What?" he asked.

"You're naked. We do not put our balls on my dead grandmother's favorite chair."

"Prissiest madam in history," August said to himself. He found his jeans and drew them on quickly, then pulled the cord from her bathrobe.

Lia couldn't believe it when he tossed it to her, turned his back and said, "Tie me."

"Are you really serious?"

He turned back around and sat on the edge of the bed. He crooked his finger at her, and she sat up to face him.

"David lied to you." August took her chin in hand. "If I can make you come with my hands tied behind my back, that will prove you are completely capable of having an orgasm with someone, and David was the problem, not you. Will you let me do this? Please?"

Lia was strangely moved by his little speech. Enough that she said—and she could not believe she was saying it—"Give me the cord."

He gave her the makeshift rope. He again turned his back to her and brought his wrists behind his back.

Lia had never tied up a man before and she had to admit—not aloud—she rather liked the process. August stood perfectly still with his hands at the base of his spine, putting up no fight whatsoever as she took the white silk cord of her bathrobe and looped it around and around his wrists. Lia found herself getting unexpectedly breathless. August looked incredibly erotic in that pose—back to her, jeans loose around his hips, shirtless and tied up. He stood in the perfect contrapposto pose, relaxed and loose as if it were the most natural thing in the world to him to be tied up by a girl.

She took her time with the cord, enjoying the view, enjoying the intimate contact with his skin.

"Too tight?" she asked as she ran her finger under the rope to make sure there was room to wiggle.

"Perfect," he said. "Finished?"

"Um…almost."

Lia checked the cord again, though it was perfectly in place, not too tight, not too loose. She just wanted to be near him like this…like he belonged to her, like he was her property she had tied up with a bow.

"You can touch me," he said.

"I can, can I?"

He looked at her over his shoulder.

"I want you to," he said. "I need it."

She shivered at the soft plea she heard under his words. When he said things like that to her, things like "I need it," she believed him. Stupid boys were always going on about how they "needed" it, but this wasn't like that. When August said he needed it, he sounded like a runner needed pavement or a swimmer needed water or a priest needed prayer.

When her fingertips touched his back, in that vulnerable place just under the rib cage, he inhaled a quiet breath. She pressed her lips to the center of his back, where the spine met the neck.

August exhaled from the depths of his soul. He faced her and brought his mouth to hers. She felt no shyness at all as she put her hands on the sides of his neck and kissed him. His mouth opened to her immediately, letting her tongue inside. He held nothing back, nothing of himself. No fear. All freedom. He kissed like a man who'd never had his heart broken. He kissed like he was never afraid he would never be kissed back.

"August…" she said against his lips.

He pressed his forehead to hers. "Are you ready?"

She nodded, eyes closed, scared but excited. "I think so." Slowly she opened her eyes.

August looked at her intently, a teacher to a student.

"You'll do everything I tell you do?" he asked.

She nodded again.

"Good." He sat on the chair. "Lie on your back with your hips at the edge of the bed, knickers off, feet on the chair arms. And trust me, your dead grandmother would approve."

She felt awkward arranging herself for him, lying back on

the sheets, perpendicular to the edge of the bed. She tried to keep her knees closed as she settled in but that didn't last long.

"Open your legs," August said.

After a pause to steel herself, Lia let her legs fall open like the wings of a butterfly.

"Beautiful," he said. "Now open yourself for me."

"Do I have to?"

"Yes."

Well, if she had to she had to.

She slipped her hands between her legs and touched herself. Slowly and with extreme embarrassment, she pulled the lips of her vulva apart and let him see the wet red flesh of her labia and vagina.

August made a soft sound, a little inhalation, a little exhalation right after. A stunningly obscene noise; she would have killed to hear it again.

"Show me more," he ordered.

"August, please."

"Briseis did it for Achilles. You can do it for me. More."

Lia pushed her hips forward, tilting them as hard as she could. A wave of desire hit her, washed through her.

"I want to see your clitoris," he said.

She moved her fingers upward, spread her legs wider, thrust her hips out harder. She pulled at the tender flesh of her hood and lifted it.

The tip of his tongue darted out and touched it, just touched it, lightly, so lightly it couldn't even be called a lick. It was electric.

"August," she gasped.

"Now that is how a man wants to hear his name spoken by the girl he's bedding," he said, laughing softly. "The next word you speak will be my name and you won't speak—you will scream it. Until then, moan and groan and pant and gasp all you want, but otherwise shut up, Lia. I'm working."

Lia couldn't believe what was happening to her even as it was happening to her. The tip of August's tongue kneaded the sensitive flesh around her clitoris, lightly rubbing it and pressing it, drawing blood into it so that the knot, that tender aching knot, swelled and throbbed like a separate heart beat inside of it. He suckled that knot a thousand times more gently than he ever suckled her nipples. So gently it was maddening. She dug her hands into the back of his hair and pushed her hips into his mouth.

A lick. The tiniest most perfect lick ever, right on the quivering tip of a nerve. A muscle inside Lia coiled tight as a spring. She panted, head back, fingers twisting harder into August's hair.

Another lick. A harder lick. The twirl of his tongue all around the edge. Then over it. A kiss. A long tender wet kiss onto it, kissing her like he kissed her mouth. He lowered his head and licked at the entrance of her body. He pushed his tongue against the hole and pushed again until the tip went inside it. Lia gasped, shocked by the pleasure and the intimacy so intense it almost felt like a violation. He turned his head slightly to the side and kissed her swollen labia again. To the other side and kissed her again. After that it seemed he wanted nothing more than to press his mouth into her. He pushed his tongue into her vagina again, and Lia lifted her hips in instinct and need.

"Wider," he ordered, and she didn't know if he meant she was supposed to open her legs wider or her labia wider. She did both. She spread her legs and her hands and August came at her with such determination she felt the chair shift under her feet. He licked the entrance of her body again, over and over a hundred times. Lia's fingers grasped at the sheets as he went at her. Sounds escaped her lips she'd never heard herself make before, not in this world or any other. Animal grunts, deep from her throat, keening pleas. He was torturing her, focusing his attention on her labia and vagina instead of her clitoris. Lia moved her hips up and down and in little spirals in the hopes of getting him to give her what her body needed. Every time she lifted her body off the bed, she felt a fresh wave of desire. He wasn't torturing her but tricking her into fucking his mouth.

The trick worked.

Finally, August licked his way up from the base of her vagina to her clitoris. He pulled the knot between his lips again and sucked; she let out a soft grateful moan. God bless the man. He should be knighted. She moaned again so he did it again. And again. Her clitoris pulsed against his hot mouth and the coil inside her tightened until it could twist and tighten no more. Every nerve seemed exposed and he found every exposed nerve and touched it with the tip of his tongue, touched and touched as she trembled and shook. Her inner muscles were clenched so hard it hurt and there was nothing left for her but release. Lia's body pressed up, up, up, and she exploded against his mouth. The sensation was so strong, a bomb in her belly, that she bent almost double, shoulders off the bed, arms around his head.

She came so hard she smelled sounds and heard colors.

Lia lay panting, nearly comatose, on the bed until August stood up and entered her field of vision. He was smiling.

Of course he was.

Then he glanced at the clock on her bedside table.

"Four minutes, fifty-two seconds," he said. "You needed that."

Lia didn't speak. She wasn't entirely sure she could speak.

"Lia?"

She held up one finger, asking for a minute to compose herself.

"Take your time," he said. "I'll be crowing if you need me."

"Crow?"

"First—I told you so. Second—there's nothing wrong with you and there never was. Third—that orgasm was so strong you almost chipped my tooth, and if you had, I would never have gotten it fixed."

Her stomach was still fluttering, her mouth was dry, her vagina wet.

"Fourth—your David's a wanker. And he's shite in bed. He probably kicks puppies, too, and is one of those bastards who creates anonymous Twitter accounts just to insult celebrities. My cock's bigger, right?"

Lia nodded as hard as her exhausted body would let her.

"Knew it."

In the background of her awareness, Lia saw August undressing again, felt the bed shift as he crawled in next to her. He gathered her in his arms and placed her back against the pillows again, pulled the covers over her shivering body. Lia managed a breathy "Thank you."

"So," he said. "Verdict?"

"Red sounds like trumpets," she said. "Blue like rain on a tin roof."

"Good. Your body did come about three feet off the bed. I measured. Did lightning strike your stomach?"

"I'm lucky to be alive."

"What about the face of God?" August asked. "Did you touch it?"

Lia raised a tired hand to his face and stroked his cheek.

"Close enough," she said. August turned his head and kissed her palm.

Then Lia tackled him. She had no idea why or where the

urge came from, but it came from somewhere and it landed her on top of August. She threw herself full body into pinning him to the bed, easy enough as he put up no fight whatsoever.

She grabbed his wrists—when had he untied them?—and pinned them to the pillow on either side of his head.

"How did you do that?" she demanded.

"What? Make you come?"

"Yes."

"I put my tongue on your clit and rubbed it there until—"

"How did you get untied?"

"I'll never tell you. You can't make me. Go on. More questions. Being interrogated by a beautiful angry spy is one of my fantasies. If you want to slap me, you can. You should."

"Who are you, August Bowman?" she asked, lightly slamming his wrists into the bed. "If that is your real name."

"It's not my real name."

"What?" Lia froze, stunned.

"It's not my real name."

"What is your real name?" she asked.

"Can't tell you. Wish I could."

"Why can't you?" Lia let his wrists go and sat next to him on the bed. "Because you're a pro?"

She knew loads of sex professionals who kept their real names secret, and she certainly understood why. But that didn't seem to be August's style.

"Long story," he said. "Boring story."

"There is no way that the story of how *anyone* becomes a sacred prostitute of Eros is a boring story. 'How'd you save all those vampire wolves from that active volcano eruption?' 'Oh, boring story.' 'Where did all those jars of human eyeballs in your kitchen come from?' 'Total yawn of a tale. You wouldn't want to know.'"

"I'm being mocked."

"You think?" Lia said.

"Fine. If you must know…"

"I must."

"My parents were going to force me to get married. I refused."

"Force you to get married?" Lia asked, stunned. "You mean, an arranged marriage or just anyone as long as you got married and settled down?"

"Mother was going to pick someone for me. I refused and ran away. My mother caught up with me and told me I either came to heel or…said goodbye. I said goodbye. And there went my home, my inheritance and my name. If I want them back, I have to let my mother marry me off and settle down."

"Are you going to?" Lia asked.

"Never," he said. "I'll die first before I bend to them."

He sounded surprisingly serious.

"Die? Really?"

"I can't do it. I can't give up my freedom. It's who I am. When I say I'd rather die than let my mother marry me off and settle me down, what I mean is…giving up this life I made for myself? It would kill me."

Lia couldn't imagine August married. She couldn't fathom what he would be like "settled down." He'd be like one of those exquisite blue-winged butterflies captured by a collector and pinned with a needle into the velvet of a shadow box—a beautiful tragedy.

"So you became a prostitute once you were kicked out of your house?"

"I was already in the Cult of Eros," he said. "You could call it my 'church' if you want. But I went pro when I needed money for the first time in my life. It's my dream job, really. I was doing it for free. Might as well get paid for it."

"But…don't you miss your family?" Lia asked. "A little? Miss home?"

Even in the darkness of her bedroom, she could see the outline of his handsome face—strong jaw, Greek nose—and the clouds forming and swarming in his gray eyes.

"It's not so bad. And my mother still talks to me. Or…I wouldn't call it talking so much. More like berating. Her two favorite words are *ungrateful* and *child*."

"She should meet Daddy. They'd have plenty to talk about," Lia said. "Your mother won't even let you use your family name anymore?"

"Part of the punishment," August said. "My family name is a bit, ah…recognizable. Comes with perks I'm no longer allowed access to."

She narrowed her eyes at him.

"Is your family famous?"

"I wouldn't call it that. Infamous, maybe."

"Who are you?" she asked again. This time, not a joke. She wanted to know. No, she needed to know.

"I wish I could tell you," he said. "But it's for the best if I don't."

"One question—would I like you more or less if I knew who you really were?"

"Based on experience…less," he said.

"All right," Lia said. "Then don't tell me. I'm starting to like liking you."

CHAPTER EIGHTEEN

August was still there when Lia woke up the next morning at nine. She hadn't expected to find him there, on the pillow next to her, but he was. Eyes closed. Heavy black lashes on peaceful cheeks. She watched him sleeping and found it a rather good show. Worth the trouble of sneaking him out of the house.

The question remained, however...how was she going to do that?

Her parents were up and about. They always were by nine. Work hard. Shag hard. That was her father's motto in life, which she'd told him to never, ever repeat in her presence. Not that he listened. Lia would simply have to hope her parents were busy at breakfast and wouldn't notice August sneaking out the back door and then the front gate.

"August..." Lia said as she stroked his hair.

He made a sound, not quite a sigh.

"August? Wake up." Lia touched his shoulder. His dark eyes flew open and stared at her in surprise.

"It's morning," she said.

"Again? Why does this keep happening to me?" He rubbed his eyes.

"You all right?" She tried not to laugh at this beautiful bizarre man in her bed.

"Temple prostitutes are not, as a rule, morning people."

"Tough," she said. "I need to get you out of the house before anyone notices you're still here."

His eyes popped wide open.

"You're twenty-one. Don't tell me your parents won't allow you to have sleepovers."

"With a boyfriend, they'd stomach it. You aren't my boyfriend, remember? You're my rent boy."

And her father would bloody kill the man, and if anyone was going to kill August, it would be her.

He narrowed his eyes at her. "Are you ashamed of me?"

"Deeply," she said.

"You'll get over it," he said, rolling up. "I need my clothes."

"They're on the floor. Except for your T-shirt. That's in Gogo's mouth."

In the corner of her room, Gogo blissfully gnawed away at August's heather-gray T-shirt.

"I didn't like that shirt, anyway."

Luckily, Lia had one of her father's T-shirts that had ended up with her clothes through a laundry error. A soft black cotton T-shirt with the name of his art foundation—The Godwick Trust—printed in polite letters on the upper right pocket. It clung to August's shoulders and stomach in all the very nicest ways. His hair was artfully mussed from sleep, and when he yawned and stretched, his shirt rode up, his jeans rode down on his hips and she spied the rose brand on his skin again. She felt a pang of desire, a deep one that nearly knocked the wind from her lungs. Why was she kicking him out of the house again?

Mother. Father. Rent boy. Infamy.

That was why.

August was standing by her fireplace mantel again, staring at her statue of Aphrodite, which seemed to fascinate him.

"August? Time to go," Lia reminded.

"This statue," he said. "Was it always kept in your bedroom?"

"I think. But I've seen old photographs where it was on the mantel in the music room before I was born. Then again, I was born in the music room—long story."

"You were born under a statue of Aphrodite?"

"Big storm," Lia explained. "Power went out. Roads were flooding. Daddy had to deliver me himself. Music room had a gas fireplace. Daddy needed the light." She paused. This was an odd topic of conversation. "Why do you ask?"

"Your father bought you the Rose Kylix—"

"Because I love mythology," she said.

"There are hundreds of kylikes on the market. He bought that one because he was told it was part of Aphrodite's cult."

"I suppose…"

"I need to ask your father a few questions."

"Write them down and I'll ask him for you."

Lia dressed quickly in jeans and a red knit jumper. She threw her hair up in a messy bun, and when they were both reasonably presentable she stuck her head out of her suite door.

She looked left, looked right.

"The coast is clear," she told August. "Just go down to the end of the hall. You'll see a set of old servants' stairs. Down those and out the door to the back patio."

"Where are you going?"

"To breakfast."

"Right," August said.

"I'll see you tonight at nine," she said.

"If not sooner." Before she could ask him what he meant by that, he kissed her on the lips and started down the hall.

Lia called for Gogo. He bounded out to her and she had to wrestle with him for a moment or two before she could get him to relinquish August's shirt. She let him outside for his morning constitutional while she headed down to the family breakfast room.

She entered the breakfast room and stopped in the doorway. August stood at the sideboard, with a plate in his hand as he examined the various foods on offer.

"August," Lia hissed.

"I was hungry," he said. "Aren't you?"

She grabbed the plate out of his hand and pointed at the door.

"Go," she said in a rasping angry whisper when what she wanted to do was scream.

"I need to talk to your father, remember?"

"I told you I'll talk to him. Go. Go."

"Are you telling me to leave or calling your dog?"

"I'm telling you to—"

"Morning, darling."

Lia froze as her mother waltzed into the breakfast room, wearing a simple yet elegant suit of red trousers and a black blouse with a bow at the neck.

"Oh, um…morning, Mum," Lia said. "You remember—"

"Morning, Lady Godwick," August said. He held out his hand to her to shake.

"Mr. Bowman." Mum smiled. "What brings you out here so early?"

"I slept over," August said.

"August," Lia hissed again.

"Oh, of course," her mother said. "Glad you could join us for breakfast."

"Thank you. Starving." He piled his plate high with food and sat down at the table next to Lia's usual chair.

Lia poured a cup of coffee she had no desire to drink. Her mother walked over to the sideboard wearing a smile Lia did not appreciate.

"I knew it," her mother whispered.

"Mother, I swear," Lia said.

"What are we swearing about?" It was Daddy who asked that question, as he walked into the breakfast room in his favorite gray suit and blue tie. No one answered it.

"Morning, Lord Godwick." August leaned back in his chair and raised his coffee cup in a salute.

"Bowman?" Lia's father said. "What are you doing here?"

She answered before August could.

"He wanted to ask you some questions about the kylix you bought me. So I invited him to breakfast."

"He spent the night, Spencer," her mother said. "Coffee?"

Daddy went silent. Lia mentally committed matricide.

"What was that?" her father finally asked.

"I spent the night," August said. "Thanks for breakfast. Wonderful spread."

Did he have to call it a "spread"?

"You spent the night?" Her father walked to the table and stood across from where August sat.

"With Lia," August said. "And Gogo. He was there, too."

"Daddy, don't—"

"I didn't catch your age, Bowman," her father said. "Aren't you a little old to be dating my twenty-one-year-old daughter?"

"I'm *much* too old to be dating your twenty-one-year-old daughter."

"That's it." Daddy slapped the table.

"Spencer," her mother said. "Sit down and eat your breakfast."

"But—"

"But nothing. You will let your daughter have her own life or you will be sleeping alone from tonight until Christmas."

"Mona, I will not just stand here and let—"

"You won't stand," Mum said. "You will sit. You will sit and eat breakfast, and that is your penance and you will take it like a man. You have been the scourge of mothers and fathers and brothers and boyfriends since you were fourteen, you hypocritical whore."

"Mum, please don't call Daddy a whore in front of me," Lia said. "It makes my mouth feel horrid—like when I taste perfume."

"Sorry, darling." Her mother kissed her cheek. "Get your breakfast. Sit and eat. We're all friends here."

"Don't feel bad, Lord Godwick," August said. "I'm a whore, too."

"August, you can stop speaking any minute now," Lia said.

"He can speak, dear," Mum said.

"Thank you, Lady Godwick."

"You're welcome, Mr. Bowman." Her mother sat next to Lia's father and started in on her breakfast.

"Please, call me August," he said.

"What questions did you have for us, August?" Mum asked. The old girl was taking it well, Lia had to admit. Daddy was red-faced and ready for mayhem, but her mother carried off having her daughter's lover at the breakfast table with aplomb.

"I'm not having this conversation," her father said.

"Then I'll have it," her mother said. "Go on, August."

"Is he wearing my shirt?" Daddy asked.

"Lia fed my shirt to the dog," August said.

"That wasn't very nice, Lia," her mother chided.

"It was my fault for letting the dog eat her—"

"Socks," Lia finished.

"You know dogs and socks." August went about buttering his toast as if this wasn't the second-most humiliating moment of her life.

"The questions, please," her father said. Lia was grateful Daddy was so healthy. At fifty-eight, he could run circles around men half his age. Otherwise he might have keeled over from a heart attack at the table.

"The kylix you gave Lia for her graduation," August said. "Where did you get it?"

"You know perfectly well. It was up for auction at Christie's."

"But you bought it in a preempt. The seller was anonymous."

Daddy shrugged. "I'd told my agent I wanted something special for Lia, something that had a connection to Greek mythology, price no object. He called around and in a few days he had some choices for me. He sent pictures. I picked that one."

"There were others?" August asked. Her father nodded. "Why did you pick that one in particular?"

"Could someone tell me why I'm answering this man's questions?" Daddy dropped his fork on the table with a clatter.

"Because I told you to," her mother said, and patted his hand.

"My daughter likes mythology. Why else?"

"But surely the other ones were painted with myths, as well, yes?" August asked. "Why that one in particular?"

"It was the prettiest," her father said, biting off each word.

"Do you remember the name of the seller?" August devoured his toast. He hadn't been joking about being hungry.

"Never got a name."

"Did you buy that one in particular because you were told it had belonged to the Cult of Aphrodite?" August asked. Her father raised his eyebrow so high Lia was having trouble telling where it ended and his hairline began. "I noticed the statue in Lia's room. That's why I ask."

"What's your interest in this?" her father demanded.

"It's unusual, isn't it? A statue of the Greek goddess of romantic love in a child's room?"

"Are you implying something, Bowman?"

"Daddy, no!" Lia cried before her father could lean over the table and beat August's pretty face into a pretty pulp. "We're trying to figure something out about my kylix. That's all. Please, Daddy?"

He could never resist a genuine "please" from her.

"Lia was the first girl born in the family in three hundred years," he said at last.

"In the music room," August prompted. "Yes? Because of a storm?"

"I delivered her," her father said. He glanced at Lia. "Storm came out of nowhere, just like the night of your graduation party, darling. Your mother wasn't due for another month. We had tickets to the symphony. Then the storm hit and your mother went into early labor. I called the village doctor but his road was flooded as badly as ours. Couldn't get out. Couldn't get anyone in. Nothing to do but do it myself."

"I've never been so scared," her mother said. "And he was so calm."

"On the outside." Daddy winced. "Inside I was a bloody wreck. But nature took her course and then there you were." He smiled at Lia, before looking back at August. "The moment I laid eyes on her, I was a changed man. It was truly the single happiest moment of my life. This tiny girl…my whole life in my two hands. Perfect except… Lia wasn't breathing."

"What?" Lia asked, shocked.

"You weren't breathing," her father repeated, meeting her eyes. "I did everything I could. I pushed on your chest, spanked your tiny arse like they do in the movies, breathed in your mouth and nose. I've never been so desperate or scared in my life. If I'd lost you… God, I would rather have lost myself."

Mum placed her hand on top of Daddy's and held it tightly.

"Mona was in and out of consciousness," her father told August. "She'd bled a lot, was nearly delirious. I didn't know what to do. I'm an old heathen, but that night I prayed with everything in me to every god I could think of. I remember looking up and seeing that little statue of Aphrodite on the mantel in the music room. I prayed to her, too."

"You called her name?" August asked.

"I might have."

"What happened when you called on her name?"

"I can't explain it," her father said. "I've thought about it for years, and it never made sense. But…it was like a miracle. A gust of wind blew the French doors open. The room filled with thousands of rose petals from the garden. Lia was in my two hands like this…" He held out his hands, miming cradling a tiny baby. "She was going cold."

Mum blinked tears from her eyes.

"It was like someone pinched Lia," Daddy said. "Or blew in her ear. She jerked in my hands. And then, by God, Lia opened her eyes and her tiny mouth and screamed her bloody head off." Her father put his hand over his heart. "I wouldn't trade every symphony and sonata in the world for the sound of that scream."

"You think Aphrodite answered your prayer?" August asked.

"I can't bring myself to believe that," her father said. "But I will say…that gust of wind was strong enough to blow the doors open and rip the petals off every single rose in the garden. It knocked over chairs in the music room and every single candle, clock and bric-a-brac sitting on the fireplace mantel. When it was all over, the one thing left standing was that Aphrodite statue." Daddy gave Lia a wan smile. "I suppose this all sounds mad."

"No, it doesn't," she said. It sounded like the fevered memories of a terrified father to her. "But…why didn't you ever tell me this?"

"I didn't even tell Mona at first," her father said, glancing at her mother. "Only after I'd spent the first three months of your life sleeping on a cot in the nursery did she drag it out of me."

"You did what?" Lia's jaw dropped open. August's arm wound around her back in comfort.

"I'd try to sleep in bed with Mona, and I'd have a nightmare about you. I couldn't sleep unless I was in your nursery or if you were in a bassinet with us in our bedroom."

"Never have children, Lia," Mum said with a wink. "You all are hell on a good night's sleep."

Her father nodded in agreement. "At night, I'd stand over your cradle and pray every new father's prayer—'Whatever god is out there listening, please make my baby immortal.'" He finally met her eyes. "Has it come true yet?"

"Yes," Lia said, smiling at him through her tears. "I'm immortal."

"Good," he said with a sigh. "That's a relief."

Lia saw August staring at her out of the corner of her eyes. She ignored his searching look, afraid she'd cry if she met his tender gaze.

"Your father and I didn't like talking about how we might have lost you when you were born," her mother said. "Bad enough it gave him nightmares the first three months of your life. We decided together that there was no reason to give you nightmares, too."

"Not sure where I got the idea…" Daddy said, "but one day I put the statue of Aphrodite in your nursery so she could look over your cradle. And once I did, the nightmares went away. Placebo effect, of course, but I was grateful for the small mercy that I could finally sleep with my wife again."

"And you've always liked that statue," Mum said to Lia. "When you were a little girl, you used to play with her like a Barbie doll. You made her marry Ken a hundred times at least."

August laughed much, much too hard at that.

"Ah, that makes me so happy," he said, wiping a tear from his eye. Meanwhile Lia squirmed in humiliation.

"Weddings, that's right." Daddy looked at Mum with a smile. "When Mona came to after passing out, she saw all the rose petals in the room. Do you remember what you said?"

Her mother smiled. "I said, 'Who's getting married?'"

Lia watched her father lift her mother's hand to his lips and kiss it. There really was something very lovely, Lia thought, about old married people still in love with each other. Even if they were her parents and she found it mostly disgusting on every other level.

"Does that answer all your questions?" her father asked August.

"Yes," August said. "Thank you, Lord Godwick."

"Good," her father said. "You can leave my house now."

CHAPTER NINETEEN

August didn't leave but her parents did. Day trip to London.

Lia stood at the window of the music room and watched her father's Bentley carrying him and her mother through the main gate. August came up behind her and peered over her shoulder.

"Breakfast went well," he said.

Lia resisted the urge to plant her elbow in his liver.

She turned around and looked up at him.

"You practically told my father you and I were shagging. At breakfast."

"Should I have saved that conversation for lunch?" August asked. She glared at him. "Your father's not the sort of man who gives up dark family secrets just by asking nicely. I needed him feeling vulnerable. Saying 'Good morning, old chap, I ate your daughter's cunt under your roof last night, and there's nothing you can do about it' tends to get a man off his game. And it worked."

"It did work." Her father was an old-school sort who was happy to laugh and joke and slap his mates on the back down at the pub—or roar at the politicians on the telly or at the players on a rugby pitch. But his fears? His secret sorrows? Those he shared with his wife and no one else, not even his children. "But why do you care so much about the statue of Aphrodite in my room?"

"I'm trying to understand how the Rose Kylix got into your possession." August wore a faraway look in his eyes.

"And you think it has something to do with that statue?"

He shrugged and came back to her. "There could be a connection. I know you don't want to believe the kylix actually belongs to a real god, but I believe it. And the toys of the gods tend to pick their owners. Aphrodite's name was invoked at your birth. You've had a shrine to her in your bedroom your entire life… It's possible the kylix picked you for a reason."

"What possible reason would make a god want me to have one of their toys?" she asked, skeptical to the core.

"That I don't know," he said. "But I intend to find out. In the meantime, keep the statue by your bed. We wouldn't want to insult Aphrodite. She's getting cranky in her old age."

He grinned but Lia couldn't, not just yet.

"I had no idea I almost died when I was born. I can't stop thinking about Daddy being so desperate he'd pray to a goddess on a mantel in the music room. You could count on two hands how many times he's stepped into a church by choice. And three of the ten times were when me and Art and Charlie were christened."

"He loves you," August said. "I envy that. My own father can't stand the sight of me."

"Oh, August, I'm so sorry."

"It's not personal. He can't stand the sight of anyone. And no one can stand the sight of him, either. Miracle he managed to get any woman to sleep with him, much less my mother."

Lia smiled, but it wasn't a real smile and it didn't last long. She pressed her head against August's chest before she realized what she was doing. She started to pull back, but he wouldn't let her. He wrapped his arms around her and held her close to him.

"It'll be all right."

"I'm being blackmailed," she said. "Because David knows I love my parents too much to tell them what he did to me. That's sick, isn't it? Using a girl's love for her parents against her?"

"It is. Makes me sick we're paying him off. We ought to be throwing him off a cliff. Times like this I almost wish I hadn't gotten myself kicked out of my family. They could take care of David with a phone call."

"Take care of? Like…mafia-style?"

"I don't mean kill him," August said. "Though it's tempting."

"Very tempting. If he wasn't such a bloody good painter, I'd throw him under a double-decker myself."

"Is he that good?"

"Unfortunately." She finally managed to extricate herself from August's arms. "He never even finished the mural in Mum's room but it's still incredible."

"Can I see it?" August asked. "Or would your mother mind?"

"She won't mind." Lia's mother had shown it off to house-guests before. She led August upstairs and into the east wing, which had been updated far more recently than the west wing—where Lia lived in the old dowager quarters. The colors were muted blues, and instead of the heavy Victorian dark wood paneling in Lia's wing, here it was mostly white wainscoting along the walls, nothing that would detract from the paintings and portraits hung in the hallway.

As she passed the portrait of her great-grandfather Malcolm, Old Number Thirteen, she stuck her tongue out at him. August caught her and raised his eyebrows.

"Sorry," she said. "I love the old boy, but this is all his fault for being too handsome."

"Too handsome?" August said. "How is that even possible?"

"This portrait used to hang over Mum's fireplace in her bedroom. Mum said Daddy caught her looking at Old Number Thirteen during...you know."

"Oh, I know."

"Daddy exiled Great-Granddaddy to the hallway and hired David to paint a mural in Mum's bedroom by way of apology. But it was a good trade, no offense to Number Thirteen. See?"

Lia opened the door to her mother's bedroom and let August in first. He did what everyone did upon entering the room. His head fell back, he stared up at the ceiling and his mouth fell slightly open.

Usually the person seeing the ceiling mural said something along the lines of "wow" or "my God" or even "holy shit." But not August. He said nothing, but his nothing spoke so much more than anyone else's words.

"It's Cupid and Psyche," Lia said.

"Eros," August said. "He hates the name Cupid."

"Why?" she asked.

"People think Cupid is a fat baby with a tiny bow and arrow. Does that look like a fat baby to you?" He pointed at the mural. Eros was a full-grown man with a bow as tall as Lia.

Lia had always been fascinated by the strange story of Cupid—strike that—Eros and Psyche. Psyche was a backwater princess from a backwater kingdom whose beauty rivaled Aphrodite's. Eros had married her in secret. She hadn't even known she was marrying a god as they made love every night in the dark.

"Why did your mother choose this myth?" August asked. "Or was it David's idea?"

"I suggested it," Lia said. "And Mum liked the idea. Said it reminded her of her and Daddy. They'd eloped right after meeting. She said being married to Daddy was like having a stranger in her bed, just like Eros with Psyche. But eventually, she saw who he really was, and she loved him."

"Why did you suggest it?"

"This myth has always fascinated me," she admitted. "The fantasy of a powerful stranger summoning you to his home to be his wife. Then having sex with that complete stranger in the dark every night so you can't see who he is. And finally you discover the whole time you've been shagging the god of sex?" Lia laughed. "Better than what happened to me. I thought I was sleeping with a god. Turns out he was monster."

"I'm sorry, Lia," August said. He touched her cheek. She smiled for him.

"Why didn't Cupid—" she began. August glared. "Eros, sorry. Why didn't Eros just tell her who he was from the beginning?"

"A few reasons," he said. "Common sense, for starters. What passes for common sense among the gods. If you love a mortal you can't tell a mortal what you are, or they'll be too frightened and run away. Or they'll love you for your power and not for yourself. Eros wanted her to fall in love with him, not his power or his majesty. They had to meet as strangers and there was only one way to do that—he had to keep Psyche in the dark. Literally."

They stood in silence, both of them, gazing up at the ceiling. David had done marvelous work. The mural took up the entire center of the ceiling. Eros, a beautiful winged youth with dark curling hair, approached a magnificent canopied bed where a girl with flowing chestnut hair sat in a gown of white—with a dark blue sash, embroidered with silver crescent moons and golden stars, tied over her eyes. The implication was obvious. Eros was about to make love to the girl on their wedding night and he'd hidden her eyes, so she couldn't see that it was a god in her bed and not a mortal prince. Of course, Psyche cheated and peeked at her sleeping husband. She was cast out for breaking the rules and nearly died trying to win back his love. Poor Psyche. Lia always felt so bad for her. What girl wouldn't want to know who was making love to her every night?

"Why the blindfold on Psyche?" August asked. "She wasn't blindfolded. They made love at night, in the dark."

"David said unless we wanted the entire mural to be one solid black square—night—he'd have to improvise. Mum suggested the blindfold. It was my idea to make it midnight blue and put little stars and moons on the fabric to symbolize night."

"Ah," August said. "You're very clever, Lia."

She blushed.

"David finished the main panel but that was it before I sent him packing." Lia pointed up at the scene of Psyche in her blindfold on the bed and Eros approaching. "The rest of the ceiling was going to be scenes from Psyche's quest to win back Eros's love. And then the frame was supposed to be all butterflies. See?" She pointed out a framed pencil sketch on the fireplace mantel that showed the completed mural, butterflies and all.

"She never lost his love," August said, staring at the sketch.

"What do you mean?"

"The writer Apuleius was a novelist, not a historian. He invented most of the Eros and Psyche myth. But there were pockets of truth in it. Eros saw the mortal princess and fell in love with her. He wanted to marry her but knew his mother wouldn't approve of him marrying the mortal girl who people said was more beautiful than Aphrodite. He had to sneak behind her back."

"What did he do?"

"He had the god Apollo give an oracle to Psyche's father, saying Psyche must go to a hill and there she would see the palace where she would live with her new husband. He didn't want to get in trouble with his mother for marrying a mortal, so he kept Psyche in the dark about his identity. If he told her his name, she might tell her sisters…eventually it would get back to Aphrodite. But Psyche found out and was furious he'd lied to her. Eros didn't cast her out because she spied on him in his sleep. She ran away from him when she learned she'd been lied to by her husband, who was too cowardly to even tell her his real name."

"You're being very hard on poor Eros," Lia said, smiling.

"It wasn't his finest moment," August said. "You can't keep secrets about yourself from the person you love. If they don't truly know you, they can't truly love you. Eros tried to win her back, and she did forgive him, but Psyche didn't want to be married to a being who would stay ageless and immortal while she grew old and died. He begged his mother to give his wife the gift of immortality, but Aphrodite refused."

"What happened to her, then?"

"Eros had to let his wife go. She remarried, had children,

lived and loved and died." August took a breath, smiled. "They were married a week, but during that week, no two beings ever loved each other so much. And Eros never quite forgave his mother for letting Psyche die. Though maybe she had a point."

"Gods and mortals don't mix?"

"Not well," he said. "Don't think of the Olympic gods as these wise, ancient beings. They're more like eternal children with much too much power. A human man betrays his wife a dozen times and she divorces him, and he never sees his children again. Zeus seduced thousands of mortal women, destroyed their lives, their marriages, forced them to give birth to monsters sometimes. Zeus carried on, no consequences except a dirty look or two from Hera." August looked at her. "Death is a gift in a way. And weakness, frailty, too, all gifts. Human actions have meaning, consequences. With gods, everything's a game. Everyone's a toy. Nothing matters. They never learn. Be grateful you're a mortal human, Lia. Even if it hurts sometimes."

Lia returned to the center of the room, gazed up at the scene of Psyche waiting for her new husband to come to bed and Eros, lovely long-limbed Eros, approaching.

"It's not fair a wanker like David gets to be such a good painter," Lia said. "Why are so many great artists such awful people?"

"Because they're people."

"I used to love watching David work. I'd bring him water and snacks while he was in here having one of his marathon painting sessions." She looked at August, blushed. "I modeled for Psyche."

"Did you?" His voice was far away, like he'd been sucked into the painting. She knew how he felt.

"David was having trouble figuring out how to paint a

woman's hair when she had a blindfold around her head. I volunteered. Glad Mum and Daddy were gone that day."

Lia remembered how she'd shivered, nearly insane with excitement when David had her sit on the edge of the bed and tied the black sash over her eyes. She had to sit so still and say nothing as he studied her from all angles, trying to decide the best way to pose Psyche on the bed. In profile? Full face? From behind? He'd chosen to paint her hair a deep dark chestnut color. Otherwise everyone, he said, would know he'd used Lia as a model if he gave Psyche the same gingerbread-colored hair as her. "Our secret," David had said, and then gave her a wink.

"That was the day I decided I was going to marry him," Lia said. She heard the sadness in her voice, the regret. "I was such an idiot."

"Human, Lia. And we've all been human," he said. "Even me."

Lia heard real regret in his voice. She knew the feeling all too well. So much regret... She didn't tell August this was the first time she'd looked at the mural since her nasty falling-out with David. She tended to give her parents' bedrooms wide berth, anyway, but also she thought it would hurt too much to see David's fingerprints in her mother's room, so to speak. But it didn't hurt. The mural was stunning. Truly. The colors vibrant and the scene so vivid Lia thought she could climb a ladder and step into the ceiling and live in the golden palace of Eros.

David said that was his goal with the mural, to make anyone lying in the bed look up and wish they could float to the ceiling and live inside his painting. He wanted to, he'd said. He would have given anything to step foot into one of his own paintings, and Lia had known exactly what he meant. She'd felt the same way when she'd read about Pan's Island in

The Wind in the Willows. All she wanted was to dive into the pages and live and breathe those words like air.

Such a pity. If David hadn't started up their war again, she might have forgiven him just for his talent alone. They could have shaken hands, apologized for how badly they'd both behaved—meanwhile, each of them secretly thinking the other had behaved so much worse—and gotten on with their lives. It did give her a thrill of pleasure to think that while David might paint Eros's golden palace and his wedding night with Psyche, Lia could live it.

If August would agree to play it with her.

She pointed upward. "Can we play that game?"

"Eros and Psyche?" he asked, and it seemed for the first time she'd managed to shock him.

"You don't want to?"

"I'd rather not."

"Wow," she said. "Didn't imagine I could find your limits. Sex in the dark too weird for you? The man who made love to a cloud?"

"The cloud started it."

"What is it?" she asked. "Did I hit a nerve?"

August shoved his hands deep into his pockets and shrugged.

"I was married," he said.

"You were married?" Lia knew she shouldn't laugh at that, but she couldn't help it. She wasn't laughing at him so much as laughing at the idea of a free spirit like August being married to anyone.

"Long, long, long ago… Brief marriage. Young love."

"When you were a teenager?"

He nodded.

"What happened?" she asked.

"Much like this," he said, nodding up at the ceiling. "I didn't tell her some very important things about me. There are some people you're not allowed to keep big secrets from—spouses, for example. But I did. She found out and left me. When I wanted to get her back, my mother talked me out of it. This all—" he pointed his finger up at Psyche in the bed "—hits a bit too close to home."

"I'm sorry," Lia said.

"I was a selfish little ass," he said. "I'm the one who ought to be sorry. But if you want to play the game, we'll play it. It would be good for me."

"You know, I could play Eros," Lia said. "And you could play Psyche as a young prince instead of a princess. I wouldn't mind seeing you in a blindfold."

He smiled that mischievous smile, the one that made her toes clench inside her shoes.

"Now that," he said, "does tempt me."

CHAPTER TWENTY

August left her for the day with a kiss and a promise to see her that night. In the meantime… Lia couldn't put it off any longer. At three in the afternoon, Lia called another meeting of the Young Ladies' Gardening & Tennis Club of Wingthorn Hall to order.

As it was a fine late-May afternoon, the young ladies of the YLG&T Club were mostly wearing gauzy floral print summer frocks. Georgy wore silver cowboy boots with hers, of course. Rani was the exception in a white skirt and pale pink polo shirt.

She also had a tennis racquet with her.

"Mum found my business cards," Rani explained. "I've had to take up tennis."

"I have an appointment in two hours," Georgy said, crossing one leg over the other, silver boots flashing. "What's up, boss?"

Lia leaned back against the fireplace mantel and took a deep breath. Not even a swagger stick would make this conversation any easier.

"I'll make it quick. We have a problem."

"Another one?" Rani asked as she bounced her tennis racquet off her white trainer.

"Another one," Lia said. "A worse one. We have a security breach."

"What?" Jane's eyes were wide and scared behind her glasses. Georgy, perpetual slouch, sat up straight in Lia's armchair, and Rani stopped making a racket with her racquet.

"It's all right." Lia held up her hands to calm them all down. "I have it under control. I think. Someone I was involved with a long time ago has a bit of a grudge against me. He somehow figured out our gardening and tennis club…isn't. He threatened to go to the police and the papers unless I paid him off."

"Bastard," Rani said. "Who is he? We'll gut him."

"Nobody is gutting anyone," Lia said. "I have the money. The end. I'm only telling you this so you'll keep a low profile for the time being."

"What does that mean?" Georgy asked.

"It means get your arse in the garden," Rani said. "Or play some tennis with me."

"Admittedly," Lia said, "we might have chosen a better name for the company, considering none of us play tennis or garden. But that's not the point. The point is I have everything under control. Just be careful and call me if anything happens. And no slipping strangers our business cards this week, please and thank you, even if he does look DTFMEL…" She looked at Georgy. "They might be someone working for my old friend, trying to get more dirt on us."

"Dirt like..." Jane began, "our boss lady is sleeping with August Bowman, the sexiest male escort in London?"

Rani laughed behind her racquet strings. Georgy stared at her in shock, horror, envy and joy, which made for quite an expression.

"Is that true, boss?" Georgy asked. "He was supposed to play tennis with me."

Lia blushed, cleared her throat and smiled.

"This meeting of the Young Ladies' Gardening & Tennis Club of Wingthorn Hall is now adjourned."

CHAPTER TWENTY-ONE

After warning the tennis club about David, Lia felt better. It would all be over soon enough and she could get on with her life. Until then, she had a date.

Lia arrived at August's house at nine sharp. He buzzed her in and called her up to his office/bedroom. In his office, she encountered a strange sight. August was nearly fully clothed—well, for him, anyway. He had on his jeans and nothing else. But that wasn't the strange part. He seemed to be placing steel chains and locks around the black iron posts of his weird space-age bed.

"Do I want to know?" she asked from the doorway.

"I had a brainstorm on the way home today," he said, dropping a few feet of chain onto his bed. He waved her over and, before she could ask what his brainstorm was, he kissed her.

"What was that for?" she asked when he pulled back from the kiss.

"For me," he said. "I like kissing you."

"Hmm. We are pleased. Now what about the chains?"

"I want to prove to you that the Rose Kylix has true supernatural powers."

"You do, do you?"

"Do I? I do."

She stared at him.

"Go on."

"Here's the idea—you'll chain me to the bed," he said.

"This is a train of thought I'm prepared to board."

"Then you'll go to any room in the house that isn't this room, as far away from this room as possible. You'll drink from the kylix there. We'll meet each other in the fantasy world. Then at some point, if you remember to do it, you'll tell me something. A line of poetry. A number between one and a trillion. And then when we both come back to our senses, I'll tell you what it was. Something I wouldn't possibly know unless you told me. What do you think? Clever plan, yes?"

Lia rocked her head back and forth, as if considering the idea.

"Hmm...no."

His eyes widened. "But it's a clever plan. Did you miss the clever part?"

"It's terrible plan. Stand there silently while I list all the reasons why." Lia held up one finger. "One, I will absolutely not chain you to a bed and then *walk off and leave you there*. What if the house caught on fire and you were trapped here while I'm off in Narnia shagging Mr. Tumnus?"

"Are we doing Narnia tonight? I thought we were doing Eros and Psyche?"

"Two." She held up two fingers. "You got yourself untied

from my bathrobe handcuffs last night without batting an eyelash. You could unchain yourself some other fancy way you have, Houdini."

"I thought of that. Set up your phone to video me the whole time. And…" He paused, turned and picked up a white envelope off the nightstand. He opened it to show her it was full of white powder.

"That's not anthrax, is it?"

She was going to be very unhappy with him if that was anthrax.

"Talcum powder."

"Why do you have talcum powder?"

"I own leather trousers."

"Right, of course."

"I'll put the key to the lock in the envelope full of talc, and that way if I need to get out, I'll have the key right there and you'll know if I've gotten into it because, well, I'll look like I've just finished eating a dozen beignets."

She had to admit the idea was ingenious. But she didn't have to admit it out loud.

"Three," she continued. "It won't work. If you're in here and I'm in another room, and you're not talking me through what's happening—"

"I have never done that," he said. "Never once. This cup has real powers. This will work."

"Why do you want me to believe the kylix is magical?" she asked him. "Why's it so important to you?"

"I want you to believe in magic," August said. "I want you to believe…"

"In what? The gods?"

"In Eros," he said, meeting her eyes. "I don't want you to think I'm a liar or a trickster or a fraud. Or just delusional.

You had one taste of the power of Eros with David, and it broke your heart."

"Beyond repair, I'm afraid."

He shook his head. "I refuse to believe that. As a duly appointed representative of Eros, god of sexual love, it is my sworn duty to heal your erotically induced wounds."

She crossed her arms over her chest. "Is that part of your mission statement?"

He furrowed his brow as if seriously considering that idea.

"We *should* have a mission statement. I'll work on that. Good call."

"August, it's sweet of you to try to heal my stupid heart. But it's not going to work. No matter what tricks you pull to try to convince me this is real, I'll find a rational way to explain it. I know you believe this is real magic or real miracles or really the gods playing with us. I respect that. I respect Catholic nuns and Buddhist monks and Jewish rabbis…all of it, even though I don't believe what they believe. Can you respect my beliefs?"

"Respect that you don't believe?"

"Right. It would take Aphrodite appearing in my bedroom wearing a crown of roses and floating two feet above the floor to get me to believe in love again, and even then, I'd think she was held up by wires. You'll just have to accept my romantic atheism," she said.

"Can you at least believe in me?" He started to wrinkle his nose and she stopped him by putting her finger on the tip.

"I'm here," she said, tapping the tip of his nose. "I'm with you. I like you. I even trust you a little, and I don't trust any man who isn't my own father and barely even him. So let's put away the chains and the anthrax before someone—you—accidentally gets hurt. Please?"

"You adore me," he said, grinning. "Don't you?"

"Not in the least. It just so happens I don't want to be in the papers for accidentally killing a male prostitute. Polite society frowns upon that for some reason."

"Shame. I had this bed frame made specifically for high-level bondage."

"I was imagining Cirque du Soleil."

"That, too. See?"

Lia watched as August stretched to his full height, grabbed the high bar of the bed frame, where a canopy on a normal bed would have gone. In one smooth, athletic motion he swung his legs over the top of the bar and then hung upside down from it, like a bat.

"Ask me what I am," he said.

"No. Because you're going to say, 'I'm Batman,' and it's not funny. He wasn't even upside down when he said that in the film. I will not laugh. Let me save you the trouble and spare us all the embarrassment."

"I can't believe you're not impressed. I'm literally hanging from my own bed by my knees."

"Why, may I ask, would you do that during sex?"

"Note the location of your mouth in relation to my cock."

Lia stood in front of him. "Ah," she said, nodding her approval. "Tab A and Slot B line up nicely."

"You can put my cock in your mouth if you want. But only if you want. No pressure."

She did want, in fact, but she wanted something else a little more. Lia pressed her mouth to the three-petal rose brand on his stomach, above his hip, and kissed it. At first only tenderly, running the tip of her tongue over the raised edges of the rose. August groaned, and Lia sucked the branded flesh into her mouth.

Then she bit it. Hard.

With a gasp, August slid down off the bed frame and onto

the bed in a heap. Lia laughed. She'd turned the brand on his stomach bright red from sucking on it.

"That dismount was shamefully executed," she said. "You'll never win the gold with that technique. Hard to believe you actually made the pros."

He grabbed her so suddenly she had no time to steel herself for it. She squealed as he threw her down onto the bed, straddled her, took her wrists in his one hand and held her down.

"What are you doing?" she demanded.

"Sticking my fingers in your cunt." His pushed his hand under her dress. Lia knew she could stop him with a word but then...that would stop him. He yanked the fabric of her knickers aside.

"You keep calling it that just to annoy me," she said.

"If you say the word *cunt* right now, I'll leave you alone," he said.

"I won't. You can't make me. And let's be honest, that's hardly an incentive."

He laughed. "You're so wet," he said. Of course he sounded pleased with himself. She trembled at the light tickling touch. He ran his finger up and down that wet seam. With his fingers he spread her open, and Lia repressed a groan. She didn't want to make a single sound while he did it. She was embarrassed enough as it was without making a fool of herself moaning all over the place. The rough tip of his finger found the entrance of her vagina, the tender little hole. He stroked it lightly, teasing it.

Her toes clenched inside her boots as August pushed one finger into her. It was dizzying. As wet as she was, it slid in without resistance, and in a second, he was inside her body. She really thought she might faint, it was all so sudden and sensual. They'd been joking, teasing, playing, laughing, and now everything was very, very serious. He pushed a second finger inside her and she whimpered, whimpered again when he spread his fingers, opening her wider...wider...until Lia was digging her boot heels into the bed to lift her hips off the sheets and into his hand.

"Not so prissy now, are we?" he said, his tone mocking. "Legs spread for me, pussy dripping all over my hand, so hot inside that your cunt could give a lesser man a second-degree burn..."

August moved his touch lower, to a soft hollow place just inside of her. He pressed his two fingertips into that hollow lightly, very lightly, but her body reacted strongly...very strongly... A muscle inside her clenched around his fingers. A nerve fired like a gunshot.

"August..." She made his name a plea.

"Tell me again," he said, gazing down at her, "how bad my technique is."

"I apologize," she said breathlessly.

"Apology accepted." He gently extracted his fingers from her body and sat back on his knees. Lia watched him, legs still spread wide, lungs burning, vagina clenching, as he put those two fingers in his mouth and licked her wetness from them.

"God," she said. He smiled, stood up and undressed before lying back naked and stretching out on the bed.

"Get the kylix," he said.

Lia was shaking so hard from arousal she nearly spilled the wine when she poured it. But she managed to get enough control of herself to carry it to August without disaster striking. August drank deeply from it and closed his eyes with a happy sigh. Lia undressed and took a deep drink from the kylix. She crawled into bed and lay very near August, her arm over his chest.

"Fair warning," he said in a sleepy voice. "Making love

while wearing wings can be awkward. You'll want to stay on top so they don't get crushed."

"How would you know?"

"Bad experience at a fancy-dress party. I'm fading fast. I'll see you in your dreams."

"Not if I see you first, Psyche," she said.

Lia felt the woozy wobbly feeling come over her again. She closed her eyes and thought of August in a blindfold. She fell asleep smiling.

When she opened her eyes again, she was in paradise.

CHAPTER TWENTY-TWO

Lia stood in a meadow on a hillside, her bare feet sunk deep in the softest green grasses. The sun hung low and red in the sky. She turned around, orienting herself to this new world and saw, at the top of the hill, a palace that shone bright as polished ivory, with gold columns and silver stairs. She walked through a carpet of wildflowers in the fading sunshine. She paused at a stream and gazed into the water. There she was... Eros. Goddess of passionate love. Her hair fell in ringlets of chocolate brown around her face and a diadem of pearls sat upon her brow. The gown she wore was the finest satin. And from her back sprang two wings of silky white feathers.

"Oh my goodness," Lia said to her reflection. "I'm precious."

She turned her head to gaze at her hair in profile and got a face full of feathers.

"Right, wings," she said, pushing the wing back down and into place. "I was warned. Watch out for the wings. Wait. Wings. I can fly."

It was just like every lucid dream she'd ever had. Once Lia realized she was in a fantasy world and wearing wings, she pushed off the earth and flew up into the air. Freed from the bounds of gravity, she rose higher and higher to watch the sun sink into the ocean.

Night was almost upon them. Her wedding night.

Lia's immortal ears heard footsteps wandering in her palace.

No one was ever to be allowed admittance into the private chambers of Eros, therefore it could only be Psyche, the young prince she'd loved at first glance and had summoned to her home.

She flew to her palace but kept herself hidden behind an ivory pillar, waiting for the prince to appear in the hallway. She held her breath and listened to the approach of two lovely feet.

Would he like the palace? She had made it just for him. For weeks, she'd eavesdropped on the people of his kingdom to learn anything she could about the prince. She knew he loved to ride horses, so she'd filled her stables with gray mares and brown stallions. She'd heard he'd laughed with a child's delight at a traveling circus and the panthers and tigers that walked on leashes like dogs, so she had every room in the palace painted with exotic animals—elephants, lions, unicorns. She'd heard a rumor that his grandmother had made him a wool blanket for his bed and had it dyed a rich rare violet, and he loved it so much that—even though it was faded and tattered—he kept it to use as a horse blanket when he rode. No surprise that she'd put a blanket of the finest silk dyed the rarest purple on their bed. Silk coverlet, cotton sheets from Egypt, a dozen pillows full of the softest feathers... She lived to please him. But would she?

For the first time in her immortal life, the little goddess worried the corner of her wing in her fingers.

She was nervous.

His shadow rounded the corner before he did, and the goddess held her breath again and made herself as small as possible as she slipped behind a tapestry.

Oh. There he was!

She grinned and bit her wing tip.

At the first sight of him she almost laughed. The part of her brain that remembered she was Lia and he was August did laugh. August had transformed himself into a teenage boy, all youthful beauty, long limbs and awkward energy. He was so lovely he made her nervous. And how silly for a goddess to be so nervous at the sight of a mortal boy of eighteen winters and seventeen summers.

Oh, but he was the loveliest of all the boys in all the world. He had black hair that waved like a nighttime ocean and a smile bright as the noon sun in autumn. He spoke rarely, taught to hold his tongue in the presence of his elders, but when he did speak, he spoke well and wisely. He always took time to pet any dog that wandered his way. Even as a boy, he'd never pulled the tails of the mouse-catching cats in his home. He blushed in the presence of pretty serving girls but never talked to them out of turn. He was happiest on the back of a horse, riding on the beach at sunrise and sunset.

If she hadn't decided to marry him, he would have joined the army. So she had summoned him to her palace to spare her sweet prince from that bitter life. She wouldn't allow him to get so much as a scratch on his knee.

"Hello?" the prince called out as he made his way slowly down the long hall. He looked up and all around him and sometimes even smiled at the sight of a mosaic chariot race on the floor or the dancing leopards on the walls. He had dressed as if for a wedding, in a fine linen chiton belted with blue leather and a simple gold circlet in his hair.

She bit her wing again, to stop herself from calling out to him. Not yet. Too soon. But almost time…

"The oracle of Apollo sent me here," he said. "I was told I am to meet my bride. I obey the will of the gods. Is anyone there? I wish to obey the will the gods."

Goodness, she thought. Goodness gracious he made her quills quiver. He wished to obey the gods. And she was a god, therefore he wanted to obey *her*.

How nice of him.

The eager goddess plucked a feather from her wing and blew it into the hallway. She peeked around the edge of the tapestry and watched the feather dance in the evening breeze toward Prince Psyche. He stood up straighter, and she delighted in how tall he was and how trim. She delighted in the red sunset shadows in his hair and the way his eyes tracked the feather dancing around his head. And oh, when he laughed as the feather brushed his cheek, she delighted in that, too.

He reached out, trying to grab it from the air but it darted out of his grasp. Her doing, of course.

The feather danced again in front of his face and the love-struck goddess blew a breath and turned the feather into a tiny white hummingbird. He gasped at the magic that had taken place just before his eyes. The bird alighted on his shoulder and nipped at his hair. Lucky bird. Then it took off, and he seemed to understand—oh, clever Prince Psyche—that he should follow it.

The hummingbird darted this way and that, but the young prince followed its lead up the spiraling stairs. Eros flew straight out the nearest window and up to the bedroom she'd prepared for them so lovingly on the highest floor. She arrived there before the prince and hid herself in the shadows.

Oh, she prayed he would admire the room she had made for them. The walls were painted with murals of wild forests and silver lakes and pretty nymphs bathing in winding streams, hiding themselves behind the dancing branches of weeping willows. The bed was big as a sailing ship with posts made of oak carved like climbing ivy. On the ceiling, she'd had painted horses running across the sky.

Too much? Probably too much. She did overdo it when in love.

She gasped. There he was.

He stood in the doorway of their bedroom peering in, his eyes wide with wonder, his posture fearful.

And then she knew she must speak.

"Don't be afraid," she said, her voice hardly more than a whisper.

He looked right. He looked left. He did not find her. She'd slipped into the mural of the nymphs and hidden behind the one with the widest hips. He'd never see her there.

"Who said that?"

"I did," his goddess said. "I mean...your bride did. That's me. Your bride."

"Where are you, my bride?" he asked. "I would like to meet you."

"I can't show myself to you," the goddess said.

"Are you shy?" he asked.

Shy? Her? The goddess of passionate love? She who had coupled with gods and satyrs and, once, even a cloud—shy? Nonsense.

"I'm not shy. Not in the least." She dropped her voice to sound sultry before breaking into a girlish giggle.

"Then why do you hide yourself from me? How can I be your husband if I'm not allowed to see you?" As he spoke he walked around the room, peering into corners, behind columns, even under the bed.

"Do you wish to be my husband?" she asked, chewing again on her wing tip. She really ought to stop that. Nasty habit.

"I wish to obey the gods. If the gods will our marriage, then yes, I wish to be your husband. Though why the gods would want the likes of me for one of their chosen ones, I can't imagine."

Handsome and humble? He was perfect. Oh, she had such good taste in husbands.

"What's so wrong with you that you think the gods strange to favor you?" she asked.

"I'm a minor prince of a minor kingdom," he said. "And why me when I have older brothers still waiting to find brides?"

"You're prettier than your brothers," she said. "I checked."

"Is my bride so shallow to be swayed by a pleasing countenance?"

"Yes."

"Oh," he said. "I suppose the gods know what they're doing."

"Not really. They're just winging it."

Ha! That was a good one. He didn't laugh. Oh, he didn't know she had wings. That's why he didn't laugh.

"Can you please come out?" he asked. "Please?"

"I can, but you can't look at me."

"Why not?" he asked. "If you are…disfigured or something, you should know I am not as shallow as my bride seems to be. If the gods want us together, then we shall be well and content if we honor them and each other."

She put her hand over her heart and sighed. She loved him. Oh, she loved him. So sweet, this young prince. Why wasn't he naked yet?

"I'm adorable, I'll have you know," she said. "Too adorable. Puppies faint at the sight of me and kittens weep with envy. Aphrodite herself said I'm cute as a button and you know she's shallow as a puddle in dry season. I'm so attractive that if you saw me, you'd fall madly in love with me at first sight, and I'd much prefer you loved me for my personality before I showed you my face."

"Can you come out and let me meet your personality, then?" he asked.

"I will," she said. "But you have to put the sash over your eyes."

"Sash?"

She untied the white ribbon from the hair of the wide-hipped nymph she stood behind. Then she took the ribbon and dipped it into the dark sky, dyeing the fabric the deep blue of midnight, and festooning it with silver crescent moons and golden stars. With a single breath, she dried the night-wet silk and sent it flying toward the prince. He caught it out of the air.

"This is all very mysterious," he said, not unkindly, almost enchanted.

"I have my reasons. Put it on." She waved her hand to hurry him up, though he could not see her gestures.

He wrapped the sash around his head, over his eyes, and neatly tied it in back and so he bound the night about his eyes.

"I'm coming out," she said. "Don't be afraid. I'm very nice."

"I'll try to be brave," he said, a smile lurking at the corners of his mouth.

The little goddess slipped out of the mural and stepped barefoot on the tile floor of their bedchamber.

At the first sound of her foot on the floor, the prince turned toward her, lips slightly parted in trepidation. Her immortal heart nearly stopped in her immortal chest. She had never loved anyone so much in her long, long life.

"You must promise," she said, "you won't try to sneak a peek."

"Sneak a peek?"

"No sneaking, no peeking."

"I promise I'll neither sneak nor peek," he said.

"Good, good, good."

"I can tell from your voice you're quite young," he said. "Are you my age?"

"I'm older than you are," she said. "A year or two…" Or several thousand.

"Are you of royal blood?"

"Oh, yes. I'm the daughter of a queen."

"Do you…" He paused, searched for the right words. "What do I call you, my lady?"

"Good question," she said. She tapped her chin as she walked circles around him. She couldn't tell him her real name—Eros. That would give away the whole game. But he had to call her something other than "hey you."

"You may call me…Ophelia," she said.

"Philia?" he repeated. "Your name means 'love.'"

She smiled. She hadn't thought of that. "Yes, it does. A good sign. But you could call me 'Lia' for short."

"I like that… Lia…"

"That'll do nicely," she said. "Would you like to touch me?"

He had better say yes.

"Yes, Lia."

Good answer.

She took a deep calming breath. Finally, she would get to touch him, this beautiful prince she'd dreamed of for days and days and days. She took his wrists gently in her hands—his skin was so young and smooth and warm, and she could feel his nervous pulse beating rapidly.

She brought his hands to her face.

TIFFANY REISZ

"You'll find I have the appropriate number of eyes and noses."

His fingertip tickled her skin as he traced the lines of her face. He touched her forehead and cheeks, her nose and even her eyelashes. Then he came to her lips and touched them tenderly. He caught a curl of her hair between his fingers and brought it to his nose.

"You are a beauty," he said. "I can tell how fine and graceful your features are and your hair smells of heaven."

"I told you so."

"You're quite cocksure for a lady."

"Am I? I'll try to do better."

"No, I like it," he said. "Makes me feel less scared that you're so confident. Are you a maid? Or a widow?"

She saw a deep blush suffuse his face.

"Is there a third choice?" she asked.

He smiled.

"I..." he began. "I've never..."

"Never?"

He shook his head.

"Never," he said. "Not even a kiss."

"Not even a kiss?" she asked. Better and better.

"The girls I know, they're all servants in my home. My father said it was wrong and ignoble for a prince to chase a serving girl. Even when they flirt, he said, it is because they are frightened of losing their place in the household and are willing to do anything to keep it. It wouldn't be right or fair, my father said, to force myself on a frightened girl even for a kiss. But I'm afraid I come to you with no idea what to do or how to do it."

She warmed at his words. Her heart danced. Such a considerate and gentle prince. Why weren't there more considerate and gentle princes? Perhaps they would conceive one tonight. And perhaps in time she would give birth to an entire army of considerate and gentle princes who would conquer the world—but considerately and with great gentleness.

"It's fine," she said, pleased beyond words. "I'll teach you all you need to know."

"Good," he said. "Thank you."

Thank you? He thanked her? Oh, she would love him every day and every way for the rest of eternity.

"Would you like me to teach you now?"

"Yes, my Lia."

She took him by the hand and led him to the bed.

"Sit," she said as she gently turned him so that the back of his thighs touched the bed.

He sat and sank his hands into the soft covers.

"It's nice," he said.

"I had it made for you. I had everything made for you. There are horses for you in the stables, and a hound waiting to walk with you every day and the foods you love to eat and all the wine you wish to drink."

"You will spoil me."

"Every day," she said as she placed her hands on his face.

She tilted it up and stole a kiss from his lips, a deft theft she repeated a dozen times. At first as they kissed, he did nothing but sit there with his lips parted to let her kiss him. But as the kisses grew deeper and hotter and heavier, he began to pant, and his hands reached up to the hands that held his face. He found her wrists, her arms, and stroked them.

"Your skin's like silk," he said. And she wanted to say, *I know*, but she didn't. She was learning.

"Thank you, my prince," she whispered, and stole another kiss or ten.

As the kisses went on and on, he inched closer to her and even closer and dared to press his legs against hers. She ran her hands through his hair and removed his golden circlet, tossing it over the top of the bedpost.

She caressed his neck, his throat, his shoulders, all through his linen shirt.

"The shirt has got to go," she said as she tugged on the fabric.

"Of course, my lady," he said, and tried three times to untie the knot at the neck. She batted his hands away.

"Let me."

"I don't mean to be so nervous."

"I like that you're nervous," she said. "It's lovely to me, your modesty. To see a boy covered in maidenly blushes is a joy. More painters should paint virgin grooms, but all they care about are virgin brides, and frankly, I'm a little sick of them."

"I'm no Hercules," he said. "I fear I won't impress you."

"If I wanted Hercules, I would have married Hercules. I wanted you."

She lifted his shirt and he raised his arms to let her pull it off. He was thin, of course, but not sickly or weak, only young. His arms, however, were sinewy with new muscle and his chest was beginning to broaden as he neared full manhood.

"You please me very much," she said. He smiled. "But what is this?"

She touched a mark on his stomach.

"A birthmark," he said. "They say it looks like a butterfly. That is why I am called Psyche. Does it displease you?"

It didn't look like a butterfly to her. It looked like the imprint of a kiss made by burning lips. Did it displease her? She answered that question by going down onto her knees in front of him and pressing her own lips to the mark. He inhaled sharply at the touch of her mouth on his skin and she saw his long fingers dig deep into the bed.

"My lady," he said, his voice pained. Against her will—

and better judgment—she pulled away from him and rested
back on her knees.

"Yes?"

"I nearly... I was almost undone. Forgive me."

"You're allowed to enjoy your bride making love to you,"
she said.

"I don't want make a fool of myself."

"If you spill your seed from one of my kisses, I'll take it as
a compliment."

"You will?" he asked, sounding relieved.

"You are young. In time, you'll learn to control yourself.
But you don't have to do anything tonight but let me touch
you and kiss you and please you. And know you cannot displease me as long as you lie there being sweet and lovely all
night long."

He grinned. "I'll do my best," he pledged.

"And I will do my worst. Now let's get you more comfortable," she said as she untied the straps of his sandals and tossed
them aside. His skin bore crisscross marks, and it gave her great
pleasure to rub his calves and massage the marks off his skin.

He breathed hard as she caressed him. He enjoyed her touch,
that was plain. How wonderful to please her prince. And to
think she didn't have to prick him with one of her arrows to
make him like her or desire her. Even now, as she soothed the
skin of his strong calves, she felt his heart turning toward her
like the face of a morning flower toward the first rays of sun.
All she needed was for him to love her, truly love her, and
then it would be safe for her to reveal her true self to him. She
pressed one long kiss on the top of his thigh and he inhaled
again so sharply she thought she'd hurt him.

"Too much?" she asked.

"I...don't know. Everything's so new. Your hair tickled me."

"You liked it?" she asked, letting the tips of her curls brush his knees and thighs again. He laughed. She didn't want him to laugh. She wanted him to moan and groan and writhe and scream her name.

She pushed her hand under his chiton.

He stopped laughing. His entire body tensed as she slid her hand up his long inner thigh until she touched his organ. She didn't grasp it, not at first. Lightly, carefully, she ran her fingertips over the length of it while her prince went as silent and still as a fawn startled in the woods.

From the corner of her eye she watched his hand on the bed, watched his fingers tighten in the sheets as she lightly stroked him. His cock was stiff and thick and warm to the touch.

She was dying to see what her fingers felt. She shoved his chiton up to his hips.

Out of embarrassment or instinct, her prince tried to tug it back down again.

"Don't do that," she said, swatting his hand away. "I'm allowed to hide myself from you. You're *not* allowed to hide yourself from me."

"I'm sorry, my lady," he said.

"You're shy. I like shy princes." She touched him again with her fingertips. Beautiful cock sitting at the apex of two long, muscled thighs. Dark with arousal and so sensitive that he flinched with her every littlest touch. She touched the base of the shaft and stroked a vein that throbbed under the wide tip—and the tip she gave extra attention to, especially the wet slit where his seed was beginning to pool.

"Do you...do you like it?" he asked, his voice nearly breaking in nervousness.

"It's perfect."

"Is it? I mean, I wouldn't know. Never shown it to a girl before and you always wonder if it's what it's supposed to be and—"

She put her mouth on him and that brought an end to his nervous chattering.

All he said then was "Uh." The most beautiful sound ever whispered by a young prince on his wedding night. *Uh*…

She wrapped her fingers around the shaft and held it still as she lavished attention on the tip with her tongue. He gasped softly, gasped again, and she thought she'd die of joy at each and every one of his tiny inhalations.

And the taste of him…salt and sweet. And the scent of him, like he'd just bathed in the clear cold waters of a high mountain stream. And the feel of him deep in her mouth. And the sight of him fighting against his modesty with every lick and flick of her tongue.

She took her mouth from him, though she still held him in her hand.

"Do you like it?" she asked.

"Is it…are we allowed to do that?"

"We're married. We're allowed to do anything we want together."

"It feels like it shouldn't be allowed."

"So you don't like it?"

"No, I like it too much. My father, the king, says the pursuit of pleasure leads men astray down evil paths."

"Your royal father is mostly right," Lia said. "But he was speaking of idleness and drunkenness, gambling and chasing serving girls. It's a man's duty to please his wife. You know that."

"Does this please you?" he asked. "Putting my…me in your mouth?"

"I wouldn't do it if it didn't please me," she said. "You'd be the best of husbands if you let me continue."

"And the worst, I presume, if I made you stop?"

"You're a very wise prince," she said, and was glad he was

blindfolded and couldn't see her laughing at him. Since she didn't want him to hear her laughing, either...she put him in her mouth again.

She drew him deeper, past the tip and down to the shaft, and once she had him where she wanted him, she lightly sucked on him as she stroked underneath his cock, the testicles and the sensitive patch of flesh behind them. If there were a painter in residence, this would make quite the mural. A winged goddess on her knees in front of a mortal prince wearing the night tied around his eyes. And his lovely thick organ in her mouth and his fingers twisting in the bedsheets and the muscles of his flat stomach twitching and his head falling back as he moaned...

No matter. She didn't need a mural to commemorate her wedding night. She was a goddess. People would be telling the tale of her marriage to Prince Psyche until the world ended.

As well they should...

"You have to stop," her shy prince said. His voice sounded pained, pained from the pleasure. "Or I'll spill."

She raised her head and smiled, though he could not see it.

"I want you to. You must."

"I must?"

"You absolutely must."

"Oh, well...if I must."

He collapsed flat on his back, in utter surrender to his bride's erotic ministrations. Soon he was lost in the ecstasy of her mouth on him. She rose up higher on her knees to take him deeper in her mouth. His back arched on the bed once and then again as she pulled harder on the shaft until it nudged the very back of her throat. Her shy prince wasn't so shy anymore as he neared climax. He breathed heavy and hard, and groaned with every breath. His cries filled the room to the rafters and she imagined that the whole world could hear the sounds of their lovemaking in the far distance. What would it sound like to them? The cry of a hawk swooping down on a dove? A coming rainstorm? An army marching to war?

Or would they hear and know the truth—that Eros had at last been felled by her own arrow and this was the sound of Love Itself falling in love?

With a final cry, almost loud enough to be a shout, the young prince grasped the sheets and came in her throat. His head lifted off the bed as every muscle in his body contracted in his coming.

She swallowed every last drop of him and would have taken more if he'd had it to give. When it was done, she remained on her knees between his thighs as he lay panting on the bed. She gently kissed his fluttering flat stomach and the butterfly birthmark received a thousand tender kisses all its own.

"How is my prince?" she asked, resting her cheek on his hip.

"Happily married," he said, chuckling.

She laughed with delight and she delighted in his laugh. She rose from the floor, still delighted, still laughing.

"You should lie on the pillows," she said to her smiling Psyche. "And rest a moment."

"Will you lie with me?" he asked as he moved carefully to the head of the bed, finding his way by touch until he lay back on the pillows and stretched, happy as a black cat caught by a sunbeam.

"My lady?" he whispered.

"Oh," she said. "Sorry. I was staring at you and forgot I should be speaking."

"It's hardly fair you've enjoyed me so much and I've barely gotten to touch you."

"You're right," she said. "I'm a selfish monster. I'll simply have to join you in bed and let you touch me. Would that help?"

"It wouldn't hurt."

Ah, clever boy. Lovely boy.

She straddled him. This seemed to please him. He inhaled deeply when she rested her bottom on his lower stomach. She unbound the bodice of her gown and lowered it—well, tried to. It got caught on her bloody wings. Lia wrestled with the fabric and finally managed to get her bodice down to her waist.

"Give me your hands," she said to Psyche, taking them and putting them on her throat.

He smiled when his skin touched hers again. Smiled and stroked her neck and shoulders. Had anything, she thought, ever felt so good in all the world as this prince's gentle hands on her body? His fingertips tickled her skin and she shivered and quivered and sighed.

"My dear modest prince." She grasped his wrists and lowered his hands to her breasts. He inhaled sharply again—oh, he was a sensitive boy—and she held her hands over his so that he would know she wanted his touch, demanded it even.

"Beautiful," he said.

"You can't see my breasts. How do you know?"

"They feel beautiful."

"Do they?"

He nodded. "They're so soft," he said, lightly squeezing them. "And hard, too." He then traced her nipples with his thumbs.

"Would you like to kiss them?"

"Yes, my lady."

She lowered herself over him and let her nipple dangle at his mouth. He caught it between his lips and sucked it gently, oh…too gently. She would never stop shivering. He slid his hands to her shoulders and that was dangerous. He was far too close to her wings.

The clever goddess knew what to do. She pulled a ribbon from her hair and ordered her prince to place his hands over his head. He obeyed—she'd given him no reason not to trust her, after all—and she tied his wrists to the bar of the headboard.

"You don't want my hands on your body?" he asked.

"I do," she said. "Always. But we have all our lives to play all our games together. And it pleases me to see you there, like a gift tied up with ribbons and bows."

"A gift for you alone."

"Yes. And no better gift have I ever been given…"

Lia raised her skirts and straddled him once more. Young and virile, he'd grown hard again already. He inhaled sharply as her wet flesh came to rest on his stiff organ. She moved on it and her folds parted. Her prince was as eager for her as she was for him. He raised his hips off the bed, lifting her with him in his need to bury himself inside her. She shifted and spread her thighs wider until the tip found the entrance of her body.

"Uh…" he breathed. Beautiful sound. Heavenly sound. She wanted to hear it again and forever. She pushed down onto him and he slid into her slick passage. In his male instinct, he lifted his hips again to push all of himself into her and then cried out in pleasure as he fully penetrated her.

Her shy prince lost his shyness then. He took her hard from beneath her, entering her with long slow strokes as he pumped his hips. He shivered against her, and his breathing was ragged. She balanced herself on his chest, her fingers digging so hard into his skin she knew she would bruise him. She gasped, suddenly—shockingly—so aroused she could have come simply by willing it. She pushed her hips into his and he said, "More," and she did it again. She lay on his chest, pressing her breasts against his warm skin as they consummated their marriage, silent after his "more," though she could hear his cock moving in her wetness. She meant to kiss him once and quickly, but as soon as their lips met, the kiss turned wild, hungry. He bit her lips, sucked on her tongue.

She rose up again, and rocked on his cock, riding him, riding him hard, and as she did her wings began to spread on their own. They spanned the room and cast a shadow over the bed. She couldn't help it. She kept her heart in her wings and they spread as her heart filled with unbearable, impossible love for the prince inside her.

Her head fell back. She called his name. With a soft sob she came and came and came.

Beneath her, her new husband shuddered with his own coming, and when he came into her, he gasped her name.

Ophelia…

She collapsed onto him. Her heart kicked against her chest like the hoof of a wild horse. He must have felt it.

"Gods," he breathed. "I love being married."

"So do I," she said. "I married very well."

"I wish I knew who you were."

"I can't tell you. It's against the rules."

"Tell me *something*, then," he begged. "Tell me something that tells me who you are."

"I am she who loves you," she said, touching his face. "My prince."

"Ah," her shy prince said with a brazen smile. "That tells me all I need to know."

CHAPTER TWENTY-THREE

Lia opened her eyes. She lay on her back and August was at her side, looking down at her face.

She started to say hello, but he stopped her words with a kiss. If she'd been expecting a quick kiss, she was wrong. The kiss was rough and passionate and dirty, and she couldn't get enough of it. Suddenly she needed to have sex. Not wanted... needed. August must have felt exactly the same because he paused in the kissing only long enough to roll on a condom. With his knees, he pushed her thighs wide and with one thrust he was inside her.

But it wasn't enough for him to simply be in her. He slid his arm under her right thigh and yanked it up and over his shoulder. She lay there under him, completely open, spread out and impaled. His cock rubbed every tender spot within her. Pinned down as she was, she couldn't even move. All she could do was lie there and take it and take it and take it. August loomed over her. His shoulders were like iron, his arms like steel and his cock rock hard and splitting her in two.

Lia groaned and panted. She hadn't known it could be like this outside of her fantasies. She'd known passion existed, and pleasure and desire and orgasms, but she didn't know they existed for her.

"You like it?" August demanded. "Don't lie to me."

"Yes," she said, breathing hard. Her nipples were so tender as they brushed against his chest. The harder he pounded her, the harder she wanted him to. Just as in the fantasy they'd shared, she whispered, "More." And he gave her more. He braced himself over her on his elbows and knees and rammed his cock into her in a frenzy of rough rutting thrusts. Lia had to grab the bar of the headboard with both hands to brace herself so she could take what he gave her. She was so close… her stomach was in a knot, her vagina dripping wet and her heart galloping like it would run away with her.

"Come for me," he ordered as he pounded away at her.

"I don't know if I…"

"You can. You have. You will." He dug his hands into her hair and tilted her head back. He met her eyes and held her gaze as he slammed into her.

"You will," he said again. "For me."

A part of her wanted to close her eyes to hide from him. But another part of her couldn't bear to look away from his storm-wild eyes. She pumped her hips into his, hard as she could, meeting his every thrust. Her clitoris was swollen and throbbed as the shaft of his cock rubbed against it.

"Hold my neck," August said. "Don't hold the bed. Hold me."

She released the bar and clung to him, one hand on the

back of his neck, the other on his shoulder. His knees were under her now as he pulled her into him.

"I can go as long as it takes," he said into her ear. Then he kissed that ear, her neck, her throat, all the while fucking her as hard and deep and dirty as any man had ever fucked any woman since the beginning of time. Everything disappeared in that moment, with August on top of her, driving into her without mercy. She lost her mind and her shame, her past and her future. Nothing mattered except the cock inside her and the climax building there, brewing like a storm, ready to burst. The bed rocked under them. August groaned as he rammed her endlessly. Lia lifted her head and buried it against his chest.

She came. She came like a tornado, like an earthquake, like the end of the world. Her entire body shuddered as her inner muscles contracted so sharply it hurt, so sharply August cried out. He slammed his own climax into hers and it seemed the ecstasy would never end, that she'd be lost in it forever. She wasn't afraid. As long as she was lost with August, she didn't care if she ever found her way back again.

When it all finally ended, August rested his full weight on top of her, trapping her under him. In a daze of orgasm and afterglow, Lia laughed drunkenly.

"What was that about?" she asked in a small sleepy voice. "You had fun playing virgin groom or something?"

"You told me you love me," he said.

Lia stiffened in shock. He couldn't believe that, could he?

"That was a fantasy."

He raised his head and then stroked her cheek with the back of his hand.

"We are most ourselves in our fantasies," he said.

"Or least ourselves," she said. "That's why they're called fantasies, not memories."

He met her eyes. "I'm going to make you fall in love with

me. I don't know how, but I am. Before this week is over, you'll tell me you love me in this world."

"Why?"

"Because you will believe in Eros."

She touched his face, his lips, his sweat-damp hair.

"I believe in you," she said. "Isn't that enough?"

"It's a good start."

PART FIVE

Ariadne & Dionysus

CHAPTER TWENTY-FOUR

When Lia got home that morning, she attempted to sneak to her room and avoid her parents. Her father would be cross the rest of the day if he knew she'd spent the night with August, and her mother would ask wildly inappropriate questions that Lia had no intention of answering.

She slipped in the back door, the old servants' entrance, and crept past the kitchen. She'd made it halfway up the stairs to her suite when she heard her mother's voice.

"It's 6:00 a.m.," her mother said. "You're up early."

Lia turned around slowly on the steps.

"I have got to get my own flat."

"Shall we go for a run? That's why you're up so early, isn't it?"

"You think you're one of those funny mothers on telly," Lia said. "You are not."

Her mother laughed a mocking laugh. A good old-fashioned ha-ha-ha-ha-*haaaa*.

"Stop being smug about it."

"You look exhausted, dear," her smug mother said smugly.

"I had a long night."

"I bet you did." More smugness. "How's Mr. Augustine Bowman?"

"Fine. Dandy. I'm going to bed now."

"Not a bad idea," her mother said. "I may go back to bed myself."

"Do that," Lia said. "We'll all just have a lie-in. And none of us will tell Daddy where we were last night."

"Oh, Daddy knows where I was last night."

"Ugh, don't call him Daddy," Lia said, wincing. "Why do you do this to me?"

"Because it's so fun to watch you squirm," her mother said. "My own mother used to torture me, too. This is cosmic payback."

"Can't you please let me complete my walk of shame in peace, Mother?"

"Walk of fame, darling. Walk of *fame*. We do not buy into those sexist and outdated notions that girls aren't allowed to have as much fun as boys are."

"Thank you, Gloria Steinem. I'm going to walk my famous way to bed."

"Aren't you even going to ask why I'm awake so early and loitering by your staircase?"

Lia sighed heavily. "Why are you awake so early, Mum?"

"Because August called."

"What?" Lia was suddenly wide-awake.

"He called your father's mobile. Said you weren't answering yours and it had rained a little and he wanted to make sure you got home safely."

"Out of juice," Lia said. "I'll charge up and text him. Now can I go to bed?"

"You can."

Lia turned and started—gingerly—up the stairs. She'd need to put an ice pack on her twat after the things August had done to her last night.

"He's in love with you, you know," her mother called up to her. No more smugness. Now her mother was absolutely crowing.

"He is not," Lia called back.

"He called your father's phone to make sure you got home safe. Either he's in love with you or he has a death wish."

Lia went to the top of the stairs and glared down at her mother.

"Today is Wednesday," she said. "I met him on Saturday. That is five days."

"Five? That's a lifetime. I was already married to your father and pregnant with you two days after meeting him."

Her mother had a point. Why were people always making good points when she didn't want them to?

"Going to bed, Mum. Alone and not pregnant. Please stop talking."

"Fine, fine. But you should know, even if your father disapproves, I like your boyfriend."

Lia walked back down the stairs, put her hands on her mother's shoulders and smiled.

"Mother, he is not my boyfriend. I am using him for sex. Gobs of very weird sex."

Mum raised her eyebrows.

"See?" Lia said. "Two can play this game. Not so smug anymore, are we?"

"You are *definitely* your father's daughter."

Lia's mother walked away. Thank the gods.

As soon as Lia was in her bedroom she plugged in her phone, as she promised she would, pulled off her clothes and collapsed into her bed.

Two seconds later, Gogo jumped onto the bed and stretched out next to her.

"He's not in love with me," Lia said to Gogo. He seemed to sort of nod in agreement. Or maybe he was just trying to lick her arm. Hard to say.

But Lia did know this—her mother was a loon. August was not falling in love with her any more than she was falling in love with August. The Rose Kylix or whatever the hell it was had aphrodisiac effects. She'd gotten swept up in the moment. That was all.

When her dead phone came back to life, Lia sent a quick message to August.

Psst...home safe.

Please get a decent car so I can sleep after you leave me.

It's Wednesday, she replied. Our deal ends Friday, remember?

I can't see you after Friday? he wrote.

I didn't think you'd want to.

I want to, he replied.

Lia grinned at her phone screen. Then she wiped that stupid grin off her face.

We'll talk about it later. Good night/morning, she wrote.

What do you want to play tonight? Zeus and Io?

Wasn't she the one he turned into a cow?

Leda and the Swan, then?

August added several bird emoji. He was never going to let her forget the bird noises.

I'm not shagging a swan, Lia wrote. Surprise me.

You sure about that?

Was she? Letting August surprise her would mean she trusted the man. Did she?

I'm sure. Goodbye.

Apparently she did trust him.

See you tonight, August replied. In your dreams. I'll see you right now in mine.

Lia set her phone on the nightstand and cuddled down into her blankets. She couldn't quite stop smiling long enough to fall asleep.

CHAPTER TWENTY-FIVE

Lia arrived at August's flat just before nine. Eight-thirty, in fact—8:29 to be precise. She might have been the slightest bit eager to see him, though she wouldn't admit that to herself. Instead she told herself a gargantuan lie. She was early because she was worried about hitting traffic. Or a water main could have burst. August lived near Camden. Real risk of rogue parades breaking out. Lia was not eager. She was simply using good common sense.

Lia went to ring his bell, but she saw a note taped over the buzzer.

Come in, Lia. All others stay out, please.

Good thing he said "please," otherwise the house would surely be overrun with burglars and murderers. Why did men always think they were immortal?

Lia slipped in through the door, taking the note with her, and locked it behind her.

"August?" she called out. No answer.

She ran upstairs and found August already in bed, covers up to his hips and no farther, head on his white pillow, eyes closed.

"August?" she whispered.

No answer. She waved her hand in front of his face.

Nothing.

She placed her hand on his chest.

Warm skin. Beating heart. Not dead. Good news there.

The Rose Kylix sat on the bedside table. Propped against the kylix was a cream-colored notecard with the words "Drink me, please" written on it.

Interesting. He must be trying to prove to her again that their nightly adventures were really trips to a fantasy realm as opposed to what she knew they had to be—a delectable combination of hypnosis and erotic hallucinations.

Lia smiled when she saw August had also placed live roses on his night table next to the Rose Kylix. A dozen exquisite pink roses in a ceramic vase painted with dancing fawns. A white ribbon was tied around the neck of the vase, and sewn onto the ribbon—embroidered, in fact—was the name "Lia."

"Stop trying to make me fall in love with you, August," she said, stroking the silky petals of the pinkest rose. "It's not going to work."

August remained silent, sleeping on, lost in a dreamworld already.

She picked up the Drink Me card. On the back August had written, "If you want, you can take your clothes off and get into bed with me, please."

Of course he'd added a "please" at the end.

Since he'd said please…

Lia undressed, placing her jeans and T-shirt over the back

of the love seat next to August's clothes. He'd nicely folded the T-shirt she'd loaned him the morning before, clearly intending to return it to her. She picked it up and held it to her face. When she inhaled, she smelled cypress and juniper. But it wasn't cologne, because she'd smelled it on his skin Monday night after his shower in her bathroom.

Lia placed the shirt with her clothes and told herself she would wash it as soon as she got home.

Or maybe sleep in it. And then wash it.

Or maybe she just wouldn't wash it at all.

Once Lia was naked, she walked to the bed, lifted the cup to her lips and then paused. Usually August said some kind of prayer or something before drinking but he always said it in Greek. She had no idea what to say. Cheers? Bottoms up? A good old Irish *sláinte*?

Cradling the cup in her palms, Lia took a deep breath.

"Eros," she said, thinking August would like it if she invoked his deity's name. "Thank you for letting August and me into your good graces." She glanced down at him, at his hand on his pillow, his naked shoulder, his lips lightly parted, his lips she wanted to kiss. "And bless August, please. Even though he is a madman who has sex with clouds, he is a very lovely madman. Please help him do whatever he needs to do to get back in his family's good graces. And let me help him if I can."

Then she drank.

As soon as she put the kylix back on the nightstand, now empty, she felt a sudden sleepiness, heavier than ever before. Quickly she lay in the bed next to August. She didn't feel right holding him while he slept, but she didn't think he'd mind if she lay very near him, close enough just for their toes to touch under the sheets and their faces to face each other. When he woke up, he'd see her there. This time she wouldn't leave while he was still sleeping. He might follow her home again. Gods forbid.

A thick fog seemed to fill the room, scented with the sea, electric as a storm. She inhaled the salt and the wild wind and closed her eyes as sleep took her like a rough lover.

She woke up on a beach.

A beach?

Yes, of course, a beach. Why was she surprised? She'd fallen asleep on the beach the night before. Why would it seem strange to wake up there? She didn't want to open her eyes quite yet. The journey by ship had been hard. Too hard. Strangely hard. The storm that had blown up last night was like no storm she'd ever seen before. A small but furious squall, it had surrounded their ship like the storm bore it a grudge. No matter how hard they fought it, with sails and oars and prayers and supplication to the gods, there had been no fighting the rage of wind and rain.

Thank the gods it seemed the storm had not wanted to destroy them, only steer them. It had forced them onto a sandbar where Theseus had dropped anchor. Once their feet had touched the soil of this island, the storm passed. But it was late and dark, and they were tired and hungry. Theseus had found a small dry cave to serve as their shelter. Their shelter. She and Theseus would sleep in the cave along the beach's edge while the six men slept outside on the warm sand, standing guard. They had no desire to sleep in the cave, anyway, they said, and be kept awake by the sound of Theseus and his witch lady celebrating their victory.

She had not dressed again after Theseus had finished with her. She'd hoped to bathe this morning in a spring before returning to the ship. Standing, she clasped her cloak around her so that nothing of her body could be seen but her face and feet. She left the cave.

The morning was pure and bright, and as soon as she left the cave and stepped onto the beach she saw a terrible sight before her.

The ship was gone.

"No..." she breathed. "No..."

Not this. Anything but this. Anything but to be left behind, abandoned and without a word...

Why? She ran up a grassy hill. Perhaps from a high ridge she could spy the ship or Theseus. She reached the ledge and saw empty ocean everywhere she looked.

"I saved you in the labyrinth," she whispered. "I guided you with my thread. I helped you slay the Minotaur and free the people of Crete from his wrath. I made your name for you. The great wide world will know the name of Theseus for centuries to come because of what we did together in that terrible maze. And you leave me? You said you would make me your queen... I would have had your child... I would have had your son..."

"Count your blessings, my princess," came a mocking male voice from behind her. "I could have killed him. Or turned him into a dolphin. So tempting..."

She spun to face the voice.

A man stood under a cypress tree, not twenty paces away from her. He wore a scarlet sash tied around his hips and a crown of grape leaves in his curling brown hair—and nothing else. His body was tall and long and lean, and he loosely held an amphora by the handle.

"Who are you?" she demanded. "What have you done with my fiancé?"

He left the shade of the tree and walked toward her. He walked slowly, no hurry in his steps at all. He had a fine male form, she couldn't help but notice. The muscle of Hermes in his thighs, the beauty of Apollo in his bearing and the seductive smile of Zeus on his lips.

When he came to stand before her, he lifted the amphora. "Wine?"

Before she could reply, he lifted the amphora to his lips and took a long drink. He offered her the jug and she shook her head no.

"You must," he said. "You're surely thirsty."

"I can't..." She held the cloak together around herself. If she took her arms from under it to drink, she would reveal her nakedness to this strange man.

"Allow me."

He lifted the amphora to her mouth. When he brought it to her lips, she nearly cried out with the sort of pleasure she'd felt when Theseus had taken her against the rough stone walls of the labyrinth. The wine was like none she'd tasted before. Sweeter, tarter, brighter. It burst in her mouth like a fat fresh grape. It was thick as blood and cold as a winter river. One sip had satisfied her strongest thirst.

"What is that?" she asked as he lowered the amphora from her lips.

"Wine," he said. "Wine from blessed grapes."

"I've never tasted its like," she said, panting, amazed. "Who blessed these grapes?"

"I did, of course."

"And who are you who blesses the grapes of the vine to create wine like none other?"

He smiled at her again, a wild animal smile. She took a step back from him in fear.

Only gods could bless crops.

Only one god would bless vines.

"Dionysus," she breathed.

"At your service, my lady."

CHAPTER TWENTY-SIX

With a flourish, Dionysus lifted her off her feet and swept her into his arms.

"Where are you taking me?" Lia asked the god of wine and revelry.

Dionysus held her against his chest easily, though she squirmed like a house cat trying to escape the unwanted affections of a child.

"I'm taking you to my vines," he said in a tone that warned her such a thing ought to have been obvious.

"Where is Theseus? What have you done with him?"

"He's gone to Athens, of course."

"He would not have left me behind," she said. "Not by choice."

"No, he wouldn't have. But I gave him no choice."

Lia shivered. Though his words were threatening, his tone was light. He spoke like a host at a symposium, regaling his guests with his best and brashest stories that he told first before they were deep enough in their cups to find everything funny. She stopped squirming in his arms when she realized she would not escape him. Instead she studied her new surroundings.

Lia had never seen such a place as this island of Naxos. The trees they passed to their left looked hazy, like a watercolor forest. And the silver brook they followed on their right glinted as if the shallow bottom were diamonds instead of river stones.

"What do you want with me?" she asked the wild god.

"You, of course," he said, and laughed. Such a laugh to set birds to wing.

"Me? Why me?"

He shook his head, laughed again, softer this time.

"I watched you with that foolish boy. Ah, I was insulted seeing that short prince touch you. What you see in him is beyond me." He set her on her feet at last.

"He's the son of Poseidon," she said. "And he is not short!"

"Never marry the son of Poseidon. Your children will smell of fish."

Lia punched him in the arm.

He made an exaggerated face of pain and looked at her.

"You struck me!"

"He doesn't smell like fish. You smell like wine."

"I'm the god of wine, for my sake!"

"You're the god of pissing me off," Lia said. She slapped a hand over her mouth.

Then she laughed.

"Ariadne?" Dionysus said, eyeing her with narrow eyes. "Have you gone mad? Already?"

She lifted her hand and whispered, "So sorry," before putting her mouth behind her palm again.

"Lia," Dionysus said.

She raised her hand over her lips again.

"I think I broke character," she said.

"You did."

"I don't know how."

"I know how," he said. "Not that you'd believe me."

"Let me guess, this has something to do with magic."

"Look at me, Lia. Are you really going to stand here in this world and tell me this is nothing but a hallucination?"

"It's a very silly hallucination." Then she gazed around at the strange isle. "But a pretty one." She met his eyes. "Sorry I ruined it, August."

"August? Who? No!" He slapped his chest. "I'm Dionysus, god of wine, women and song!" His voice echoed across the valley.

"You're August and you're adorable," she said, still laughing.

Dionysus/August's shoulders sagged. His chin dropped to his chest. He shook his head.

"Here I am, trying to throw you a nice orgy, and you're mocking me."

"Guess I didn't drink enough? Bit too sober for Dionysus?"

"This was my fantasy," August said. "I suppose I wanted to be with you more than I wanted to be with Ariadne."

Lia suppressed a grin of pleasure at his words.

"I like your grape leaf crown."

"Do you?" he asked, turning his head left and then right. "Fetching, is it?"

"I'm envious."

"Want one?"

"Can I?" she asked.

"Of course." He wriggled his fingers in front of her face.

Lia raised her hand to her head and felt fresh cool leaves growing out of her hair.

"Very posh," she said. "Can you manage a wardrobe change?"

"The ladies who serve Dionysus wear sheepskin."

"Like condoms?"

"Those are sheep's guts," August said. "Sheep*skins*. Suede."

"Maybe something in cotton? Little warm for suede."

"If you insist, but we're being *very* historically inaccurate."

Lia tossed the cloak off her shoulders and found herself now wearing a soft white cotton gown exactly like those she'd seen in a hundred Renaissance paintings of Ancient Greece.

"Pretty frock," she said. "Thank you." She glanced around the scene before her—the meadow, the stone gate, the buttercup sun in the Aegean blue sky, August at her side in his crown and Pre-Raphaelite curls. "Why did you pick this place for us to play?"

"You said you wondered why Theseus left Ariadne on the island of Naxos while she slept, even after declaring his love and promising to marry her. He was forced to by Dionysus, who had seen Ariadne and wanted her for himself."

"Didn't Ariadne get a say in it?"

"She did," August said. "She said, 'Yes, I'd rather marry a god than a short half-mortal philanderer.' Worked out better for her than Psyche. Dionysus and Ariadne had one of the few rare happy marriages in Greek mythology. Meanwhile Theseus continued to womanize all his life and died heartbroken after the death of his wife, mistress and son."

"Ariadne dodged a bullet," Lia said.

"No bullets back then," August pointed out. "She dodged an arrow."

"So did I." She nodded with the realization.

"Did you?"

"With David. What if I hadn't caught him kissing Mum? I might have spent weeks sleeping with him, falling more and more in love with him, totally oblivious that he was a complete bastard. And I never would have met you, then, right?" Lia asked. "Both Ariadne and I got screwed over. Then again, both Ariadne and I got to look 'with mortal eyes on things rightly kept hidden.'" She smiled at August. "Just quoting *The Wind in the Willows*."

He put his hands lightly on her shoulders, met her eyes.

"Do you trust me?" he asked.

"Not even remotely," she said.

He looked at her, lips now pursed in disapproval.

"A little," she said. "Why do you ask?"

"Because," he said, "I want to do something for you. Here. Now. Will you let me?"

"Does it involve shagging with grape leaves on our heads?"

"It doesn't involve shagging at all."

Lia's eyes widened in shock. "I'm almost scared."

"You should be." He grinned maniacally. Mad as a hatter, this one was, Lia decided. Good thing she liked mad hatters so much.

"Please?" he said. "You'll like it."

"It will scare me *and* I'll like it? That makes no sense at all."

August took her face in his hands and held her gaze. His eyes appeared darker here, in this place, bluer, truer, as if the August in the real world were a pale shadow of the August in this world. It seemed he belonged here, and she almost wished they could stay in this place forever. The colors were more vibrant, the winds sweeter and stronger, and the woods full of secret beasts no mortal had ever seen nor tamed.

"All right," she said. "I trust you."

"Close your eyes."

She closed her eyes.

"Don't peek."

She didn't peek.

"Tell me your favorite color."

Lia said it was pink most days, sometimes yellow, like sunrise.

"The colors of sunrise will do nicely," August said. "There. I've got it. Open your eyes."

Lia opened her eyes.

She looked at August. He'd changed clothes and now wore the garb of a turn-of-the-century country squire, ready to muck about on a wet Sunday ramble. Mud-brown trousers, a matching waistcoat, a linen shirt, neck buttons undone and sleeves rolled up to reveal his wrists.

"You approve?" he asked.

"You look nice," she said. "Like a duke's gamekeeper."

He pointed at a red curtain that hung seemingly on nothing and for no reason in the middle of the meadow.

"What?" she asked.

"Let's see behind the curtain. I've got a surprise for you…"

She raised an eyebrow at him but let him take her by the arm and lead her through the red curtain.

As soon as they passed through it, they were in a new world.

Lia glanced around… The landscape had changed entirely. Gone was the lush Mediterranean paradise. Where they stood now looked like the Lake District of England. A little river wound around them from a source unknown and into a thick forest of oaks and willows. A wind kicked up, a winding wind that wound its way through reedy trees. Finally, birdsong. Goldfinch, song thrush and wren.

The sky…it was no longer late afternoon in this pastoral paradise. The yellow sun poked its head through the pink petals of dawn.

And floating toward them on the silver morning waters was a rowboat painted in stripes of pink and yellow and white.

"All aboard," August said, offering his arm out to her.

"You're up to something," she said.

"I absolutely am, yes."

Warily—though more amused than afraid—Lia took August's arm and let him lead her to the edge of the river. He waded into the water and held the boat steady as she stepped inside and sat quickly on the pink silk cushion in the bow. August shoved them off and sat down on a cushion of his own in one smooth motion.

"Where are we going?" she asked, leaning back to enjoy the ride.

"Down the river and into the woods," he said as he placed the oars and started to row. He rowed well, and the trim little boat skimmed along the top of the river, swift as a water strider bug. Must have been the magic of the fantasy as they were slipping into the woods mere seconds after they'd set out.

Once they'd passed into the forest, Lia shivered. The shadows were thick and cool here, and August stopped rowing to hand her his corduroy jacket from the floor of the boat.

"Thank you," she said as she put it on, touched by his gallantry.

"I could have made it warmer," August said. "But I'd rather lend you my jacket."

Lia smiled as she wrapped the jacket around her and held it to her body. She was glad he hadn't raised the temperature, and not simply because she liked wearing his coat.

This is how it should be, she thought. But what? How what should be? She didn't know where she was or where August was taking her, but somehow she already knew it should be like this—a cool shadowy spring morning with garden birds waking up to sing. As August rowed them through the woods,

Lia felt as if she'd stepped into a painting or into the pages of a fairy tale.

Everything was perfect…the pink-and-yellow-dawn boat, August's sleeves rolled up just so, and the trees by the water… a million willows, there had to be. Lia had counted, and they came to a million exactly.

"Willows," Lia said. "August?"

""'Believe me, my young friend,'"" August said as he pulled on the oars. ""'There is nothing—absolutely nothing—half so much worth doing…'""

""'As messing around in boats,'"" Lia said, finishing the famous quotation from *The Wind in the Willows*.

She knew then exactly where they were, and so she began to cry.

August smiled at her, said nothing and pulled again on the oars.

The river widened from not much more than a twelve-foot trickle and turned into a pond that was almost dignified enough to be called a lake. The sun shone down and warmed them enough that Lia slipped off August's jacket. In the center of the almost-lake sat an almost-island. August rowed to the island, and with a splash of two boots in shallow water, he pulled the boat ashore.

He helped Lia to her feet.

She could not speak, and August was kind enough to ask her no questions. He let her weep, though he did use the sleeve of his shirt to wipe the largest of her tears from her cheeks.

"Weeping like a willow because she's in her favorite bed-time story," he said, shaking his head. "This girl who told me her heart died. I don't believe a word of it."

He kissed her cheek to show her how silly she was and then took her by the hand.

"Come, Lia," he said. "We have a date."

Gently he tugged on her hand, but she dug her feet in the soft soil and wouldn't budge.

"Lia?"

"I can't."

"You can. Watch. It's easy." August lifted his feet up and down. "Just like that. March on. He's waiting."

"I can't go in there."

"In there" was a copse of trees, trees that looked as old as Mother Nature herself, old as Father Time. They were hoary with emerald moss, and ivy dangled like crepe paper at a party from every branch. She saw the face of the old Green Man beaming at her from between the branches before he disappeared again with a reedy laugh. And from within the circle of those trees came a sound she'd never before heard but recognized at once. The sound of panpipes played softly and so well that Lia knew she heard them played by the creature who created them and who had given them his name.

"It's not real," she said.

"It's not?" August said, bemused. "Then why are you crying?"

She didn't answer. August took her in his arms and kissed her forehead. Lia heard the music, closer and clearer, and she stepped forward, unable to resist the song any longer. August walked at her side, near her but not touching. Lia knew she must choose this moment—it could not be chosen for her. August could offer it to her, but it would not happen until she accepted the gift.

The sun had risen to high dawn—the full yellow disc of it stood tiptoe on the edge of the horizon. The shadows in this primordial glade were long and gray. The breeze smelled sweet as strawberry blossoms. Lia's heart beat outside her body. She had never felt so much in her life. So much so much so much, she felt everything at once. She couldn't have stopped walking forward if someone tied iron chains around her ankles.

They came to a creek, no wider than a puddle. August skipped over it first, then helped her across.

She wobbled her landing and ended in his arms. Lia clutched his shoulders to steady herself and, once steady, his shoulders remained clutched.

She kissed him.

It was a sweet and tender kiss and over in three breaths, but Lia knew that kiss changed something inside her. Not changed something really, but healed something. And that something was her heart, and the kiss healed it because the kiss meant she had a heart again. And she knew she had one because she hadn't kissed August out of passion but passionately kissed him out of love.

She pulled back from the kiss and met his eyes.

"Don't look now." August whispered the whisper of a devout child in a church hiding his prayers inside his hands. "But he's behind you."

Lia looked behind her.

She gasped softly, almost silently, when she saw the shoulder of the god. He sat with his brown back against a green tree, and all she could see at first was the tree and the shoulder and the naked human back that turned to animal fur at his waist.

"Oh," Lia said, fingertips on her lips. Just "oh." She looked at August, smiling through tears or crying through her smiles, she didn't know.

"Go on," August whispered. "He won't hurt you, I promise."

She shook her head, not in disagreement but disbelief. But she went on. How could she not? What English girl who ate and drank *The Wind in the Willows* with her tea and buttered toast wouldn't? Such a thing would be as silly as Alice refus-

ing to follow the White Rabbit or Lucy Pevensies walking
past the wardrobe without giving it a second glance.

August let her go and he let her go alone. She walked past
peonies, past green willow warblers, past doubt and fear and
heartache so healed now she'd forgotten she'd ever been hurt.

She walked into the glade and there he was, still sitting
with his back to that tree and so enormous, even seated, she
had to crane her neck to see his face. Had he become bigger
or she smaller? He was the god, not she. Maybe August had
made them the size of Ratty and Mole and that's why the god
loomed so large. Or perhaps she felt so small because she had
become a child again. Not in body but in wonder and in joy.

The old god Pan played on and on, ringing lazy lullabies
from his pipes and sweet melodies made for sleeping not dancing. His horns were curved like the spirals of a seashell and
shimmered as if made from the same stuff as the insides of
oysters. They glinted like dancing water as he swayed gently
in and out of the sunlight in time with his music.

Lia stood in front of him, directly in front, and he nodded
his head, once and nobly. She saw the baby otter at Pan's feet,
curled up so tight it was as if he'd fallen asleep in the bottom
of a teacup.

August had remembered everything…the boat on the river,
the strange magic island come out of nowhere, the pipes, Pan
and the baby otter she'd come to rescue and return to his
worried father.

Pan's Island…she had finally found Pan's Island.

She knelt on the ground and gently, oh-so-gently, slipped
her hands under the otter and lifted him to her, holding him
like a human infant against her shoulder. Small as he was,
no bigger than a newborn puppy, she could hold him in one
hand. With her other hand, she reached out toward Pan's clo-
ven hoof. Trembling, Lia touched it, hard as a goat's hoof but

ten times its size. He must have felt her touch, and she froze when his eyes met hers.

Pan's face was handsome behind his shaggy beard, with lines upon lines around his earth-brown eyes, which crinkled when he smiled. She loved every last one of those tender wrinkles. Lia had never known either of her grandfathers, gone before she was born, but she knew a grandfather's love for the first time when she gazed on that kindly and timeworn countenance. Those old eyes of his had seen everything and forgiven everyone. And Lia knew that as long as she lived, he would love her, and as long as she loved him, he would live.

And oh, she did love him.

The great god Pan had played his pipes all this time, played sweetly and softly and well. When she stood humbly at his feet with the baby otter in her arms, he took the pipes from his lips. Why? August had stepped into the sacred grove, and it was when Pan saw August that he'd stopped playing for a full measure. When the music played again, it was no less lovely, but Lia found it mournful, less a lullaby and more an elegy.

Pan shook his great shaggy head as if trying not to laugh.

"You can laugh," August said to him. "I deserve it."

Pan held his pipes in one hand and with his other he ruffled August's hair like a fond uncle, then patted his cheek, then chucked him once just under the chin before he turned all his attention to his playing again.

Lia looked at August and saw he had twin tears on his cheeks.

"What is it?" she asked, though she knew. Of course she knew.

"I'd forgotten," August said, "how beautiful he is."

"I hadn't forgotten," Lia said. "I always knew."

""Are you afraid?"" he asked. Of course he had to quote the book at her.

Lia answered, "No." She was not afraid.

"I am," August said.

"Of Pan?" It seemed impossible to be afraid of Pan.

"Of you."

She laughed. "Why?"

He stroked her cheek. "You know why."

She smiled, still crying.

"Poor lad," August said, stroking the baby otter's soft sleeping head. "We should get him home to his father."

"Of course," she said. Must get the lost baby otter home. August led her from the glade and she looked back at Pan, only once but once was all it took. Pan winked at her and changed his tune again. As she and August walked away, toward the boat on the bank, the pipes trilled a wedding march.

"Randy old goat," August muttered as he put Lia and the otter in their boat.

"Not in front of the baby," she said. August laughed softly, and they set off rowing down the river. In a muddy puddle under an oak bearded with moss, a large gray-brown otter came ashore and barked. The otter in Lia's arms wriggled itself awake and returned the bark. Lia held up the baby and the large father otter dived quickly into the water and swam right up to their boat. After one quick kiss on top of the otter's small furry forehead, Lia set him down onto his father's belly, and otter and son paddled away. Lia smiled as she watched them go.

"Daddy and I wandered the woods every evening for an entire summer when I was little, looking for Pan's Island. He read the story to me every night. He told me once he'd sell everything he had to buy me a ticket to Pan's Island if he could. And you just…you just brought me here with a wink and a snap of your fingers. I dreamed…ever since I was a little girl I dreamed of this…and here I am. I wonder if he'd be heartbroken to know I made it here with you, not him. Even if it's not really real...it feels real."

"He wanted to find it for *you*," August said. "Not for himself. He's a good father, and good fathers hold the doors open for their children that only their children can pass through. All that matters is that you found it and you're happy. You are happy, aren't you?"

"I've never been so happy," she said, fresh hot tears running rivers down her face. She let herself weep without trying to stop, and she knew she wept not because it was over but because it had happened.

August smiled, and it was a smile to steal a young girl's heart, and as Lia was a young girl, her heart was stolen by it. And that wasn't even the mad part. The mad part was that Lia didn't want it back. He could keep the heart he'd just stolen. He could keep it forever, in a box or on a shelf, though she hoped he'd keep it in his chest, next to his.

"I thought the Rose Kylix made erotic fantasies come true," she said to August in a teasing tone. "This is the wrong kind of fantasy."

He smiled again, a different smile. A shy sheepish smile. She loved that smile because she knew what it foretold. He locked the oars and pulled her to the floor of the boat. Lia laid her head back on the pale pink cushion as August moved on top of her slowly, careful not to tip the boat.

She shuddered in pleasure as his body met hers, the warmth of his skin, the weight of him on her and over her...it satisfied a hunger in her too long ignored. August's mouth met hers and kissed her with almost delicate kisses, as if he understood her fragility and the fragility of the moment. This was her dream, her deepest sweetest dream, and she would have to wake soon but not yet. *Please*, she thought, *not yet*...

August braced himself, his weight on his elbows as he kissed her lips and neck and throat. "Do nothing," he whispered into her ear. "Just lie there and let me make love to you."

She nodded, smiled a shaky tearstained smile. He kissed the tears and returned the smile. As he lifted her gown to her waist, she watched his face. His eyes were hooded with his dark lashes and he wore an expression of the most intense concentration, like an archer with his arrow in the notch and the string pulled back to its tautest point.

Lia unbuttoned two more buttons of his shirt as he opened his trousers. He lay on her again and this time she could feel the thick hard length of him against her stomach, pressing in and down. He pushed her gown to her stomach to bare her breasts. When naked to his gaze, he ran one hand over them, not to squeeze or to grope but simply to stroke and stroke gently. Her nipples hardened against his warm palms and he lowered his mouth to her left breast. He licked the nipple once before drawing it into his mouth, and Lia tensed as he sucked it.

The pleasure was sharp, intense, focused in the tender tip that he drew on again and again. The slow draw, the tug, the moist heat on her breast, was bliss but paled before the bliss of watching August as he did it. His eyes were closed, and his lashes lay heavy on his cheeks. He looked almost pained, like he'd waited eons to kiss her breasts and the relief was so utter and complete he had to hold back tears. This display of raw emotion surprised her.

Lia lifted a hand, heavy with languor, and pushed his hair off his forehead and stroked his cheek.

"It's all right," she whispered, arching her back to press her breast harder to his mouth. He didn't break the contact, but he did glance up at her once, and she smiled tenderly at him as she lightly touched the lips that suckled her. August paused only long enough to whisper a few words before taking her nipple into his mouth again.

She lay back under him, ran her fingers through the thick soft waves of his hair and then slid her hands down his back, pushing his shirt off his shoulders and to his waist. His skin was smooth and sun-warmed. She couldn't stop touching him. Her body rose under his, almost of its own accord. August released her breast at last, but it seemed he hadn't gotten control of his emotions enough to meet her eyes again. Instead he nudged her thighs wide and nestled between them.

August's cock throbbed against her as if trying to find its way to her opening. Lia shifted under his chest and pushed against the tip until it slid through her wet folds and entered her. He shivered in her arms, and his breathing was ragged, his eyes still closed tight. Then he raised his head and looked at Lia, and she didn't know who he was.

For the span of one single breath, Lia was afraid of him. His eyes had gone cloud wild. She'd never seen such a blue as that. And she knew in an instant, and no one had to tell her, that she had been wrong when she'd thought that August's eyes were the color of storm clouds. No, no, no.

August's eyes weren't the color of storm clouds...

Storm clouds were the color of his eyes.

He smiled, and in a second breath he was August again.

"You should always be here," he said.

"I'll stay if you stay," she said, touching his cheek.

He kissed her again, gently, and as he kissed her, he found her clitoris with his fingertips and stroked her with such precision she clenched hard around him, hard enough his breath caught in his throat. She lay back again and let herself enjoy the terrible sweetness of being the cause of a man's undoing. He was older, a mystery to her and vastly more experienced, and she could conquer him utterly while lying flat on her back. This was power even a god would envy.

August rested his forehead against the center of her chest as he moved in her. No thrusting—that might tip the boat. They made love an inch at a time, barely moving and yet pushing so hard against each other Lia could hardly bear the tension.

When she came, her climax wasn't like last night's. It was gentler, quieter, and far more tender and dear. August's back bowed once before he came inside her. He stayed in her afterward, holding her in his arms.

"August?"

"Yes?"

"Thank you."

A slow smile spread across his face. His eyes softened. He laid his hand on her forehead and tenderly stroked her hair. Gently he began to move inside her again.

""There is nothing—absolutely nothing—half so much worth doing,""" he said into her ear between sweet kisses, """as messing around in boats."""

PART SIX

Aethra & Poseidon

CHAPTER TWENTY-SEVEN

Lia spent the next day in a hazy-headed daze. She sat at her loom from midmorning to evening, embroidering a white-winged horse onto her tapestry's dark evening sky. The work was absorbing, a perfect distraction from her thoughts, thoughts that troubled her nearly as much as her feelings and more than her memories.

Every stitch required her complete concentration. She was painting a Pegasus with needle and thread, no easy task. Between each stitch, however, she had time to think, to feel, to remember.

August. She couldn't even hear his name echoing in her mind without needing to stop and catch her breath. Something had happened last night that she hadn't expected, hadn't asked for, hadn't realized she wanted so much until August had given it to her.

When she'd come to in August's bed, she hadn't felt the usual high she'd come to expect as a standard side effect from drinking from the Rose Kylix. She'd glanced around and seen his bedroom and begun to cry.

August had pulled her into his arms and held her against his chest.

"Why are you crying?" he'd asked. She had liked the way he'd asked her, as if he simply wanted to know why she cried, not because he wanted her to stop.

"I want to go back," she'd said. And then said, "With you."

She fell asleep only after he'd promised her he'd take her back as often as she wanted.

Perhaps that was why Lia had spent her waking hours at her loom, weaving herself again into a myth by day, the way August wove her into myths by night.

A good thing she'd left the Rose Kylix at August's flat by his bed. If she'd had it with her, the temptation to drink from it would be nearly overwhelming. She would drink and dream her way back to Pan's Island. She would sit at the feet of Pan and listen to his piping, perhaps dance in the woods among the trees and the flowers. But it wouldn't be the same, of course, without August there.

Since coming home last night—this morning, really—she'd felt like a veil had gone up between her and the real world. She and August on one side of the veil, everyone else on the other. Including her parents. Her brothers. Her friends. David, too. It scared her how much she wanted to stay behind that veil with August. Or…if she was honest with herself…it scared her how much she wanted to stay *with August* behind that veil.

Lia had just put the final stitch into the left wing of the Pegasus when she heard a soft knock on her sitting room door.

"Come in." She lifted her head from her embroidery and realized it was evening already. Where had the day gone?

Lia wasn't surprised to see her mother standing in the doorway. But the outfit...that did catch her off guard. Her mother, usually dressed to the eights if not the nines, was wearing black yoga bottoms and a white T-shirt.

"What are you doing, Mum? Why are you dressed like that? Did you lose a bet?"

She had concerns this was a bizarre sex thing involving her father, but she was too curious not to ask.

"I thought if I put on exercise clothes I might accidentally do some exercise."

"Exercise? What happened? You aren't dying, are you?"

"I stepped on the scale." Mum patted Lia on her cheek. "Word of advice—stay young as long as possible, then immediately get old. Skip right over being middle-aged. It's hell on the metabolism."

"Don't be melodramatic, Mum. You're beautiful and you know it. Men throw themselves at you all the time."

She snorted a laugh. "They throw themselves at your father's bank account and hit me on the way there." Lia didn't believe that for one second but she didn't say anything. "So... are we seeing our Greek god tonight?"

"We are," Lia said. "But if you're here to interrogate me about him, you know where the door is."

"Oh, fine. I'll keep my questions to myself. Although... I do like him for you."

"I like him for me, too," she confessed. She smiled as she stretched her back. Her mother came and stood behind her sewing stool and rested her chin on Lia's shoulder. She peered at Lia's tapestry.

"My daughter is very talented," Mum said. "Sometimes I wonder how you're mine. I can't sew on a button."

Lia rolled her eyes but not unkindly.

"You could if you practiced," she said, and then realized she sounded exactly like someone she knew—her own mother. Her mum ignored that comment and started nosing through the books on her side table.

"What's all this?" she asked. "Planning a new tapestry?"

"Maybe," Lia said, though that wasn't true. But she was hardly going to tell her mother she'd been thinking about other erotic adventures she wanted to go on with August.

"Poseidon and Aethra," her mother said, looking at the page Lia had left open on her sewing table. "I know Poseidon, but who was Aethra?"

"The mother of Theseus," Lia said.

"Ah, you know better than that," her mother said. "Who was *she*? Not who did she give birth to or who did she marry. Believe it or not, I'd had my own life and adventures before I met your father and you were born. Some that would turn your hair white."

"I actually do believe that, Mum. You have adventures *now* that turn my hair white. This is a wig."

"It's flattering." Her mother tugged a curl of Lia's hair. "Who was Aethra?"

Of course Mum wasn't going to let it go.

"She was…a mystery," Lia said. "She's known for having had sex with her husband and a god in the same night and being impregnated, somehow, by both of them. That's the story I was reading."

"Now we're getting somewhere. I assume Poseidon was the god? Who was the husband?"

"A king named Aegeus. He came to visit her father, King Pittheus. Aethra's fiancé had just been exiled from the country for murder. Pittheus must have wanted to foist her off on someone else, fast. He got King Aegeus pissed on undiluted wine and sent him to his daughter's bedroom to shag and sleep."

"Parenting was very different in those days," her mother said.

"Mum, you gave me a vibrator for my eighteenth birthday."

"There wasn't a drunk king attached to it."

"Anyway…" Lia continued. "King Aegeus and Aethra slept together. Maybe they hit it off so well because they both had names starting with *Ae*. Whatever it was, they shagged and fell asleep after. They were sound asleep in bed when the goddess Athena appeared and woke Aethra. She said Aethra needed to hie herself over to the Temple of Sphaeria. Why? Athena didn't specify. But Aethra went, presumably after cleaning the royal sperm off her legs."

"A wet flannel works best," her mother said. Lia ignored that comment.

"She went to the temple and offered a sacrifice to, well… somebody. Athena, most likely. And while she was there, Poseidon appeared, all wet and naked and in the mood. They shagged in the temple. Or he raped her. Several versions of the myth say it was rape, but in those same versions, she's the one who's telling everyone that her son was fathered by Poseidon. I don't know how to reconcile a woman bragging about her son being the child of her rapist."

"Do you think it was rape?"

"Possible," Lia said. "On one hand, he was a god and she was mortal. That's a big power imbalance. Hard to imagine she could properly consent to an immortal. On the other hand…if you had the chance to shag a god, wouldn't you take it? Don't answer that, Mum. Rhetorical question."

"Oh, I definitely would," her mother said. "I'd start with Thor."

The good countess clearly needed a refresher course on rhetoric.

"Look at that. Could you resist that?" her mother asked. She'd turned to a page in the book, a full-color photograph of Bernini's most famous sculpture, *The Rape of Proserpina*. Bernini had lavished all his talent and attention onto the body of Pluto—Hades to the Greeks. He was massive, naked and impossibly strong. Proserpina—Persephone to the Greeks— squirmed in his grasp but in vain. No woman—goddess or mortal—could escape such a being. Utterly male but more than male. Human but more than human. Merciless in his beauty. Savage in his lusts.

"No." Lia stared at the god and the poor girl helpless in his grasp. "I wouldn't even try."

"Poseidon and Hades were brothers," her mother said. "If Poseidon looked anything like that, Aethra probably volunteered for the job of having his child."

"You know the maddest thing?" Lia asked. "There's no artwork depicting the encounter—Aethra and Poseidon in the temple. Theseus is one of the most famous Greek mythological heroes and, according to his mother, he had two fathers— one a king and one a god. But no artwork at all? Not a single famous painting or kylix or amphora or anything that depicts Aethra and Poseidon in the temple? So strange."

She tossed the book and it landed neatly on the love seat.

Mum smiled and sat down next to the book.

"Suppression," her mother said as she drew her legs under her into a position that could have been called almost-yoga. "It's the most dangerous form of flattery. When a story like that gets ignored by male artists, that always means they're afraid of it for one reason or another."

Lia turned on her stool and gave her mother her full attention.

"What do you mean?" she asked.

"Ever heard of a book called *Mathilda* by Mary Shelley?"

"No," Lia said. "I only know of *Frankenstein*."

"The reason you've never heard of it is because it's the story of a teenage girl whose life is destroyed when her father falls in love with her. Mary Shelley's father was a book publisher. He read her new manuscript, was horrified by the implications of it—guilty conscience, probably—and confiscated it. He wouldn't allow it to be published, and it wasn't—for over a hundred years. If a story is suppressed or obscured, it's because somewhere along the way it scared the shit out of a man. And that story of Aethra sounds like a prime candidate for suppression by men. On one hand," her mother said, holding up her right hand, "you have a woman who's trying to tell anyone who would listen that the father of her son was the god Poseidon. On the other hand, you have a mortal man humiliated that his young bride left their marriage bed on their wedding night to have sex with someone else. Who benefits by calling it rape?"

"The husband," Lia said. "If she had sex with Poseidon willingly, then he's a cuckold. If she was raped, well...you can't sue a god for adultery."

"More important," her mother said, folding her hands into her lap, "King Aegeus would have been humiliated to have his wife telling the world she'd left him sleeping in bed to go have sex with someone else. If he called it rape, he saved face. And the best evidence that nobody buys the rape story is the lack of artwork about it. The old masters loved painting rapes. Walk through any art gallery of Renaissance paintings and it's a history of rape on the walls. They adored subjects where women were being hunted, chased, kidnapped, raped. The artists wanted to enshrine male power over women. They chose what myths they thought were worthy—the rape of the Sabine women, Apollo and Daphne, Medusa—"

"Hades and Persephone," Lia said. "Leda being raped by Zeus in the form of a swan. Europa. Helen of Troy." Lia had seen dozens of paintings of those subjects.

"The old male masters would never choose to preserve the story of a wife who got to have more fun than her husband. Not only that, she isn't punished for it. She's not turned into a tree or some reeds or a cow. In fact, she's rewarded for her adultery by giving birth to the most famous hero in Greek mythology."

"I hadn't thought of it like that," Lia said. "You're probably right."

"You should weave it," her mother said. "As talented as you are, you don't need an original source to work from. You can do it all by yourself. And Aethra and all the badly behaved wives in history will thank you."

Lia felt a surge of love for her mother. Sometimes she forgot how nice it was to talk to her about art, life, love, nonsense. She had a much different perspective than her father, who cared more about the value of an artwork than the substance of it.

"I'm going to tell Daddy you said all that."

"Do it," Mum said, laughing. "He loves me because I'm so badly behaved, not in spite of it. As a good husband should. Or a wicked whore of a husband like mine."

"Mother."

"Sorry."

"You are not."

"Not really. Your father might be a handsome whore but he's also the love of my life, the father of my children, my best friend and, well, all the clichés. But I can pretend he's a normal saintly husband for your sake if you like."

"It's all right," Lia said. "I don't want you to pretend."

"You don't mind having two wicked parents?"

"I'm getting used to it."

"Good, because we aren't changing anytime soon," her mother said. She got up and kissed Lia on her cheek. "Better two parents who can't keep their hands off each other after twenty-two years instead of two parents who can't stand each other, right?"

"Much better," Lia said. "As long as you keep your hands off each other in my general vicinity." She waved her hand in a circle to indicate the general vicinity of the entire house.

"No promises." Her mother kissed her cheek again and then started to leave. Lia wanted to stop her and ask her something. She wanted to ask if it really was possible to fall in love in a week. She wanted to ask who was supposed to say stupid stuff like "I think I'm in love with you" first in a relationship. She even wanted to ask if it was all right to fall in love with someone you never went on a real date with but had fantastic sex with...or was that just infatuation?

Her mother would know the answers to all those questions, but Lia couldn't bring herself to ask them. What if Mum wanted to know why Lia was so unsure of herself with August? The answer was David, of course. Lia kept her mouth shut and hated David Bell a little more. He hadn't just broken her heart, he'd bruised her relationship with her own mother.

"I should go change," Mum said. "Don't forget drinks with David before his show tomorrow night."

"Oh, don't worry, Mum. I haven't forgotten."

Her mother left and Lia dropped her chin to her chest.

She would be a very happy person the minute David was out of her life forever.

But would he be? Ever?

As long as she stayed silent about what had happened between them, her parents had no reason to not pick up their friendship with David where they'd left off. Her father might even talk David into finishing the mural. He'd be under their roof again. Lia would move out—her parents had a town house in London—but that would mean leaving David alone with her parents here at Wingthorn. She was sick at the thought of her parents being friends with the man who'd crushed her heart under his heel, who'd nearly beaten down her door in fury, who'd hurled horrible insults at her, who'd blackmailed her the second he'd gotten dirt on her.

Or worse, her parents being *more* than friends with him again.

But what else could she do? Maybe she could quietly hint to her parents she'd heard rumors about David, that he'd screwed over a "friend" of hers? She'd have to figure something out to protect her parents from a blackmailing lying bastard like David Bell.

That would have to wait, though. First things first.

Lia hated to do it, but it was time. Thursday evening. She couldn't put it off another day.

She found her phone and called David's number.

"Lady Ophelia," he said when he answered. No hello. Just his sneering voice sneering out her name and that ludicrous courtesy title of hers. "To what do I owe the pleasure?"

"I'll have your money tomorrow," she said. "I suppose you'll want cash?"

"You have the money?"

"Yes."

"A million pounds?"

"As you demanded." August had promised it to her. She knew he'd have it. Nice to be able to trust a man again.

"Who'd you sleep with to get a million in cash in five days?"

"A male prostitute," she said.

"Usually doesn't work that way," he said. "Usually you pay the prostitute, not the other way around."

"I'm just that good."

"You've improved, then."

"Your manners haven't."

"That hurts, Lia."

"No, it doesn't."

He laughed. She hated his laugh, like he'd won the lottery on a stolen ticket.

"Listen, I've given the whole thing a lot of thought, and I've decided I don't want the money, kid."

"You don't want a million pounds?"

"Nah. I'm no blackmailer."

Lia didn't believe him for one second.

"All right," she said, and waited for the other shoe to drop. He dropped it very quietly.

"I'd rather just tell the papers about you. That's worth more than a fortune to me. Good night, Ophelia. See you tomorrow."

He rang off before she could get in a last word.

Lia stared at the phone in her hand.

That utter bastard.

She should have known. She absolutely should have known he would play her like this. He'd probably never even wanted the money from her. He just wanted to make her panic and scramble and beg, borrow and steal the money while he sat back and laughed and laughed.

Lia thought she might faint. Her lungs burned. She was dizzy. She sat down, still clutching her phone. She called August right away, before she could pass out.

He answered after two rings and she told him what David had told her.

"I don't know what to do," Lia said, eyes hot with tears. It felt like she had a hand around her throat, choking her. "What do I do? What should I—"

"Lia," August said, his voice sounding preternaturally calm. "Listen to me. Stop panicking."

"I can't. I can't. If he calls the papers, it'll be front-page news all over the country, probably the world. My brothers will get tortured at school. My parents will get ostracized. Georgy's family will never speak to her again. I—"

"I'll figure something out," he said. "Sit tight. I'll get it sorted. And please, don't panic."

"What should I do instead?" she demanded. Not panic? Like telling someone jumping off a bridge not to scream.

"The statue of Aphrodite in your room?" he suggested. "Say a prayer to her."

"You're joking, right?"

"I've never been more serious in my life."

"What…what am I supposed to pray for?"

"Ask her to help you."

"Why? What good will that do?"

"She won't listen to me," August said. "She might listen to you. Will you do it?"

How could she tell him no? She'd do anything for August, and she told him that.

"Thank you," he said.

"August, I'm scared."

"I know. But I'll protect you any way I can."

"Right," she said. "He comes at one of us, he comes at all of us."

August had said that Monday night when she told him she was being blackmailed.

"That's not why I'm helping you," he said.

"Then why are you?"

"You don't know?"

"No."

"I'll tell you next time I see you. Go pray. Please."

"I'll pray as hard as I can."

Lia hung up and immediately went into her bedroom.

Gogo sat up in his dog bed and gave her a curious worried stare. She wished she could reassure him but couldn't. Visions of headlines ran through her head. All the horrible jokes. The puns. The salacious details of a peer's daughter who started an illegal escort agency at age eighteen. Clients would be outed. People would lose marriages, jobs. Her friends would be mortified, humiliated, tossed out of their homes. She didn't even want to think about how her brothers would fare, away at school. Daddy would never be able to look her in the eyes again. Her mother would want to know why this was happening, and Lia wouldn't be able to tell her. Lia would have to stand there in silence and let her world crumble around her while David watched and laughed and patted himself on the back.

Nausea overwhelmed her. She wanted to throw up. She needed to throw up. But she wouldn't. She'd promised August, for some insane reason, that she would say a prayer to Aphrodite. And if she was doing it for August, she would do it right.

Lia gathered the candles. She knew she ought to offer something. Tradition and all that. She found the note from David that still had the lock of hair she'd cut and given him after he'd taken her virginity. According to myth, Artemis and Aphrodite were sisters and rivals. Maybe Aphrodite would appreciate having an offering that belonged to Artemis offered to her instead.

"This is mad," Lia said to herself as she lit the candles and arrayed them around the statue of Aphrodite. Surely this was just busywork August had given her, something to do to calm her down, to make her feel better or to shut her up for a few minutes so he could figure out how to help her. Even so, she picked up the lock of hair, and as she dipped it in the flame, she prayed her heart out.

"Aphrodite, goddess of love," Lia began, "please help me." After that Lia wasn't sure what else to say. "David used my love for him against me. A man who likes hurting women shouldn't be allowed to win, right? Um… I'll shut up now. I don't know what I'm doing or why I'm doing it, anyway. That's not true. I know exactly why I'm doing this. Because August asked me to. And I'm in love with him. So, please bless August, too, and keep him safe and happy… Amen."

Lia let the curl of gingerbread-colored hair burn to nothing.

And that was that.

But that wasn't that. That wasn't that at all.

A wind kicked up.

A gust of wind that rattled Lia's ancient windows, rattled and beat against them, beat against them until they finally blew open.

The wind rushed into the room and doused all four candles at once. The photos fell off the mantel. Her phone blew off her nightstand and onto the floor. Her lamp tipped over. Books blew open. Even Gogo looked windblown. He barked, but it wasn't a scared sound. He barked the way he did when he'd treed a squirrel. A bark of joy. Lia ran to the windows to try to force them to shut and latch, but the wind was too strong, so strong it blew the petals off the roses from the bouquet August had given her. The pink petals swirled around her dark bedroom.

Then it just…stopped.

Just like that.

Over.

The wind died, and Lia was able to get the windows closed.

She set her lamp upright and checked to make sure the candles had really gone out before they burned the whole place down.

When she had everything set to rights, she finally sat down in her grandmother's armchair. Gogo put his head in her lap and whimpered.

"Yeah, I don't know what the hell that was, either, boy." Whatever it was, it was terrifying, and Lia could do nothing but hold Gogo and pet him and comfort herself by comforting him.

About an hour later, her phone rang.

CHAPTER TWENTY-EIGHT

The call was from August. Lia answered immediately.
"August?"

"Can you come over right now? I have good news for you."

"Good news?"

"Very good news. You won't have to worry about David anymore."

Lia was so stunned she couldn't speak at first.

"What are you saying, August?"

"I'm saying your prayer worked."

He rang off, and in record time she was on the road to London.

Did she dare to hope August was right? What had he meant when he said it had been taken care of?

For the first time since getting her license, Lia wished she'd let her father buy her that Jag or an Audi or anything that went faster than a 1980 Metro. But finally, she turned onto August's street. She ran to the front and didn't bother to knock. August was expecting her, after all. She went in, calling out his name as she did.

"In the living room," August said.

Lia ran down the entry hall and burst into the living room—where she came to a quick stop when she saw August had company.

A woman stood by the fireplace, facing the mantel, her back to Lia. She was tall and elegant with enviable curves and thick black hair worn in a loose knot with tendrils galore trailing over her shoulder. She was dressed in a skirt suit of spring pink. A wrap of faux ermine was draped over one shoulder and one arm. *Venus in furs*...that was Lia's first thought as she looked at the woman, and she couldn't remember where that phrase came from—was it a book or was it a song?

August also wore a suit—three-piece gray with the jacket off and his sleeves rolled up. A suit? And the woman dressed so fashionably, as well? Lia wondered what the occasion was.

"So sorry," she said. "The door was open. I didn't mean to interrupt."

"You didn't," August said.

She waited in the doorway, afraid to go into the living room, afraid to leave. She kept waiting for the woman to turn around and greet her, but she didn't. Lia could only catch the smallest glimpse of her face, but she was a great beauty, that was obvious.

The woman said something then in a low sultry voice and August replied to her. They were speaking Greek, which Lia recognized but didn't understand. A great beauty. Greek. And powerful enough to make August nervous.

"You're August's mother," Lia said. "How do you do?"

The woman didn't answer. Perhaps she didn't speak English.

Lia looked at August for help. He smiled, but it wasn't a happy sort of smile.

"Lia," he said. "I had a talk with my mother. She's agreed to take care of your situation with David."

"What does that mean?"

"It's for the best if you don't know. Nothing illegal, though, I promise. But my mother has connections. She'll pay Mr. Bell a visit in the morning. You're not going to get arrested. You won't be in the papers. By tomorrow evening, it'll all be over. You can relax."

Lia wasn't relaxed, not at all.

"But how?"

"How will they do it?" August asked. "Like I said, nothing illegal. That's all you need to know."

"No." She lowered her voice. "How did you talk your family into helping me?"

August had been persona non grata in his family ever since he'd refused the marriage his mother had arranged. There was no way they'd do anything for him, not like this…not helping one of his patrons. They'd been so furious at him he'd had to change his name. How had he talked them into helping her?

Then Lia knew.

She knew exactly what August had done.

"You're getting married," Lia said to him.

He raised his hands in surrender, faked a smile. "I suppose I am."

"No, no." She shook her head. "You can't…not for me. You can't mean it. He doesn't mean it." Lia said that to his silent mother, who still had not turned to face her. "August…" Lia breathed. "No."

"Can you go and wait for me upstairs? We can talk in a few minutes. We can, can't we?" He asked that of his mother.

The woman nodded tersely, held up one finger. One fin-

ger meant one minute. That's all the time she would allow Lia
and August to be alone together. One minute to say goodbye.

Lia wanted to kill the woman. She wanted to strangle her
where she stood with her own ermine wrap.

This woman who was going to save Lia…

"It's not worth it," she said to August. "I'm not—"

"You are," August said softly. And then louder as if he
wanted to make sure his mother heard and understood. "You
are."

Her lips quivered, tears burned her eyes. She couldn't speak,
could only shake her head as if to deny it all.

"Please, Lia," he whispered. "Please go up and wait for me."

How could she say no to him? How could she not do anything he asked of her after he'd done this terrible, beautiful
thing for her?

She went upstairs to his office/bedroom. She stood by the
bed and did not move. For a long time, she simply stared at
the sheets they'd made love on, the pillows they'd slept on,
the Rose Kylix they'd drunk from…

"I will never see him again."

She knew that for a fact. August would come up the stairs
and enter the room and they would sit in the same chairs
they'd sat in on the day they'd made their deal, and he would
say he was sorry for hurting her. She would thank him for
helping her and he would thank her for understanding. Then
she would leave and go home and go to bed and she would
wake up tomorrow and the first thought in her mind would
be, *I will never see him again.*

If she were a little stronger, a little less well-bred, she'd have
beat on his chest and screamed in his face and told him he
was an idiot, a fool—that she would rather have spent the rest
of her life in hiding or in jail than to let him do this for her.
Hadn't he said he would rather die than give up his freedom?

It was all her fault. She'd told him too much. She'd told him how much David had hurt her and how scared she was for her friends and her brothers and her parents. Did he feel responsible for her now?

Lia heaved a quiet sob. Her guilt consumed her. She would give anything—her heart, her soul, her life—to go back in time, back to Pan's Island, back with August, and never leave.

Without thinking, Lia walked to August's bedside table and pulled the cork from the wine bottle. She poured not a sip, not a swallow, but a full glass of Syrah into the Rose Kylix, lifted it and drank.

Why? Because she couldn't bear the moment anymore. She couldn't bear her guilt and her love for August. She had to go away, disappear, be someone else, anyone else. She had to go back to Pan's Island one more time. Being there last night had healed her heart. Maybe it could work its magic on her again.

She didn't take her clothes off or lie on the bed. She sat instead in the armchair in front of August's stupid fish tank fireplace and watched the blue flames dance behind the glass. Those flames really did look like water, like ocean waves dancing to the tune of an evening storm. Lia stared at those waves, those waves, those endless dancing waves. She could hear them now, the waves rising and crashing, lapping at the stony shores of an ancient kingdom. She could see the blue waves and hear them rise and crash and now…now she could smell them, salt and copper.

Lightning struck Lia.

She gasped and opened her eyes.

This was not Pan's Island.

That was Lia's first thought when she awoke. But where was it? It took a moment for her eyes to adjust to the dark. Such deep dark that she knew she was in the past, in a world lit only by the moon, stars and torch fires. Luckily it was a bright night and a full moon, and soon Lia could make out her surroundings.

She was in a bedroom lying on a soft feather bed with a gauzy mosquito netting hanging overhead like a canopy. The walls were pale stone, the ceilings high and outside the large low window she saw the ocean.

Lia heard a voice. A male voice, soft and incoherent. She looked over, next to her, and saw a man sleeping. She wasn't afraid of the sleeping man, although he was naked in the bed. So was she. Somehow, she knew he belonged there more than she did. He wasn't unhandsome, simply older than she'd wanted in a husband.

Husband? Yes…that's who he was. Her husband. Brown hair with enough silver in it that she saw it shimmer in the moonlight. A close-cropped beard. A broad back and shoulders, strong arms, the rough hands of a man who held the reins of a team of horses every day, and the reins of a kingdom.

Lia pressed her hands between her legs and touched herself. She felt fresh semen dripping out of her body onto the linen sheets.

What was she doing here?

And who was she?

It seemed she should know but she couldn't…it was on the tip of her tongue, but without August here as a guide, she was lost.

She would simply close her eyes and wait for morning. She thought if she fell asleep, when she woke up she would be back where she belonged, wherever that was. Where was that again? She couldn't remember. Didn't matter. Wherever she'd come from, she must not have liked it much if she'd left it. She settled back into the bed, next to her sleeping husband, and closed her eyes.

Thunder.

Lia gasped and sat up in bed. Was there a storm? She reached out to wake her husband, but then she saw something.

A woman stood by the window, the large square stone window, and stared out at the ocean. She was tall and extraordinarily beautiful. Her bearing was noble, imperious, almost military in her white gown overlaid with a thick leather breastplate and a sword sheathed on her hip. Whoever she was, she was no servant. Whoever she was, Lia must greet her. All strangers in this kingdom must be greeted as if they were gods traveling in disguise.

Lia slipped from the bed and wrapped a sheet around her naked body as she approached the waiting woman.

"My lady," she said. "Who are you and what brings you to my chamber? Tell me so that I might make you most welcome."

"You carry a son inside you," the woman said, not meeting Lia's eyes.

"A son?" she repeated. So soon? She'd been married only a few hours.

"Are you not pleased?"

"Too pleased for words," Lia said. "But how do you know?"

"It is my place to know and tell and yours to hear and believe."

"I do hear. I do believe. But…who are you?"

The woman at last turned her face from the ocean to look upon Lia. Her eyes were the gray of dove's wings.

"Pallas Athena," the woman whispered.

Lia gasped and sank to her knees.

The woman stepped close and Lia rested her head against a thigh as strong as marble.

"Your piety is pleasing to me," Athena said, and she touched her fingertips to Lia's hair. "I will bless the child you carry."

"Thank you, great lady," Lia said.

"Your son was conceived within a stone's throw of the ocean. He should be a great seafarer. Salt water shall flow in his veins. His name will rise like the tide but never retreat."

Lia looked up at the goddess.

"Bless you, my lady."

"Go," Athena said. "Go now to the temple if you wish to claim this blessing for your child. Go now and offer a sacrifice, and your son's name will be remembered for eons as the greatest of all the heroes of Athens."

Then Athena was gone.

Lia did not hesitate to obey. She rose from her knees and found her discarded gown on the floor by the bed where her new husband had tossed it.

She dressed quickly. Barefoot—she had no time to lace her sandals—she slipped from her bridal chamber. Her naked feet made no sound on the stone floors as she ran down the long dark hallways. She found the door that led to the stable yard and slipped out of it. She could not be stopped. Even if her father or her husband found her now, she would run away from them. Not even a king's command could outrank a god's.

Once free of the palace grounds, she had only to take the cobblestone path to the temple. She saw it a mere half mile away, white as a dove in the moonlight. Lia felt Athena's protection around her as she made her way down the path. Her feet struck no rocks. She encountered no bandits or brigands. And though it was clear a storm was brewing, the rising winds pushed her on like a ship at full sail. She reached the temple so swiftly she wondered if she'd been carried part of the way by the winged feet of Hermes.

Like every temple in the known world, the entrance faced the rising sun, but it was hours until dawn. Surrounded by a shroud of night, Lia climbed the cool marble stairs. She found a brazier left to smolder by night and lit a torch with the remnants of the fire. By her small fire she found her way to the altar. Warm air rose from between the tiles of the temple floor, tickling her feet and setting her skin to shiver.

She lit a fire at the feet of the statue of Athena and knelt before it to pray.

At your command, Athena, I have come to your temple. Bless my son with your good blessings.

Even as she thought those prayers, Lia wondered why... Why was she here? Why was she praying? Why was this happening?

She wasn't married. She wasn't pregnant. She was Lia Godwick, and she shouldn't be here. She went and stood at the western-most end of the temple.

Water.

Not down below the cliffs where the water belonged. No. The water had risen ten...twenty...fifty feet high.

The tide was rising higher than she'd ever seen it rise before, and if it kept rising, soon it would make an island of the temple and then wash it away.

In terror she sank to her knees, offered a thousand wordless prayers to Athena and any god who would hear her. In the black sky, Zeus made himself known with bolt after bolt of jagged lightning. The temple slowly began to shake as if Hades, deep below the earth, were holding tight to the pillars that held the world steady and shaking them.

And still the water rose.

She ran to the northern edge of the temple.

Water.

She ran to the southern side.

Water.

She ran to flee from the eastern entrance where surely the water hadn't risen yet.

Water.

Water.

Water.

Athena, she prayed silently. *Is this the blessing you offered me? The blessing of death? Speak to Poseidon, beseech him on my behalf to be merciful. Tell him I carry a child who I will dedicate to his service if he will spare us death this night at his hands.*

She spun in a circle, in a panic, helpless and desperate.

The temple trembled again.

Before warm air had escaped through the cracks and tickled her like the gentle hot breath of August's kisses.

Now the cracks between the tiles steamed.

And there in the archway next to the altar of Athena where Lia had knelt to pray…stood a man.

But not a man, for no man she had ever seen looked like this man.

Lia's eyes widened at the sight of him, looming in the arch, filling both its width and its height, though that meant the man had to be seven feet tall at least.

He stepped into the temple.

Water surged and steamed around his feet.

Lia saw it steam, saw the steam rise, watched it rise from his ankles to his mighty thighs, past his massive muscled stomach, huge broad chest and all the way to his head. Iron-colored hair down to his shoulders. A thick gray beard.

Eyes like the fathomless sea…

She stood rooted into place, frozen, unable to scream or speak or move. She could not blink. Her lips trembled. She could faint any moment.

He stepped toward her, rivulets of water running down his naked body from chest to stomach, down impossibly long thighs.

He towered over her, gazed down upon her.

"You called me by name," he said, his voice the low rumble of ocean waves.

"Poseidon," she whispered.

He stretched out his hand, his enormous mighty hand, and touched her cheek.

He was so large it seemed impossible he could be anything but a statue come to life, but when he touched her cheek he was warm, made of flesh, if not human then more than human.

Her skin burned where he touched her. All around her the temple floor steamed and breathed with wet heat. Lia knew she should run away, run anywhere, run nowhere, but run. Yet her feet remained rooted in place. Distantly she recalled she had a husband in her bed and that she must return to him. But she couldn't move. She was Poseidon's slave. But not from fear or force, but desire.

He was magnificent.

So she stayed.

And he touched her more.

Both hands came up to her face, his fingertips stroking her from her neck under her ears to her lips and again. His touch tingled with lightning. She shivered, and the hairs on her arms rose. She felt so insignificant standing before him, so small in comparison to his enormity that she might as well have been a child. But she didn't feel the fear of a child, a child's horror of seeing a naked male form in front of her, but a woman's hunger.

As he touched her face, she told herself this was simply another dance in a dreamworld so she had no reason to be afraid. Might as well enjoy it while it lasted, until she woke up from this impossible dream.

The thick long fingers of his enormous hands lightly stroked her parted lips. He pressed a fingertip, only one, into her mouth and touched the tip of her tongue. She allowed it. She would allow him everything. A drop of water slid from his earlobe and dropped to his chest. She watched it run over the hulking pectoral muscles and into the ridges of his stomach. Everything, yes. She would allow him everything. How could she not?

She a mortal and he a god?

Lia looked up and met his eyes. He studied her face like a jeweler examined a diamond, seeking out the flaws, but finding none. He ran his fingers through her hair, grasped it gently and pulled it to bare her throat to him. She was a rag doll in his hands, small and helpless and limp. Even his lightest touch overwhelmed her. He could have lifted her with one hand.

With her throat bared, he bent down low and pressed his nose against her skin, inhaling her scent. In the steaming heat of the temple, in her terror and desire, she had begun to sweat. Salt water glistened on her skin. The scent seemed to please him like a perfume. He pressed in closer to her, inhaled her scent again. But it was not all he did to her. Before she knew it had happened, he'd found the knotted belt around her waist and untied it. He didn't bother with the ties at her shoulders. He simply pulled, and the gown came off her body, puddling at her ankles.

She wished he would speak to her and was grateful when he didn't. What could he say to calm her hammering heart? What could she hear that would make this encounter any less strange or terrifying?

Nothing.

He placed his hands on her shoulders and pushed her to her knees.

Of course she should kneel before him, he a god and she a mortal.

And of course he should push the head of his enormous

organ into her mouth. The head was all her mouth could take. She wrapped both hands around the shaft—solid as marble— and held and squeezed it. She was well aware of his huge solemn eyes watching her as she sucked him. Did she even please him with what she did? Was this about pleasure for him? Or did he want her obedience?

Or did he want her worship?

Or her love?

The immense tip of his cock strained her mouth. Her jaw ached around it, but she had no desire to stop her work. To simply kneel and stroke the great length and breadth of his cock was divine. He towered over her. She understood prayer now, the desire to kneel before immensity and to please the great being with her kneeling.

Without so much as a shudder or a sigh, he released into her mouth and she swallowed what he released, tasting the salt and finding it sweet to her tongue. A god's semen would be sweet, wouldn't it? And when it was done, she already craved more.

It was nothing for him to reach down to her, to cup her head and caress her face. Her hands were still around his cock, and he took both of them into one of his and lifted her off her feet, lifted her easily until she stood with her back arched and breasts thrusting forward. She hung from his great left hand as if from a hook while his mighty right hand made a survey of her body.

Poseidon took each breast in his palm and held it a moment, squeezed it and released it. He swept his large palm over her quivering stomach, up and down her arching back and bottom, down her thighs and up again. Then the moment came she'd known would happen. His long thick fingers, large as a normal mortal man's cock, spread the lips of her vulva and pushed into her vagina. She didn't cry out but she whimpered. His touch was probing, searching. She wondered if he was measuring her inside, to see if he could take her and she him. On the fulcrum of his fingers, he pivoted her this way and that as he explored the wet inner chamber of her body. He turned his hand to force her hips to tilt forward and her vagina contracted around his fingers and she cried out from the sudden shock of pleasure.

She thought she saw him smile, but just the once and then it was gone before she could be sure she'd seen it. But she must have pleased him. He withdrew his fingers from her vagina and took her around the waist with both hands. His hand span was as wide as her waist and he again lifted her effortlessly off her feet. At once, she put her hands on his shoulders and her legs around his waist as he brought her down onto his cock.

She cried out, a sound that the whole kingdom must have heard as he pressed the enormous head of the granite organ into her body—the tip alone, for it was all she could take at first. But he was no more content with that than she. He lifted and lowered her, lifted and lowered her, as she pushed and pulsed her hips until she opened enough to take the length of it inside her.

His huge hands slid up her back—one hand cradled her head and neck, the other arm and hand supported her back.

She released her desperate hold on his shoulders and hung limp in his arms, impaled on the massive organ that speared her. When he lowered his great head to her breasts, she dug her fingers into his wet hair. His vast mouth encircled her breast, enveloped it, sucked it into the hot slick cavern, and his rough tongue sought her nipple and lapped at it endlessly as she hung in his grasp, split open on his cock.

It was bliss, the purest mindless bliss, to be held in his enormous arms, sucked and penetrated to the deepest parts of her. It seemed hours passed while she was suspended off the ground, in his grasp, as the organ inside her made slow and deep inroads until it had filled her as completely as her body could be filled without bursting at the seams.

Lia could do nothing but pant, and pant she did, as wave after wave of pleasure rolled over and through her. It would take nothing to make her come, almost nothing. What it did take, finally, was one thrust. One sharp thrust of his cock into her, and the gratified grunt of the god who coupled with her. Her body exploded with deep delicious spasms, and as she came, the god released his seed into her—thick, scalding waves of fluid that he poured into her so hard she could feel each fresh rush against her shuddering cervix.

After her climax, she lay still as a corpse in his mighty hands. Her breasts throbbed, swollen as they were from the intense suckling of his mouth, and her vagina pulsed around the shaft that still filled her.

But was he done with her?

No. He had only begun to school her on what it meant to give oneself to a god.

Still holding her, he went slowly to his knees and brought her back down to the floor. Delicious warm water encircled them as they copulated again. She was allowed movement now and she braced her feet on the floor to lift her hips in offering. His stony expression began to crumble as they made rough love. Sounds escaped his lips. Desire hooded his dark eyes and turned them glassy. The whole of her sex—her vulva and vagina, clitoris and cervix—all throbbed with one heartbeat around his organ. She couldn't believe she could take so much into her. She rolled up a little and touched the tender flesh where he was joined to her and wrapped her hands again around the impossibly thick shaft. She measured him as he measured her. Even fully and completely embedded in her, she could take little more than half his length. She wanted every inch of it but knew he'd have to open her womb to fit it in, and he seemed content with what he could get of her.

As he rammed her with his cock, she gazed upon his body with adoration. The tendons in his arms moved and strained, as did the veins in his neck. His body was a mountain, his chest the cliff face, his shoulders like peaks and his head the snowcapped summit. Beautiful god...not less human in his goodness but more...more...taller and stronger, with a man's eyes and a man's hungers but a thousand times more virile than any mortal man.

"Lovely," she whispered, and he laughed at her praise, rewarded it with a fresh burst of seed into her womb. She felt it, the thick hot fluid as it filled her and filled her. She sensed a quickening deep inside her, like lightning inside her belly. His godseed invaded her womb and staked its claim there.

"Yes," he said into her ear. "Your son will be my son."

So this was Athena's blessing...her son would be a great hero with salt water in his veins. Athena had sent Poseidon to her in this temple, to claim the child already in her womb. And what would she say to that, to a god who would deign to bless the mortal seed of a mortal man and his mortal bride?

"Thank you, my lord."

"You will tell your husband whose seed made your son great," he said.

"I will."

"And you will tell him you were more a wife to me than you were to him."

His arrogant laugh filled the temple, and the mighty and terrible god began to thrust into her again.

He wrapped his arms around her back and hips and lifted her from the floor. Her legs were spread out over his massive thighs. Again and again he lifted and lowered her, spearing her on his iron-hard organ. She arched back and offered her breasts to him, which he roughly suckled, pulling the tender tips into his mouth and lavishing them with his tongue. Pleasure swept over her in wave after wave. She couldn't stop her climaxes even if she'd wanted to. They were too powerful and there were too many of them.

She whimpered when he withdrew his cock from the wet cleft he'd been penetrating for what felt like hours. But she found he was not done with her, merely moving her for his own pleasure. He put her on her hands and knees and spread her thighs. With one smooth, long stroke, he speared her again. Her back bent and her head lifted like a supplicant in prayer. He ran his hands up her back and around her body to take her breasts in his hands. He held them in his palms as he pumped into her. The feeling went beyond pleasure into sheer obliterating sensation. She felt everything, and she felt it all at once—the humbling of being used, the fullness of the enormous organ in her as it pumped and spurted into the core of her. The god wrapped his arm around her and pressed his chest against her back. She was overtaken, he dwarfed her; her much smaller body disappeared beneath his. At last she released the cry that had been building inside her since her first sight of him looming naked and erect in the archway.

The god who impaled her did not scream. But like the ocean he ruled, he roared as he emptied himself into her for a final time.

She hung limp in his arms. He remained embedded in her, his nose to the back of her neck, breathing deep the scent of their coupling.

It was over. She knew it was over. She knew he would release her and she would be forced to stumble in her torn gown from the temple back to the palace, and she would return to her marriage bed still wet with his seed.

And for the rest of her life she would carry the memory

of this insane encounter in the temple of Athena. Every time her husband touched her, she would remember that a god had once touched her there. When her husband gave her pleasure, it would pale in comparison to the pleasure given to her by this god. She would mourn the memory of this night until her death and, by this god, she would tell everyone who the true father of her son was—even if it brought shame upon her and made her own husband abandon her and their child.

No.

She would not allow it.

"Take me with you," she said to Poseidon.

"Where I go you cannot come," he said as he withdrew from her body. She was too empty without him inside her.

"Take me with you," she said again. She turned over and faced him. She spread her legs for him, let him see the seed he'd spilled inside her. "Take me with you, as a bride or concubine or even a slave. It is no matter to me. But I cannot go back. How can I live the rest of my life seeing the world by candlelight now that you have shown me the sun? How can I spend the rest of my life drinking from a thimble when you have shown me the ocean? How can you send me back to the bed of a mortal man when you have taken me in a temple? No god would be so cruel."

"It would be crueler to take you from all you've ever known."

"I would rather have a god's cruelty than a mortal's love."

Slowly the regal head nodded.

Without a word, the god Poseidon lifted her from the floor and held her to his chest. He strode purposefully to the westernmost end of the temple. The tide had risen so high that water pooled at the feet of Athena and all the burnt offerings were extinguished. He stepped from the temple directly into the water. The sea surrounded her at once.

Passion fled. Panic took its place, seizing her heart as Poseidon has seized her body.

What had she done? The shore receded in the distance and the world was nothing but black water. She screamed in terror, but the water muffled the sound. Would she drown? Would she die? Was this the cruelty Poseidon had offered her? Would she close her eyes and wake again in the kingdom of Hades?

She squirmed in Poseidon's grasp, but he did not release her. She beat against his shoulders, pounded her fists into his hands. It was like trying to raze a forest using a feather.

A heavy current surrounded them and lifted them to the surface. The white cap of a wave broke over Lia's head and she tasted air. She was going to die if he took her down again. She had one chance to save herself. No one could best a god except, perhaps, another god. What god would she call upon? Athena, who had sent her to the temple? Zeus, who would take any chance to best one of his brothers? Aphrodite, who would take any chance to spite one of her sisters?

Lia filled her lungs with air and cried out a name in prayer. "Eros!"

She cried out to Eros, for Eros alone would understand the desire that had driven her mad. Had he heard her cry? Would he help her?

Something flew past her head and into the water.

Something long and sharp and vicious, tipped with sharp stone and poison.

An arrow.

She looked up and there on the rocky ledge of the cliff stood a man.

No, not a man. A god. White wings sprang from his shoulders and spread twenty feet wide. He was all sinew and muscle and pure concentration. He held a mighty bow in his mighty hands. He notched an arrow and pulled back the string.

He let it go and it struck home, right in Poseidon's back. The god of the seas cried out and blood bubbled in the waves, turning them red. He would not die from the wound, but he did let her go so that he could tear the arrow from his shoulder.

Lia swam away from him as fast as she could. Waves crashed over her again, but she fought them until her strength failed her. Her arms were leaden and her lungs burned. She was a mortal girl, not a goddess. Eros had saved her from Poseidon for nothing.

She began to sink again, deep, deep into the cold black sea. As she faded, the last of the life leaving her body, she thought of her mother and she wished she had kissed her goodbye and told her how much she loved her.

"Lia, Lia..."

She knew she was dying or already dead, because an angel hovered over her. Had to be an angel. What other creature had white wings with a twenty-foot span that shimmered like silver in the dawn light?

"Lia? Lia, it's me. Speak, Lia. Breathe... You have to breathe. If you die in this world, you'll die in the other."

Die? Wasn't she already dead? Her eyes slowly focused.

Olive skin, boyish smile, eyes the color of a storm-wild sky.

"August..." she breathed. "I thought you were an angel. You had the most beautiful wings."

The world went black.

CHAPTER TWENTY-NINE

Lia wasn't dead. She knew that for certain. After a few breaths, a few blinks, she saw she was back in August's bedroom, on his bed, and August held her in his arms. He was rocking her slowly, speaking softly in Greek. He touched her chest, felt her heartbeat, kissed her face, her forehead, her hair, a thousand times.

"August?"

"Lia…" he breathed. "I thought I lost you. I couldn't find you anywhere. I've never been that scared. I would rather lose me than you. I would rather lose the whole world."

"I have to…" She took a ragged breath. Her entire body ached like she'd been slammed against a wall. "I have to sit up."

Carefully he held her into a seated position. She swung her legs off the bed and rubbed her forehead.

"Are you all right?" August asked, and before she could answer he pressed a glass of water into her hands. It shook so hard she almost spilled it, but he steadied it and brought it to her lips. She drank deeply, and when she'd finished, she felt better. Not good. But better.

"What happened?" she asked.

"You tell me," he said. "I came up here and you were out cold, and I had no idea where you had gone. I told you never to drink from the kylix alone. You could have died, Lia."

"Died?"

"When the mind dies, the body dies," August said. "If you hadn't shouted my name, I would never have found you in time."

He ran his hand through her hair, kissed her temple. She felt him shudder. Had he been more scared for her than she was for herself?

"But I didn't…"

"What?"

"Nothing." She didn't remember shouting August's name, but apparently she had.

"Where were you?" He took her face in his hands. "Why was Poseidon trying to drown you?"

Lia couldn't bear to be touched anymore. She pushed his hands aside and staggered to one of the club chairs.

"Sit," she said. "Please?"

She pointed at the chair opposite her. He sat on the floor at her feet.

Typical.

"Lia, talk to me," he said.

"I had been talking to Mum this evening about the story of Aethra and Poseidon. It was on my mind, I suppose. I meant to go back to Pan's Island. I ended up getting shagged in a temple by Poseidon. Oops."

"I warned you the cup was dangerous."

"Right," she said. "Don't play with a god's toy without permission. Never again. Promise."

"How was the sex, though?"

"Not half-bad." Classic understatement.

"Good girl," he said. "If you're going to get swept up in one of your own erotic fantasies and nearly die doing it, you might as well enjoy some top-notch cock first." August laughed. He laughed until she thought he might cry.

He picked up a book off the other chair and showed her a picture. "That's what I had planned for us tonight." He'd chosen the famous painting of Zeus visiting Danaë in the form of a shower of liquid gold.

"Good choice," Lia said. "I always wondered what it would be like to have sex with a precious mineral in liquid form."

"Liquid gold can hit all those hard to reach places."

"Sounds fun. Too bad we can't…"

Lia blinked, and a tear ran down her cheek. She hastily wiped it away.

"I should go home. I shouldn't be here with you anymore. It's not right. You're engaged."

"We're allowed to talk," he said.

"Allowed. We're *allowed* to talk. That's nice of them to let you talk to me," she said, meeting his eyes. "How could you? You didn't even ask me what I wanted."

He looked sad but not guilty. "I didn't think I could tell you no," he said, hanging his head between his knees for a moment. "If you'd begged me not to do it, I would have given in just to please you. And your safety is more important than your happiness."

He looked back up at her.

"Forget about me," Lia begged. "You said you would rather die than bend your knee to your parents, than give up your freedom and your life here to marry a woman you don't know, like or love. And now you're doing it."

"I was being selfish and stupid when I said that," he said. "I cared only about me and my feelings and my freedom. Then I took you to the island and the way you looked at Pan and the way you looked at me... I saw you there in that sacred grove in that white dress with tears running down your face, and I thought my heart would burst from love. I would have married you in that grove, built you a palace of gold or a cottage of river stone, and we would have lived there and loved there until the end of days."

"Marry me? Because I got weepy when you put me inside my favorite book?"

"Because I love you, Lia," he said as if it were the most obvious thing in the world. "And I'm not afraid to tell you that here and now in the real world with you standing in front of me."

"You love me?"

"Yes," he said, then louder, "yes. I love you."

She laughed. "Why? I'm surly."

"Charmingly surly."

"I'm bitter."

"Tart."

"I'm a kitten with a switchblade," she said, weeping openly now.

"I like kittens. I'm not afraid of your switchblade."

Lia slowly stood up. She picked up her bag and slung it over her shoulder. She was still shaky but steady enough to walk and see and drive home.

"I should go."

August came to his feet, and when it seemed inevitable that he'd try to hold her one last time, she held up her hand to warn him away.

"You're engaged," she said. "For the sake of whoever she is, please don't touch me. Enough girls have gotten their hearts broken this week. Let's not throw another on the pile, all right?"

"I don't even know who she is. She might not even be a girl. Could be a nymph. A satyr. A fawn."

"A cloud?"

"Could be a cloud," he said.

"Whoever it is, they're still your fiancée. You should respect that."

"Prissiest madam ever," he said. "I'm sure my cloud and I will be very happy together."

"You are?"

"No," he said. She appreciated his honesty.

"I don't think you'll believe me but it's true… I hope you're very happy. You made me very happy, happier than I ever thought I could be again."

"You do love me, don't you, Lia?" he asked, his voice almost breaking on her name. "Even a little?"

She looked at him and shook her head, not to say no, but so he'd know what an idiot he was being asking her that.

"Of course," she said. "Of course I love you, August. Of course I do."

Lia started to leave again. She made it as far as the door where she turned around and looked back at him. One last look. One last smile.

"I'll never see you again, will I?" she asked.

"No," he said. "When I go back, it'll be for good."

She nodded. "You can have the Rose Kylix," she said. "You can keep it, I mean. I'm giving it to you, no million pounds necessary. You should have it. It belongs to your people."

"Too nice for your own good." He tried to laugh but it didn't come out quite right. "Lia," he said. Just Lia, her name.

"I'll, um…" she began, but stopped when her words caught

in her throat. She took a deep breath. She would not fall apart. She would not. What she had to say was too important.

"I will remember our trip to Pan's Island as long as I live," she said. "I'll remember that beautiful thing you did for me. When I'm so old I don't even remember my own name, I'll remember..." She heaved a sob.

"What, Lia?" August asked. Tears streamed down his face, his lovely beloved face.

"You," she said. "I'll remember you, August Bowman. If that is your real name."

"It's not," he said.

"Too bad," she said. "It's a very nice name."

She smiled one more time.

Then she left.

PART SEVEN

Danaë & Zeus

CHAPTER THIRTY

L ia didn't cry all the way home. A small miracle, but she
    was grateful for it. If she came home crying, her mother
might see, and if her mother saw, she'd want to know why.
As fragile as Lia was feeling, she knew she'd tell Mum everything. No, she would go home and take a long hot bath and
go to bed and sleep for a couple days. And when she woke up,
she'd get on with her life, because what else was there to do?

By the time Lia made it home, it was nearly ten. She must
have lost a very long time in the fantasy world of Aethra and
Poseidon. Usually after her jaunts with August, she'd felt high
as a kite—happy and carefree, fearless and free. Not tonight.
How unfair… August had to go and get engaged to some random girl. What a buzzkill.

See? She was making jokes about this awful situation already. Such a good English girl. Stiff upper lip. Never surrender. Keep calm and carry on. Churchill would be so proud of her.

Lia parked in front of the house and went in the front entrance, too tired and dejected and cold to bother hiding the fact she'd gone out. As she walked past the music room on her left, she heard laughter.

Her mother's laugh, like she'd just been pinched in a tender spot.

Her father's laugh, like he'd won a hand of poker and was raking in the chips.

And another laugh, like a man who'd just gotten away with murder.

David.

CHAPTER THIRTY-ONE

That bastard was here.

Too furious to be afraid, Lia walked into the music room and found her mother standing by the sofa, pouring David a glass of red wine while her father sat back in an armchair, nursing a Scotch on the rocks.

Her mother looked up when Lia came in, and her father grinned.

"There's our girl now," her father said. "Come in, love. Say hello to David. We were just telling him about how good you'd gotten at your weaving."

"Lia," David said. He wore dark jeans, a black jacket and a T-shirt splattered with paint. "Great to see you, kid."

"Two for eight."

"What?" David's brow furrowed.

"Two T-shirts for eight pounds at Tesco," Lia said. "You have paint on yours."

He chuckled a mad king's chuckle. "Right. I should get some new shirts. I'm always so busy, I forget to do it." He grinned up at her mother. "Mona, sit. I can pour my own wine."

He patted the seat on the sofa next to him, and Mum sat there.

David put his arm on the back of the sofa, just behind her mother. Lia mentally murdered him with a railway spike through the head.

"Where's Gogo?" she asked. He usually curled up with her mother when Lia wasn't home.

"Had to put him outside," her father said. "Wouldn't stop barking at David. You know how strangers make him nervous."

"August didn't make him nervous," Lia said. "He loved August from first sniff."

"Who's August?" David asked, grinning behind his wineglass.

"Lia's boyfriend," Mum said in a conspiratorial whisper.

"August and I broke up tonight." David's fault. She looked at him so he'd know that. So he'd know and be afraid of her. And if he wasn't afraid yet, he would be soon.

"Oh, sweetheart. I'm so sorry," her mother said.

"It's fine." It was not fine.

"Sorry, darling," Daddy said. She appreciated that he'd managed to say that without smiling.

"Tough break, kid," David said. "I've been there myself. Why don't you have a drink with us? You'll feel better."

Then he dropped his arm around her mother's shoulders.

Had it been any other man—any of her father's friends or

mother's friends or even the bloody plumber—Lia would have let it go. But it was David.

Lia wasn't about to let that go.

"Get your fucking hands off my mother."

"Lia!" Mum said. David raised his hands in mock surrender. Only August was allowed to mock her.

And August was gone.

"Rough night," David said to her mother. "She's allowed to be in a bad mood."

"I don't think so." Her mother glared at her. "Lia, let's give the bad attitude a second thought, shall we?"

"This isn't attitude, Mother. I have to tell you something."

"You sure you don't wanna go to bed, Lia?" David asked. "Rough night and everything?"

She saw it. A flash. A tiny spark of fear in his eyes. He'd been counting on her not telling her mother they'd slept together. He'd been banking on it. He'd been so certain that Lia was more noble than he was…

Well, he was wrong.

"David and I had sex when I was seventeen, Mum. That's why he ran away from England. I told him to go after I found out he'd slept with you, too, the night after he had me."

"What?" Her mother spun and faced David as her father came to his feet.

"That's not true," David said, almost sputtering in his fury. "You know it isn't true. I would never…" He stood up and pointed at Lia. "She was obsessed with me. She told me so. I told her I wasn't interested. She told me I had to leave the country or she'd tell you all I'd raped her."

Her mother rose from the sofa and slapped him.

Slapped him. Just like that. One hard beautiful slap right across the cheek.

Guess her mother didn't believe David's story.

And her father sure as hell didn't.

"You hurt my daughter?" he said. Not said so much as *roared*. A good old English roar.

"You both need to calm down." David had his hands up now, not in mock surrender anymore. "You don't want to make this ugly."

"I'll show you ugly when I'm done beating your face into a bloody pulp," Daddy said as he approached David with murder in his eyes. "You're twenty years older than she is. You were a guest in our house. We put a roof over your head. We paid you a fortune for that mural you didn't bother finishing and that's how you repay us? By hurting our daughter?"

Her father grabbed David by the shirt.

"Daddy, stop it!" Lia screamed. She couldn't bear the thought of her father going to jail for attempted murder. "Stop it right now. He's not worth it."

"It's worth it to me," he said, looking at her with so much pity it ached.

"She's the sane one in the room," David said. "You do not want to get on my bad side here, okay? I can make life very difficult for all of you."

"What's he talking about?" her father asked. "Lia? What the hell is he saying? What's going on?"

She saw David inching toward the door as if to make a break for it. Her father grabbed him again by the shirt and pushed him against the wall, not hitting him, but holding him there.

"I can have you arrested for this," David said.

"Shut it," her father said. "Lia, talk. Now."

"Daddy, listen. Mum…I'm sorry. I'm not sorry about what I've done, but I'm sorry it's taken me so long to tell you. I was in love with David and I did flirt with him and I did tell him I was in love with him, that's true. He came to my room that night and we slept together. And the next night, I saw him with you, Mum."

"Oh, Lia…" Her mother's eyes swam with tears.

"It's okay, Mummy," she assured her. "It's not your fault. You didn't know. He knew." She pointed at David. "He was using us both because he could. I was so angry and hurt that I told him he had to leave the house and never see you all again or I'd tell you we'd had sex. I never said I would tell you he'd raped me. You know I never would do that." She'd never even considered doing something like that.

"Of course we know that, angel," her mother said in the same tone Lia had said to August, *Of course I love you.*

"Angel?" David repeated. Her father shook him a little. Lia didn't try to stop him.

"I wrote him a note and promised him if he left and never spoke to you all again, I would never tell you what he did to me," Lia said. "I knew you'd blame yourself, Mum. I knew you'd be heartbroken, and I didn't want you paying for what he did."

"Sweetheart, I'm your mother. You always have to tell me things like this. You have to. You just… You're my child. I protect you. You don't protect me."

"And I protect the both of you," her father said. "I'm going to throw this bastard out on his head and make sure he never steps foot in this country ever again."

"You don't want to do that," David said. "You absolutely do not want to do that."

"And why is that?" Daddy demanded.

"Because he knows something about me," Lia said with a heavy sigh. "He knows I did something illegal."

"Who hasn't?" her father asked. "What did you do? Slap a bobby? Steal the crown jewels?"

"Since I was eighteen I've been running a sort of…escort

service with my friends," Lia said. "Well, not sort of. I've definitely been running an illegal escort agency with my friends.
I handle all the arrangements. They're the, you know, the service providers. A few of your friends are clients."

"My friends? Who?"

Lia saw the fire in his eyes. No time to be discreet when
her father was ten seconds away from either a murder or a
coronary.

"Um… Xavier Lloyd. Jack Raymond. Derek Jones. Lord
Pomeroy. Should I go on?" Her father's attorney. A billion-
aire investor. An art gallery owner. An old friend of her father's from Eton.

"I think that's more than enough," her father said.

"David found out and he told me I had to give him a million pounds to make up for the commissions he had to cancel
because of me, or else he'd expose me," Lia said. "But when
I was ready to pay him, he said he didn't want the money. He
just wanted to tell the world."

It was shockingly easy to tell her parents the truth. It all
just came out in a big whoosh of words.

"You got those commissions because of me," her father
said to David, then shook him a little again. "This is how you
thank me? Hurting my wife? Hurting my child?"

"Lia," her mother said. "Go to your room and wait for us.
We're going to have a little talk with David."

"There's no point," David said. "You know you aren't going
to kill me. And trust me, even if you do—which you won't—I
have friends who will make sure the truth still gets out about
her. I'm not an idiot. I've got my ass covered."

"We'll see about that," her father said. "Lia, you heard your
mother. Go."

"Please don't hurt him, Daddy," Lia said. "Not for his sake,
but for yours and mine."

"Do as you're told," her father said.

Lia did as she was told.

She would have stayed and listened at the door, but she didn't have the heart for it. Once she'd said it all, the fury went out of her and she was left with nothing but the terrible need to tell August what had happened.

She got to her bedroom and dug her phone out of her bag. Maybe…just maybe, if she got to August in time, she could tell him she didn't need his mother's help anymore. She'd already told her parents. They knew everything. They were with David right now, and her father was either going to beat some sense into David or bribe him into silence. Lia would believe either of Daddy in the mood he was in. But whatever happened, at least now there was the tiniest chance she could keep August from having to get married and give up his freedom to some girl—or fawn or cloud—he'd never met.

She called his number and put the phone to her ear.

Immediately she heard a strange tone followed by, "This number is no longer in service."

Lia held out her hand and stared at the phone.

She was too late.

He'd told her his parents were powerful. They must be some of the richest, most powerful people in the world if they could shut down August's life that quickly. He was probably on an airplane at that very moment, heading toward Greece or Cyprus or a yacht on the Mediterranean. There were probably already movers in his house, packing up his things so that by tomorrow morning the existence of "August Bowman, sacred prostitute of Eros" would be completely erased.

Lia dropped her phone and rested her head on the fireplace mantel.

She'd ruined August's life and hurt her parents, and all for nothing. For nothing at all.

Lia raised her head and the first thing she saw was her statue of Aphrodite, sitting so pretty and placid on her mantel.

She grabbed the statue and threw it into the fireplace grate where it shattered into four pieces.

"That wasn't very nice."

Lia spun around.

A woman sat in her grandmother's armchair, a woman in pink with a stole wrapped around her arms. She had a perfume bottle in her hands and was spritzing herself.

Lia knew that perfume, that scent. Hermès.

And she knew that woman, too.

"You're August's mother. How did you get into my room?"

"Oh," the woman said as she rose to her feet and then... began to float two feet above the floor. A crown of roses sprouted on her regal head. "I have my ways."

"Oh my God," Lia breathed.

"Oh your goddess, you mean. Aphrodite. Very pleased to formally make your acquaintance, my dear."

CHAPTER THIRTY-TWO

Lia didn't faint, though she wished she could.

The woman, Aphrodite, came back down to her feet with a smile.

"Do you want to check me for wires?" she asked.

Her voice tinkled like wind chimes in a spring breeze.

"No," Lia said. "That's fine." She was backing away, backing…backing…until she could back away no farther. Her back was to the door.

"You're having a bad day. I'm sorry, darling," the woman said.

"You…you said you're Aphrodite."

"Yes." She smiled bright as the evening star.

"And you're…August's mother."

"Obviously."

"So August is…"

"You know exactly who he is." She snorted a very ungoddess-like laugh. "August Bowman. The august bowman? The exalted archer?"

And Lia did. At once. It all made sense, though none of it made sense.

"Eros."

Aphrodite nodded. "Well, he hasn't been Eros for about, oh, thirteen years? That's when he had a massive strop and quit. Retired his wings and his arrows, gave up the immortal life on Olympus and came here to play human for a bit."

"He told me you all kicked him out of the family because he wouldn't submit to getting married."

"He wouldn't submit to tea and cake," Aphrodite said. "All right, so the truth is, he gave me one sleepless night too many. He was always shooting people with his arrows—making kings fall in love with commoners, handsome vain men fall in love with poor plain girls. He shot Zeus with an arrow and made him fall in love with a cloud. A cloud! I still don't know what ever became of that poor cloud. Probably traumatized for life."

"I'm sure it found love again," Lia said.

"His father and I finally had enough after Eros did the cruelest thing ever."

"What was that?"

"He made us fall in love with each other."

"That's bad?"

"You haven't met my son's father. I don't recommend it."

Ares. Mars, to the Romans. God of war.

No, Lia didn't have any desire to meet August's father.

"We had to teach our son to behave. Mortal parents take away the television and video games. We stripped him of his immortality and his powers. We thought after a day or two, a week or two at most, he'd repent and come to heel. But no…

turns out he liked being a mortal. Took to it like a fish to water. When he was Eros, he looked about twenty years old, if that. Now he looks, I don't know, eighty?"

"He looks thirty," Lia said. "Thirty-three tops."

The goddess shuddered. "He's always been a difficult child. Prince of Mischief, we call him. He's his father's son. More war than love. Not happy unless he's causing trouble and making everyone miserable. Ungrateful child, after all we've done for him."

"He was very kind to me," Lia said. "And I would appreciate it if you kept your opinions about him to yourself."

She couldn't quite believe she'd said that to a goddess.

The goddess didn't seem to mind. She grinned broadly.

"Such a nice girl," she said.

"I'm the madam of an escort service."

"I'd hardly hold that against you, dear. I had a whole cult of temple prostitutes in Corinth in service to me. Ah…the good old days." She patted Lia's cheek.

Lia recoiled.

"No, don't touch me. You're making August get married to someone he doesn't want to marry. You have to let him out of it. I've already told my parents everything, anyway. I don't need your help."

"Do you like my perfume?"

"What?" Lia asked, shaking her head in supreme confusion. She had conversational whiplash from the sudden change of subject.

"My perfume? Do you like it?"

"It smells very nice. Hermès. My mother wears the same sort."

"I thought it was very kind of you to give it to me," Aphrodite said.

"Give it to you?" Lia asked. "When did I... Rita. With the catering company. That was you? No..."

"Yes," she said, and curtsied in honor of her own acting prowess. "Just a disguise. My own son didn't even recognize me. You read your myths. I know you know how it works. If you do a kindness to a god or goddess in disguise as a lowly mortal in need, the god or goddess will reward you. I was about to get sacked for stealing from you and you defended me against your housekeeper's accusations and even gave me the perfume. Because you showed hospitality to a visitor in your home that even Zeus would applaud, I will honor you by granting you a boon. I can either release my son from his promise to come home and get married and give up all this mortal mischief he's been doing the past thirteen years. Or... I can pop downstairs and take care of your little mess you've made. I'll blow in David's ear and make him forget all about you, blow in your mother's and father's ears and make them forget everything that happened tonight. I can even paint over the mural on your parents' bedroom ceiling, and it will be as if David never stepped one foot into this house or your life. What shall it be?"

Lia didn't even have to think about that for one second.

"Let August go," she said. "I mean, Eros."

"You want him for yourself?"

"Of course I want him for himself. But even if I never see him again, I don't want him forced to be someone and something he doesn't want to be—especially because of me."

"You're certain? All Hades is about to break loose downstairs. Your David is threatening to call the police on your father. Perhaps he already has. Is that a siren I hear?"

Lia heard the siren, too. Her stomach sank. But she had no choice.

"August said the gods envy mortals because our actions

have consequences. Even when the consequences are bad," she said, "they're still good because they give weight and meaning to our lives and choices. I don't believe I did anything wrong—everything that happened was consensual, nobody got exploited, everybody had fun. But I know what I did was illegal. I'll take the consequences, no matter how ugly it gets. And…what happened this week with August and me, I want that to mean something, too. I don't want to magically make it go away, not even the pain. Even the pain of losing him reminds me I had him for a while… As for the mural, yes, David's a wanker but the painting is magnificent. And it's August and me, I suppose. Leave that alone, too." Lia squared her shoulders. "I'm sorry to rush you off, but if it's as bad as you say, I better get downstairs and stop Daddy from committing murder."

"Your father does love you more than life itself," Aphrodite said. "I saw that the moment you were born, and he called on my name to breathe life back into you. You've been like my own goddaughter. You make me very proud."

"Thank you," Lia said. "I think."

"Before I go…" The goddess bent to pick up the broken statue of herself. Except it wasn't broken anymore when she placed it back on the mantel. "Your great-grandfather loved this little statue of me. And I loved your great-grandfather. He would have been very proud of you, too. Defying convention, thumbing your nose at all the stupid rules imposed on women that never get imposed on men, living the bawdy life of a…what did you call it? A congenial pervert? My kind of girl. I like you so much better than Psyche—pretty girl but no backbone. You, child, have backbone." Aphrodite placed her hands on Lia's shoulders, and this time Lia didn't brush her off. She couldn't, not with the way Aphrodite was looking at her, her great dark eyes full of love.

Aphrodite bent and kissed Lia on the forehead.

"All I ever wanted," the goddess said, "was for someone to love my son as much as I do. You've made me a very happy lady."

And with those strange final words, Aphrodite was gone.

CHAPTER THIRTY-THREE

Stunned by what had just happened, the dazzling strangeness of it all, Lia could only stand there in her room basking in utter astonishment. She felt like she'd been staring straight at the sun for an hour and it was going to take a long time before her vision cleared. She leaned back against the door, pressed her hand into her stomach and breathed and breathed.

She nearly jumped two feet into the air when someone knocked on her bedroom door. She turned and threw the door open. Her mother stood across the threshold.

"Mummy," Lia said. "It's you." She slapped a hand over her heart in relief.

"The craziest thing just happened," her mother said.

"What?" Lia asked, panicking again.

"A police officer showed up and arrested David."

"Arrested David?" She nearly shouted the words.

"I know." Her mother raised her hands in surrender to fate. "Insane. Said David hadn't paid his taxes on some paintings he sold a few years ago."

"A police officer. Tonight. Arrested David. For evading tax."

"That. Is. Correct."

God, her mother was a wisearse.

"You didn't get the cop's name, did you?" Lia asked.

"Officer Arren, I think. Officer Ariss? Something like that. Why?"

"No reason."

Arren? Ariss?

Ares?

"I guess we won't be going to his art show tomorrow night," her mother said.

"I didn't really want to go, anyway. His new work looks like a bunch of wank."

Mum laughed, nodded. "It really does. Past his prime already. My mural was his best work."

"And it wasn't even his idea. It was mine."

Lia hoped it would stay like this, just casual conversation, nothing deep, nothing serious. But she should have known better.

Her mother suddenly reached for her and pulled her into an embrace.

"Why didn't you tell me, sweetheart?" she asked, holding Lia so tight it almost hurt. "You know you can tell me anything."

"Because I love you?" Lia said. "And I know you. I know you'd blame yourself. I know you'd… I know it would have broken your heart to know you and David broke my heart. I guess there were enough broken hearts lying around."

"It does break my heart," her mother said. "If I had thought for one single second… I mean, he was old enough to be your father… Never occurred to me you'd have feelings for him. I should have known. I should have asked you. I should have—"

"Been psychic?" Lia pulled back to face her. "See? You're doing it. You're blaming yourself when none of it's your fault. Even when I was angry at you I knew I shouldn't be. All David had to do was not come to my room. Or tell me to back off. Or tell you I'd been flirting with him when you and Daddy weren't looking and you all needed to have a talk with me. But there you are, standing there, blaming yourself, and this is exactly why I didn't tell you."

"I'm a mother. This is what we do. We blame ourselves. You could trip over Gogo tonight on your way to the toilet and break your nose, and I'd tell myself it was my fault for letting you have a dog."

"If I couldn't have Gogo, I would have moved out of the house and lived with him on the street and then you would blame yourself when I got myself murdered in a knife fight. 'Damn. That's what I get for not letting Lia have a dog.'"

There. Her mother laughed a genuine laugh. Finally.

"He told me I was crap in bed," Lia said. Now that she'd confessed a little, she needed to get it all out. "And you were a goddess in comparison."

Her mother took her by the shoulders and stared at her.

"David didn't care about me. He used me for your father's money and connections. You have to know that."

"He did?" Lia asked in a small hopeful voice.

"He said as much downstairs. I knew it then and I know it now. I just didn't care." Her mother exhaled heavily. "Please don't believe his lies for another second. Please?"

"Okay," Lia said, smiling through tears. "August told me to tell you a week ago. I should have listened to him."

"Why didn't you? And don't say it's because you didn't want to hurt me. You know there's more than that to it."

"I…" Lia looked down at the floor. "I never told anybody. Not until August. It was just too humiliating."

"My poor baby."

She collapsed into her mother's arms and cried.

Mum stroked Lia's hair like she had a million times before. The daughter did the crying-her-heart-out and the mother did the comforting-with-all-her-might. The whole thing was horrible and awful and sad, but Lia thought it was almost worth it. She'd told her mother all her secrets and when Mum now said, "I love you, my darling," Lia could believe—because now her mother knew the real her. And Lia knew who her mother was, too. A weird, half-wild, wonderful woman.

"I love you, too, Mummy."

"You forgive me?" she asked.

"You didn't do anything wrong," Lia said.

"You forgive me, anyway?"

"Yes," she said. "If you'll forgive me."

"For what? Not telling me when you should have four years ago? Or running an escort agency with your friends under our noses?"

"Um…both."

"All right," her mother said softly. "I will, however, have to ask you to kindly cease and desist all illegal activities. If you end up in prison for pandering, I'm going to age very quickly overnight, and then I really will never forgive you."

Lia laughed between her sobs.

"No more crying now," her mother said. "David's not worth it."

"He was crap in bed, wasn't he?"

"Total crap. Or are these tears for August?"

"August," Lia whispered.

"What happened? He seemed mad about you."

"He's, ah, going back to Greece."

"That's what planes are for."

"It's family stuff," she said. "I can't be part of it. He's gone for good."

"I'm so sorry, my darling," Mum said, wiping the tears off Lia's face with her own bare hands.

"Now, that's what I want to see." Those words were spoken by her father, standing in the doorway of Lia's suite. "Genuine remorse and tearful contrition. Ashes and sackcloth would also be appreciated."

Gogo trotted into her room then and sat at Lia's feet. He didn't care if she was in trouble. He knew who put the kibble in his bowl every day.

"Sorry, Daddy," Lia said.

"Sorry? You're saying sorry? You've been running an escort agency with your friends for the past three years and I get a 'sorry'?"

"I'm *very* sorry?"

"When I said there was nothing you could do to disappoint me but die, did you have to take me literally?" he asked. He pulled her pink business card with her tennis racquet and rose logo out and tossed it on the coffee table. "Young Ladies' Gardening & Tennis Club, my arse. I should have known when you never played any bloody tennis."

"A little suspicious, I admit," Lia said.

"I thought it was a drinking club," her mother said.

"What?" Lia asked. Where on earth had Mum gotten that idea?

"Gardening & Tennis? G&T? Gin & Tonic?"

"Close," Lia said. "But no cigar."

Her father pointed at her face. "No more gardening. No more tennis. You understand me?"

"Yes," Lia said.

He pointed at her bedroom.

"Bedroom, *madam*. Stay there. Forever," he said. "At least a week. Meals will be brought to you. Otherwise do not step foot one out of your suite until we've figured out what to do with you. I don't care if you're an adult. You still live under my roof, and I will send you to your room if I want."

A week?

"Mum?"

"Don't look at me," her mother said. "He sends me to my bedroom all the time, whether I'm in trouble or not."

"Mother, now is not the time for that."

"Do as your father says. And don't worry. It's going to be all right. We won't let anything happen to you."

"I know," Lia said.

"Are you all right, darling?" her father asked, anger momentarily put away. She gave him a small smile, a little nod.

"Yes, Daddy."

Mum kissed her forehead and patted her cheek. "Get some sleep." Her mother crooked her finger at her father. "Take me to bed, spouse. I was very impressed with how you handled that asshole painter."

"You liked that, did you?" He wagged his eyebrows at her.

"Parents, go away, please."

"Ungrateful child," her father said. But her mother blew her a kiss. He put an arm around her mum's waist and ushered her into the hallway. As they left Lia heard Daddy saying, "She takes after her great-grandfather."

Her mother replied with unconcealed pride, "No, darling, she takes after me."

CHAPTER THIRTY-FOUR

Lia took a long shower and put on her pink cotton nightie and got into bed. By the time her head hit the pillow she had convinced herself the whole thing with Aphrodite had simply been a temporary break with reality caused by over-whelming stress, the lingering effects of whatever hallucino-genic substance coated the Rose Kylix or a combination of both. Lia certainly would never break her great-grandfather's Aphrodite statue. Proof—there it was, sitting on her mantel like always, in perfect condition.

As for David? Well, you had to pay tax. Odd that the arrest-ing officer had come to Wingthorn to haul in David, though. How had he known David was here? At least it seemed Au-gust's mother had kept her end of their devil's bargain and called in the necessary favors to get David out of Lia's hair.

He'd probably get deported by Monday morning. Or August's mother would offer him a deal—she'd make his legal troubles go away if he promised to keep his mouth shut. Either way, it was done. Lia knew in her heart her troubles with David Bell were over for good.

So why couldn't she be happy?

Because August was gone, that was why. He was gone and she would never see him again.

Lia patted the bed so Gogo would join her, but for some reason he didn't want to leave his dog bed. Ah, fine. Be that way, stubborn puppy. She'd sleep alone. She'd done it for most of her life. Wasn't so bad. Wasn't so bad at all.

She turned the light off and pulled the covers to her chin— the covers that still smelled like August, like cypress trees and his skin. Lia ignored the tears that streamed from her eyes and onto her pillow as she willed herself to sleep. She'd be doing a lot of sleeping the next week while she was a prisoner in her own bedroom.

Like poor Danaë, the daughter of a king who locked her up to prevent her from falling in love and getting pregnant with the son who was prophesied to kill him. Locking his daughter up didn't work, of course. Never did. Lock up a girl in a tower or a dungeon and it was like catnip to the gods, Lia knew. Might as well hang a sign over the house that said Get It Here, Gods!

That thought made Lia smile. Or maybe it was exhaustion making her loopy.

But something was definitely wrong with her.

Why was she hearing…bird noises?

Was that it? Bird noises? Not birdsong or crows cawing, but she knew she'd heard the fluttering of wings. Wings?

Lia rolled up and turned on her lamp.

August stood by the foot of her bed.

."August!" She stared at him in gobsmacked wonder, her lips parted and her eyes wide as the sky. "You're here. And… naked."

"Did you miss me?"

"Yes," she said. "But you can't be here. Or naked. You're getting married. Go away. Put clothes on, too. Not in that order."

He laughed and climbed on the bed. He crawled to her and loomed over her on his hands and knees.

"What are you doing here?" she rasped. "I'm under house arrest. You're going to get me murdered. And you…you're supposed to be in Greece getting married to a cloud or something."

"I'm free," he said. "My mother let me go."

"She did? Oh…" Lia was so happy she could do nothing but reach for him to hold him and never let him go.

But he stopped her. He took her wrists in his hands and pressed them down into the pillow at either side of her head.

This she did not mind.

"Do me a favor, Lia," he said. She lay under him, pinned down and basking in her joy. "Don't scream."

"Scream?"

Two massive white wings sprouted from August's back and filled the room wall to wall.

Lia started to scream. August slapped a hand over her mouth.

"You are very bad at following instructions."

He took his hand off her mouth.

She stared up at him, at his strange changeable gray eyes and his dark waving hair falling over his forehead and his smile nearly as wicked as he was, and she knew him, she knew who he was. August Bowman. Her love and her lover.

"You have wings."

"You like them?"

"Where did you get them?"

"Born with them. Weird, aren't they? You just never know what'll happen when two gods make a new god."

"You cannot be a god," she said, gazing at his wings. They certainly looked real enough, though they could just be clever props.

"You still don't believe me?" he asked.

"I'm struggling," she said. "Though trying to maintain an open mind."

"Don't care if your mind is open," he said as he put his very human knees between her thighs and pushed them apart. "As long as your legs are."

"No, stop. We have to discuss this," she said. "The wings for starters. Start with those."

He kissed her. All was forgotten. The kiss set her heart to throbbing and her heart set her lips to kissing. She wrapped her arms around his strong neck and he wrapped his arms around her back, raising her from the bed and against him to kiss her even more, to kiss her until her skin flushed pink as a rose in spring.

August released her from the kiss and she lay breathless beneath him.

"Okay, so what about the wings?" she asked.

"I am done with your doubting Thomas ways," he said. "I'm going to prove to you once and for all who and what I am. And you're going to like it, young lady."

"I'll be the judge of that," she said. Or she'd planned to say that. The words were on the tip of her tongue when August simply disappeared in a flutter of feathers.

The room seemed empty, terribly empty, and Lia sat up and glanced around, looking for any trace of him. She found nothing but one white feather on her bed. And even that was no definitive proof. She slept on feather pillows.

Except the feather was softer than silk and smelled like the purest water from the highest mountain stream.

"August?" she called out softly. She wanted him back so badly she'd believe anything he said. She'd believe he was a king or the pope or the prime minister of Canada if that was what it took to get him back and keep him back.

"August?" she called out again, a little louder this time.

Then she saw something sliding in through her window and snaking up the ceiling. Lia narrowed her eyes at it and saw it seemed to be…gold. Liquid gold. It oozed across the ceiling, shimmering in the lamplight.

"August?" she whispered. She held out her hand and one drop of pure liquid gold landed in her palm.

No…he wouldn't…would he?

But she already knew he would.

Another drop fell from the ceiling. Then another and another. They landed on the bed all around Lia. Drop. Drop. Drop. Like pennies from heaven. The drops kept coming and coming, and as they fell, they found each other and formed puddles of gold, shining gold, glimmering gold…

One puddle slid across the sheets toward Lia. Her chest heaved in fascinated horror as it approached. She held out her hand to it and touched it as gently as she'd ever touched a soap bubble blown in summer on the lawn. The liquid gold puddle was warm but not hot, and satiny to the touch. She plunged her fingers into it and laughed as it formed a ball in her hand before dropping back down to the sheets.

More drops fell from the ceiling onto the bed and created more shimmering, glimmering golden puddles. One oozed its shining way to her thigh and Lia let it crawl—if that was the verb—onto her leg. It felt heavy, solid, but it didn't hurt. And she wasn't afraid. Either this was August doing something wonderful and bizarre to her and for her or she had simply gone mad. Either was acceptable to her after the day she'd had.

The puddle on her thigh slid up her body, up her hip and over her stomach...and it was heavy enough that Lia had to lie down on her bed. It slid through the valley between her breasts, and one golden tendril extended like a long finger to stroke her cheek and brush her lips, as if in a kiss. Lia murmured a soft sound of pleasure. It felt so solid on her, so heavy and so strange but sensuous, too. Her skin tingled everywhere the gold touched.

She had her little pink nightie on, but the magical golden puddle didn't seem to mind. It slipped under the bodice of her gown and covered her breast with a thin layer of gold. Lia closed her eyes as gentle heat seeped deep into her skin. Her nipples hardened, and she could swear it felt like heavy hands held her breasts, squeezing the nipples, pulling and pinching them.

Her hands grasped at the sheets as two more of the gold slicks slid across the bed and onto her legs. Now it felt like six large hands on her body—two on her breasts, two on her thighs, one on her belly, one on her chest. The golden hands explored her skin, every inch of it. They eased up and down her legs, over her feet and even between her toes and up again to ring her ankles. They glided over her throat and around her neck, up and around her ears and across her lips, then down her shoulders, down her arms, down to her hands where they tickled all ten of her fingers.

More golden drops fell from the ceiling and the golden hands on her grew more solid, larger, heavier and even more intent on exploring every part of her body. Lia went limp, overcome with the pleasure that was beyond words and reason. The golden hands lifted her, pushing her gown off her body and her underwear down her legs. There were ten golden hands now on her body, twelve. Too many to count. They turned her onto her stomach and flowed all over her from her neck to her back, over her bottom and thighs and calves, and kissed the very bottoms of her feet. Lia gasped and panted, panted and gasped, as those sinuous golden hands poured over her body like water.

Lia luxuriated in the touch of the hands on her body. She yielded completely to their explorations. The gilded hands pushed her onto her back again and she let them cover her from knee to throat. Every nerve in her body tingled and every muscle in her body sang as the hands stroked and caressed her. When the hands crept up her inner thighs, Lia lay there, legs spread wide, in a stupor of purest sensual pleasure.

One golden hand cupped her between her thighs. She inhaled hard as a tendril of gold found her clitoris and encircled it. Pressure, gentle pressure. Kneading. Her clitoris throbbed as fingers of gold pushed under the hood of flesh that covered it and pushed back. A tongue of gold, a thousand times more precise and careful than any human tongue could be, ran over the exposed organ, teasing it until Lia's lower back came off the bed in her ecstasy.

Another one of the gold slicks pushed through her swollen labia and poured into her vagina. Lia flinched as she was slowly but incessantly filled and filled. The liquid gold inside her grew in volume as more of it entered her. It kneaded at the inner folds, pushing through them, pushing them apart, until it felt to Lia like she had the largest supplest dildo in the world inside her.

But that wasn't enough for August.

Lia gasped, stopped breathing, when she felt the thinnest slightest tendril of liquid gold pass through her cervix, going deeper inside her than any man ever could. It should have hurt, but didn't, feeling instead like the most tender intimate penetration...

But that wasn't enough, either. Another hand of gold slid

over her hips and over her vulva and down to the other, tighter, entrance of her body and began to work its inexorable way inside her. And yet another hand of gold danced up her chest and to her mouth where it entered her even there, like a blunt thick finger on her tongue, and Lia couldn't help but suck on it like a cock in her mouth.

Two hands of gold covered her breasts and squeezed them, tugging and twisting her nipples until they were hard as diamonds, diamonds and gold. Her vagina was filled to bursting, her womb infiltrated, her arse, her mouth. No woman in history—except for perhaps Danaë herself—had ever been so penetrated. Every part of her was conquered, every hole filled. She could take no more. The golden finger on her clitoris never ceased to knead and mold that swollen knot of tissue while the golden organ inside her vagina pulsed and throbbed. Immobilized by the impossible weight upon her, Lia could do nothing but lie there and let the golden hands work her entire body, inside and out, into a frenzy. She was squeezed and rubbed, pressed and pleasured, invaded and lifted, and filled and filled and filled.

When she came, it seemed her entire body rose off the bed, and perhaps it did, with hands of gold under her. Her hips pumped, and sensation burst from her clitoris and along every nerve, up her spine and into her back and thighs and womb. And when the obliterating orgasm struck her, all she could do was gasp August's name once.

She might have passed out. She thought she had. When she came to again, she lay naked on the bed. The golden droplets were all gone. Instead August lay on his side next to her, head propped on his hand.

He smiled wantonly at her.

"Now do you believe me?"

CHAPTER THIRTY-FIVE

"That was the dirtiest sex in history," Lia said, lying across August's seemingly human chest.

"Top ten at least."

"You went in places you're not supposed to go," she said. "Will I need to see a gynecologist? Or a metallurgist?"

"Want to do it again?"

"Yes, please," she said.

August wrapped them in his wings, and she held out a hand to stroke the walls of the feathery cocoon.

"I'm so afraid I'll wake up tomorrow and this will all have been a dream," she said.

"I just made insane love to you in the form of liquid gold. And you still doubt?"

"It's not doubt," she said, rising up to look down at him. "Only fear."

He stroked her cheek and grinned.

"Nothing to be afraid of. I'm here now," he said softly. "I'm not going away. And if I do, I will take you with me."

"Yes, very sweet. But how did you talk your family into letting you back in?" she asked.

"Mother's behind all of this," he said. "I had a feeling she was when I saw the statue of her on your mantel. She arranged for the Rose Kylix to come into your possession. She knew it would get my attention."

"She was playing matchmaker."

"Of course she'd pair me up with one of her acolytes."

"I didn't even realize I was," Lia said.

"Mother said all she ever wanted was for me to learn how to really love so I'd know how wrong it was to play with hearts. When I gave up my freedom to help you and you chose my happiness over getting yourself out of trouble… Well, Mother thinks I've finally learned my lesson. She's very happy I found a girl who loves me."

"I do love you," she said, gazing down at him in adoration. "Although I am so furious at you for not telling me you're bloody Eros."

"I tried telling you a, oh, million ways," he said. "I mean, come on now, Lia, I named myself August Bowman."

"I was told August was short for Augustine, not a synonym for 'exalted.'"

"You didn't want to believe," he said. "That was the problem."

"I do believe now, though. I think." She scratched her temple.

"I'll make you believe," he said, and dragged her down to his chest again and held her tight to his body.

"What happens now? Never been in love with a Greek god

before," she said, smiling. She really had gone mad. It was fine. August was here, being completely mad with her.

"I'm supposed to keep a low profile, but as long as I do we can come and go as we please," he said. "And you'll be treated like Ganymede, the beautiful youth the gods found so lovely that Zeus took him up to live in Olympus."

"As long as I'm with you," she said. She thought of something and hated to bring it up but…she had to know.

"What about David?" she asked.

"Oh, he'll be a free man in time for his art show," August said. "But Mother had a word with him while he was in the clink. She put the fear of goddess in him. She said you were her son's lover, and if he tried to hurt you, she would have him chained to a rock and she'd instruct an eagle to peck out his liver for all eternity."

"Harsh," Lia said.

"She told him we're a Greek mafia family, not entirely inaccurate. After the death threat, he went very quiet. But we let him go," he said. "He won't be bothering you anymore."

"Thank you," she whispered, then kissed the center of his chest.

August put a finger under her chin, raised her head to look at him.

"If you want me to," he said, "I can make you forget what happened with him. And I can make your mother forget. I can make it all go away. I know how."

Lia considered it. Then she discarded the idea. Tempting as it was to make the painful memories disappear, getting rid of them would mean discarding the good memories that came after. Yes, David hurt her and her mother, but now she and her mother loved each other even more. And she cherished the memory of her father leaping to her defense without hesitation and her mother slapping David across his smug face.

"No," Lia said. "I'm fine. I'll keep my memories as they are. If I forgot the hurt, I'd forget the healing."

"Good choice," he said, stroking her back.

"Will you miss being a prostitute in your own cult?" she asked.

"Fun while it lasted," he said.

"I wouldn't stop you if you wanted to keep doing it," she said. "As long as you love me the most."

"I think I've played enough for a few centuries at least."

"I haven't," Lia said. "But I'm forbidden from being a madam anymore. Mum and Daddy are opposed to the idea for some reason."

"They're very conservative for a couple of married perverts," he said, then snapped his fingers. "Oh, speaking of married perverts...we have to get married."

Lia sat up, shoving his wings aside.

"We have to do what?"

"Don't worry. Not right this minute. One of Mother's conditions. She was very serious about me getting married and settling down. If I was going to get my crown and wings back, I had to agree to get married. But I got to pick the lady—or fawn or cloud. And the lady I picked was you. Do you mind?"

"When exactly?"

"Not today. But a short engagement would be preferred. Say...five years?"

Lia's shoulders slumped in relief. "Five years isn't considered a short engagement."

"When you're several thousand years old, five years is nothing."

"But what happens when I get old and you're still this?" She pinched his too-handsome cheeks.

"Mother would make you immortal, if you want. Or I'll quit being a god again, and we'll grow old together."

"You'd do that for me?" she asked.

"I would," he said. "Mother wants a grandchild, but we have plenty of time to figure all that out. Eons…"

Lia straddled his stomach and sat on his hips.

"I love you, August Bowman."

He wrinkled his nose at her. "Do you?" he asked. "Tell me how."

"With all my heart," Lia said.

"And?" He batted his eyelashes.

"All my…soul?"

"And?" He batted his eyelashes harder.

"And all my…"

"Starts with a *C*," he said.

"All my concupiscence?"

August threw her on her back and entered her with a stroke.

"I'm going to pound that prissiness out of you if it takes eternity," he said.

"Good," she said. "My cunt can't wait."

When August stopped laughing he made passionate love to her.

Though if anyone was standing outside the door listening, all they would have heard was bird noises.

Aphrodite, goddess of love, the universal mother and evening star, was too busy crowing to eavesdrop on Eros and Lia. The Godwicks had long been worshippers of hers, and she'd planned for decades to marry her son to one of them if they'd ever hurry up and have a bloody girl child. But of course her son wouldn't marry anyone she told him to marry. Oh no, gods forbid! Yet, it was all too easy to trick him into thinking he'd picked out his own bride. And she supposed he had, but she put them together. Full marks for Aphrodite. She patted herself on the back. The old girl still had it.

Still…she did regret hurting her sweet, wicked son. In a show of affection for the young lovers, Aphrodite took a page from her sister Athena's playbook. She pinned the night into place to give her son and his fiancée more time together in the intimate dark…a romantic gesture that went entirely unremarked by the lovers who were too busy making love to even notice what Aphrodite had done for them.

Ungrateful children.

CHAPTER THIRTY-SIX

Lia called the final meeting of the Young Ladies' Gardening & Tennis Club of Wingthorn Hall to order. She looked at her friends, her "ladies," and smiled with genuine affection.

"Well, boss?" Rani said. "What's the news?"

"We have a problem," Lia said.

"I'm really starting to hate these meetings." Georgy slouched deep into Lia's armchair.

"Is it that bloke?" Jane asked. "The ex of yours Rani wanted to gut?"

"No," Lia said. "He's all taken care of."

Rani's eyes widened.

"Oh, I didn't have him killed," Lia said. "He's just out of the picture. God, it does sound like I killed him. The point is, it's over and done with without a drop of blood shed."

"Then what's the bad news, boss?" Georgy asked.

This was the hard part, the part she'd been dreading.

"Ladies…the time has come for me to retire my nonexistent garden shears and my invisible tennis racquet," Lia said. "I'm quitting the biz."

The three ladies stared at her with heartbreak in their eyes.

"Lia," Rani said. "Why?"

"Um…because my parents told me I had to."

"You really have got to get your own place, boss," Jane said.

"Working on that," Lia said. "But there is good news. You won't be left alone and without protection. I found you a new boss."

"A new boss?" Jane sounded very skeptical. Lia didn't blame her. "Who?"

"She's a bit older and she's had loads of experience at this. She's got more connections than I do, more money. Also—"

Lia heard a tap on her bedroom door.

Before she could answer it, the goddess Aphrodite threw open the door and sashayed inside, wearing pink faux furs in June and towering over them all on her hot-pink high heels with diamond-encrusted roses on the toes.

"Hello, ladies," Aphrodite said, a wide smile on her cotton candy lips. Jane, Rani and Georgy stared slack-jawed and wide-eyed at the goddess of love herself. "Call me Mrs. V. We're going to fuck beautiful men, make enormous amounts of money, and be worshipped night and day like the goddesses we are. Shall we get started?"

Georgy looked at Lia and nodded her approval.

"Well done, Lia," Georgy said. "She'll do nicely."

PART EIGHT

Daphne & Apollo

CHAPTER THIRTY-SEVEN

"What are we doing?" Lia asked August—she would never get used to calling him Eros—as he put her in his Tesla.

"Indulge me," he said, then kissed her. "Just one more bit of unfinished business."

August had made love to her all last night and all morning and even that afternoon. But, by evening, he'd nudged her awake and told her to get dressed in her very best. She reminded him she was under her father's house arrest.

He reminded her that he was a Greek god.

Lia wore a vintage burgundy gown that had belonged to her grandmother. She pinned her hair in a loose knot with tendrils flowing, and August put a pink rose behind her ear.

He'd slipped into a trim black suit, and she was amazed how neatly his wings disappeared when he folded them into place.

"After a couple thousand years, you learn a trick or two," he'd said.

On the way to wherever he was taking her, they stopped by his house.

"I have to pick up one thing," he said.

"The Rose Kylix?" she asked.

"Mother's confiscated that—again. This is something else."

He ran into the house and emerged minutes later carrying a longbow as tall as he and a quiver of arrows.

Back in the car, Lia looked at him.

"I don't want to know, do I?" she asked.

"You're going to like this," he said.

The next stop was the Attic Gallery.

"It's a good thing I love you," she said as he helped her out of the car. "I really do not want to see David again. Trust me, I don't need closure."

"This isn't for you," he said. "This is for me. And don't worry. You won't have to talk to him."

Funny that no one tried to stop August from entering the gallery with a bow and quiver slung over his back. Either no one could see it, or they simply assumed it was all part of David's surrealistic art show.

Once inside, Lia paused by a massive canvas. The plaque said the title of the piece was *The Forest of Apollo*. The painting was nothing but women who were human from the waist up and trees from the waist down. Ah, the story of Daphne and Apollo. Eros had struck Apollo with a golden arrow of love and he'd struck Daphne with an iron arrow of hate… Daphne ran from Apollo as he pursued her, prayed to the gods to save her from the obsessed deity and she was turned into a laurel tree.

"Mum was right," Lia said, staring at the painting. "Male artists really do love painting horrible things happening to women. And you should be ashamed of yourself."

"That," August said, pointing at the canvas, "was not my work. Apollo was royally miffed when Daphne wouldn't go out with him, and he turned her into a tree to punish her. Then he had the balls to blame the whole thing on me."

"Really?" Lia asked. She wondered what other myths about him were and weren't true. "What happened to Daphne?"

"I turned her back into a nymph," August said.

"And then you made love to her. Right?"

"No," he said, sounding insulted she'd even suggest it. She raised her eyebrow at him. "I didn't want to get splinters."

Lia looked at the painting again, all those poor tortured Daphnes…

"If you were going to paint one scene from any Greek myth," Lia asked August, "what scene you would paint?"

"You," he said. "You at the feet of Pan, holding a baby otter in your arms."

Lia's heart rose half an inch in her chest.

"I'm not in a Greek myth," she said.

He kissed her on the mouth. "You are now, my love."

That's when Lia knew she and August would be happy together forever.

"Come on," August said. "Let's get this over with so we can make love again."

The Attic Gallery had a mezzanine level that was home to the artworks that were always on display. Most of the guests at David's show were on the main floor. She and August walked around and around the mezzanine.

"What are we doing up here?" she asked.

"Waiting…"

"For?"

"Perfect justice," he said, and winked at her. "Ah, here we go."

Lia peered down at the party below. She saw the crowd parting to let a woman through, a beautiful woman in red, so beautiful one could rightly call her a goddess.

"That's your mother," Lia whispered.

"I invited her as a sort of peace offering."

"That was nice of you," she said.

"Not really," August said. "I'm going to shoot her in the heart with a great big arrow."

"What? Why?"

"Oh, look, there's our *artiste*," August said, pointing out David working his way through the crowd, glad-handing as he went. Though his smile was broad, it appeared forced to Lia. He was likely still recovering from having Aphrodite, in the form of a mafia queen, threaten to kill him in all sorts of gruesome ways. "Cover me."

Lia glanced around, not knowing how to cover him. August didn't seem to care. He took off his jacket and laid it over the banister. He rolled up his sleeves to his elbows. This could not be good. Then he reached behind his head and pulled two arrows from his quiver.

"August…" Lia said.

He notched them both on his bow at the same time.

"This is not good…" Lia winced.

He pulled back the string. He wore a look of purest concentration. Two arrows, one bow, and his aim had to be perfect, just perfect.

"I can't look," she said.

She covered her eyes but peeked through her fingers.

The string thrummed as he let the arrows fly. Gifted with his sight, Lia saw one burning arrow stream into the chest of David, right through his heart.

And the other arrow, black as iron, struck his own mother, right through her heart.

Then...

"Oh my gods..." Lia breathed.

David looked at Aphrodite like he'd seen the sun for the first time.

Aphrodite looked at David like he smelled of dung.

David started to make his way through the crowd, fast as he could, pushing people aside, while Aphrodite drew away from him even as he took her hand in his and kissed and kissed and kissed it...

"August, you didn't."

"An arrow of love. An arrow of hate. Now he'll know what it's like to be brutally rejected, and my mother will think twice before interfering in my sex life again. A job well done."

"You really are the Prince of Mischief," she said.

"I'll show you mischief, my lady." He kissed her. "Let's go."

"We can't just..."

"What?"

"We can't leave them like that. They're in love-hate with each other," she said.

"The arrows weren't very potent," August said with a shrug. "The poison will wear off soon."

"Like...in an hour?"

"For Mother? An hour. For David Bell? More like a week," he said. "But trust me, he deserves it, and Mother can more than handle herself."

He slung his bow over his back again and took Lia's hand. They went out of the gallery, not through the main entrance but through a back door and upstairs to the roof, where they stood and looked out on the lights of London.

"That was kind of sexy," she said as he slid his arm around her waist. "The archery thing. Good look for you."

"I'll teach you how to shoot."

"Where? Olympus?"

"Is that where you want to go?" he asked.

"What are my options?"

"Let me think…" He nodded thoughtfully and started ticking off places on his fingers. "Olympus. The Underworld. Maybe you can get some weaving tips from Arachne—unless you're afraid of human-size spiders. There's Arcadia. Ancient Crete. Elysium. The Land of a Thousand Dances. Delphi. Your pick. We have all eternity."

"Pan's Island?" Lia asked.

August looked at her through narrowed eyes. "The real Pan's Island, you mean? Or the fantasy version from the storybook?"

"The real Pan's Island," she said. "If it exists, I mean. But if you exist I suppose Pan must exist, and he must live somewhere."

"He does," August said. "On an island, in fact. We're old friends."

"He likes you?" Sounded like August—Eros—had managed to piss off most of the Olympians. They had better go somewhere August would stay mostly out of trouble.

"He's the god of nature and sex is natural. I'm the god of sex and nature is very sexual. We have loads in common."

"What's his island like?" Lia asked. She didn't want to be disappointed if it wasn't like she'd dreamed.

"Wilder and stranger and more beautiful than you can imagine," August said as he drew her to him. "You'll probably go mad there."

"Can we go there first?"

August waved his hand and suddenly a red curtain hung on the roof of the gallery, a red curtain held by nothing.

"Shall we?"

Lia crept over to the curtain. She put her ear to the velvet, and from behind it she heard pipes playing a tune so lovely and lively that she thought if she started dancing to it she might never wish to stop.

August took her hand in his, and he slowly began to draw the red curtain aside. She spied a river running silver, and a forest greener than any green her eyes had ever seen, and young girls in diaphanous gowns of baby blue, palest pink and sunshine yellow dancing in circles around a laughing bearded satyr.

Lia looked at August in delight. He stared at her with love in his eyes, with unutterable love.

"Are you afraid?" August asked.

"No," Lia said as she passed through the curtain and into the realms of magic and myth.

And yet.

Oh, and yet...

She was afraid.

Ω

ACKNOWLEDGMENTS

I'd be remiss if I didn't thank the various and sundry maniacs who helped bring this book to fruition. We have to start with my humanities and aesthetics professors at Centre College. I'm finally making something out of my liberal arts education with *The Red* and *The Rose*.

I also have to thank Mr. Bulfinch wherever he is for his fine compendium known commonly as *Bulfinch's Mythology*. Also, I extend my gratitude to authors Catherine Johns (*Sex or Symbol? Erotic Images of Greece and Rome*), Robert Garland (*Ancient Greece: Everyday Life in the Birthplace of Modern Civilization*) and, of course, Homer (*The Odyssey, The Iliad*). Homer, the world owes you a donut. Sorry. I bet you hate that joke.

Massive piles of gratitude to freelance editor Mala Bhattacharjee for her brilliant suggestions and eagle-eyed editing. I can't recommend her services to other authors enough!

Very special thanks to author Kira A. Gold (*The Dirty Secret*) for her astute editorial suggestions and costume corrections. Thank you, Jenn LeBlanc (*The Rake and the Recluse*), for help with English titles. I probably still got them wrong. Silly American.

Thank you, British comedian, author and TV presenter David Mitchell (*Back Story*, *That Mitchell and Webb Look*), for his entire oeuvre, which I devoured while writing *The Rose* in order to better reproduce the voice of a posh and whimsical (and adorably stuffy) English person.

Enormous thanks and love to the Eagle Creek Writers Group of Lexington, Kentucky, and our fearless leader, Jennifer Barricklow, for the constant encouragement and helpful critique. Much *philia* ("brotherly love") to Earl P. Dean, Andrew J. Cole, Bob McKinley, Banning Lary and K. F. Lee, and all my other Eagle Creek writing buddies!

Thank you to the Carnegie Center for Literacy & Learning in Lexington, Kentucky, for the opportunity to teach creative writing. The more I teach, the more I learn.

Of course, great thanks is due to Michelle Meade, my fearless editor who was especially fearless when letting me loose on another erotica project. Eternal gratitude as always to my literary agent, Sara Megibow. Kudos to the cover designers at MIRA Books for my beautiful cover. It's better than I dreamed.

Many kisses to everyone who read *The Red* and loved it enough to demand another adventure of those wicked Godwicks. Shall we go for three?

Of course I must thank the ancient peoples of Greece for the richness and beauty of their stories, myths, culture and legends. Now I raise a cup of wine to you and drink deep in your honor. *Dii propitii!* May the gods be propitious!

And finally, *agape* ("unconditional love") and *eros* ("passionate love") to my husband and fellow author, Andrew Shaffer (*Hope Never Dies*). Cupid got me good when I met you.

I mean, Eros.